For my mum, Irene, who opened the door.

1

Jen held the umbrella over her head and listened to the rain drumming on the canvas. It would be cosy inside the pub. The wind blew hard through the material of her jacket. She'd thought she'd be warm enough, but there was ice in the February gusts that sifted around the corner and lifted her hair, rearranging it across her face. She'd spent the afternoon in the hairdresser's and had been pleased with the glossy style, silver strands streaked through the chestnut locks. In the grey suit and neat heels, she'd thought she'd look smart, but the cold weather and the sharp breeze had taken the edge off her preparations and she was sure her nose would glow red beneath the light dusting of powder. But Eddie wouldn't mind – the first thing he always said was how nice it was to see her and how lovely she looked.

There were posters in the windows of the Olive Grove, huge red hearts and cute Cupids with arrows, proclaiming the evening's special Valentine dinner. Jen could hear the hushing of the waves breaking against the sea walls in the distance and, from down the road, the crisp sound of approaching footfall. It was Eddie, in his pale mackintosh, the collar up, looking debonair, just like Inspector Morse. It was seven thirty, sharp.

* * *

Half seven, thought Rose. The torture must end soon. Little Amelia's nimble fingers pressed the pristine ivory keys on the piano: the discordant jangle made a pulse in Rose's head throb.

'Try again from the beginning, dear,' she murmured, watching the second hand twitch on the wall clock. It would soon be over and Amelia would leave her in peace. Rose sighed and spoke through clenched teeth. 'Shall we call it a night, dear? I think Mummy's here – someone just rang the doorbell, I'm sure.'

Amelia slammed the piano lid down without turning round and stood up, still in her school uniform, tidy in the crisp white blouse and tartan skirt, her blonde plaits neatly secured with bows. Rose held up the child's coat and led her to the door where a tall, slim woman with dark hair in a no-nonsense cut and a smart coat was standing in the porch, the rain teeming behind her. Amelia went straight to her and took her hand, a dutiful six year old. But Rose was sure that the child wrinkled her nose and stuck out the edge of a pink tongue at her. Amelia's mother smiled, although her eyes remained cold.

'How was Amelia's lesson, Mrs Grant? She's been prac-tising all week. Is it time for her to be put forward for a grad-ing?' She held out two notes, a ten and a five.

Rose noticed Amelia scowling. She was unsure what to

say, her hand fluttering in front of her face. 'She's making progress, Mrs Bassett. Soon, I hope.'

Amelia's mother frowned. 'My friend, Sally, tells me that Joni Yates puts all her pupils in for grading early. They all seem to pass with distinctions too.'

Rose sighed. She wished she could tell the woman to take her child to Joni Yates, then, and see how she coped with Amelia, who clearly didn't practise anything from one week to another. But her pupils were becoming scarcer: she had no idea why she didn't just retire. After all, it wasn't as if she needed the money. Bernard had left her comfortably off and piano teaching was a routine that left her feeling unfulfilled, flat, without energy. 'Keep practising *Für Elise*, Amelia, and maybe we'll discuss grade entry next week.'

Amelia gazed up at her mother, her tiny brows meeting in a knot. 'Furry Liza is boring, Mummy. Can I learn the violin instead? Elsa in my class goes to violin. She says the teacher is really cool.'

Amelia's mother met Rose's eyes, as if her daughter had just made up her mind for her, and turned on her heel, tugging the child towards the pouring rain and a dark car parked by the kerb. Rose closed the door, locked it securely with the bolt and chain and muttered, 'Minx.' As an afterthought, she mumbled, 'What a blessing that Beethoven was deaf. If he'd heard Amelia slaughtering his *Für Elise* for the last forty-five minutes, it would raise him from the grave.'

She stood in the hallway, thinking. Half past seven. She hadn't eaten since lunch, and then just a slice of toast. She wasn't really hungry, but she ought to look after herself better. Her skirt was hanging off her, the waist baggy, and her legs felt weak. She would find something in the freezer, something with calories. There was a box of macaroni cheese for one. She could heat it up in the microwave. Rose sighed again. She didn't like February. Spring was too far away and the house was too cold. Besides, Bernard had died in February two years ago and each year she felt the cold, haunting loneliness grasp her by the shoulders and whisper in her ear that she was by herself and companionless and that was how it would always be now.

Of course, she had her new friends, the four women she'd met at aqua aerobics last October when the club first started. They were nice women, but they only met for coffee once a week and then she came home alone and it was back to the silence again. She shuffled into the lounge and picked up a yellow duster, rubbing it over the piano. It had been hers and Bernard's. He had been a wonderful musician, a church organist too. She replaced their wedding photo lovingly on top, over the circle left by a wine glass years ago. Not hers, of course – it might have been made by their son, Paul, one Christmas when he'd visited with the children. His visits were a rare thing nowadays – he was a busy man, of course, he had an important job.

Rose stared at the photo, black and white in the silver frame. It all looked so dated now. Bernard was in his suit, a flower in the lapel, his hair wavy, a broad grin on his face, and she was much shorter than him, gazing up in the lacy dress, her eyes full of love. That had been in 1967 – it was so long ago and yet, strangely, she could remember exactly how she'd felt, her heart fluttering, the thrill of becoming Mrs Grant and not Miss Rosemary Tucker. They'd had almost fifty good years, well, mostly good. She'd done her best as a wife. She couldn't really complain.

Rose shuffled forward to the kitchen and opened the freezer. The macaroni cheese meal for one was next to the loaf of bread and the half-empty bag of frozen peas. She'd need to do some shopping. She plucked out the cardboard meal and headed towards the microwave.

* * *

Della heard the knocking at the door. 'Sylvester? You forgotten your key?' She rushed to the front door, wiping her hands on a tea towel, patting the dark curls smattered with grey sprinklings. 'That man,' she muttered under her breath. 'He's out too late again. His dinner is ruining in the oven.'

She pulled the door open and he was standing there, his pork-pie hat on his head, water dripping from the brim onto his misted glasses, his lips pursed for a kiss. He held out a bunch of roses. 'Come to me, my valentine,' he purred.

'Get in out of the rain and stop the foolishness.' She laughed, tugging at his sleeve and helping him out of his damp coat. 'I wish you'd give up this crazy snack-van job. You're late again and drenched through...' The flowers were thrust in her arms and he had her round the waist, waltzing.

'Come here, my valentine girl. I bring you flowers and what do you do but all this nagging me again?' Sylvester giggled, kissing her full on the mouth. He pulled away, whipping off his hat. His head was smooth and shiny, but there were tufts of grey whiskers on his chin. Della hugged him to her.

'I prepared your favourite. Salt fish.'

'Ah.' He wrapped an arm around her shoulders. 'My mommy's salt fish and ackee, I remember it so well, when I was a boy. Life in Jamaica was good before we came to this godforsaken cold country.' They walked into the kitchen and he sniffed exaggeratedly. 'No wonder I married you, Della Donavan – you cook just like my mommy used to.'

Della turned to him and put her hands on her hips, frowning. 'You telling me there are no other benefits, Sylvester?' She swirled away, reaching for a vase, unwrapping the flowers and arranging them carefully. She knew he was studying her, the sway of her hips, the way she moved with a roll – it was the first thing he'd ever noticed about her when they'd met in Stepney fifty years ago. 'The flowers are beautiful.'

He pulled her to him in one expert move and she was on his knee. 'You're beautiful,' he murmured. 'We eat first, then how about an early night, my valentine?'

She pulled off his glasses and gazed into the soft brown eyes. 'You think you're still the man you were at twenty-five?'

'You put fire in my belly, woman.' He put his mouth against hers, crushing their lips together. Della pushed him away, laughing.

'Your technique still needs work,' she said, grinning. 'But you're the sexiest man I ever met, Sylvester.' She levered herself up, rubbing a hard hand across the ache that had started to settle in her lower back, and moved awkwardly towards the cooker. 'And I've made your favourite ginger cake for pudding, with rum.'

She lifted a pot from the hotplate although her wrists ached with the weight of it. Her husband was sitting back in his seat smiling. 'You have a fine figure on you, Della.'

'I'm not the slim girl I was at twenty-two.'

'You are still the same to me.' He lifted his knife and fork and winked at her. 'Come on, then. Let's eat first. Afterwards I'll chase you round the bedroom.'

She laughed. 'I look forward to it. And when you catch me, will you still remember what to do?'

* * *

Tess stared at her plate. She had no appetite. She'd been on her own all day, cooking, tidying, watching daytime television, looking forward to Alan coming home. But now he was here, and they were sitting across the table from each other, she had nothing to say. The only sound was of Alan chewing, a wet sound, slurping mixed with the snapping of teeth. He had gravy on his chin.

She tried a question. 'How are the chops?'

'A bit tough, Tess,' he mumbled, his fork in the air.

'Oh.' Tess concentrated on her plate. She hadn't started on the chop yet but it looked all right to her. The potatoes and peas looked fine. She tried again. 'How's the mash?'

He said nothing for a moment and then shrugged. 'Mash is mash.'

Tess clanked her knife and fork against the porcelain plate, cut the chop and chewed. It seemed tender enough. She gazed at her husband across the linen tablecloth. 'The weather's not good, is it?'

His eyes sparked with sudden interest. 'No, it's not. This rain is forecast for the whole weekend. I won't get out on the course if it carries on teeming down. I have a new iron I want to try out. I've been practising the swing with Cliff's club. I think it might improve my game. Cliff always buys the best for himself. My handicap would improve vastly if I just...'

Tess scraped back her chair and stopped listening. She collected his plate, now empty, and took it to the dishwasher. 'Shall I make coffee, Alan?'

Alan frowned, leaning back in the chair and rubbing his portly belly. 'If you like, Tess.'

She felt strands of platinum-blonde hair loosen from the clip at the top of her head and she pushed back the silky skeins. 'I could open a bottle of port if you like.'

Alan pressed the black-framed glasses towards his eyes. 'Port? Whatever for?'

'It's Valentine's Day,' Tess chirped. She'd bought him a card, a blue tie wrapped in tissue paper; they were upstairs, next to the bed.

Alan shook his head. 'It's just commercial rubbish,' he grunted. 'I was going to get you some chocolates, but I thought with you being on a diet you wouldn't appreciate it.'

Tess looked down at herself, at the baggy pullover and comfy jeans. She didn't remember telling Alan she was on a diet – she thought she was fine; her waist was a bit thicker than it had been before the children, but she was not bad for her seventy-two years. She met his eyes. 'Do I need to go on a diet?'

He shrugged. 'It's an after Christmas thing, I suppose – you had too much wine and chocolate and cake.' He sniffed. 'Tess, bring the coffee into the lounge, would you? There's some golf on Sky Sports. I thought I might...'

He shoved back his chair and mumbled as he moved towards the door. Tess stared at him – the dark hair, sparse on the top – and sighed as she watched him go. There had been a documentary she'd wanted to watch about a woman who had travelled to Egypt, an archaeologist in search of evidence about the life of Nefertiti. Tess had wondered what it would be like to travel and research, to go somewhere exotic and interesting. But now she'd have to take her book in the lounge and read while Alan watched golf and gabbled a ridiculous running commentary on each shot, speaking to himself as he always did. Tess filled the kettle and thought about Nefertiti. She'd been a mysterious and powerful woman in Egypt. Tess was a skivvy in Exmouth to a man who was a slave to golf.

* * *

'Elvis. Elvis, I'm home.'

The black cocker spaniel rushed towards her, his long ears swinging, and leapt up at her knees. Pam reached down and fondled the curly fur on his head. 'I haven't been too long, have I, Elvis? I just wanted to do a mile – the weather's awful.'

To prove her point, Pam ran her fingers through her hair. The usually blonde spiky cut hung in dark dripping clumps over her face. 'A man at the bus stop shouted at me: "You must be bloody mad, woman, running in this weather at your age."' I just laughed. But I'm freezing now. I must get out of these jog pants and into the shower. Come on up with me, Elvis – no, I'll feed you afterwards, I promise. I must get this clobber off and get warmed up.'

Pam rushed up the stairs, the spaniel bounding behind her. She peeled the damp layers from her body and hurried under the stream of hot water, reaching for soap and lathering herself. Through the steam and the glass, she could see the dark shape of Elvis, sitting patiently on the bath mat, waiting for her.

Swathed in a fluffy dressing gown, her feet bare, Pam padded downstairs, Elvis at her heels. In the little living room, the wooden table had been set with one plate, one knife and one fork, and a fire was blazing in the hearth. Pam curled up on the colourful rug, pushing a hand through her hair. Elvis snuggled down next to her legs, placing his wet nose on her lap. She rubbed his head and met the soulful eyes.

'OK, it's dinner time soon, Elvis.'

The spaniel wagged his tail, a steady drumbeat against the rug. She smiled at him. 'I've got some food for you in the kitchen. And I was going to make a nice Buddha bowl for myself but guess what? I've just remembered. It's Valentine's night. I'll do a pizza and open a bottle of red wine and afterwards we can both have a treat. Mine's ice cream. What's yours?'

Elvis bounded up towards her, his front paws on her chest. The dressing gown sagged open. Pam laughed.

'Elvis, really! I know you're the best valentine I've ever had but you need to keep your passion under control.' She hugged him close, the fire warming her face, and she offered him her wide smile.

'I must be the only woman in the world sharing Valentine's night with Elvis. But it has to be said, although you look gorgeous...' she kissed his damp nose '... your breath is terrible.'

2

Jen had offered to pay half the bill, but Eddie had insisted. He'd reached for his wallet and taken out cash, winking at her conspiratorially as he added an extra five pounds on the silver tray. He'd smiled towards the waiter. 'That's for the good service. The pie was particularly tasty. And I'm a great believer in coming back to somewhere if the service is of a good standard.' He'd held up her coat as she slipped it on. 'Shall we go, my dear?'

He presented his arm and Jen poked her wrist through the crook of his elbow as they strolled along the path. The rain had stopped but there was a strong breeze from the seafront and the streetlamps reflected light from neon signs in the puddles. Jen and Eddie turned the corner towards Barley Mow Avenue, where she lived. Jen raised her eyebrows. It was gone ten o'clock and Eddie lived half a mile's walk from her house. She turned to face him. 'Eddie, you don't need to walk me all the way home. I'd hate you to be caught out in another rainstorm...'

He chuckled. 'It's Valentine's Day. I thought I might get an invite to come in for a coffee.'

'Oh.' Jen frowned. He hadn't been in her house, not yet. He usually walked her to the corner of her road, pecked her cheek and turned away, discreet and polite. But then, most of their dates had been lunchtime meetings or strolls on the seafront or an afternoon tea. She had met him for the first time on Boxing Day; they'd both been wandering on the beach and he'd started a conversation, invited her to join him for a warm drink in the Olive Grove before enquiring where she lived and walking her halfway back. They'd talked about how quiet it was, being by themselves over Christmas – he was a widower – and he'd invited her for a drink the next day, then they'd met twice a week for lunch, then recently more frequently: a cream tea, a brisk walk. He was charming, good looking, good company. But he'd never asked to come in for coffee before.

'Oh,' Jen repeated. 'All right.'

She wondered what he meant by coffee. He was walking next to her, an impatient roll to his stride as if he was in a hurry. She could smell the tang of his aftershave. He'd clearly sprayed on a good deal more when he'd visited the Gents just before they'd left. And he'd combed his hair. Jen thought he was well groomed, smart, suave even, but she hadn't considered the wider implications of coffee.

They rounded the corner to Barley Mow Avenue, walking at a pace towards her little semi-detached house with the green front door. Jen's thoughts were racing. She had coffee in the kitchen: an instant ground mix in a jar, some decaff at the back of a cupboard. She even had a cafetière and some Machu Picchu beans. She wondered what sort of coffee Eddie would drink. Or if he'd prefer tea.

There was an unopened packet of custard creams somewhere too.

She glanced up at him and he winked again. She wondered if coffee mightn't mean something completely different, not coffee at all, but an innuendo, a euphemism for something else. Jen caught her breath. She had no idea what to say to him. She pulled the key from her handbag, opened the front door and muttered, 'Well, what takes your fancy, Eddie?' He raised his eyebrows. 'I mean, do you want it hot and strong, sweet, milky or just as it comes out of the spout?' She felt herself blushing and fluttered her hands in front of her face.

'Shall we take our coats off and sit down?' Eddie glanced around the hall, at the thick carpet and velvet door curtain that kept out the draughts. 'You keep it nice here, Jen.'

He sat in the lounge on the sofa, his feet on the rug. His shoes were damp and Jen wanted to tell him not to get mud on the carpet. He was glancing around the room, taking in the furniture, the books, the photos on the sideboard, her wedding photo with Colin in 1970. Jen was holding a bouquet as if it was heavy, a smiling bride with her long chestnut hair and the flowing white dress; Colin with sideburns and a fringe over his eyes.

She retreated to the small kitchen, banging open the cupboard door and clutching a small jar of freeze dried Costa Rican. Her hands shook as she filled the kettle. It had been a long time since a man had been in her house – there had been no one through the door since Colin had died and that had been four years ago, apart from her brother-in-law, Pete, and the young lad who'd serviced the boiler, of course. Jen wondered what Eddie might want to service. The porcelain cup slipped from her grip. She caught it just in time and placed it carefully on the saucer, on top of the tray with the jug of milk and the sugar lumps. Her heart had started to thud. She was not sure whether she was feeling excitement, passion or just unbridled fear.

She'd been married at twenty-three and, before Colin, there had just been one boyfriend, Ricky, who she'd loved from the age of fifteen until they'd broken up five years later, when he'd taken off to a pop festival, met some new friends and left to 'find himself' on the Isle of Wight. Jen had lost him and herself too, for a while, then she'd met Colin, an assistant in the local fishmonger's shop, and settled for a quiet life. Colin had been promoted to manager; he was a good businessman, buying their house then purchasing the shop for himself. They had been comfortable, although it would always be a regret that they weren't blessed with children. Colin had been kind, thoughtful and she'd never wanted for much. Then he'd had a stroke four years ago. He'd lasted three months. The second stroke had finished him off. Jen admitted to herself that she'd felt lonely ever since.

She missed the warmth of him more than the passion. Colin had been moderate in his desire for her. Her first love, Ricky, had been young, a sloppy kisser and a fumbler of buttons, more interested in his guitar than lust. She'd missed out on it really – mad passion, frantic sex. Sex had never been on her mind much at all, until now. Eddie had kissed her before, on the cheek at first then, several weeks ago, on the lips, briefly, every time they parted. There was warmth in his hugs, but she'd never considered that there might be something else. And now she didn't know what she was feeling. Afraid? Glad to be desired? Perhaps she simply felt happy in his company. She wasn't sure. She carried the tray into the lounge, her breath a little ragged. Eddie had taken off his jacket and loosened his tie. She put the tray down and he patted the seat next to him, grinning.

'Jen. Come and sit here. The coffee can wait a minute, can't it?'

She wondered why her legs were being so obedient as she moved to the sofa and plonked herself down next to him, her shoulder against the arm he had draped across the back of the seat. His grasp circled her and he pulled her next to him.

'Jen...' He pecked her cheek. 'Jenny.'

She wondered whether to sit up straight, wriggle away, feign a sudden interest in conversation and start gabbling about the lounge carpet, the deep pile, and the difficulties of finding a good hoover, one that would pick up all sorts of dust and get into the tricky corners. He nuzzled her cheek, his lips against her ear. Jen closed her eyes; the sensation wasn't unpleasant. She inhaled the heady cinnamon and musk scent of his aftershave and wondered if he would kiss her. He pecked her on the lips and she blinked. He was staring at her, his blue eyes huge, his tidy grey hair framing a handsome face, his lips pursed to speak. 'Jen...'

She wondered what would come next. The excitement and trepidation had turned into puzzlement. 'Eddie... your coffee will get cold.'

'I haven't come here for the coffee, Jen.' He moved his face closer to hers. 'I ought to tell the truth. It was a ploy to get you here alone, just us, by ourselves.'

Jen felt her heart bump. She was thrilled, intrigued. He was going to kiss her, perhaps tug at her clothes. Her mind raced; she had known him for two months – she liked him a lot. But what if it wasn't passion on his mind? What if he intended to steal from her, or worse? She did trust him though. His face was serious and kind. He surely couldn't be a serial killer, but she'd read about such people in the papers, making widowed ladies trust them and then... No, surely not Eddie. His eyes were full of kindness.

'I wanted to say something, Jen. I mean, we get along well...'

She caught her breath. He was going to tell her that he wanted to end the relationship. They got along well but that was all there was to it – she was expecting too much of him, a widower, set in his ways. Jen shook her head – no, it wasn't that. He'd taken her out on Valentine's night. Perhaps he was going to confess that he'd fallen for her, that he was in love. Then perhaps he'd rip open his shirt, fall on top of her and sink his lips against her neck.

Jen exhaled. She'd been reading too many romance novels. She reached out, patted his hand in an encouraging way. 'What is it, Eddie?'

'When we met on Boxing Day, we talked about how difficult it was being alone. You lost your husband. My wife, Pat, passed away two years ago. I've never become used to being by myself, to tell you the truth.'

He must be miserable, Jen thought. His face was serious, his eyes those of a lost puppy. She patted his hand again.

'How can I help, Eddie?'

'We get on, don't we?' He had suddenly become breathless, his words rushed. 'I mean, we like each other. Jen, we're not young. There's no time like the present. Not a second to waste.' He fumbled in his pocket, his face flustered, his lips open, panting. Jen wondered what he was searching for. An inhaler? Her eyes widened; she was astonished. He pulled out a handkerchief, unwrapping the neat folds, and held something out towards her. It was a ring, three diamonds in a row on a gold band, an antique style.

'Jenifer Hooper, would you do me the honour...?'

She frowned, unsure what he wanted. The thought flicked into her mind that he was trying to sell it to her. Perhaps he had money problems. 'Eddie...?'

'Will you marry me?'

She gasped, falling back into the sofa, against the soft cushions. She did not know what to say. Her mind was blank, waiting for the flood of emotions that would follow. 'Me? You're asking me...?'

He grasped her hand, holding the ring up, sliding it onto the wedding finger. It was a little loose. 'It fits well. Real diamonds. The best money can buy. So – would you do me the honour of becoming my wife?'

Jen was aware that she hadn't said yes. Not yet. But he was right: it was a good idea. They were both in their seventies. Jen was seventy-three and Eddie a little older. They were both alone, widowed. Neither of them liked solitude. And Eddie was a nice man, dapper, suave, well dressed, and pleasant company. Thoughts were rushing, crashing against each other in her mind. It would be good to have someone there when she woke up, someone to share meals with, to talk to, to share the warmth of an embrace. And he was such a nice man, so caring, so considerate. She'd be mad to refuse.

But it had happened so quickly she couldn't catch her breath. In some ways, Eddie was still a stranger: she'd only known him since Boxing Day. They'd been on pleasant dates and enjoyed each other's company; he was courteous, kind, always complimenting her, offering her his arm as they strolled along the beach. It fluttered into her head that he was nothing like Colin, her Colin, whom she'd known so well, who had fitted her married life like a comfortable sock, who had become such an essential part of the fabric of her life that she knew every stitch. Eddie was unknown to her, a fit that wasn't yet snug.

'What do you say, Jen? Will you be Mrs Bruce? Will you accept...?'

An expression of confusion etched itself across her face. Her fingers shook; the ring was loose on her wedding finger. She stared at Eddie. 'I'm not sure – I mean – I don't know. It's early days yet. Can I think about it?'

He slid the ring from her finger and held it in his open palm, meeting her eyes with his serious blue ones. 'Of course. Take as long as you need. But neither of us is getting any younger...'

He pressed his lips against hers. They were cool. When he pulled away, he seemed composed.

'Just let me know when you're ready, Jen. You know I'll wait for you to decide.'

Jen nodded energetically. 'All right, Eddie.'

He glanced around the house. 'You've made it so nice here. A feminine touch. But of course, I could tidy it up a bit, you know – I'm good with DIY.'

Jen nodded again. She wasn't sure what to say. It was as if a whirlwind had lifted her up – she was buoyant and moving out of control. Her limbs had gone numb. Her lips too. She could only nod. Eddie eased himself upright.

'Well, I'll get off now, shall I? Perhaps we can meet tomorrow and we can talk about it again when you've had time to give it some thought? It's a good offer, my dear. What do you say, Jen?'

She stood up, facing him. 'Yes. Yes, all right, I'll think about it.'

He kissed her lips lightly again. 'Well, that's it. Do take it seriously, though. You and I are very good together. We make a good couple and we'd make each other very happy.' He reached for his coat, tugging it over broad shoulders.

Jen blinked, then fussed with his collar, fidgeting with the buttons. 'Are you going home now, Eddie?'

'It's eleven o'clock,' he said, smiling. 'I need my beauty sleep. You too.' He lifted her chin. 'Well, you just need sleep.' He shuffled towards the door. Jen wondered if she should invite him to stay. She wanted company. She wanted him to hold her tight, to kiss her properly. He hadn't said he was in love with her yet.

'You wouldn't like to stay... a bit longer?'

He pecked her cheek again. 'I'll phone you tomorrow and we can meet for afternoon tea.' He put a finger to her face. 'What a wonderful evening this has been. It's so nice to spend time with you. I just thought it would be lovely if our arrangement was a bit more – permanent.'

Jen nodded. She wondered if she should have said yes, if her refusal had made Eddie's feelings cooler towards her. He kissed her cheek and put an affectionate arm around her. She clung to him but he eased himself away.

'It'll be cold outside. I'll see myself out. I don't want you to catch a chill. Goodnight, my dear.'

And then he was gone. Jen squeezed her eyes closed, not sure if she was disappointed, in love or just confused. All three, perhaps. But she would have liked him to stay. She'd have enjoyed more conversation and a sense of closeness. Then perhaps she would be sure she loved him; she'd know if she should have accepted his proposal. But there was always tomorrow. She was suddenly filled with a thrill about the future, and what it might bring.

She picked up the tray. The coffee was untouched, but it had gone cold. Jen sighed. She'd wash up, tidy a little and then she'd go to bed, alone. She gazed at her finger where the diamond ring had stayed for almost a minute. She'd had the chance to become an engaged woman, a bride-to-be. It had felt strange, frightening and just a little bit exciting. She wasn't sure what she'd tell her friends at aqua aerobics — that Eddie had proposed and she'd turned him down? The room was cold and Jen was alone. For a moment, she imagined that Eddie was her husband, that they'd finished cups of cocoa and they were on their way upstairs to bed. He'd take her small fingers in his large hand and they'd go up together. Jen suddenly felt a chill in the air and she realised how lonely she was.

Rose played *Für Elise* again, perfectly. Her fingers drifted easily over the piano keys and the sound of the music flowing, confident and loud, was somehow reassuring. She finished with a flourish, sat back and looked at her hands. Small, neat, well-shaped, a single gold band on her left hand. She still missed him, Bernard, especially at this time of night, although there had been times he'd annoyed her and they'd bickered. But it was too late for feelings of regret. She had no one to be annoyed with now, and that made her sad. When the last vibration of the piano had faded, it was replaced with empty silence and she felt cold and alone. Rose stood up from the piano stool. She'd throw away the half-eaten macaroni cheese, wash the plate and go up to bed.

* * *

Della lay on her back, listening to the nasal rattle of her

husband, Sylvester, who was sleeping by her side, his glasses still perched on his nose. It was his usual nightly practice to snore, an adenoidal snort that lasted for fifteen seconds, stopped and then started up again. Like a chainsaw. Della smiled. She waited through the silence, the seven seconds' respite, counting him down and then, bang on time, he started again, the persistent wheeze assaulting her ears again. She reached over, patting his shoulder lovingly. 'Sylvester... Sylvester. Stop snoring and go to sleep now, will you, my love?'

He paused and then mumbled through soft lips. 'Love you too.'

Della grinned. She breathed out, rolled over, tugging the duvet with her, and snuggled down into the cocoon of warmth. She closed her eyes, sighed, and started to drift. Seven seconds of blissful silence. The chainsaw rattle began again, stretching out into a fifteen second rumble, pausing for seven seconds, then starting up all over again.

It was past eleven now and Alan was still watching golf. He was still making comments aloud, analysing each whack of the ball, the angle of each curve on the air, the descent towards each hole. Tess clenched her teeth – as if she'd be interested. She'd recorded the documentary about Nefertiti. She'd watch it tomorrow, when Alan was out with his other golf buddies, after he'd left in his jacket and ridiculous cap, carrying his bag of clubs to the car. Tess groaned. The television screen illuminated his face and his eyes shone with happiness. She didn't care. She had her friends, her own thoughts. She picked up his teacup, the plate she'd put the biscuits on, and took them through to the kitchen to wash up, avoiding his eyes. As she passed him, he gave a little grunt of thanks.

She washed the dishes, staring out of the kitchen window. The sky was dark blue, dotted with shining specks of stars. The moon slid behind a cloud and emerged again, a pale silver hook. Tess felt very small inside her quiet house, with no sound except for the dripping tap in the kitchen, and the rattle of the television from the next room. She shook her head sadly and told herself again that she didn't care what Alan did. She'd carry on trying to make her own life fun, as she always did, just for herself.

* * *

It was one of those precious moments that could be held still, like a scoop of fresh water in cupped hands, and treasured. A second of pure peace, followed by another. Elvis was curled up at the bottom of the bed and soothing music from the smart speaker filled the room, the gentle melodic voice of Enya. Pam closed her eyes and thought of woodlands, leaves draping their tips in gurgling streams, the sunlight filtering through branches. She reached down to stroke Elvis's soft fur and felt a damp nose, the wetness of a tongue. She breathed out, grateful for the warmth of a thick duvet and the intense burning of her toes against a hot-water bottle. The past was in the distance. The present was all that mattered. Life, she decided, was good. How could anything be simpler and better than this?

* * *

Jen woke early in the morning; her eyes immediately opened wide and she listened. She sat upright in bed, her heart pounding. She'd heard a noise downstairs. She held her breath. The digital alarm said it was almost seven o'clock. She listened harder, her ears straining against the silence. There it was again, a soft bump like a footfall. It had come from the living room. Jen breathed out imperceptibly. It hadn't come from outside; it wasn't the soft gliding of a milk float – there hadn't been one in the street for years – or the heavy rumble of the bin men's lorry. It had sounded like someone bumping against furniture. It was a burglar.

Jen called out, 'Who's there?'

The fear in her own voice made her tremble. She slid out of bed and reached for her dressing gown, pulling it over her nightie. Somehow a second layer made her feel safer. She edged to the top of the stirs, her feet barely touching the carpet. She held onto the banister, supporting each step she took. At the bottom of the stairs, the front door was locked; she'd locked it last night after Eddie had left. Jen listened; empty silence rang in her ears, and then the noise came again, a brief brushing sound, once.

'Who's there?' Her voice was a little stronger but her legs were trembling. She edged towards the door, pushed it open slowly and turned the corner into the living room. Her heart leapt as she saw a hunched shape and a pair of green eyes narrowing in her direction.

'Gus!'

Jen glanced from the black and white cat to the open curtains: she had left the top window open and the neighbour's cat had clambered through. She blew air from her mouth in relief as Gus scuttled towards the front door to be let out. She turned the key and opened the door, watching him rush out into the quiet street.

Jen decided she needed to settle her nerves: she'd make herself a cup of strong tea; perhaps she'd have toast and marmalade. She sank onto the sofa and put her head in her hands.

She'd left a window open. It was a small gap, but a burglar could have easily crawled through into her home. She was by herself, vulnerable, prey to all sorts of dangerous people.

At once she wanted Eddie to hold her in his arms, to pull her to him and tell her she was safe. If he'd been there, she wouldn't have been so afraid. He'd have stood up to a burglar; he'd have been strong.

It was suddenly crystal clear. She loved Eddie; she needed him. They should be together. Not only would she be safer, but she wouldn't be alone. It made complete sense. Eddie was right, she knew it. He was sensible; he was just what she needed in her life: stability, comfort. Jen took a breath. She knew what she had to do, and at once. She reached for her mobile and dialled his number. Eddie answered almost immediately, his voice a crackle, concerned and reliable.

'Jen? It's half past seven. Are you all right, my dear?'

'Yes.' That was the word she wanted to say. Jen was breathing rapidly. 'Yes, Eddie – I've never been better. And if you want to ask me again, that's my answer – yes.'

He was quiet for a moment and then he chuckled softly. 'Are you saying you'll marry me, Jen? Really? Well, that's wonderful news.'

She was smiling, her face stretched with happiness and relief. The warmth in his tone told her she had made the right decision.

'Eddie... yes, I'm sure.'

'Excellent. This calls for a celebration. Can you meet me in the café on the seafront – Coffeelicious? It opens at nine. I'll buy you breakfast.'

Jen nodded, her heart pounding. She realised Eddie couldn't hear her, so she added, 'Yes, yes, yes,' and beamed again at the sound of the word.

'Oh, then I'll see you soon, my dear,' Eddie whispered. 'And I'll bring the ring along, shall I?'

3

The five women emerged dripping from the pool, their skin tingling from the exercise. They formed a line unintention-ally, five different heights and shapes wearing five different colours. Tess Watkins, blonde hair tied back in a little plait, was short and curvy in a turquoise blue tankini; Rose Grant, her grey-brown hair almost black now drenched with water, was in a sensible navy-blue swimsuit, neat and tidy. Della Donavan clambered out next, shapely in an orange floral swimsuit, her frosted dark curly hair glistening with pearl droplets of water. Then the smallest of the five, Jen Hooper, her shoulder length chestnut hair clipped to her head, wet tendrils dripping, her body slender and delicate in a cream swimsuit. Finally, towering over them all, Pam Marshall stood tall and willowy in a racer-back black swimsuit with blue and red stripes down one side. With her blonde pixie cut flat-tened against her head and her hands on her hips, she was athletic and broad shouldered. The friends giggled together, shaking water from tired limbs, moving towards the changing rooms, water dripping from their swimsuits. Tess's voice rose over the laughter. 'Well, Kathy certainly made us work hard today. I think we deserve some refreshment. Who's up for a coffee and a slice of cake?'

Rose nodded. It was better than being home alone. Pam breathed out. 'I'm gasping for a cool drink.'

'I'm not surprised.' Tess's voice was mock-indignant. 'You were doing aqua aerobics for the five of us today.'

'I'm worn out.' Della puffed air from her mouth. 'It was hard work. It's supposed to help the aches in my bones but I'm exhausted. I thought it was meant to be gentle exercise.'

Pam snorted. 'Exercise should never be gentle. It's like life – we should throw ourselves in, give it 100 per cent, grab it by the balls.'

Jen's face was thoughtful as she linked her fingers together and glanced at the new ring.

Tess hooted. 'I can think of better balls to grab.' She flicked water from her platinum hair. 'Did you see the young man with the dark hair and the broad chest at the other end of the pool? Tight white Speedos? Just like Patrick Duffy in *The Man from Atlantis,* Remember him, girls?'

Della chuckled. 'Oh, yes – he was very handsome.' She nudged Pam, rolling her eyes. 'But shouldn't you be thinking about Alan's balls, Tess?'

'Alan knows where he can stick his balls. And his golf clubs.'

Tess and Della turned to each other, howling with laughter. Rose's eyes were etched with concern. 'That's a terrible thing to say about your husband, Tess.'

'It may be, but it's true. That man is driving me mad.' They were in the changing rooms, sorting through their sports bags. Tess picked up her towel, flinging it around her shoulders. 'Alan's at golf. I'm out with my friends, free and having fun. I'm going to start by enjoying an invigorating shower. Then I'm having a massive slice of cake.'

Pam turned to Jen, who was standing next to her, fidgeting with her hands. 'Are you OK? You're quiet today, Jen.'

Jen was distracted. 'Oh, sorry – yes, I'm fine.' She forced a giggle. 'I'm looking forward to something sweet and tasty in the café.'

Tess squealed. 'I bet. Are you still going out with that handsome man you met on the beach? Freddie or Eddie or whoever he is.'

Jen nodded, twisting the ring on her finger. She reached for her towel and smiled.

* * *

The table in the café was a mess: Rose wouldn't have allowed the polished wooden one in her dining room to get in such a state. Tess covered her lips as she smiled – there were cake crumbs, paper wrappings, slops of coffee across the plastic surface. She imagined Alan's face if he came home and their oak table was in such a state of disarray. Della swept crumbs into her hand. Pam was more concerned with finishing the contents of a second bottle of sparkling water and, when she dumped the empty container back on the table, it toppled over on its side, spattering little puddles in its wake. Rose wondered if Pam's house was as untidy. She supposed since Pam had always been single, as far as she knew, no one had been around to complain about untidiness. But then, Pam had never had anyone to keep the house nice for either, she thought. Jen was unusually quiet, staring at her fingernails.

Della dabbed her mouth with a paper napkin and

dropped it on her plate. 'That was such good cake. Nearly as good as I make myself.'

Pam sank her teeth into her slice. 'We deserve a treat.' She thought for a moment. 'It's a shame we haven't got a bottle of wine or two. I haven't had a good celebration in ages.'

'Are you thinking of a girls' night out?' Tess chewed at a fingernail. 'What a lovely idea. We could get all dressed up, go somewhere nice...'

'Dancing...' Della suggested.

'Clubbing,' Tess offered. 'There are some really great places for a rave-up in Exeter.'

'Rave-up?' Pam spluttered, wiping her mouth. 'What decade are you in, Tess?'

Tess winked. 'I don't care as long as there are plenty of drinks flowing and some fun to be had.'

Rose pulled a thoughtful face. 'What about a birthday? Who's next? I'm not until December.'

'A girls' night out would be fab.' Pam drummed her fingers on the table. 'Do we need an excuse?'

'We could just go out and party – without any excuse at all.' Della chuckled.

Jen took a breath. It was time. This was her cue. She held out her left hand to reach for a slice of cake, wiggling her fingers exaggeratedly. Light caught the diamonds and they winked, shooting flashes of rainbow colour. Della sat up straight. 'What's that on your finger, girl?'

Three voices trilled at the same time. Tess leaned forward. 'Oh my God, no! Tell me she hasn't...'

Della sighed. 'It's a diamond ring. How beautiful...'

Pam screeched. 'When did that happen?'

Jen's face broke into a wide smile she couldn't hold back.

'Two days ago. Valentine's night. Eddie asked me... and the next day, I said yes.'

Rose frowned. 'It's a bit quick, isn't it? You've only known each other since Christmas. It takes me longer than that to decide which cut to get at the butcher's.'

'I think it's lovely,' Tess breathed. She was thinking of the emptiness of her own life when Alan was at golf, and how the walls held cold silence in them every day.

'Congratulations.' Pam banged a fist on the table. 'Well, here's our excuse for a night out.'

Della grabbed Jen's hand. 'What a wonderful ring. The diamonds are huge. Where did you buy it, Jen?'

Jen waved her hand for all to examine. 'Eddie chose it. He just sprang it on me. He came in for coffee...'

'Coffee...' Della laughed.

'I bet he did.' Tess snorted.

'... and he asked me to marry him and produced the ring. Of course, I did the sensible thing and asked for more time to think about it.' She wiggled her finger again. 'Then the next morning, I said yes and Eddie took me to breakfast to celebrate. It was really lovely.'

Pam leaned back in her seat, stretching out long legs in jeans. 'Well, how exciting. Congratulations, Jen. So, when's the big day?'

Jen giggled. 'We've been talking about it. Eddie thinks we should get married in six weeks or so. Late March, early April. A spring wedding...'

'I hope we're going to be your bridesmaids,' Tess butted in.

'Oh, we'll probably just have a simple do. No fuss. A few friends – you're all invited – and a quiet meal somewhere – probably the Olive Grove. Eddie wants us to live in my house.

He said he can rent out his place and we'll get a good income from it. He's written all the figures down on a piece of paper.'

'He sounds like a sensible man.' Rose thought for a moment. 'But there's no fun in maths – what about the exciting bits like the honeymoon?'

Pam fluffed her short hair, making it stand up. 'Eddie certainly sounds like he has it all worked out.'

'And how do you feel, Jen?' Della leaned forward. 'Are you all excited?'

'It's like being caught up in a whirlwind...'

Tess grimaced. 'Oh yes, it's like that at first. All lovey-dovey. Then after a year or so, it's smelly socks to wash and "the chops are a bit tough, Tess" and golf clubs in every corner of the room.' She noticed Jen's anxious expression and laughed, too high. 'Oh, but that's just Alan. I'm sure your Eddie will be completely different.'

'Does he snore?' Della asked, wrinkling her brow.

Jen pouted. 'I've no idea. We haven't...'

'You haven't sampled the goods yet?' Tess giggled. 'Is that a good idea?'

'Eddie's very proper... and respectful,' Jen insisted. 'We talked about a honeymoon. A long weekend in Lyme Regis. We'll wait until then.'

'Oh, I'd want to know he was man enough for the job before I married him.' Tess winked.

Della's face was serious. 'I think you're all missing the point.' She met everyone's eyes in turn, then she smiled at Jen. 'It's a wonderful thing. Our friend Jen is getting married. And we should all rejoice for her.'

Rose nodded. 'Yes, congratulations, Jen.'

'To years of happiness,' Pam murmured.

'I'll drink to that.' Tess nodded. 'And that means a party.'

* * *

'Have you met him, Tess?'

Pam and Tess were walking home together. It was well past five and the light was fading already, the sky streaked with indigo and crimson wheals. The two women lived several streets away and it was their habit to walk home briskly together after aqua aerobics and put the world to rights. But today there could only be one topic.

'No – but Jen seems very taken with him. I've never set eyes on him – have you?'

'Yes.' Pam took a breath. 'I was out with Elvis, jogging on the beach a couple of weeks ago. They were walking along in the other direction, arm in arm. I stopped to say hello and Jen introduced me.'

Tess wrinkled her nose. 'What's he like?'

'Handsome, mid-seventies – a tall man, broad chested, well mannered.' Pam shrugged. 'I can see why Jen would like him. He seemed very – protective, you know, the sort of old-fashioned-gentleman type who wraps a woman in cotton wool.' She thought for a moment; somehow she had sensed all this within moments of meeting Eddie. 'He didn't seem to like Elvis much when he leapt up at him. He seemed more concerned with his expensive coat. I had to carry on with my jog pretty quickly after that.'

Tess increased her pace to keep up with Pam. They were going up a steady hill. 'I'm amazed how fit you are, Pam, at seventy-three. Jogging, yoga, swimming – you never stop. You're just amazing.'

'I believe that we either use it or lose it.' Pam grinned. 'It's not all plain sailing. I have aching knees sometimes and a sore heel most mornings. I love to get out though, in the fresh air. Elvis loves it too.'

'It's too cold for me.' Tess shivered. 'Alan is happy to be out in the winter chill though. He's moody as anything when he can't play golf. And as for me, I'm glad to see the back of him, when he's out on the course. I get a bit of time to myself.'

Pam's brow was furrowed. 'Do you really not get on, Tess?'

'To be honest, we see so little of each other now, it's hard to tell. We just bumble along really.'

'Why don't you leave him if it's so dull?'

'Habit, I guess.' Tess shrugged. 'I used to love him once.' She chortled. 'Passionately. Then we had the kids. Lisa's forty-seven now. Gemma's forty-five. Once they came along, I just seemed to be involved in their lives. I suppose Alan and I grew apart. Then he gave up work, retired, took up playing golf in all his spare time and we only saw each other first thing in the morning and late at night.' The pounding of their feet on the pavement was the only sound for a while, then Tess said, 'It's normal now, I guess. And breaking up would be difficult, selling the house, being alone, like poor Rose. I'm not sure which would be worse, being with Alan or being lonely.'

Pam chewed her lip. 'I'm happy by myself.'

'Have you never lived with anyone?'

'There have been – you know – people in my life...' A small laugh escaped Pam's lips. 'Nothing ever worked out though. I always became bored – it was always too claustro-phobic. Or people got bored with me, or things went wrong. I wonder sometimes if I ought to be sensible, settle down, just like everyone else...' She sniffed. 'But really I'm glad I'm single.'

The mood had become a bit morose. Spaces between

conversations seemed to fill with thoughts, regrets. Then Tess said, 'Well, Jen's getting married. How about you and I plan something for us all this weekend – a girls' night out for the five of us? What do you say, Pam?'

'Perfect.'

They had arrived at Pam's front door, a little terraced cottage in the middle of the street. Tess had two more streets to cross then she'd be home. They hugged, feeling the warmth of the other's cheeks, then Pam said, 'I'll ring you. We'll sort out a great night to celebrate Jen's engagement.'

Tess nodded, pushing her hands deep into her coat pockets, her voice trailing back to Pam as she strolled away. 'I think we could use one. It might cheer us all up a bit.'

* * *

Della was peeling plantains. Sylvester's favourite. He had such a sweet tooth. He'd be home soon from the snack van on the seafront, which he managed most days at lunchtime and sometimes into the evening. Oil was sizzling in the pan. She was thinking about marriage. She and Sylvester had married in a tiny church in Stepney, forty-nine years ago. She'd worn a lacy gown she'd made herself. Sylvester was all done up in a second-hand suit and his pork-pie hat. He'd looked so handsome. She diced the plantains, throwing the pieces into the oil, listening to the fizz.

Linval had been born less than a year later; Aston one year after that. They'd never had much money as a family. Sylvester had worked hard, two jobs sometimes, but they'd been happy. Throughout their marriage, laughter had kept them entwined. They'd talked together, tucked up in bed on cold nights, about going back to live in Jamaica. Sylvester had left St Ann's Bay at sixteen. Della had arrived in the UK earlier, as an eight year old, her parents leading her by the hand from the boat onto the bleak windy quay. She'd never known such bitter cold weather and she'd never got used to it.

But their love had kept her warm, Sylvester's embrace, his cheerful smile, his kisses. She didn't want for much else. She put a hand to the ache in her lower back. The oil spat and hissed in the pan as she flipped the golden plantains over. She hoped Jen and her Eddie would be as happy as she was.

* * *

Rose sat at the piano and stretched out her hands. Bertie Small would be here in ten minutes for his lesson. He was quite good, a chirpy ten year old, but Rose suspected that his mother was keen for him to progress at a faster rate. Apparently, Bertie's grandfather had been a good pianist. Rose wriggled her fingers. She had neat hands – they could fly across the keys nimbly. She was glad she'd never inherited the arthritis her poor mother had to endure, fingers twisted into brittle claws at sixty-five. Rose was seventy-five and, despite or perhaps because of the constant use, her fingers were as deft as ever. She began to play, Tchaikovsky's piano concerto No 1. She loved the way the notes filled the room with resonating sadness. It was somehow pure, soothing, as if the rest of the world could understand and share her melancholy.

Rose smiled sadly, regret curving her lips, as she watched her fingers move lightly, the fluttering left hand, the finger with the gold wedding band. She missed Bernard terribly but, more than that, she hated the cold ache that filled her body when she was alone in empty spaces and silent rooms. She hoped Jen would be happy with Eddie, but she, Rose, was feeling more alone than ever, unwanted, dowdy, someone who would spend solitary days playing beautiful music for herself until her last hour. She felt a single tear roll down her cheek.

Her fingers thrummed on the keys, more and more heavily until she was making the notes reverberate. Suddenly, the melody lifted into the air and the room was filled with energy, with powerful music and a new strength and direction. A thought popped into Rose's head: things only became stronger if you made more effort. Perhaps her life should be about making more noise and demanding to be heard. Her jaw clenched; she pressed down firmly on the keys and felt the music soar and it lifted her spirits. Perhaps it was time for a change.

4

It was almost eight o'clock. It was dark outside and a wind was buffeting a branch against the panes. The taxi would be here soon. Jen squinted in the mirror, fidgeted with her hair and glanced at the clock again. She wondered what everyone else would be wearing and whether the pretty blue dress she'd chosen would be too formal. Pam would be in jeans; Della would look glorious whatever she was wearing and Rose would have picked something sombre, preferring plain colours.

Jen couldn't guess what Tess would wear: for a woman whose marriage was so dull, she always seemed full of surprises and was guaranteed to be colourful and bubbly. She'd probably wear something stunning. Jen wanted to shine tonight, as bright as the three diamonds on her finger. It was only going to be a simple meal in a restaurant, cock-tails first in some trendy bar, but the girls had organised it for her to celebrate her engagement. They were becoming closer as friends – this was their first real night out together, if she didn't count the drink in the Olive Grove on Christmas Eve, and she wanted it to go well. It was as if a good girls' night out would lead to a good engagement between her and Eddie, a great wedding and then a successful marriage. She had to admit she felt nervous. The doorbell rang. Jen grabbed her handbag and plastered a smile on her face. No pressure, then.

Pam, Tess and Della were already in the taxi, which was filled with the heady aroma of too much perfume. Jen took her seat next to Della and fastened the safety belt. The taxi driver mumbled something about going to Jubilee Road next then they'd head for Exeter. The women paid little attention to him, the back of his head a dark silhouette of bristly hair. Tess was already outlining the cocktails available at the Havana Bar from the menu on her phone. She cackled. 'I don't care what's in it – I'm definitely up for a Drunken Sailor or two tonight.'

Della chortled. 'Dances with Wenches... I wonder what that is...'

'I'm going to have a couple of Cement Mixers.' Pam waved her hands to show how the alcoholic drink might be whirled around in the glass. The taxi slowed down to a stop and the door was pulled open. An anxious looking Rose climbed in, wearing a heavy coat.

Tess waved the phone and called out, 'Hello, Rose. We're just contemplating our orders for the night. How do you fancy a Screaming Orgasm or two?'

Rose's face froze in horror. Pam helped her to her seat and patted her hand. 'It's Irish cream, vodka and amaretto. A really sweet cocktail. I might have to try one.'

Tess burst into peals of laughter. 'It's going to be a fabulous night, girls. And it's all down to Jen, our awesome bride-to-be. Congratulations to Jen and Eddie.'

Five voices whooped and screamed. There was a round of

applause and someone started singing Queen's 'Crazy Little Thing Called Love', almost in tune. The taxi driver, a man in his forties with designer stubble, glanced in his rear view mirror at five women in their seventies, mostly dressed to the nines, hooting with laughter, and he shook his head and glanced back to the road.

The Havana wasn't full; there were one or two couples at tables and a group of several young people who were possibly students in the corner, but the place seemed quiet. Pam led the way to the bar and grinned at the barman, a tall young man whose name badge proclaimed that he was called Sam. 'We're celebrating tonight, Sam.' Pam rummaged in her purse and handed over a twenty pound note and a ten. 'Will that get us five cocktails?'

Sam seemed a little perplexed. 'It's happy hour until nine. So, if you order two each, buy one get one free, that's twenty-five pounds.'

'Righto.' Pam flourished the notes. 'Five Drunken Sailors and five Dances with Wenches, please.'

Tess screwed up her face. 'And six Screaming Orgasms...'

'Six?' Jen shook her head. 'There are five of us.'

Tess giggled. 'Happy hour – three plus three free ones – if no one can drink the spare one, I'll have it.'

Pam shook her head. 'I think we should just stick with two each, Tess – we'll need some space left for a glass of wine over at the restaurant.'

'You can have mine, Tess,' Rose wailed. 'I'll never drink a whole one.'

'I only want one,' Jen insisted.

'They don't put much alcohol in them.' Tess patted her arm. 'But you're right, Pam – let's pace ourselves.'

Sam shrugged. 'I'll bring them over – where are you sitting?'

Pam pointed to the quiet corner. The bar had dark wooden floors and tables, red strip lights on low ceilings and brick walls. Rose felt a new determination to enjoy herself as she followed Tess to the table with six seats, but she was anxious. It was not an environment she was accustomed to. Music was blaring from speakers overhead – a woman with a husky voice was singing a song about not wanting to go to rehab. Rose thought it didn't bode well. She would just sip her first drink slowly. She took her place next to Jen, who she was sure would be the most moderate. Della gazed around her. 'Nice place. Good choice, Pam.'

'Someone told me about it – apparently it gets really busy here later, but we'll be eating by then.'

'Where are we having food?' Jen wrinkled her nose. 'I hope it's not too far to walk.'

Pam shook her head. 'Across the road – the little Italian place. Felipiano's. It's supposed to be lovely. Our table is booked for half nine.'

'That's very late to eat.' Rose gazed at Sam as he arrived with a tray of drinks. Her eyebrows shot up – the cocktail glasses were much bigger than she'd expected and they were filled with colourful liquid that reflected the bright light. She watched Sam place them skilfully on the table. Tess was giggling and flirting with the waiter, telling him he had huge biceps and it must be a by-product of his job, carrying so many full glasses. Rose felt her cheeks tingle and she glanced away. She was wondering where she fitted in with the abandon of a girls' night out and she determined to try harder.

Music began to play. It was Dexy's Midnight Runners,

'Come On Eileen', and Tess jigged around in her seat, waving her arms and leaning over, selecting a glass, taking a huge sip. She made an audible sound of pleasure. 'I love this song.'

'Rolling Stones for me,' Della lifted her glass. 'I always thought Mick Jagger was gorgeous.' She took a sip of cocktail. 'He still is.'

'Too dangerous.' Jen was staring at the glasses, selecting one. 'Mick Jagger, I mean. I liked the Beatles. Lovely Paul McCartney with his handsome baby face.'

'You know me – Elvis every time.' Pam winked, taking a sip of her Drunken Sailor.

'Abba.' Rose stuck a finger in her glass and tasted the liquor tentatively. 'I like Abba best.' She was shocked by the peal of laughter that came from the four friends' mouths in one loud gush. She suddenly felt annoyed. 'What? I like their music – the tunes, the songs, the piano playing.'

Tess leapt in with a chorus of 'Dancing Queen', waving her drink so energetically that the cocktail slopped over the lip of the glass. Jen's face was serious. 'You like Abba? Seriously?'

'Their songs are clever – well composed, well structured.'

'But aren't they just pop songs?' Tess wrinkled her nose as if the idea smelled awful.

Rose was persistent. 'I've got a book with all the songs in for teaching piano. I use them in some of my lessons. They are quite popular with some of the children.' She picked up her glass and her eyes flashed defiance. 'Well, I like them.'

'And why not?' Pam smiled encouragingly. 'Well, this is nice – we have plenty of time to have some fun. Our table isn't ready for another half hour. Are you enjoying yourself, Jen?'

'Mmm.' Jen was halfway through a mouthful of Dances

with Wenches. She wiped her lips delicately. 'I'm not sure what Eddie would think of me if he could see me now though.'

'Sylvester wanted to come with me.' Della grinned. 'He said he'd put one of my dresses on and a wig if it meant he could have a night out with us. He said he'd love to be a fly on the—'

'Alan wouldn't want to be here.' Tess finished the contents of one glass and reached for another. 'He'd ruin it anyway – in a dress or otherwise.'

Half an hour later, Tess was regaling them with the fact that she hadn't even received a card from Alan on Valentine's Day and he hadn't worn the blue tie she'd so carefully wrapped in tissue paper. Pam reached for her handbag. 'OK – everyone ready?'

Tess grabbed the three unfinished cocktails and drained the glasses, taking Rose's almost full glass that she was offering from her fingers and inverting it. Jen glanced at the glinting ring on her third finger and smiled – she felt sudden warmth towards the women who had dragged her out on a cold February night to celebrate. Tess was still singing 'Dancing Queen' when they left the bar. By the time they were seated in Felipiano's, she had started on 'Mamma Mia', accompanying herself on the cutlery.

The restaurant was beautifully furnished, rustic white walls and tiny candles in jars, pretty checked cloths on each table. But it was busy, waiters rushing between crammed tables with menus and plates of food, smiling apologetically. Jen pulled a face. 'We've been here ten minutes and no one has come to take our orders.'

'We'll just spend more time chatting – it's so nice to be

here with you all.' Pam indicated the menu. 'I'm having the veggie linguine.'

'Red wine?' Tess asked. 'Shall we get two bottles?'

'At least.' Della put her hands over her ears. 'It's very noisy in here.'

A screech had just filled the air. Two tables away a group of eight or nine young women were raucously waving their arms, shrieking, talking too loudly over one another. Rose sighed. 'They're drunk.'

'They're having a proper girls' night out,' Tess remarked, before launching into the chorus of 'Waterloo'.

Della waved a hand. '*This* is a proper girls' night out. I haven't had so much fun in ages.'

Jen agreed. She was watching the group of young women, confident in short dresses, bright lipstick, glossy hair, clutching colourful handbags. 'I feel my age…' she sighed.

'Not at all.' Pam frowned. 'Age is nothing. We're here – we're having fun. We can make as much noise as they can.'

'More,' Tess whooped, resuming the Abba chorus.

Rose studied one of the young women in a white dress and a pair of fluffy pink rabbit ears. 'I think that one has just passed her driving test…' She chewed her lip. 'She's wearing L-plates.'

A young waiter hovered by the table, a young man with dark hair slicked back and a professional smile. 'Sorry about the delay. What can I get you, ladies?' He indicated the table of young women who had just raised their glasses and screeched again. 'Hen party, I'm afraid.'

Pam was about to tell the young man that they were celebrating Jen's engagement, but he was eagerly brandishing a pencil and note pad while Tess was telling him he was a dead

ringer for Johnny Depp. Rose glanced at the young women.
There were empty bottles, streamers strewn across their table
and the conversation was deafening. The bride-to-be, a very
tall dark haired girl whose skirt came to the top of her thighs,
pushed her way out behind her friends, muttering something
vulgar about needing the toilet. Rose smiled and was momen-
tarily envious of the abandon the young women were display-
ing. They clearly didn't care who was listening or what people
thought and she remembered her own mother's insistence on
decorum and politeness, how others judged your behaviour if
it was unseemly. Rose decided that times had changed for the
better and wondered what her mother would have made of
the hen party. She wouldn't have been impressed.

The food arrived more quickly than expected and the
friends began to eat, Tess filling everyone's wine glass as soon
as it became half empty. She was enjoying herself tremen-
dously. It felt good to be out with friends; in truth, it felt good
to be without Alan. She launched herself across the table to
refill Jen's glass, belting out 'Take a Chance on Me' as she did
so. Rose grinned, thrusting out her chin.

'You know all the words, Tess – that makes you an Abba
fan.'

Tess nodded, filling up her own glass, spluttering, 'Too
right,' before bawling out the one about needing a man after
midnight.

Pam lifted her glass, which was brimming over. 'A toast,'
she called out. 'To Jen and Eddie.'

Della raised her red wine. 'Jen and Eddie – happy
engagement.'

'To Jen,' Rose yelled. A new determination filled her
lungs. She was enjoying herself.

'To wedded bliss – may you always have a man after

midnight.' Tess leapt up, roaring at the top of her voice before sinking back into her seat.

Jen beamed. She was having a wonderful time. She was going to be Eddie's wife and she felt surrounded by friends, warmth and the promise of a new beginning. She glanced around. The young women two tables away were sitting up straight, staring in her direction. The blonde one next to the woman in L-plates guffawed. 'Bloody hell – I hope we can all still party like that when we're their age.'

Jen raised her glass in their direction, a bride-to-be herself now, and winked. 'Practice makes perfect,' she mouthed.

5

'I've got no sympathy for you, Tess. You brought it on yourself.'

Alan folded his arms and brought his chin down to his neck so that he looked severe. Tess was feeling terrible. It wasn't just the sore head and the feeling that she never wanted to drink again unless it was pure cool water, but the sense of having overstepped the mark last night, having been too loud, too exuberant. Perhaps she had offended her friends or – worse – ruined Jen's special night. She was wondering if she should buy them all little presents or flowers or if she should ring everyone and apologise. She leaned back on the sofa and rubbed her eyes. Alan was still in the doorway, grumbling.

'... completely over the top. I've never seen you like that. I had to go and sleep in the spare bed. I thought you might be sick over me.'

Tess felt sad. 'You might have looked after me?'

'You were drunk, Tess. It's not very appealing to sleep next to someone who is drunk, mouth open, snoring.'

'You snore all the time,' Tess retorted.

'I can't imagine what the women you were with are like. A group of harridans, screeching and baying and drawing attention to themselves, no doubt.'

Tess expelled air sharply. 'No, they weren't, Alan. I just drank too much. I was enjoying myself. Anyway, perhaps you and I should go out more. It was ages since I'd been out – before Christmas – and I really needed to let my hair down.'

Alan shook his head. 'I wouldn't want to go to a cocktail bar. I don't like Italian food much either.'

'No, all you seem to like is golf.' Tess didn't mean to say it. Alan's eyes widened. For a moment, he seemed cross, then his expression softened.

'Tess... there are social evenings up at the golf club some-times. Some of the wives go down with their husbands. Cliff takes Celia most weekends. You'd like Celia. She's friendly enough.' He took a deep breath. 'To be honest, love, I think she might benefit from having you as a friend. She's a bit dowdy, you know, a bit frumpy, dull. You'd cheer her up – you have so much more fun than she does. You should tag along.'

Tess didn't feel that she had any fun. She felt inclined to shout at him, to tell him that she'd heard enough about his golf during the daytime and she didn't want to spend her evenings talking to an equally bored, dull golf wife while the men chatted about irons and caddies and whatever else it was that obsessed them. She stared at her husband and he smiled softly. Something about the twinkle in his eyes, the gentleness that used to be a light in his gaze when he looked at her took her by surprise for a moment. Then a wave of tiredness or nausea came over her, the toxic tingling of too much alcohol. She sighed.

'Maybe, Alan. Or maybe we could go out somewhere together, just the two of us.'

He came to sit next to her on the sofa, resting his hand on her shoulder. 'You're right, Tess. We must do that, soon. We need some quality time together. I need to make more fuss of you.'

Tess thought about covering his hand with hers. Her fingers fluttered, ready to move, then he folded his arms and his hands were lost to her...

His eyes were sad. 'Tess, I know it's Saturday and we usually spend the evening together. It's just – well, the weather is really good today and a few of the chaps are meeting at the golf course this afternoon. I said I'd go down with Cliff. I might be a little bit late home, so – perhaps it might be wise not to cook anything for me this evening.' He smiled at her, raising his eyebrows. 'I'll grab a sandwich. Perhaps you can get an early night. You know, so you feel a bit better tomorrow.'

Tess nodded. 'OK. I'll do that.' She glanced at him. 'But I thought Sunday was the day you played golf all day.'

His voice was light. 'Oh, yes – tomorrow's Sunday session is still on.' He stood up and shifted back to the doorway. 'But we'll go out somewhere next week, love. I promise.'

'Alan...' Tess rubbed her temples. 'Do you ever think you neglect me?'

He shrugged, sauntered back to the sofa and placed a kiss on the top of her head. 'I'll make it up to you, Tess.'

With a hint of an apologetic smile, he turned and walked away, towards the hall where he kept his coat, his car keys and his golf clubs.

Tess shook her head sadly. 'How?' she asked, but the room was empty.

* * *

The spring sunshine streamed into the lounge, pale as melting butter. Rose smiled and tugged the hoover into the centre of the room, switching it on and searching for dust. She'd air all the rooms today, give the house a good spring clean; she'd polish the piano, dust the photos and perhaps even treat herself to a cream slice from the baker's later. She moved her feet nimbly as she manoeuvred the machine, shoving the nozzle in all nooks and crannies while she was doing a little dance.

Her heart felt light. She'd really enjoyed the evening out with the girls. The half a cocktail, a glass of Valpolicella and most of a spaghetti carbonara had left her feeling very sophisticated. She had no pupils for piano lessons today – the one she usually had on a Saturday morning, eight year old Candice, had cancelled, so she was determined to pamper herself. A hot bath with scented bubbles would be in order.

Rose hoovered around the sofa, pushing it back to reach the carpet underneath. Despite the roar of the machine, she was humming a sprightly tune. She paused a moment to recollect what it was: Abba's 'Gimme! Gimme! Gimme! (A Man after Midnight)'. Rose thought about the very idea of a mysterious stranger sneaking into her bedroom and she smiled.

* * *

Sylvester hugged his wife, almost sweeping her off her feet, although they were almost the same height when Della wore heels. She giggled. 'What foolishness is this now?'

'I'm taking you out for lunch.'

'We can't afford it, Sylvester. Besides, you should be out in the snack van by the sea wall.'

He lifted a lip in a pretend sneer. 'The van can go to hell right now. I'm taking my pretty wife to lunch. She deserves it.'

'Are you crazy?' Della rolled her eyes. 'I was out last night, partying with the girls. I don't need two treats in a weekend.'

'And you came home in such a good mood. I love it when you wake me up for cuddles at midnight.'

'I didn't mean to wake you, Sylvester.'

'Your feet were cold – I had to warm them up.' He took her hand, kissing the back of it gently. 'So today, I want to treat you. I'm taking you for lunch. I can do the van afterwards this afternoon – there are enough customers to make it worthwhile. I have a good reputation to keep up – Sylvester Donavan is always out there with hot coffee and rolls, in all English weathers, the cold, the freezing, the ice and the snow.' He smiled, his eyes crinkling. 'But I want to spend some time with you today, look into your beautiful eyes across a table and...'

'... eat fish and chips,' Della spluttered.

Sylvester was serious. He held up Della's jacket, waiting for her to slip it on. 'I want to show my appreciation for my wife. Then we'll go for a stroll along the headland, just like we did when we were twenty-something and we used to go walking together.'

'When we were twenty-something we were young and energetic, living in Stepney, strolling through the streets in the dark, with nowhere to go, nothing to do. It was lovely though. We were poor then. That seems so long ago.' She sighed. 'We're still not well off though...'

Sylvester reached for his coat, shrugging it on and

pushing his hat on top of his head. 'I am a rich man, Della. Rich with love. And I can afford to take my lovely wife out for a romantic lunch.' He offered the crook of his arm. 'Come on, sweetheart. Let's paint Exmouth red.' He cackled. 'We can put ketchup on our chips.'

* * *

Jen moved her coffee cup out of the way to the side of the desk and wriggled the mouse. An image came up on the laptop screen – a wedding outfit website, a page showing a glamorous woman in her thirties wearing a cream suit, nipped in at the waist, neat, knee length. The suit was expensive and not available in size ten. Jen sighed and clicked the mouse again. Perhaps she'd try something less conventional. Last night's celebrations with the girls had left her pulse racing. She felt a twinge of rebellion. She could be any kind of bride she liked. It was her wedding, after all.

She clicked on another page. An ivory dress, long, sweeping to the floor, caught her eye. Short sleeves – she'd be too cold in March. Besides, the model in the photo was clearly in her twenties and Jen was seventy-three. She should pick something more appropriate. Eddie would have a smart suit on, impeccably groomed. Jen thought about how she would look by his side: she'd need to be neat, traditional, well presented, in a pale suit and a stylish hat.

She whirled the mouse again. An image caught her eye. A bride was wearing a long red dress, a coronet of tiny flowers in her hair. Jen gasped. The robe was scarlet, vermilion, and in plush velvet with wide sleeves. The woman looked like a sprite, or one of the Celtic brides in the Middle Ages, her hair in ringlets down to her waist and her eyes huge with happiness. Jen wondered what she would look like in such a dress and how Eddie might react if she arrived at the register office looking like Lady Macbeth. She stifled a smile and reached for her coffee. She'd get herself a refill, maybe a sandwich. She didn't want to eat too much. She was going round to Eddie's for dinner tonight. They were going to talk about the wedding. He'd prepared a spreadsheet of all the costs involved and they were going to plan the day and finalise the details. Eddie had said they should consider getting married sooner rather than later.

Jen picked up her mug and headed for the kitchen. She imagined herself in the long dress, her face luminous, glowing, and flowers in her hair. A smile widened across her face. She was going to have a wonderful wedding – it would be her day, and she was really excited about every single thing to do with it. She actually felt like a bride-to-be.

'I think I might be coming down with something, Elvis. My throat is a bit sore.' The little black spaniel yapped from the back seat of the car as Pam brought the Volvo to a halt. She held out a hand and he licked her fingers, his tongue slobbering across her palm. 'I'll only be a minute. Stay here – be a good boy. I'm only just in the shop here.'

She locked the car and Elvis watched her walk away. His eyes were round and he leapt against the window, putting his paws against the glass. Pam felt the usual tug of guilt at her heart whenever she left him, even for the briefest of moments. But dogs weren't allowed in Earth Grains Wholefoods. The doorbell rang with a tiny jingle as she rushed into the shop. Everywhere was stacked with goods: toiletries to the right, bagged-up dried foods to the left. Two women were standing at the counter. The taller one, her hair tied in a bright scarf, was weighing out spices for a short woman in a mackintosh. The other, a woman in her thirties with gold-rimmed glasses and short dark hair, was writing something down. Pam approached her. 'Hi, Anthea – I need some Echinacea.'

The dark haired woman straightened, pushing her glasses back against her face, and grinned. She twirled round and found a packet from a shelf, holding it up.

'This is the best if you feel a bit under the weather. We use it all the time in here.'

Pam rolled her eyes. 'I was out on the town last night. I went for a run this morning and felt a bit fuzzy around the edges.'

Anthea winked behind the glasses. 'Are you sure it's not alcohol related?'

'Oh, it definitely was.' Pam beamed. 'An engagement party. We had a whale of a time. But my throat is a bit sore so...' She reached for her purse.

'What about some yogi tea? I recommend the spice mix for sore throats.'

Pam nodded. 'I'll go and have a look. I won't be a minute.'

She strolled over to the tea display, gazing along the rows of colourful boxes. Chamomile tea, fennel tea, women's blend. She picked out a box called Throat Comfort. Behind her, the doorbell pinged. She turned round with her purchase. A man in a smart coat was talking to Anthea, his back to her. Pam thought she recognised the voice, although the man was talking in almost a whisper.

'... so I wonder if you could recommend something to help – you know – the older man.'

'What did you have in mind?' Anthea pushed a hand through her short hair. 'Do you mean a vitamin supplement to increase energy levels?'

'Well, yes.' The man paused. 'Energy and – well – I need something to make me more, you know, active. Er, active as in – virile. You see, I'm getting married soon and I'll probably need to...'

Pam compressed her lips, stifling a smile. She recognised the man, his handsome, confident appearance. She'd seen him once before; the colour and texture of his coat were familiar. Elvis had leapt up at him when she was jogging on the beach and the gentleman had been arm-in-arm with Jen. Pam wondered if she should call out to Eddie and remind him that they had met.

Anthea was reassuring. 'Oh, yes, I have the very thing. These are specifically designed for all aspects of male health for gentlemen over forty.' She handed him a packet of something that looked like vitamin pills. Eddie reached for his wallet, handed over a note and slipped the magic pills in his pocket. Pam hovered behind him, grasping the tea, trying not to smile.

Eddie turned brusquely and lurched forward, brushing against Pam. 'Oh – so sorry – I didn't see you.' He showed no sign of recognition or remorse as he blustered towards the door.

'Oh, don't worry – it's the story of my life,' Pam called after him. She grinned as she heard the doorbell jingle and moved to the counter. 'Women become more and more invisible as they get older.' She held out the box of tea. 'Thanks, Anthea. And the Echinacea and a packet of healthy doggie treats, please. How much do I owe you?'

6

Eddie had prepared a delicious dinner with red wine. He'd placed a bowl of salad with tomatoes and cucumber to one side of the table, another bowl of new potatoes with a knob of butter and then his showpiece, the boeuf bourguignon, in the centre. He'd put out crystal glasses, silver cutlery and white serviettes. Jen wondered if this was how they would eat when they were married. It was quite formal and it felt special, cultured, but Jen doubted that it would suit the mid-week meals she usually served herself, which were quite relaxed affairs in front of the television. She wondered how much her life would change when Eddie was living in her house. She pushed the thoughts to the back of her mind. He was talking.

'I can get six hundred pounds a month for this place, apparently. That's not a bad income. And I can put my car in your garage – we can sell the little Fiat you have. You won't need it – I can drive you wherever you want to go.'

Jen nodded. It was a nice thought, having a husband, a chauffeur, someone to cook for and to share the cooking with. He clearly doted on her; he'd take care of her and make sure she wanted for nothing. She caught his eye and smiled. He was wearing a blue polo-neck shirt with blue jeans. He looked relaxed, attractive, his eyes crinkling at the corners as he gazed at her. And she had made a special effort – a pretty dress with a slightly low neckline, her hair swept up.

'You're looking nice tonight, Jenny, my dear.'

She wondered if he'd ask her to stay and her thoughts drifted to the toothbrush and the tube of face cream she'd popped in her handbag just in case. He offered her more boeuf bourguignon and she shook her head. 'Thanks, Eddie – it was lovely though.'

'I'll get the spreadsheet, shall I, Jen? Or maybe we should have a coffee first? We can talk about the wedding. How does March thirtieth sound? Or April sixth? They are both available at the register office.'

Jen felt a little tremor flutter across her skin. 'That would be nice, Eddie. Do you think it'll give me time to find something special to wear? After all, I want to choose something really nice.'

Eddie smiled and inspected perfectly trimmed nails. 'I know you'll be smartly turned out, Jen.'

'But I want to look especially good.' She met his eyes. 'I mean, I want to co-ordinate with you, and on the photos...' She gave him a hopeful look. 'We are having photos, aren't we?'

'My son, Harry, will do those. I've asked him already and he said he'd be delighted.'

Jen nodded. 'I haven't met him yet.'

'Oh, you will, on the day. I don't see him that often, although he's only up in Chester. It's not as if he's in a foreign country. He has a family and a busy life. In fact, I've been persuading him that he ought to take a break from his work – he has his own antique business. We spoke on the phone earlier. He'll take a snap or two of our big day for us.'

Jen glanced around the dining room. There were no photos of Harry or his family. There were no photos of Eddie or his wife, Pat, the one who'd died. In fact, there were no photos at all, just the polished wood dining table, the fireplace with the gas stove with synthetic flames, two armchairs and a gold-framed copy of Constable's *The Hay Wain* on the wall. Jen tried again. 'What will you be wearing, Eddie?'

'My dark suit, probably. A carnation. So really, Jen, you can wear what you like. Get yourself a smart suit, cream maybe, or a light blue to complement my dark colour. Oh – and a hat is the way forward, isn't it? For a mature woman at a wedding.'

She nodded. Eddie stood up purposefully and left the room. He was in the adjacent kitchen. Cups were clinking, a kettle was on. Jen gazed around the room. There was little sign of Eddie's personality, although she knew he had one. He was warm, light-hearted, good-humoured, and affectionate. He was going to be a wonderful husband and the simple sparseness of his home proved to Jen that he needed a feminine touch in his life. He'd find her home so much cosier when they were together as husband and wife. It would be a haven of love and stability for them both.

Eddie returned carrying two china cups on saucers. 'I thought we'd have tea... I can't drink coffee before I go to bed. I'd never sleep.'

Jen wondered whether to suggest that that they drink coffee and forget completely about sleeping. She grinned shyly at Eddie and he placed a palm over her hand. It was a complicit gesture, she thought: he shared her state of mind;

he was feeling warm and fuzzy too, with a mixture of desire and anticipation, as she was. Jen sipped her tea. His hand was still resting on the fingers of her left hand, touching the engagement ring gently. He murmured. 'Jenny – there's something I wanted to say...'

She met his eyes and there was a melting feeling in the pit of her stomach, a little lower even. 'Yes, Eddie?'

He was going to ask her to stay the night. Her heart beat harder – she had forgotten her nightie. But it wouldn't matter: she could ask to borrow one of his shirts. Or maybe she could break the habit of a lifetime and sleep as nature had intended. She gave him an encouraging grin, a stare that she hoped smouldered a little.

'Jen – I was going to leave this until later but, well, I'm not sure it will wait...'

Her heart thudded. She wondered whether to leave the seat and creep over towards him, to curl up on his lap and stare into his face, share a kiss, more kisses. His hand was still over hers. It hovered. He patted her fingers softly.

'The thing is... there's something I've been planning – something I'd really like to do. It would mean a lot to me if you said yes.'

'Eddie?'

'I hope you won't mind me asking, Jen.'

'Oh, no – I'm sure I won't.'

'The thing is...'

'Eddie?'

'Well, I'll need to get tickets organised.'

Jen stared at him. 'Tickets?'

Eddie chuckled. 'My son, Harry, said I should have a stag night and I agreed. We discussed it and we've decided to go to Las Vegas together.'

'Las Vegas?' Jen pulled her hand away. It flew to her mouth.

'A stag night, just my son and me.' He rolled his eyes. 'We'll stay for a few days, do a bit of sightseeing, and maybe have a little flutter in the casinos.'

'Oh.'

'You don't mind if I go, do you, Jen?'

'Oh. No, not at all.'

'I thought it would be nice to spend some quality time with Harry. To catch up, just boys together. It'll be real fun. But I wanted to ask you first – to check that you didn't mind me going.'

Jen nodded. She felt a little numb. It was not what she had been expecting him to ask her at all. Eddie was holding her hand across the table again. He murmured, 'No doubt you'll have a dinner out with your aqua aerobics friends? A hen party of sorts. You seemed to enjoy the last night out with the girls.'

'Yes.' Jen moved her head slightly in agreement. She didn't understand why she was so stunned. She was not jealous of Eddie's relationship with his son, Harry. It was good that they wanted to spend time together. But the idea of them gambling in Las Vegas shook her a little. Eddie had always seemed so frugal, so sensible. Their wedding was going to be a modest one; the honeymoon weekend in Lyme Regis would be cheap in comparison with Eddie's stag night. But she was being silly: of course Eddie should celebrate with his son. And it was right that he was frugal and wise. It would be too easy for Jen to let her excitement run away with her and Eddie was her voice of reason. She felt a little awkward that her first reaction had been uncharitable. Jen wished she had her friends around her now; it would be good to talk this over with some sympathetic women.

Eddie had moved away from the table; he had come to stand behind her; his lips brushed the top of her head. 'My dear Jenny.'

Her anxiety disappeared in a moment. She felt him leaning against her chair, the warmth of his cheek against the top of her head. His arm touched her shoulder gently. She slid up from her seat, turning round into his embrace. A kiss would make everything all right. An embrace, the crush of his lips against hers. They would kiss and kiss. Then she would stay the night.

'Jen, my love, you look tired.' He was holding up her coat. 'I've called a taxi for eleven. I could walk you back but I thought it would be easier to organise a lift. We've both had wine.'

Jen struggled into the sleeves as he buttoned her up. She felt like a child being dressed warmly before being shipped off to school. He kissed her lips briefly. 'Well, it's almost eleven. We'll say goodnight, shall we? I'll walk you to the door.' He slipped an arm around her; she felt the weight of its protection. 'Shall we meet tomorrow? There are still lots of things to organise for our wedding. We need to confirm the date. Maybe we can talk about finances too, and have a proper look at the spreadsheet?'

* * *

'I wouldn't mind at all if Sylvester went to Las Vegas with Linval and Aston.' Della kicked her legs hard against the water in synchronisation with everybody else. 'It'd be nice for him to be able to afford to go with the boys.'

The aqua aerobics class was in full swing, Jen and her friends on the front row, five other ladies of mixed ages, one heavily pregnant, behind them.

'Knee to chest,' called Kathy, a pretty, freckled woman in her fifties with short blonde hair, standing by the side of the pool. She pressed a button on the CD player and a strong female voice sang a rhythmic song about a milkshake. Kathy waved a muscular arm. 'Knee to chest and push the leg down strongly again; exhale slowly. Now repeat ten times. That's it. Get those hearts beating fast. Go for it. Keep going.'

'I don't really mind,' Jen spluttered. 'It's nice for Eddie to have bonding time with his son.'

Rose frowned, thinking. She didn't want to say anything to upset Jen, but she wondered if Eddie shouldn't have included the cost of his projected stag night expenditure on the spreadsheet along with the budget honeymoon and the £300 limit for Jen's wedding attire that she had just told them about.

'Men and their boring hobbies.' Tess panted, raising a knee. 'Why can't they pick something cheap and fun like... aqua aerobics?'

'Now tread water, ladies,' Kathy hooted, her voice bouncing an echo on the blue walls of the swimming-pool complex. The women immediately responded, treading water furiously. The smell of chlorine and steam surfaced and hung on the air.

'It's not as if I'd like Las Vegas though – I mean, I wouldn't want to go with them.' Jen gasped, her face pink with effort. Pam thought her friend looked disappointed, but she concentrated on pushing her strong legs against the water.

'Alan spends so much money and time on his golf,' Tess muttered, her face dripping. 'I don't get a look-in.'

'Poor Sylvester spends every penny he can spare all on me.' Della kicked her legs hard. Aqua aerobics always eased the pain in her lower back. She pushed against the water even harder. 'I'm not sure he's the Las Vegas type though. A pint and a pie in a London pub and a bet on the football is more his style – or enjoying my home cooking and a night in, watching television.'

'Jumping jacks – cardio workout. Then we're into scissor jumps,' Kathy yelled and the women leapt and fell, splashing water everywhere, Pam bouncing higher and displacing more water than anyone else in the group. 'Helen, at the back, take this one easy, please – I don't want a water birth today.'

The women giggled, and the splashing increased. Next to her, Pam felt the water rising more energetically than usual. She looked at Rose, who was waving her arms angrily, a frown on her face. 'Are you OK, Rose?'

Rose nodded, without changing her focus, staring into the distance, flapping her arms like a demented flamingo in a new pink swimsuit.

'OK, ladies. To the edge of the pool now. Let's finish off the session with a butt kick.'

'I could kick his butt,' Rose muttered to herself. Pam shook her head. She had no idea what Rose meant, but she was certainly thrashing around in the water with added energy.

'I'm exhausted.' Tess gasped as Kathy declared the session over. 'I just hope my figure is improving after all this exercise.'

Della made a snorting sound. 'Your figure's perfectly fine, Tess.'

'Alan doesn't think so.'

Pam put an arm around Jen as they clambered out of the water. She grinned, recalling Eddie's purchase of vitamin pills in the wholefood shop. 'Well, Jen – I bet your Eddie appreciates you as a beautiful woman.'

Jen pushed wet hair back from her face. 'Oh, he's really sweet. He's so attentive and protective – I feel completely safe with him around. But he's very respectful of me too.'

Tess squeezed Jen's arm as they walked to the changing rooms. 'You were telling me things were becoming very lovey-dovey last week. Did you stay over at his place?'

'Ah, well, we've decided that we're leaving it until after the wedding.' Jen stared at the stone flags on the floor, water dripping from her swimsuit.

'He's such a gentleman.' Pam grinned. 'When can we meet him?'

Della shook water from her face, reaching for a towel. 'Sounds like he really cares for you, Jen. He's so respectful.'

'Well, I don't agree,' Rose spluttered, her face shining with water above the new pink suit. The four friends stared at her. She stamped her foot. 'I mean, if he really cared he wouldn't be able to hold back on the passion. And it's Jen's wedding and all she gets is a spreadsheet and a cheap wedding gown and he goes swanning off to Las Vegas with his son. It's not fair.' Her eyes were beads, tiny in her wet face. 'And you didn't pick the ring, Jen. It wouldn't surprise me if he didn't buy it bargain basement. Or perhaps it was the one he gave his first wife.'

Jen gasped. 'Eddie loves me with all his heart.' She frowned at Rose. 'He is a perfect foil for me. I'm the passionate one, the hot-headed impulsive one, and he is calm, grounding, protective. Really, Rose – you know nothing about him.'

Rose mumbled, 'I'm not sure you do, either.'

The friends were silent. Tess was staring at Rose, amazed.

Della's hands flew to her hips, her expression one of shock. Jen shook her head and gazed down at her feet. There were tears in her eyes.

Rose put out a hand, touching her friend's shoulder, and muttered, 'Sorry, Jen. You're right – I don't know Eddie at all. I shouldn't have said anything – it'll all be fine.'

Pam took a deep breath. 'OK, ladies – we need to move forward, and have some fun. Jen's getting married and we are celebrating. You're all invited to my house for supper. We can crack open a bottle or two and talk about Jen's hen night. When are you all free? How about tomorrow?'

7

Pam was still cooking when the first guest rapped at the door. She frowned. 'They aren't due until half seven. It's barely quarter to. Stay there, Elvis – don't touch the cheese, please. Or the salad – I know how much you like to pilfer.' She ruffled the fur around his ears and he pushed a wet nose into the palm of her hand. 'OK, come with me to the door, then.' She scooped him up and went into the hall. Someone had knocked again. Rose was huddled on the doorstep in a pale pink faux-fur jacket and jeans.

'Hi, Rose. New coat?'

Rose nodded from the doorstep. 'I went out over the weekend – I bought myself this jacket and a dress, a swimsuit and some underwear – all in pink. I wanted to cheer myself up – it's spring, almost. Besides, my name is Rose, not Dullard.'

'This is Elvis. Are you all right with dogs?'

'Fine.' Rose nodded as she followed Pam through the little lounge and into the kitchen. 'What a sweet house, Pam.

The thing is – I don't know – this business with Jen. I'm not happy...'

'Red wine OK?' Pam lifted a bottle of Cabernet Sauvignon.

'I don't usually drink much wine, but OK, I'll have one glass, Pam.' Rose took the wine and swallowed a mouthful hastily. 'You see, I've been thinking about things. Since the dinner, since the night we went out. I bought myself some new things. I just wanted to treat myself. I've been in the doldrums a bit and I thought it might be time to get out of them.'

'Well done you.' Pam smiled. 'We're having aubergine and butter-bean tagine and a salad – is that OK?'

'Sounds wonderful.' Rose sipped more wine, leaning over to tickle Elvis's chin. The little spaniel stared at her with round eyes, unblinking. 'Pam – I hope you didn't mind me coming here early. I wanted to talk to you about something. If it's all right.'

'Of course.' Pam stirred the tagine, replaced the lid and gave Rose her full attention. 'What is it?'

'I wanted to talk about Jen – to try to get my own head round this thing with the engagement. I said too much yesterday – opened my mouth and spoke my mind. I felt awful afterwards. But I'm a bit worried. She's such a sweet-natured person, so kind, and this whirlwind thing with Eddie...'

'You don't trust him, Rose?'

Rose stood upright, placing her hands on her hips. 'I might be wrong – I hope I am – but what if he's a skinflint, a pinch-penny, going to Las Vegas with his son and gambling while she has a limited budget for her wedding dress and her honeymoon is a paltry weekend in Dorset? That's not exactly the doting fiancé, is it?'

Pam shrugged. 'I see what you mean but I'm sure he cares for her. He's a pensioner – they both are – he probably just wants to economise. And she clearly adores him.'

'Pam.' Rose placed the wine glass firmly down on the countertop. It was only a quarter full. 'I was fortunate in many ways to share my married life with Bernard. I loved him and he was a good man. We had a son, Paul, and we were happy. But there were problems.' Rose took a breath. 'Generosity wasn't his forte. Or thoughtfulness. You know what I mean? I rarely had birthday presents or Christmas presents. He said he cared and that was enough for me, but he never showed it. I'd be upset to get nothing on my birthday and he'd say, "Oh, sorry, Rose – here's a ten pound note – treat yourself." I loved Bernard, but he wasn't very thoughtful or generous and years and years of it affected my confidence – I thought myself not to be worth spoiling or being treasured, if I'm honest. I denied myself because I was being denied. He came first and I was second best, and it became a habit, feeling not worth much. We had holidays, on his terms, but I never had independence – I never bought myself new clothes or had much fun.'

Pam nodded, a little surprised to see Rose so animated, her words tumbling out quickly. 'You think Eddie is like Bernard?'

Rose brought her lips together. 'Yes, I do. Bernard was a kind man even if he was a little too careful with the contents of his wallet. We were happy enough, good company for each other and he was appreciative even if, although I shouldn't say so now he's gone, our life could be a little boring. And I do miss him, although I don't think I knew how much I would when he was alive. We bickered a lot. I suppose we both just took each other for granted, slipped into a rut. Now I miss him being around the house, his smile, his silly jokes. But Jen is a sensitive soul. She needs someone who will cherish her and Eddie puts himself first.'

'Rose...' Pam lifted the lid of the tagine. Steam rose in front of her face like a potion. 'I'm sure Eddie adores her.'

Rose's voice became higher. 'Look at Tess. She's a strong woman and her Alan never gives her the time of day. He plays golf all the time. She is a lovely person, but you saw her the other night. She's lonely, starved of fun. I mean...' her voice became louder as she finished her glass of wine '... I'm alone and desolate and sad and dowdy but I'm better off than both of them.'

'You might be being a bit hard, Rose. Jen seems happy with Eddie.'

Rose nodded. 'I'm sure you're right, Pam, yes – I'm probably seeing it all wrong. And I'm overprotective. I thought that too – it's in my nature. That's why I married Bernard, to care for him and put him first. My fault, I suppose. But times have changed now. And I'm worried. I thought I'd come early, Pam – to talk to you. You are wise and sensible and I know you'll be able to calm me down and help me think straight. At the moment, I'm just a little bit edgy – I'm probably being unfair and you seem so grounded.'

Elvis barked in agreement, lifting his front paws high and tottering on his hind legs. Pam offered him a morsel of cheese, which he dropped to the floor and snaffled up greedily. Rose's face was serious. 'Do you think I'm overreacting?'

Pam shrugged her shoulders. 'I don't know, Rose. You may

be right. We've all only known each other since the class started last autumn but we seem to get on well. We're all protective of Jen and we hardly know Eddie at all.'

'There's definitely a bond developing between the five of us – and that's why I thought I'd talk to you about my feelings. Jen's known Eddie less time than she's known us.'

'Maybe Jen will be fine.' Pam recalled the image of Eddie on the beach, Elvis's sandy paws on his jacket. She remembered Eddie buying the vitamin pills in the wholefood shop and she realised she had no idea about his suitability as a partner. 'They'll be company for each other, won't they?'

'I'm in my seventies now and I'll admit it – I'm lonely. But I'd rather have no company at all than a man who didn't put me first and treat me like I was special.'

Pam stretched a hand down and tousled Elvis's fur. He licked her palm. 'Maybe you're right, Rose.'

They were thoughtful for a while, and then the sound of the knocker being rapped at the front door jolted them. Pam rushed to the hall, Elvis yapping at her heels, and tugged open the door to see three smiling faces, three women holding up bottles of wine and chorusing, 'Hello.'

Pam held the door open and Della, Tess and Jen tumbled inside, full of delight at the compact prettiness of Pam's cottage, the glowing fire in the hearth, the cuteness of Elvis, whom they were immediately showering with kisses, and the warm smells of a succulent tagine. Rose unfolded her arms, plastered a smile on her face and hurried into the lounge to embrace her friends, saving a special warm hug for Jen.

* * *

'Anyone for more apple cake and cream?'

'I couldn't, Pam.' Della blew air from her lips. 'I'm full. But it was delicious.'

'That was lovely.' Jen smiled, helping herself to more water.

'I'll have a sliver, please – it was so nice.' Tess held out her plate. 'Anyone else for more wine? Rose?'

'A little.' Rose nodded. 'Thank you. Now – what were you talking about just before, Della?'

'Second chances. I was saying how nice it was that Jen has a second chance at love. You know, I believe life offers us opportunities every now and then. A meeting with someone, an opportunity to do something new. And we should take our chances with both hands.'

'Like bungee jumping, do you mean?' Tess pulled a face. 'Like a bucket list?'

'Bucket lists depress me,' Rose mumbled. 'I don't like the idea of doing something quickly, before you die, in case you miss out. But I do like the idea of doing something because the opportunity is there and the desire is there, spontaneously.'

Della thought for a moment. 'I think I'm guilty of drifting – you know, just putting things off until tomorrow.'

'But you are happy, Della.' Tess sipped her wine. 'Life is good for you. I spend far too much time being disappointed, disgruntled.'

Rose laughed. 'So do I, Tess. We should make a change.'

'But I don't know how to change for the best. If I left Alan, it would be chaos. Besides, we do get on, sometimes.'

'Is that enough?' Rose raised her eyebrows. 'Bernard and I used to bicker. I thought it was enough to make me happy, a marriage, and another person around the house, but is it really the only option?'

Elvis barked, leaping up on Pam's knee. She rubbed his ears and he settled down. 'I often think how times have changed.' She sighed. 'Young women now do their own thing so much better than we did. We thought we had it all in the 1960s – we were independent, we had freedom. I was a bit of a hippy – you know, free love and festivals and all that. But it was just another excuse for men to have everything on their own terms. They can be a bit controlling, some of them.' She sighed again, her face temporarily sad. 'We were still chattels, something to look good on their arm – second best in terms of opportunity, despite Germaine Greer.'

Della nodded. 'I was glad I married early. But although motherhood is a blessing, my boys wore me out. Young women nowadays have it much better than we did. They have cleaners, childminders, house-husbands.'

'And wonderful careers.' Tess leaned forward. 'They can own their own cars, houses. They keep their own names when they are married, they do as they please. We got it all wrong. Did you see those women in the restaurant at Felipiano's? Short skirts, lashings of lipstick – in touch with their own sexuality. Flaunting it. I'd love to be like that. They were loud, proud, enjoying themselves.'

Jen grinned. 'We gave them a run for their money that night, though.'

'We did.' Tess laughed. 'There's life in us all yet...'

'Right.' Rose put her elbows on the table. 'That's it. We can do what they did – better, even. We need to organise a hen party for Jen.'

'Just like theirs – what a great idea.' Tess scooped up the last of her apple cake.

'We could do cocktails again,' Jen agreed. 'At the Havana Bar and Felipiano's. It was a lovely night.'

'I'd go there again. I really enjoyed it. We could have L-plates, angel wings.' Tess licked her lips. 'What about a stripper? You know, a fireman... with a hosepipe and a thong?'

'Maybe...' Pam shrugged. 'But perhaps cocktails and an Italian meal don't make a real hen party.'

Jen raised her eyebrows. 'The women at the other table seemed to be having a great time. I'd be happy with us going there, all together, having fun.'

'Yes.' Pam glanced at Rose, who had closed her eyes and was thinking. 'But it's hardly the same as Las Vegas. Eddie will be away having a special time, bonding, seeing shows, gambling – not doing something anyone could do any weekend. We should come up with something else – something a bit more fun.'

'Something a bit wilder?' Della put her hands to her face. 'Like a nightclub? There are some good ones in Exeter.'

'Or what about a hen party in London?' Tess sat upright. 'Goodness me – we could do an overnight in London.'

'Good idea.' Pam smiled. 'A whole weekend. That would be a real chance to let our hair down.'

'Rubbish.' Rose opened her eyes wide. Her face was set, determined. 'A night in London? We can do better than that.' She looked from one face to the other. 'We're going to the City of Love itself, Paris. That's what we'll do. We'll have the best hen party possible. We'll make our own plans and it'll be tailor-made by us for the most fun we can have. Let's grab this opportunity. Say yes – let's do it.'

The women looked at each other, their eyes wide. Then Pam raised her wine glass. 'All right. Let's all go to Paris. What do you think, Jen?'

Jen's face shone as she lifted her tumbler of water. 'Why not? Paris it is.'

The five of them held their glasses aloft and chimed them together. 'To Paris,' they chorused.

8

'I said I'd go to Paris, but I'll have to tell them I can't go now.' Della's face was sad as she pushed the trolley down the frozen-food aisle. She reached for a bag of peas.

Sylvester took over trolley duties. 'I don't see why. You've never been to Paris before. You should go.'

Della threw the peas in the trolley, as if she was throwing away the idea of a holiday with the girls. 'It's not right.'

'How so?'

'You work every day in that shabby old van on the seafront. You deserve the holiday. If anyone should go it should be you.'

Sylvester chuckled. 'You're sending me on a hen holiday with four women?' He flapped his arms like a chicken's wings. 'Sounds fine to me.'

'We should go, you and me, just the two of us. It's the city of romance.'

He paused in front of the battered fish and put his arm around her. 'I have romance every day with you, Della. I have enough put by, a few pounds, but it's enough for you to go to

Paris with your girlfriends. I'll be just fine. I might even enjoy the freedom.'

'You mean you'll be drinking every night while I'm gone?'

'I could go to London to see Aston and Cassandra, maybe meet up with Linval. It's tough for him since he split with Sariah and she took the kids. We could go to the Carpenter's Arms together. I could take a long weekend to catch up.'

Della sighed. 'OK, but I'll miss you when I'm in Paris.'

He kissed her on the lips. 'And I'll miss you. So, it's decided, my sweetheart. You go, have the time of your life. Just stay away from all those French Casanovas, or they'll have me to deal with.'

'Are you sure it's all right, Sylvester?'

He adjusted his glasses and studied a bag of oven chips before throwing them in the trolley. 'You deserve the break. Of course, you must go.' He winked at her. 'And if you enjoy it, then maybe we can save up some more and the two of us can go together next time. A sort of second honeymoon.'

'Second honeymoon? We never had the first one.'

He glanced round to check if anyone was watching, then he patted her bottom. 'The first honeymoon isn't over yet, woman. You wait till I get you home.'

Rose searched through her list of long-playing records. She hadn't played an LP in the house since Bernard had been alive, but she knew what she was looking for. She leafed through the stacks of old records organised alphabetically; she flipped past Abba, Bach and Bizet, The Beatles, Beach Boys, Beethoven, Berlioz, Brahms, Buchner, John Coltrane, Chopin, Dire Straits, and there it was – next to Dylan.

Debussy's 'Danse bohémienne'. Rose reached up to the record deck, lifted the arm and placed the needle at the edge. Immediately she heard the rhythmic sound of the throbbing grooves through the speakers, then music filled the room. She flopped into an armchair and closed her eyes. Piano keys bubbled with sounds light as feet stepping on air, an energetic tripping dance that transported her to Paris at the end of the nineteenth century. Rose imagined cafés, painters in berets, women in long robes and coquettish hats, a crowded room, people drinking wine and absinthe and sharing laughter. She saw dark streets, a couple in love, spilling from the busy café, the woman's voice a soft gurgle in French; the man, his words low, strangled by desire, wrapping his arm around her as they walked down towards the Seine. The dark river swirled and they were alone and in love. *Amoureux.* It sounded wonderful.

Rose sighed. Paris would be a rich experience, a heady mix of new tastes and scents and stimulating sights and sounds. She would see the Eiffel Tower, the galleries, the churches. She had been to Paris before but that was forty years ago, a weekend break with Bernard, and they had argued about whether to have dinner at the hotel or in a little bistro that Rose would have preferred. She imagined a tapestry of new sensual delights that would transform her life for ever. She breathed deeply, imagining herself as the bohemian woman in the dance, her eyes dark and flashing as she swirled and seduced in a crimson dress. Her movements were confident, provocative, and powerful – she was in touch with her true self. Rose smiled. She would make herself a special meal tonight. She had found a recipe book and it was full of all sorts of delicious options – duck à l'orange, Brie en croute, coq au vin, tarte Tatin. She had bought a bottle of

Beaujolais. She had no idea what it was going to taste like, but it was French – it was preparation for Paris and Rose was ready. This was going to be the trip of a lifetime.

* * *

The red clay cliffs topped with tufts of grass sprawled in the distance. Jen picked her way across the beach, avoiding the dark streak of sand that held puddles of water. Eddie took her hand in his gloved fingers. 'No, I can't say I'm entirely comfortable with it, Jen.'

She glanced up at him; his handsome craggy face and serious blue eyes held an expression of concern. She took a breath. 'I've researched it on the Internet. We can get a taxi to the airport and a plane directly to Paris, then another taxi to the hotel. We can leave on the Wednesday morning and come back on the following Monday. That will give me four whole days here to prepare for our wedding.' She gave him a hopeful smile. 'And there won't be much to prepare – the date is booked, March thirtieth, and the Olive Grove have agreed to do the meal. We'll just pick up the ring from the jewellers on Thursday, and the flowers – that's all there is to organise now.'

He sighed. 'Call me a bit old-fashioned, Jen, but the idea of you in Paris with four other, well, let's say, older women – it worries me, quite frankly. I mean – I'm just concerned for your safety because I care...'

'Oh, we won't go off the rails.' Jen giggled. 'A gallery, a show – we'll behave ourselves.'

His frown deepened. 'It's not just that. Paris is a huge city – there are all sorts of people there who will see you as – basically – five naïve women whom they can take for a ride. You'll be sitting ducks. Do you all speak the language? Do you have any idea about the price of a taxi? And what about the scammers and the thieves on the Metro? What if the hotel is awful, next to a strip club, or there are bugs in the bed?'

'I've picked one out – the Sirène – it seems a nice hotel.' Jen had started to feel worried. 'I'm sure we'll be all right. We'll be very careful.'

'Five vulnerable women in their seventies.' Eddie shook his head. 'I'd be worried sick. I wouldn't even be in the UK to help you if you got into trouble.'

'But you're going to Las Vegas. That can't be the safest place…' Jen heard the whine in her voice and felt annoyed with herself.

'That's different, it's just me and Harry, and we're both capable of taking care of ourselves. We're…' He paused. Jen wondered if he was about to say, 'We're men.' Eddie breathed out. 'We're more experienced in the ways of the world. I'd just be so worried that something might happen to you.'

Jen stared ahead at the cliffs, reds and ochres merging against a dappled sky flecked with milky clouds. She didn't want to upset Eddie; she had no idea what to say next. She had already paid the deposit.

* * *

Tess sat in the bath listening to music on the tinny radio as she squirted huge spurts of essential lavender in the water. Little pools of oil floated, thick and iridescent on the surface. She lay back in the darkness, hazy candles flickering on the window ledge, the smell of sandalwood hanging on the air. She breathed in, determined to relax. She was still furious. Alan had gone out to the clubhouse.

She suspected he was in the bar, still complaining to Cliff about his foolish wife.

She had told him she was going to Paris. He had replied that she could go where she liked but it was a waste of money and it would be wiser to spend it on some new curtains for the lounge. She had argued that he was always out playing golf and it was her turn to have fun. He had grunted, suggesting that the last time she went out with her four women friends she had drunk too much and he thought that once she was in Paris, she wouldn't know where to draw the line. Basically, she was a social liability to her friends – if her friends were, indeed, the sort of women she should be going away with at all.

Tess had retorted that she never went anywhere with Alan, she seldom enjoyed herself and she was determined to go. It was Jen's hen celebration and she, Tess, would do as she pleased. Alan had raised his hands in the air; he was not about to stop her – he wasn't that kind of man. But he thought the whole escapade was pretty silly, if the truth were told; she was far too old to go gadding about, behaving like a foolish teenager. He added that, although he'd never met any of her new friends, he imagined them to be loud, flighty types and Tess would be a lot better off to try to pal herself up with some of the golf wives, like Cliff's wife, Celia, who was very dull and frumpy and in need of a good friend. Tess had told him to go to hell and he'd replied that he'd go off down the golf club for a drink instead and give her time to come to her senses.

Tess closed her eyes and sank beneath the bubbles, letting the water swirl over her face and into her nostrils. Under the water, she could hear the low vibration of the sounds –moving water thudded; music from the radio thrummed, dull and low. She slid upright, blinking until her eyes were clear, and reached for a bar of scented body scrub. Suddenly, she laughed out loud, a heady peal that rose to the ceiling and filled the bathroom. Tess thought her laugh was maniacal, hysterical, a laugh of abandon. But she couldn't help it. As soon as Alan had left, she'd phoned Jen and paid the deposit. That was it. She couldn't turn back now – she was off to Paris.

Elvis leapt out of the Volvo and turned in circles, chasing his tail with delight. He loved evening walks on Woodbury Common. Even more so, he loved to run with Pam and she was ready to go, in her jogging bottoms, T-shirt and trainers. She took off at a steady lope, Elvis close to her ankles. Her knee had been aching this morning, so she would start slowly. They left the car park behind them, their feet on the soft turf, the common wide open in front of them, an expanse of scrubland, gorse and heather, stretching to trees and ending in the silver curve of the coastline. They kept to the path, smiling at the occasional dog walkers they met, Elvis dutifully remaining inches from Pam's heels, however loudly other dogs barked or wanted to play.

Pam increased her pace slightly as she jogged downhill towards a shady forest. The wind was cold but she was warm, the easy movement of her long limbs generating their own heat. She turned onto the path that led between sticks and puddles, running under the overhanging branches of wood-land. Her skin tingled, chilled by the moving air. She had something on her mind. Elvis was close to her, his soft black ears swinging, his stride bouncing and enthusiastic, matching hers. The light in the woodland was serrated, the dying sunlight illuminating branches and new buds, shadows lurking behind bushes and inside dips and ditches. She jogged into a clearing and turned left, back onto the path.

'What am I going to do, Elvis?' she murmured.

She recalled the phone conversation with her sister, Sharon, who lived in Bridport with her husband. She was usually only too delighted to have Elvis for a few days on the rare occasions when Pam was away, but they were going to London, to the Bridge Theatre to see a play. She'd asked Frances, a friend and neighbour, three houses away, but her grown-up children were visiting that weekend, and a lively spaniel together with the grandchild, a new baby, was not a good idea.

Pam frowned; she didn't want to put Elvis in kennels. He had never been in kennels before and she'd vowed when she brought him home from the rescue centre five years ago, a nervous and tentative one year old, that she'd always protect him. She glanced at the cocker spaniel as he bounded by her side, velvet ears rising and falling, and she knew that she wouldn't let him down.

'It's no good, Elvis,' she gasped between breaths. 'They'll have to go without me.'

9

Jen had it all worked out on the laptop screen. She set the printer to make five copies, one for each of them. They'd fly out from Bristol on the Wednesday morning, the twentieth, and they'd be in Paris in the early afternoon. Jen couldn't help the little flutter in her chest. Paris! She'd been to Paris but it had been many years ago, she and Colin. It was 1995, their twenty-fifth wedding anniversary. She'd loved it – buying souvenirs near the Eiffel Tower, an evening at the Moulin Rouge. She'd planned for the friends to visit all the usual places before they returned on Monday the twenty-fifth, days before the wedding on the following Saturday. The day before Eddie returned from Las Vegas.

Jen was excited. She'd pencilled in tentative plans for every day. After all, as Tess had said, it was her party. They'd visit the Eiffel Tower and the Louvre; they'd take a boat trip down the Seine, maybe go to a club or a show. Then they'd have free time on the Sunday to relax and have a big hen 'do' somewhere in the evening. She'd made a lovely spreadsheet and she'd offer it to everyone, to invite them to make changes, add comments and then let her friends plan the final night out as her proper hen party – Eddie would be proud of her organisation. Jen sighed. She knew Eddie didn't really want her to go to Paris. He hadn't said so specifically since their dinner together, but he *had* asked her why she didn't choose a pampering spa weekend in Taunton or perhaps a cookery day with her friends. He'd shown her a website for a murder-mystery evening where friends dressed up in crazy costumes and had to find clues about who had killed one of them.

She'd suggested that she didn't think murder was very appropriate before a wedding and Eddie had laughed and said that an arts and crafts weekend might be more appropriate than swanning about in a foreign city with four other women. Jen had felt a little piqued, although she hadn't said so to Eddie, but it made her even more determined to go. And the spreadsheet was full of ideas. She would meet the others in the Olive Grove at six thirty to discuss it, to share ideas and make final plans. She secretly wondered whether they shouldn't fit in an evening in a casino and have a little flutter, all dressed up in their glamorous evening wear. After all, what was good enough for the gander…?

Jen folded the five copies of the spreadsheet and popped them in her handbag. It was almost six o'clock and, if she left the house now, she'd be there early to greet her friends as they arrived. She shrugged on her jacket and stepped out into the March air, feeling independent and sophisticated. After all, it was Jen who had been to the travel agents, researched brochures, rifled through various hotels and prices and come up with the bed and breakfast and flight package. She'd checked with the others, paid the deposits and drawn up the ideas for a choice of activities. For the first time in a long time, she felt confident, self-sufficient and strong. She was going to be a bride again soon.

She breathed out in excitement; the wedding was less than four weeks away. She ought to order her dress. She had found a good site online, De' Borah's reasonably priced bridal wear for second-time marriages, and she had found two budget choices she liked: a scoop neck, floor length chiffon dress in pale grey and a knee length satin dress in navy and cream with a cream satin jacket and a navy pillbox hat with a jaunty feather. She wasn't sure which to choose, if either. She resolved to ask the girls, but the Paris hen night was at the top of the agenda for now.

She arrived at the Olive Grove and bought herself a glass of chilled rosé wine. The barman, Tom, was as friendly as ever – more so now that she was holding her reception in the function room at the back. Jen was feeling very much the cultured, chic and liberated woman as she took her place in a cosy corner of the lounge, crossed her legs neatly and thumbed through her iPhone. Tess had messaged to say that she was on her way with Della. Rose had sent her an email an hour ago to say that she was out shopping but she'd be on time. There was no message from Pam, but Jen knew she was the most reliable of all the friends.

A text pinged in from Eddie. It read:

✉ Have a lovely time with the girls planning your hen night. I look forward to our date tomorrow. Your Eddie x

Jen sent him an affectionate reply, saying how she was excited about having lunch with him the next day and checking through the guest list for the reception. So far, with

Jen's friends, her younger sister, Anna, and her brother-in-law, Pete, in Plymouth, their son, James, and his partner, and Eddie's friends and family there would be twenty-five people. Eddie had wondered if they could cut the numbers back to around twenty but Jen couldn't think of anyone she wanted to leave out.

She glanced up from her phone as Tess tumbled into the lounge bar, followed by Della, all smiles, and Rose. Jen stared. Rose had put her hair up in a French roll, the fringe sweeping and long; chips of diamanté sparkled in her ears. She had on a faux-fur jacket, faux-leather trousers and her lips were vermilion. Jen stood up and gasped. 'I didn't recognise you, Rose.'

'I've been shopping. I've read a book about Coco Chanel. If I'm going to Paris, I'm going to look the part.'

'Doesn't she look wonderful?' Della breathed.

'Wine for everyone? My treat.' Tess was already on her way to the bar. She called over. 'Where's Pam?'

'On her way, I guess.'

At that moment, Pam rushed in with Elvis on a lead. Tess mouthed, 'Red wine?' and Pam nodded, taking her place next to Jen, who was already handing out spreadsheets excitedly.

'We'll do all the usual places. And I wondered if we couldn't push the boat out, go to a casino or a show? Both.'

'I might have a problem.'

'Don't worry, Pam.' Jen beamed. 'I've booked us all a continental breakfast in the hotel. They can cater for vegetarians so you'll be fine.'

'No, it's not that. The thing is, Jen – I can't come.'

'Why ever not?' Rose frowned.

'It's Elvis, bless him.' Pam stroked the velvet ears and the little spaniel licked her hand in return. 'I have no one to leave him with.'

'Can't you find kennels?' Rose's fingers smoothed her long fringe. 'It's just for a few days.'

Pam's face was sad. 'I can't do that. Not to Elvis.'

'I'd ask Sylvester – he'd love to – but he works in the snack van by the seafront and of course he couldn't take a dog with him.' Della leaned over, patting Elvis's soft fur. 'Not even one as beautiful as Elvis.'

'So that's that. I can't come.'

'What?' Tess stood at her elbow, holding a tray of drinks. 'Of course you can come, Pam. Here – dig in, girls – wine all around.'

Rose picked up a glass and pulled a face. 'Next time I might try a pink wine, like Jen has. Rosé. It looks very sophisticated.'

Tess squeezed in next to Della and pulled out her phone, ringing a number and holding it close to her ear. The others watched as her face took on a business-like expression. 'Alan. It's me. I wonder – could you look after a little dog while I'm away in Paris at the hen do? No, a spaniel. Of course he's tame.' She winked at Pam. 'Can't he go to golf with you?' Her face was concentrating now, listening. 'Ah, right. Yes, the Olive Grove. I don't know when we'll finish – about half seven, quarter to eight. Yes, there's something in the oven for supper. What? Oh, really? OK, see you then.' She showed the friends a baffled face. 'That was Alan. He said he'd call in, in about an hour. He's just packing up at the golf course. He said he'd have a think about having Elvis.' She paused, then let out a peal of laughter. 'Wonders will never cease.'

'Will he be all right to look after Elvis while he's playing golf?' Pam knitted her brow. 'Elvis is no trouble but I'd hate to think he'd be left in a car…'

Pam swallowed a gulp of wine. 'Alan is a lot of things – but he's not unkind to animals. He'd never neglect Elvis.' She gave a little laugh, a soft bray. 'Only his wife.'

'Right.' Jen waved her copy of the spreadsheet. 'Let's assume you can come, Pam, shall we? Now, to plan the party. We have six days.'

'Five nights.' Tess rolled her eyes.

'It's going to be glorious.' Rose nodded.

'Glorious,' Jen agreed. 'And organised.'

An hour passed quickly, full of good-natured banter and debate. Rose wanted to take in an opera; Tess didn't. Jen wanted a shopping spree but Della wondered whether that wouldn't be expensive. Jen said there were spa treatments available in the boutique hotel across the road and she wanted to treat everyone to a facial, but Pam said they should be treating her, as she was the bride. Tess wanted to go to a nightclub and Jen thought a visit to a casino would be fun; Della was quite happy to walk around Paris and see the sights but Jen wanted to see them from the top of the Tour Eiffel. The spreadsheets were a mass of scribbles and crossings out when Alan arrived, standing by their table, giving a little cough to let everyone know that he was hovering.

Tess noticed him and had to look twice: he was wearing a smart new jacket in dark material and casual jeans, his hair newly cut. He smelled of a spicy aftershave. 'You're looking good, Alan. Have you made all this effort just for me?'

Alan planted a kiss on her head and put a hand to his hair, preening. 'Of course –I popped home after golf to make sure I was presentable for my gorgeous wife and her friends. Aren't you going to introduce me, Tess?'

'Everyone – this is Alan.' The four women stared at Tess's husband, who was clearly much more presentable and pleasant than she'd made him out to be. 'Alan, this is Della, Jen, Pam and Rose.'

Alan greeted each woman in turn, smiling broadly at Della, kissing Rose's hand. His eyes lingered on Jen and, when he came to Pam, he said, 'Pleased to meet you. And this must be your little spaniel.'

'Elvis.' Pam grinned.

'Well, Elvis.' Alan patted the dog. 'I'm sure you and I can get along together fine while my wife is having a lovely time with her friends in Paris.' He winked at Jen. 'You and I, Elvis – two single men, left alone. Who knows what mischief we'll find? Maybe you can come to the golf club with me and sit in the bar? You're clearly fine in social settings.'

Elvis barked and the five women chuckled. Then Pam looked anxious. 'Are you sure? What about when you're playing golf though?'

Alan waved a hand. 'Oh, it's no problem. I've had a chat with my golf pal, Cliff. His wife Celia is often down at the golf course and I'm sure she'd be glad to take Elvis for a walk. She'd probably be glad of the company – she never gets a look-in when I'm chatting to Cliff about our game. Poor woman looks bored stiff most of the time. They'll be fine for an hour or two each day and she'd be glad to have a stroll with a handsome dog.' He chuckled. 'Come to think about it, Elvis is probably the better conversationalist.'

Tess sat up straight. 'I thought you weren't happy about me going to Paris, Alan?'

'Whatever made you think that, Tess?' He waved his hands, flabbergasted, exaggeratedly so. 'At first, I was a bit concerned for your safety, especially after your wild night out drinking, but I'm sure you'll have a wonderful time, you and these charming friends of yours.'

'So that's all sorted.' Tess folded her arms. 'Brilliant.'

Pam was reluctant. 'If you're sure... That's very kind of you, Alan.'

Alan took a seat next to Tess, draping his arm around her shoulders. 'Oh, anything for my lovely wife. It's important that you all go off to Paris and have a fantastic time.' His eyes moved to Jen. 'After all, a hen party has to be done properly. Now – can I buy you ladies a drink?'

'Alan?' Tess was confused by Alan's affable nature, his new delight at her going to Paris, his charming behaviour. She blurted the first words that came into her head. 'The supper is in the oven...'

'I popped home to leave the car after golf and turned it down low– it's only a casserole. And we're just ten minutes away. So – ladies – what's your pleasure? Wine? Cocktails? On me.'

10

Tess opened her eyes. The curtains had been splayed wide and light was streaming around a shadow standing at the side of the bed, his shoulders hunched. Tess blinked. Alan was carrying a tray with a coffee pot, a mug, a plate with a boiled egg and a piece of toast, pale in the middle and charcoal around the edges. He was smiling. 'Breakfast, Tess.'

Tess frowned. She immediately wondered if it was sex he was after and this was a distracting prelude. In her mind, she tried to make a joke of it: it couldn't be – it wasn't his birthday. Besides, he was fully dressed, in jeans and a polo shirt. He laid the tray on her knee. There was a flower in a little glass. His stretched smile made a dimple in his chin. 'Everything all right, my love?'

Tess thought it unwise to comment that her immediate thought had been that breakfast was a tentative prologue to marital relations. It was particularly sad because he had shown little interest in her for a while and, in fairness, she hadn't felt the urge to tug him upstairs to the bedroom. It was the best she could do to peck his cheek. She sighed, thinking about the old adage that suggested that if you don't use it you invariably lose it, and 'it' in this case meant that she and Alan had drifted apart; she had lost confidence in herself as a woman and he had turned to golf as his main source of enjoyment. She forced a grin. 'This is nice, Alan.'

She was about to ask him what had prompted such rare spontaneity and kindness. He seldom brought her breakfast in bed. When the children had been young, she and Alan and Lisa and Gemma had tucked up in bed on a Sunday morning with a plate of toast and marmalade and a pot of tea brought up by the girls. Tess remembered it sadly: Gemma with her long nightgown, plaits swinging, carrying the heavy tray, her brow knitted in concentration while Lisa, twelve, two years older, bossed her from behind, cups tinkling against the teapot, all precariously balanced on a chopping board. She had loved those times. They'd been a happy family mostly. She and Alan had shared laughter, good times and so much more. Now the girls were grown with families of their own and Alan had his golf. Tess was left with emptiness; her strong, confident personality had become diluted and was dribbling away.

'Penny for them, Tess?' Alan was gazing at her, his face troubled.

'Sorry?'

'Your breakfast is going cold.'

'Oh!' She pulled the pallid toast apart, crumbling the burned edges to a dust and dipped the morsel into the egg. 'Lovely.'

He beamed. 'Just thought I'd tell my little wife that she is special.'

'Thanks.' Tess chewed thoughtfully. 'It's a lovely day, Alan. Are you off to golf now?'

'Not at all.' He sat on the edge of the mattress and tapped her hand. 'I thought we'd spend some time together, have a little drive today – go over to Woodbury and walk on the common. Then maybe we could stop somewhere nice for a pub lunch?' He raised his eyebrows. 'What do you think, Tess? It's quality time together, because you are worth it. And you said I'd been neglecting you. I want to show you how important you are – how loved.'

Tess met his eyes and carefully brought the teacup to her mouth, sipping the liquid. It was very milky and a little too cool. 'Yes – that's a nice idea.'

'Great – that's decided, then – a wonderful day together, just you and me.' Alan stood up, caught sight of his reflection in the wardrobe mirror and smoothed his hair. 'Let's do that, then. Get yourself up and showered and dressed. Put something nice on. I'll be downstairs waiting in the living room.' He grinned at his reflection, pleased with his idea. 'I'll see you when you're ready.'

Tess watched him walk away, his bottom shapeless in the blue jeans. She thought about how much she'd enjoy the spring sunshine, going for a walk, then lunch in a cosy country pub. Tess breathed out slowly. Alan was trying hard: she couldn't complain about his attitude. She wondered why she felt so sad all of a sudden. She pushed the tray away and swung her pyjama clad legs out of bed with a sigh.

An hour later, Alan parked the white BMW in the car park next to a neat Honda Civic, slid out of the driver's seat and rushed round to open the door for Tess. She smiled and wriggled out. The BMW was in immaculate condition. Alan had bought it new almost ten years ago when he'd retired at sixty-five and he'd kept it spotless. He offered Tess his arm. 'Are you ready for a walk, Tess?' She nodded and linked her wrist through the crook of his elbow. He smiled down at her. 'It should give us an appetite for lunch.'

Tess wondered if he intended playing golf later. Perhaps she should ask him, but it was easier to say nothing and to listen to her feet in walking boots making a steady rhythm on the firm ground. She looked down at the strong brown lace-ups, and tried to think of something to talk about. Nothing came to mind.

* * *

Half an hour later, Jen and Eddie returned to his car from a brisk walk across the common. Jen's chestnut hair had blown free from the jaunty scarf she'd wound around her head but she was snug inside her warm coat. Eddie opened the door of the blue Honda Civic, his face unimpressed. 'The owner of that white BMW has parked a bit too close.'

Jen snuggled into her seat. 'I don't think twenty-six people to dinner is too many, Eddie. It's a round number.'

He smiled and patted her knee. 'So is twelve, my dear. And much cheaper.'

'But I want to invite the aqua aerobics girls. We've become really close.'

'You've known them for... how many months? Five?' Eddie knit his brows together. 'And anyway, you're going to Paris with them. That should be ample really.'

Jen pressed her lips together. 'We're becoming really close friends. And I've known them since October. That's longer than I've known you, Eddie.' She closed her eyes. They had been a couple for such a short time. But Jen was sure he was everything she needed in her life, to make it warm and safe and happy. She sighed.

He slipped an arm around her shoulders. 'But we're different, my dear, you and I. We're going to be married.' He offered her his most charming smile.

'I thought we could invite Tess's husband, Alan. I met him in the Olive Grove.' Jen pouted, brushing her windblown hair from her face with smooth fingers. 'He seems really friendly. He bought us some drinks and he was quite charming. Tess always says he neglects her but, really, he was so attentive to her. And I think you'd like him, Eddie. He might become a good friend...'

'That's not a good reason for giving someone a free meal, Jen – that you might become friends with them.' Eddie took a deep breath. 'I know how kind-hearted and generous you are. But we need to set a limit to the numbers. Seriously, I think we should just keep it to close family: your sister, Anna, and her husband. My son, Harry, and his wife, a few close friends. Let's keep it simple, shall we, Jen?'

Jen shook her head. 'We can afford to invite more people though, can't we? You said it would be all right at first.' She thought for a moment. 'I want the hens there, really I do.'

'Hens.' Eddie squeezed his eyes tight as if the sound of clucking women irritated him. 'It might be nicer to spend quality time with Harry, for you to get to know him, and I could get to know Anna and her husband. Keep it familiar, intimate. I want to avoid the noise of too many guests...' He beamed at her. 'After all, Harry will be like a son to you, won't he? That will be nice, Jen, won't it – having another family, grandchildren, so to speak?'

'Yes – I can't wait to meet Harry, but...' Jen leaned back in her seat. 'Please, Eddie – just the hens?'

Eddie frowned, his face serious. 'It's important to be frugal, Jen. The Olive Grove isn't cheap. We could invite your friends to meet us in the pub for a drink after the meal, how would that be? Then you can bring all the women and all their husbands and whoever you want.' He moved her face towards him, taking her chin in his hand. 'How is that, my dear? That would be nice, wouldn't it?'

'I suppose so.' Jen looked disappointed. 'After all, I am having the hen do, and six days in Paris won't be cheap.'

'Exactly.'

She sighed. 'But then, Las Vegas won't be inexpensive.'

'That's different – it's a special bonding opportunity for Harry and me.' Eddie's blue eyes met hers. 'It's a chance for us to spend time together, father and son. I want to treat him to something he'll always remember. He's a good lad and I know he'll enjoy being spoiled a bit, dressing up, the roulette, nice dinners.'

Jen took a deep breath. The question had been in her head for a while, but she made it spring from her lips before she lost the confidence to say the words out loud. 'How much will it cost? The stag do to Las Vegas?'

'Oh, it's more than just a stag do, Jen. It's a holiday. I explained that. Harry and I want to—'

Her voice was a whisper. 'How much?'

'I've estimated around five thousand.'

'*Eddie...*'

He smiled at her, patted her hand. 'In truth, my dear, that's one reason why I wanted to economise a bit. I've let the Las Vegas trip run away with funds a little – because of Harry. And I knew you'd be fine with it all. You're going to Paris with the girls and – well, it's not as if it's your first wedding, is it?'

'No, you're right.' Jen's mind flitted back to her wedding to Colin. He'd adored her; he'd said often enough he'd give her the moon if he could. She remembered her father paying for the church, the reception, and Colin doing his best to contribute to everything. She recalled him, skinny in his wedding suit and nervous, stammering through the vows, pushing the ring onto her finger and kissing her tentatively. Colin had been a doting husband, full of tenderness, generous and good humoured, but very different from Eddie. Colin had been so young when they'd married, so earnest; Eddie was mature, suave and sophisticated and in control.

Jen knew he had a point – he was the sensible influence she needed in her life. Eddie was the perfect gentleman., affectionate, proper, that was the word for it, and assured. Jen told herself that he was right: she didn't need a big reception; Eddie would enjoy his Las Vegas trip and she'd have fun in Paris. She nodded. 'All right, Eddie.'

He started up the engine, a soft purr filling the car, and turned the dial on the radio to bring up some classical music. 'That's settled, then, my dear. Shall we go back to your house now? We could make a sandwich for lunch, perhaps?'

'Lovely,' she agreed. Eddie reversed carefully, keeping the white BMW at a safe distance, and he swung the Honda Civic around in the car park, giving Jen a warm smile. She offered him a small smile back, but something at the back of her mind was niggling her, like a damp toad squatting on her shoulder. She wriggled it away and thought about what food she had in the fridge, what sandwich filling she had to tempt Eddie with for lunch. But two toads had bounced back, squatting on each shoulder, scratching at her thoughts, suggesting in her ear that maybe there was something unre-solved that she should think about during the journey back to Exmouth, something that felt a little bit like a trifling worry, but one that was going to stick with her for a long time and would refuse to go away.

Jen gazed up at Eddie and his eyes met hers briefly. He stretched out a hand and squeezed her knee, leaving it there. Jen breathed out. It was good to be in a warm car, sitting next to someone who was decisive, wise and a foil for her own frivolous nature. She felt the pressure of his hand on her skin and closed her eyes. She and Eddie were perfect for each other. Married life was going to be glorious.

11

Soap suds covered the small kitchen table as the spaniel shook his wet fur and barked with excitement. He stood in the large bowl filled with clean warm water, expectation in his eyes. Pam rubbed his fur gently, massaging him clean. Elvis's dark curls were plastered close to his body, making him look bedraggled and thinner, but his huge eyes shone as he stared up at Pam, his pink tongue hanging out. Pam rinsed him several times with warm water from another bowl before wrapping him lovingly in a towel, lifting him out of the water and hugging him close to her chest. 'There you are, my gorgeous boy. All done.'

Elvis learned towards her, resting his head against her neck. She placed him carefully on the table, removing both bowls and putting them in the sink. As she returned, the little spaniel shook himself vigorously and the last water droplets flew in all directions. Pam's clothes and face were damp as she lifted a clean dry towel and rubbed at Elvis's fur. 'You're full of mischief, Elvis, but at least you're clean. That was a great run we had on the common this morning.'

Elvis barked agreement. Pam moved her leg to test out her knee. It had been sore this morning during the run. Her face contorted with the twinge of pain that shot down her leg like electricity. 'Maybe I'm too old to keep this up, Elvis?' She towelled him with added vigour. 'Maybe I should just stick to gentle exercise – yoga, aqua aerobics.' She gazed into Elvis's face, the brown eyes round with adoration. 'What do you think, Elvis? I'm seventy... something. Am I getting past all this?'

Elvis sprang towards her, his paws hitting her full in the chest, and she lifted him up and swung him round, laughing. 'You keep me young, my gorgeous boy.' She planted a kiss on his forehead and plonked him down on the floor. 'There you are. Nice and clean for when the girls arrive at six o'clock. OK – come and give me a hand with supper. I'll need three plates – me, Della and Rose. I don't know why I couldn't raise Tess this morning. I hope they all like aubergine lasagne and a hearty green salad.'

She opened the cupboard, selecting three dinner plates. Elvis leapt up at her ankles and barked. 'Yes, I'll rest the knee, Elvis. Maybe I'll take tomorrow off running and just do some yoga, some stretching.' She glanced down at the little dog, whose eyes were fixed on her face. 'I was wondering whether to take my running shoes to Paris with me. I might get a mile in each day before breakfast. Imagine jogging down the Champs-Élysées.' Her smile faded as she gazed at Elvis, who had decided to turn in circles, chasing his tail excitedly. 'I'm going to miss you for six days and five nights.' She hugged the plates and sighed. 'But you'll love it – walks on the golf links every day...'

The doorbell chimed and Pam dragged herself from her thoughts.

Della was in the doorway, laughing, wrapped in a warm red jacket. Pam had to blink for a moment at her companion – she didn't recognise Rose straight away. Her hair was shorter, a feather cut, and the salt and pepper dull brown had been laced with honey blonde. She was wearing a cashmere wrap over a sweater and smart dark jeans and, most strikingly, her lips were vermilion. Della giggled. 'Look who I just bumped into. Doesn't Rose look like Helen Mirren now? Or is it Jane Fonda?'

Rose shook her head. 'Coco Chanel is my role model. Seriously – this trip to Paris in the springtime has been a wake-up call. Shall we go in and make a start?'

In the living room, Della sniffed the air. 'What smells so gorgeous?'

'I made a veggie lasagne – it's in the oven.' Pam waved her hands as if in apology.

'I'm so looking forward to Paris. I've spent too long moping. Now it's time to live a little.' Rose delved into her handbag, a capacious Burberry lookalike, and pulled out Jen's spreadsheet, neatly folded. 'Right – how long do we have before the lasagne, Pam?'

'Half an hour.'

'OK – let's make a start, shall we?'

They sat down at the table, pushing the plates Pam had set out aside, and Rose pulled out a pen. 'Now, first point – the hen do on the final night. This list of Jen's is what she wants, although it's bound to change when we're actually in Paris, but we'll stick to it as best as we can for now, shall we?'

'Things will change as we become more familiar with the environment,' Pam suggested, lifting Elvis onto her knee and massaging his ears. 'So we ought to keep it flexible, although what Jen wants is our priority.'

'True,' Della murmured. 'But the objective this evening is to plan something special for Jen's last night. She's leaving it up to us, right?'

'Right.' Rose lifted the pen. 'So, we need something that won't clash with anything else we're doing during the rest of the break. Something she'll enjoy and remember.'

'They do spa treatments at the hotel.' Pam ruffled her short hair so that it stood up in spikes. 'We could treat her to a surprise spa day from all of us.'

'But what about in the evening?' Rose frowned. 'We need a really special night out.'

'How about the Folies Bergère?' Pam raised her eyebrows. 'We might be able to book in advance for a show?'

Della sighed. 'It's a shame Tess isn't here. She knows how to have a great time – she'd be full of ideas.'

Rose brought her lips together. 'You're right – she's such good fun. But I didn't think that much of her husband, Alan. He seemed a bit of a slime-ball.'

'He seemed very pleasant.' Della remembered his generosity, buying cocktails for the group in the Olive Grove. 'He seemed very fond of Tess too.'

Pam shook her head; she wasn't sure whether dapper Alan had been the genuine article or whether he'd put on a show for Tess's friends. Another thought was creeping into her head. 'Have either of you met Jen's bloke, Eddie?'

Rose folded her arms. 'I'll be accused of being anti-men here, but I think he's being a bit controlling over the wedding.'

'Perhaps they have a tight budget?' Della's thoughts flitted to Sylvester working longer hours in the lunch van, scraping together the extra money for her to go to Paris.

'He's a selfish man, I think.' Rose was not one to mince

her words. She made a huge tick on the spreadsheet, as if she'd dealt with Eddie with one slice of the pen. 'Right – we arrive in Paris on the Wednesday, so we'll have a gentle evening and get our bearings. Jen's put dinner and drinks. That's fine, isn't it?'

'Can't wait until we get to Paris,' Della leaned forward. 'What happens on the Thursday?'

'She's scheduled sightseeing during the day –of course, that means the Eiffel Tower. Jen's put down to visit a gallery too. Do we all agree the Louvre is a must-see? As long as Jen agrees.'

Pam pointed at the page. 'She's put down a trip to a casino on Friday evening, with a question mark next to it. I'm fine with doing what's on Jen's plan, but I can't imagine myself in a casino.'

Della agreed. 'I won't be gambling, that's for sure.'

'Perhaps it's Jen's chance to get even with Las Vegas Eddie?' Rose ticked the page again. 'We can all dress up and take in the atmosphere. Buy one cocktail each and make it last. It will be an experience, if nothing else.'

Della frowned. 'Why has she put a graveyard visit down for Friday after the sightseeing? It seems a bit morbid.'

'It's Montparnasse, Della – lots of famous people are buried there: Sartre, Baudelaire, Saint-Saëns, Beckett.' Pam smiled as Della pulled a disbelieving face.

Rose agreed. 'My research says there's a big tower near Montparnasse and you can go up it and see Paris from the top – you can see the Eiffel Tower and at night it looks beautiful. I wondered if we could perhaps persuade Jen to go there and then have dinner.'

'It might be just perfect, and cheaper than the Eiffel

Tower, probably with less queueing.' Pam leaned forward. 'Saving more money for the shopping Jen's put down for us on Saturday. Jen definitely did mention going up the Eiffel Tower though.'

'I want to see the Eiffel Tower and buy Sylvester a T-shirt with "I heart Paris".' Della grinned.

Rose wrinkled her nose. 'There will be plenty of those around, I'm sure.' She pointed to the spreadsheet. 'What about we do late lunch after the shopping, then a boat trip on the Seine – unless we all decide to move that back a day. It'd fit better on Saturday, and then on Sunday we can have free time in the hotel or a spa treatment and make our outsides beautiful, then go somewhere really special in the evening and give Jen a proper send-off.'

'Not a show?' Pam furrowed her brow. 'I'd love to see a proper Paris show.'

'Tess will want to go to a club.' Della leaned a hand against her chin. 'I'd rather go somewhere quiet and have a meal.'

'A jazz club would be lovely,' Rose suggested.

'Whatever we do,' Pam said thoughtfully, 'it must be a night Jen will remember – a proper send-off.'

'Agreed.' Rose ticked the page. 'Right – I'll pencil all those ideas in and we'll talk to Tess. But let's make Sunday evening a surprise for Jen, shall we? A real razzle-dazzle hen night.'

Della closed her eyes. 'It's such a privilege to be going to Paris. We've only known each other since last autumn, but it will be so nice to spend the time together. It's great to have made such nice friends.'

'Definitely,' Rose agreed.

Pam's eyes were on Elvis. She tangled her fingers in his

shiny black curls and breathed out softly. 'I smell lasagne.' She met Rose's gaze and smiled. 'Right. I'll dish up, shall I?'

* * *

It was six thirty by the time Alan and Tess reached home. They had eaten a lovely lunch in a country pub, all oak beams and mellow lighting, and then Alan had insisted that he drive Tess around the coastline towards Dorset, to take in the pale March sunshine and cloudless skies before heading home. They pulled into the drive and Alan sat back in his seat and grinned at Tess. 'Have you had a nice day?'

Tess smiled. 'It's been lovely.'

Alan leaned over and squeezed her shoulder. 'We're good together, you and me, Tess.' His lips brushed hers. 'And you're right – I need to make more of a fuss of you. Today has been special. We should do this more often.'

He kissed her again. Tess closed her eyes. She felt her phone buzz in her pocket but she ignored it, concentrating on the brief sensation of Alan's mouth against hers.

'It's been wonderful.' She opened her eyes and he had moved away; he was checking his phone for messages. She touched his arm. 'And the day isn't over yet, Alan. We have the whole evening ahead of us. We can do whatever we want.'

As he stared at the screen, he grunted. 'That's right, Tess.'

Tess checked her own phone and gasped. 'Alan – I've missed lots of texts from Pam, and one from Della. They're meeting this evening to sort out the finer points of Jen's hen do, and what we were going to do for her on the last night. A final hen bash. I'm too late.'

Alan beamed, opening the door of the BMW. 'Well, you can call them now. Did I mention, I told Cliff I'd meet him at the club for a swift one?' He opened the door on Tess's side and put out an arm to help her. 'You don't mind, do you?' His eyes met hers. 'But we've had such a perfect day though, Tess – if you'd rather I stayed…?'

'No.' Tess felt surprised he hadn't asked her to go with him. He'd been pleasant all day, in a light-hearted mood and quite attentive. 'No, of course not.'

She clutched her phone, deep in thought. Alan had been good company and Tess felt warmth towards him, a resurgence of the old feelings of something – closeness, familiarity. She followed him as he moved to the back of the car, opening the boot lid. She wondered whether she should put her arms around him, offer him a kiss or some show of affection. He bent over to lift his jacket from the boot and, as Tess leaned against him, she saw the glint of something shiny, a box. 'Alan. What's that?'

He dropped his jacket back in the boot and turned to her, a smile on his face.

'What's what, Tess? I was just picking up my jacket.'

'No – underneath.' She'd definitely seen a gleaming packet, gold-wrapped, the bright paper winking from the depths of the boot.

Alan moved his jacket and pulled out the small square package. 'Oh – this, you mean?' He held up a glossy carton. 'Ah. You weren't meant to see this. It was meant to be a surprise.' With a smooth movement, he handed her the box and grinned at her. 'For you, with all my love.'

There was a label attached to the box, with neat writing. She recognised Alan's script. *Your favourite*, followed by a small *x*.

'Why have you got me a present?' Tess felt flustered. 'My birthday's in November.'

Alan leaned back against the car. 'A show of my undying affection for my wonderful wife.' He rubbed his chin. 'I've been neglecting you lately. I wanted to make it up to you, Tess.' He watched her unwrap the box, her fingers fumbling, and he added, 'I was going to give it to you before you went to Paris. So you could think of me every time you put it on. It's French, of course, because you're off to Paris.'

She ripped the paper off to reveal a white box. 'It's perfume. Chanel. Alan, that's so lovely.' She hugged him closely and felt a little awkward. 'It's not my favourite, though – I usually wear Dior...'

Alan held her at arm's length and smiled down at her. 'I'm sure it will be your favourite when you get used to it.' He pressed her arm. 'The smell is so sophisticated – it reminds me of you. Put some on now.'

Her hand shook a little as she eased the perfume from the box and sprayed some on her wrist.

He inhaled, closing his eyes. 'Delightful. A really sexy smell. Whenever you wear it, it will remind you of me. Oh, I'm going to miss you, Tess.'

Tess hugged him again, leaning against him, her face resting against the smooth material of his shirt. It was the old, affectionate Alan and for a moment, Tess felt her heart ache for past times when they had been so close. He felt warm and smelled of sweet aftershave. She wondered if she shouldn't have a long bubble-filled bath while he was out and then put on the perfume and very little else. She could go to bed and wait for him.

Alan led the way towards the door, the keys in his hand. 'You wouldn't rustle something up for tea, Tess? A sandwich or something? It's well past six now and I said I'd meet Cliff at half seven.'

They were in the hallway. Tess heard his voice drift back to her as he started to climb the stairs. 'I'll just have a quick shower; freshen up while you put something together. I don't want to be late.' He was on the top step, turning towards the bathroom. 'Thanks, Tess. Ham and salad would be nice. Not too much mustard this time.'

12

'Eleven days to go...'

Jen sat on her bed, a comfortable double with a pale grey duvet cover, and stared at the dress. It was on its hanger, on the front of the wardrobe door, sheathed in its plastic cover. It was perfect. She and Eddie had been to Plymouth, where she'd introduced him to her sister, Anna, and her brother-in-law, Pete. The men had taken to each other immediately, chatting and guffawing, clapping each other on the back and settling with a drink in front of the cricket while Jen and Anna had gone shopping. She'd found the dress straight away. Anna had led her to a little shop in a side street and she'd spotted it hanging on the rack: it was a long ivory tube of pale silk with long sleeves and pearl buttons at the wrist. She'd loved it at once but she was afraid to buy it. 'I'll only wear it once, Anna, and it's four hundred pounds. That's over budget.'

Anna had laughed and suggested that she buy the matching shoes too, hugging her and telling her that she was worth it – that it was probably the last time she was going to get married and she should feel special. Jen had taken a breath and bought the dress and the shoes. They'd driven home, the silk dress carefully wrapped in tissue and placed in a box, and Jen had taken the dress straight to her bedroom and hung it up carefully. She'd planned to remove the price label and dispose of it carefully as soon as she arrived home.

It was Tuesday, March nineteenth. The wedding was scheduled for the thirtieth at three thirty and everything was organised: the register office, the small reception at the Olive Grove just for close relatives, with friends invited to join them afterwards for drinks in the bar. Jen felt a tremor of nervousness at the thought of her own wedding. Being a bride, standing next to Eddie, wearing her silk dress and carrying the small bouquet of lilies she'd ordered – the idea made her skin tingle. Then afterwards, they would drive to Lyme Regis in Eddie's car and stay in a hotel. There would be a wedding night and a special breakfast the following morning. Jen felt her heart beat faster in her chest. She was suddenly nervous.

She moved from the bed to the wardrobe to stare at the dress, sliding her hand inside the plastic cover and touching the soft fabric. She closed her eyes, imagining herself wearing it. Even in her seventies, she'd be radiant, modest, and Eddie would be next to her, tall and proud and dignified. She'd booked to have her hair done early in the morning and she'd chosen a swept-up style, little pearls in her hair to match the buttons at her wrist. She hoped she'd take Eddie's breath away. Her mind moved to the wedding night, the hotel, Eddie holding her in his arms and murmuring her name. 'Finally, my love, we're together...'

After the honeymoon, they'd drive back to Jen's house but it would be their house. Eddie would move his things in once they'd returned. He'd arranged to let out his house from the beginning of May. He'd be living with her all the time – he'd be her husband. Jen thought that it was hard to believe, somehow. He'd be there, at mealtimes, when she woke, and for much of the day. He'd tidy the garden, put his clothes in her wardrobe, his toiletries in her bathroom. She wondered how that would feel and told herself that it would be wonderful, that the house wouldn't be so empty.

There was a click downstairs; the front door opened and she heard him call, 'It's only me.' Jen remembered that Eddie had his own key now.

'Don't come up, Eddie – the dress...' She scuttled downstairs and he was standing in the hallway in a smart suit and a dark overcoat. He opened his arms and she slipped into his embrace. He kissed the top of her head.

'Just popped in to say I'm off now, Jen. The car's outside. I'm meeting Harry at the airport.'

Jen gazed up into his eyes. 'Enjoy Las Vegas.' She thought for a moment. 'Enjoy your time bonding with Harry.'

'I will.' He grinned at her. He smelled of aftershave, leather and soap. 'And you're off to Paris first thing tomorrow.'

Jen nodded. A little tremor wriggled up her spine. She would pack this afternoon and then she and the four friends would be off for an adventure. 'I'm looking forward to it.'

Eddie's face became serious; shadowed with concern. 'Promise me you'll take care, that you'll be all right, Jen.'

She giggled, too loudly. 'I'll be fine. The girls and I will have fun...'

Eddie frowned. 'That's what I'm worried about. I hope they behave themselves, and that they don't do anything improper. The idea of my wife-to-be with women who are screeching and cavorting, mutton dressed as lamb—'

'Eddie, really. It won't be like that at all.' Jen tittered into her hand. 'It'll be a very sedate affair. Very cultured.'

He smiled, showing her a relieved expression. 'Well, then, I'm happy.' He placed his lips on her forehead. 'Enjoy yourself, my dear. I'll send you a text to tell you I've arrived safely. Do the same for me, won't you?'

'Of course.' Jen smiled. 'And I'll let you know when I'm back on the Monday. You're back on Tuesday the twenty-sixth.'

'Then we have the wedding on the Saturday to look forward to. And the rest of our lives. You'll be Mrs Bruce.'

'I can't wait.' Jen stretched up on tiptoe to kiss his lips. Then he hugged her, smiled briefly and was gone.

Jen stood in the hallway. She wasn't sure how she felt. She'd miss Eddie, the strong embrace, his self-assurance. She was sad she wouldn't see him for a whole week and she suddenly felt anxious about the hen trip to Paris.

Jen tried to imagine herself walking round a Parisian art gallery, sitting in a pleasant restaurant, walking by the Seine, but she couldn't visualise herself there. It was the voices of the other women that reverberated in her ears, their laughter, their energy, their mischief. She thought of Della's warmth, her giggle, Rose's mock-indignant comments, Pam's caring smile, Tess's madcap dynamism, their combined *joie de vivre*. Jen was looking forward to Paris far more than she'd thought.

She stood up straight, stretching her arms and letting a wide smile break on her face. Eddie would be so proud of her when she came home, when she told him what a successful time she'd had in Paris. She knew he'd worried that five older women in Paris wouldn't be able to cope. But she and her friends would have a whale of a time while he was bonding with his son, and a week later they'd be together again and have so many good stories to share. She imagined herself sitting in front of the television with Eddie, watching a programme about Paris, and she'd point out each place of interest and say, 'We went there...'

He would be so impressed; he'd watch the programme with his arm around her and, afterwards, he'd kiss her tenderly and tell her how proud he was that she'd organised a successful hen party in Paris. Then he'd take her hand and lead her to the bedroom...

Jen sprinted back up the stairs with a new vigour in her step. She was going to pack.

Della frowned, turning down the oven, making sure the one-pot chicken and rice was on the lowest setting to keep it warm. It was half past seven – Sylvester was late. She'd wanted to have a lovely meal with him tonight – she'd be off to Paris with the hens tomorrow. Of course, he was frequently late. He'd work long hours in the snack van sometimes and, although she'd bought him a mobile phone, he'd never use it. 'Damn fool things,' he'd say, adjusting his glasses. 'How am I expected to read those small-print messages?' And then Della would roll her eyes and tut and he'd roll his eyes back at her and laugh. But tonight he was later than usual. The chicken had been moist and tasty half an hour ago; now it would be dry. The ache had returned to her lower back and sat stubbornly, twinging every time she moved too quickly.

The rain lashed the window. The weather outside was cold; there was ice in the hard rain. Della thought about the five hearty meals she'd left in the freezer in cartons, labelled Wednesday through to Sunday. She'd cook something from fresh for him when she returned on the Monday. She wanted to make sure he ate a proper meal. Burgers and sandwiches and packets of crisps from the van didn't make a nutritious dinner – she'd told him that.

She worried about him every day, and that worry would accompany her to Paris with a megaphone. She knew anxiety would crawl onto her pillow like a nasty goblin and shout in her ear before she fell asleep. The same worry would creep up to her in the middle of her laughter, just when she was enjoying herself with her friends, and whisper to her, unsure if Sylvester was all right, if he was eating properly, if he'd done something to hurt himself and she wouldn't be there to help. Sylvester was a grown man, she told herself. He could take good care of himself. But wasn't it just like him to try a bit of DIY to surprise her while she was away? And what if he hit his thumb or bashed his head or something even worse? What if, while she was in Paris, a pipe burst, ice melting at the end of a long winter, or someone tried to steal his takings in the van or accost him on the way home? She would not be there to offer soft words and cuddles and be by his side. She felt anxious – worse – she should not be leaving him for almost a week. It was like a betrayal.

The front door rattled, the sound of a key turning and then a soft clicking shut. Della moved towards the cooker then twisted to watch him stagger, water dripping from his hat, his face shining with rain, into the kitchen. He blinked through rain-covered glasses and shivered inside his thin coat. Della ran over to him and pulled off his scarf, tugging at his outer garments. 'You're soaked to the skin.' She pursed her lips and sucked in air. 'Look at you, Sylvester. What have you been doing out in all weathers until this hour?'

He shook his head. 'It got busy – lots of people stopping

in their cars, wanting hot drinks and snacks on their way home.' Beneath the coat his T-shirt was damp and stuck to his small frame. 'I just kept working on. Then when I parked the van up and came to walk home, the damn fool wind swept a great gust of rain off the sea and I was drenched to the skin.'

Della pushed him towards the door. 'I'll keep your chicken nice for you. You go and get yourself a hot bath, warm yourself up. You'll catch your death of cold.'

'Ah, don't fret yourself, Della. I'll have a tot of rum. I'll be fine.' His face was stiff with cold; he didn't look fine at all. 'No worries – I'll eat first and—'

'Not in those wet clothes.' Della gave him another gentle shove. 'Come on. Let me get you in the bath, get you warm.'

Sylvester gave a single chuckle. 'Can you soap-sud me all over, Della? That'll warm me up nice.' But he wasn't smiling. He looked frozen, immobile. Della hugged him and the cold from his body made her shiver.

'Come on, Sylvester. Let's get you in a steaming-hot bath and back to normal. Then you can eat.'

'A tot of rum'd be nice.'

'Afterwards, when you've eaten.'

He closed his eyes for a moment, as if he'd fall asleep where he stood. 'To be quite honest with you, Della, I might just skip dinner and go to bed. I'm feeling tired out.'

She propelled him towards the stairs and up into the bathroom, passing him a large towel and flicking the taps so that steaming water gushed into the bath. She helped him peel off his T-shirt and jeans. In front of her, he was bent over, skinny, a little naked man with a smooth head and wet glasses. Della sighed. She was even more worried about leaving him now. How would he cope with her away in Paris?

13

Jen was disappointed that they weren't sitting together on the aeroplane. She hadn't realised that they'd have to pay more to reserve seats together when she'd booked. Pam was seated next to a corpulent man in his sixties whose broad shoulder hung over her seat, who smelled of sweat and beef pasties and who was currently tucking into a ham sandwich, grease around his mouth. Pam looked away. It had been awful handing Elvis over to Alan at Tess's house. Alan had promised to take good care of the little cocker spaniel; he had patted the soft curls on his head and called him Buddy, but Pam felt the pricking of conscience and something akin to immature irritation.

She wasn't sure what was making her so grumpy – she usually cheered others up, had a positive attitude, and was a joyful spirit. But today she felt different. She recalled how Elvis had gazed at her with adoring eyes as she handed over the bag of dog food. He had his usual trusting expression when she kissed his muzzle and promised to see him in six days. But when she'd turned to go, he had yapped, leapt up and Alan had grabbed his collar and affirmed in too loud a voice, 'We're just fine, Buddy.'

Pam had forced herself not to turn back, not to snap, 'His name's Elvis' and not to misread Alan's firm voice as a sign that he had no real affection for dogs. As she closed the front door with an empty clunk, Pam's head was filled with the idea that a man who didn't love his wife, who wasn't kind to her, wouldn't be able to look after a dog. But she told herself she was being mean-spirited. Alan had wished Tess a great time; he'd kissed her cheek and said he'd miss her. He'd hugged Pam too, told her to have fun and to 'forget about the pooch'.

But how could she? Elvis was not just a dog; he was special. She felt miserable. She pulled out her phone and thumbed through photos: Elvis on the beach, in the park, running, sitting, adorably begging with his pink tongue hanging out and his dark eyes shining. She felt tearful and she knew she was being silly. She put the phone away in her handbag.

'Can I get you something to drink?' A man in a starched white shirt, his face chubby and pink, smiled at her. His red enamel name badge proclaimed that he was called Craig and that he was cabin crew. 'Any drinks, snacks for you, madam?' he asked again, beaming. Pam stared at the trolley he was pushing, at the array of little bottles and bags of crisps. The man next to her suddenly thrust an arm out across her chest to point at the trolley. 'Scotch, please.'

The stench of sweat that wafted from his shirt as he moved his arm made Pam pull a nauseated face. She ignored him, clenching her teeth, and smiled up at the uniformed cabin crewman, gazing at his neat hair. 'Yes, please, I'll have a sparkling water.'

The passenger next to her huddled back into his seat,

bringing his chin in to his chest, making a disgruntled noise. Craig handed Pam a bottle of water and a glass almost at the same time as he produced a miniature whisky and a glass for the man. He beamed at Pam. 'Are you paying separately or are you buying your husband's drink?'

Pam was startled; suddenly, she felt alarmed. It was unfeasible that the man next to her could be her husband. She was affronted that anyone would consider her to be married to a man whose physical fitness, let alone personal hygiene, was such a low priority, but Pam was also cross with herself again for being so uncharitable. She glanced at the man. 'We're not together.'

The passenger had already poured his whisky, and was proffering a ten pound note to Craig. 'I'd be delighted to buy the lady a drink.' He gave a wide grin and suddenly he looked friendly. 'Please...' He turned his full attention to Pam. 'Allow me.'

Pam nodded and began to pour her water. 'Thanks – that's kind.'

Craig moved away and the man next to her sipped his drink and smiled. The smell of strong spirits and stronger sweat reminiscent of a meat and onion pasty oozed towards her. Pam focused on her water, the glass, the bottle. She felt awkward; she had been spiteful; she'd had negative thoughts about the kind man who was sitting next to her. And it was all because she was missing her dog. She was being grumpy, unhappy, and moody and this was Jen's hen holiday.

As she swallowed the tepid fizz, Pam resolved she'd do better and dedicate the next few days to her friends' happiness. Elvis would be there waiting for her on Monday when they returned and it was the least she could do now to buck up her ideas and have fun. She turned to the man and gave him a warm smile. 'So – are you going to Paris on business or for a holiday?'

* * *

Three rows further back, Rose was seated next to an elegant lady about her own age. The woman had short white hair, long turquoise earrings, a smart blue dress and she was reading a fashion magazine. Rose gazed over her shoulder at the glossy, colourful images. Slim young women with wild hair wore improbable clothes: impractical garments like feather jackets and glittery jeans and gold stringy vests that would never cover the average bust. Rose smiled. She wished she'd worn things like that as a teenager. In the 1950s, children dressed like miniature adults. It was only in the 1960s that Rose discovered that she could wear short skirts and orange lipstick and that she could backcomb her hair and try to become an individual.

But soon after, she had become a mother to Paul, who had been demanding as a small baby, so much so that she'd decided that she couldn't cope with more than one child. Bernard had worked at an office during the day while she looked after little Paul, occasionally seizing a quiet moment where she could rest or have a cup of strong tea.

But even *Watch with Mother* on TV would do nothing to placate the two year old ball of energy, who would scream and writhe and tantrum all day until his father came home. Then the toddler would fall into a doze on his daddy's knee after the dinner Rose had struggled to prepare all day. She'd endured Paul under her feet or screaming in his cot or wriggling in the crook of her arm. Bernard had laughed with disbelief. 'He's such a good boy, Rose. So obedient. I don't know why you complain about him.'

Once he'd said, 'Perhaps he picks up on your tension, Rose? Perhaps that's why Paul isn't calm around you? Perhaps he senses you are nervy.' That had stung Rose, hurt her so deeply that she'd been to the doctor's surgery and asked Dr Turpin for Valium; she'd believed that Bernard was right – she must be a nervous person, highly strung. But perhaps that hadn't been the case. Perhaps, she thought, she'd just been a normal mum with a hyperactive child. Paul was still hyperactive now, always working or off somewhere with his family. He'd been more Bernard's son than her own, she mused, but she contented herself with the fact that he always phoned her once a week, on a Sunday morning, without fail.

The woman in blue looked up from the magazine and noticed Rose staring at the pages of the magazine. 'Would you like to have this when I've finished with it?' Her voice was soft, a rustle of tissue paper.

Rose was alarmed. She felt a flush tingle her cheeks. 'Oh, I'm so sorry. I didn't mean to read over your shoulder.'

'Not at all.' The woman smiled. She had perfect make-up over parchment skin, twinkling blue eyes. 'You're welcome. I just bought the *Vogue* to read on the plane.'

Rose hesitated. She wanted to strike up a conversation. The woman's voice was gentle and friendly and Rose had always wanted to make conversations with unfamiliar people but she'd always been too timid. She took a breath. 'I thought you must be a fashion designer.'

The woman laughed. 'No. Goodness me. I'm eighty. I don't work now.'

'You look younger than that.' Rose brushed a hand through her newly cut and coloured hair and she forced herself to make eye contact and smile. 'We older women do take care of ourselves nowadays though, don't we? I mean, my own mother looked old at fifty.'

'You're so right.' The woman patted Rose's hand. 'I think it's because we ask for more from the world. And we ask for more of ourselves. I'm a widow now, but that doesn't mean that I have to stand still and wait for the undertaker.' She brought her face closer to Rose's and murmured confidentially, 'I'm going to Paris to see my daughter and her family. They live in the suburbs. But in fact, I'm going for another reason – I have an *amour* there too.'

Rose crumpled her brow. She hadn't understood. 'A what?'

'A new love. Someone I met at the end of last year. He's sixty-eight, so I suppose that makes me a cougar, doesn't it?'

'It makes you amazing,' Rose blurted, then she added, 'I'm a widow too.'

The woman stuck out a hand, her fingers circled with silver rings. 'Joy Scott.'

'Rose Grant.' She looked into the woman's twinkling eyes. 'What a positive name – Joy suits you.'

Joy sighed. 'It didn't always suit me. When I lost Frank, it would have been better if I'd been called Misery. The Spanish have a good girl's name for it – Dolores. It means pains, suffering. That was me for ten years after Frank died. He'd been my life.'

Rose nodded. 'It's hard to get used to someone not being there.'

'It is.' Joy raised her eyebrows. 'I tried everything. I had grandchildren; I threw myself into charity work, friends, the church, writing memoirs, baking cakes. It helped considerably but, oh, late at night... Do you know, Rose, I'd never felt so alone, so abandoned. My soul ached.'

'I know how you felt.' Rose sighed. 'But we have to go on.'

'You never get used to it – the loss is always there. But you build your life around it. I will always be Frank's widow, but I am other things too. I don't just mean someone's mother, someone's lover. I mean, I am me. I have a life to live and, do you know, Rose, I am damned well going to live it.'

'That's inspirational,' Rose breathed.

'And you too. You're inspirational.' Joy took her hand. 'You're younger than me, clearly...'

'Not by much,' Rose interjected.

'But look at you. Stylish, strong, off to Paris. Are you by yourself?'

Rose couldn't prevent the grin that was spreading across her face. 'No, I'm part of a hen party.'

'That's marvellous.' Joy craned her neck to search for a member of the cabin crew. 'That calls for a drink. What do you say? It's lunchtime but it's never too early for a celebratory gin and tonic.'

* * *

Five seats back, Della had her eyes closed behind huge sunglasses. She was trying to sleep. The occasional soft lilt, the plane buffeted by air, made her sigh and drift off. Then she would remember Sylvester, his erratic sleep last night, snoring then shifting then waking, and she would take off her glasses, rub her eyes and worry again. He'd hardly eaten the chicken she'd cooked specially for him. It was unlike him not to finish every morsel, hug her and declare it was the best thing he'd ever eaten. But he'd swallowed two glasses of rum and gone to bed early.

She knew it was as hard for him as it was for her to be apart from each other. She'd been in hospital for the births of Linval and Aston and then later for the hysterectomy, and he'd had a spell on the wards when he'd had an ulcer, but, other than that, they'd always been together. It was the way things were, and Della worried that Sylvester would find it hard to cope by himself. It would be easier for her: she had company; she'd be with her friends. But Sylvester being alone made her anxious. He seldom cooked for himself; he seldom did his own washing. He probably didn't even know where the hoover was kept.

She'd enjoyed caring for him; it was part of how she loved him and he cared and loved her back with all his energy. But the thought seeped into her head like noxious smoke. One day, one of them would be gone. How would the other manage? They were not prepared for a life by themselves, neither of them. It was unthinkable.

Della closed her eyes and breathed deeply. She tried to clear her mind, to rest and think nice thoughts, of times with Sylvester, of the boys, then of nothing at all. When sleep came, it was fitful and troubled by grating worries.

Jen stared out of the window at the clouds below: little puff-balls, threadbare streams of cotton wool in an ocean of a sky. It was beautiful. The round window framed the view perfectly: Jen could glimpse the curve of a silver aeroplane wing, white clouds like soft snow-packed mountains below, then the smudge of land, green fields scratched with a brown network of pathways. The plane tilted to one side. They would be in Paris soon. She felt excitement as a tingle in her fingers, a touch of ice against her skin. Six days in Paris was going to be glorious. It was going to be better than a gambling visit to Las Vegas – it would probably be better than a weekend in Lyme Regis. It was Paris, the city of culture, of dreams, and she was really going to enjoy herself.

* * *

Tess finished her wine. The smart middle-aged man in the window seat next to her was giving her a look of disapproval. Tess knew why. He was French: she knew this because he had spoken in French to the cabin-crew woman with the blonde ponytail as he'd sat down and his accent had been perfect. Tess sighed and wondered if she should ask for another small bottle of wine. It would have been easier if the friends could have all sat together. She'd envisaged a hen party from the beginning – laughter, drinks, chatter. Right now, in the seat next to the serious Frenchman, she felt isolated, alone and inappropriate.

She knew that she'd made a mistake, turning up for the flight in jeans, a blue and white stripy top and a black beret. She'd hand-made a huge badge that proclaimed *Je suis une poule* with a ridiculous hand-drawn cartoon of a hen in a wig and sunglasses, standing next to the Eiffel Tower and waving a glass of wine. The string of plastic garlic she'd used as a necklace had been a bad idea too. She was glad she hadn't painted on the little moustache she'd considered as a finishing touch earlier. Alan had told her she looked ridiculous. He had been back to his old grumpy self this morning until Pam arrived with Elvis and Tess had hugged him goodbye; then he'd been effusive and wished her a wonderful time. He'd even said he'd miss her.

The immaculately dressed man next to her was glowering at her from under his bushy eyebrows again. Tess didn't think it was a look of admiration. It was disapproval and, of course, he had every right to be annoyed: she was a blonde woman in her seventies dressed in parody costume, promoting a cultural stereotype. She hadn't intended to offend. She hadn't given it a thought – she'd just wanted to be in a frivolous hen party mood with all the others on the plane, sharing drinks and talking and planning and giggling, and that wasn't easy with Jen four rows away and the others near the front, in a rear seat next to a serious gentleman she didn't know but whom she'd inadvertently offended. Tess sighed. The plane rolled sideways. At least they would be in Paris soon and they could start to enjoy themselves.

She noticed a member of the cabin crew approaching, a chubby faced man with a warm smile. She beckoned him over. His red badge said he was called Craig. Tess greeted him with a grin. 'Excuse me, Craig – I wonder if you have any duty-free perfume? Any Dior?'

'Of course, madam. Which one would you like?'

Tess paused for a moment. She'd no idea why Alan had thought the Chanel was her favourite. She couldn't get used to wearing it – it was far too floral for her taste. She chuckled. You couldn't trust a man, especially Alan, to know which her favourite fragrance was. She'd give the Chanel away and not mention it to him. He wouldn't notice and Jen would probably love it. Buying herself perfume would start off the holiday well – she'd feel cheered up, indulged, pampered. She found her purse in her bag and grinned at Craig. 'I'll have the Poison, please.'

14

The taxi driver talked to them in French all the way to the Hotel Sirène, Tess nodding and agreeing with everything even though she had no clue what he'd said and she was far too embarrassed to try to use her schoolgirl French. The journey was halting, the driver stopping several times to spit out a word that sounded like 'poot' and waving his hands in a disrespectful gesture to another driver or a pedestrian who stepped out in front of him and ignored him, crossing the road and talking into her phone. Tess decided the best way forward was to talk to him in English and hope he could understand.

Della stared out of the window, watching buildings flash by in a blur. It was exciting to be in this strange city and, to her, Paris was an exotic mixture of shops and restaurants; busy people and strange place names. She felt her heart accelerate. There was no sign of the Eiffel Tower but, as the taxi swerved from street to street, sped up and halted sharply at traffic lights, Della knew she'd have so many fabulous stories to share with Sylvester when she returned.

Rose was reading the *Vogue* magazine Joy had given her, large sunglasses perched on top of her head. She looked sophisticated, a Parisienne taking everything in her stride, in her cashmere wrap and smart clothes. In truth, Rose had spent far too much of the money Bernard had accumulated, but she'd told herself it was time to live a little. She glanced up from the glossy pages and inhaled. Paris even smelled different: warm, fresh, welcoming – a beautiful spring day. Rose wondered if she was being silly but she had the distinct feeling that she was coming home.

Pam gazed at her friends: Della, intrigued by everything; Rose, so cool and relaxed. Tess was in her element, her platinum-blonde hair tucked beneath a huge black beret and a string of plastic garlic around her neck, chatting to the taxi driver, waving her arms in a monologue about how they were going to have the time of their lives in Paris and how it would be a hen party to remember and where did he recommend for five frivolous English ladies to eat? The taxi driver began to speak in English in a loud voice, his lips stitched around a cigarette, twisting his head towards the women, suggesting a good Moroccan restaurant close to the Hotel Sirène.

Pam could smell bitter smoke wafting from the front of the cab into their seats at the back. She pushed thoughts of Elvis from her mind. The little spaniel would be fine with Alan; he'd probably have a wonderful time walking round the golf course with – Pam couldn't remember the name of Alan's friend, or the name of his friend's wife. Elvis probably would enjoy himself so much he wouldn't want to come home. Pam wanted to believe that would be the case. She couldn't think about Elvis pining for her. She was here in Paris now and it was about time she started to enjoy herself.

Jen was feeling as if she were the star in a film about

herself. It was a rom-com about a woman who was marrying again after a whirlwind romance. Her husband was a tycoon, a property magnate, and she was a sophisticated, fashionable fifty-something with the world at her feet, about to enjoy some time being pampered in a luxury spa hotel. She had brought her friends with her and, in the film of her imagination, they would have a wild time, laughter and tears, ups and downs. She had even started to cast the characters in the film using movie stars. Her husband was Brad Pitt – who else? She was Jennifer Aniston or Angelina Jolie. Tess, of course, was Goldie Hawn; Della was Halle Berry and Pam would be played by Meg Ryan or Julia Roberts or maybe Jamie Lee Curtis.

Jen closed her eyes. The actors she'd chosen were a little younger than she and her friends were and they were very cultured and chic, but Jen was going to have a wonderful time in Paris, a dream time, so why shouldn't she play out the story as a spring romance performed by beautiful people? Jen couldn't cast Rose. She tried again. Meryl Streep? Barbra Streisand – she was musical, like Rose. But Jen wanted someone who would epitomise Rose's transformation. She'd been so dowdy, so stuck in the past, but the Paris trip seemed to have revitalised her somehow. Jen knew the exact words for it – Rose had a new *joie de vivre*. Yes – Rose would be played by Kristin Scott Thomas: elegant and determined and refined.

Jen was thinking of a little theme tune, some light music to accompany the opening of the movie: *Hens in Paris*. She breathed out slowly. She would be Jen Bruce in ten days, not Jen Hooper. Eddie would be her husband. It felt very unreal; it definitely felt as if she were starring in her own movie, living in the middle of a dream.

The taxi lurched around a corner and jerked to a halt. The driver called over his shoulder, 'We are here now – Hotel Sirène.' Pam paid him with several notes and he smiled and offered her a business card printed with the name Taxi Faik. The women clambered out, tugging their luggage, and stared up at the tall building above a striped red and white canopy and a vertical sign, 'Hotel'. The building stood on the corner where two roads intersected. It was white, three storeys high, sandwiched between a café-bar from which emanated the pungent aroma of ground coffee and a takeaway shop that specialised in *poulet rôti* and smelled very strongly of fried food.

Tess giggled. 'We'll be all right for lunch here.'

Traffic streamed down the road to the left; on the right, there was a cobbled shopping precinct and pedestrians ambled along the centre, carrying shopping and staring into vast windows. 'Perfect.' Rose smiled. 'And we're not far from a Metro, so we'll have access to anywhere we want to go.'

'Great choice, Jen.' Pam smiled. 'Shall we go in and see our rooms?'

'This is home for the week.' Della beamed. The word home triggered an emotion and she felt her features contort a little. This place would be nothing like her real home. She smiled broadly at her friends and made her voice brave. 'I'm looking forward to this.'

'I'm looking forward to a shower.' Tess grunted.

'Then we can plan what to do later on,' Jen suggested.

Rose's eyes flashed defiantly. 'I intend to have a look around the area and get my bearings.' She inhaled. 'Paris has a character all of its own and it's a character I think I want to get to know well.'

They pushed open a glass door and carried their cases

through into the hotel foyer. The space was small, a red carpet on the floor and huge green potted plants and a pair of armchairs in the corner, which made the reception area even more intimate. There was no one around. The five friends gazed around them. Della noticed a lift and sighed. 'Thank goodness we won't have to drag these cases up the stairs. I think I packed too much.'

'You can't have.' Tess chortled. 'It's impossible to bring too many clothes.'

Pam grinned. 'We're only here for six days. I just brought a few things and my shorts and running shoes.'

'I packed my case as full as it would go.' Jen dragged her luggage by the handle, making a face to show that it seemed heavy. 'I even sat on it to zip it up.'

Rose shrugged. 'Well, I'm not sure what I'll do on the return journey after I've bought some new clothes. I might even buy another case to put them in.'

A woman appeared at the reception desk. She was small, smart and heavily made-up with strong eyebrows and scarlet lipstick. Her hair was a dark and straight bob, cut short at one side and longer on the other with a sweeping fringe. It was difficult to tell if she was in her thirties, forties or older. She wore a well-cut navy suit and a white blouse. She raised the dark eyebrows, looking directly at Rose. '*Mesdames?*'

Jen gaped at her friends, her face suddenly tense and nervous. Pam stepped forward and took a breath. '*Parlez-vous anglais, madame?*'

The receptionist didn't blink. '*Oui.*'

'*Nous avons deux chambres réservées au nom de...*' Pam thought a moment. 'Er – in the name of Hooper. Two rooms – one double, one triple – Jenifer Hooper?'

'Of course.' The receptionist smiled confidently and

handed Pam several swipe cards. 'The rooms are reserved for you for five nights, Mrs Hooper. Here are your keys.'

'Oh. *Je suis Mrs...*' Jen paused as she thought the better of it.

Pam grinned at the receptionist. 'Thank you...' Her eyes moved to the woman's gold-coloured name badge; she was called Marion. Pam decided it was too early to be familiar. 'Thanks.'

'You are most welcome.' Marion showed small, perfect teeth. 'If you would fill in some forms for me first and show me your passports, then you can go up to your rooms. Breakfast is served from seven o'clock until ten. I wish you all a pleasant stay at the Hotel Sirène.'

Minutes later, they stood outside the lift, on the landing of the second floor.

'We haven't decided about the rooms – who's sharing with whom.' Tess looked confused.

'I really don't mind.' Pam shrugged.

'It's Jen's decision.' Rose folded her arms.

'I can't decide between you all. How can I do that?' Jen leaned against the vast wall with high ceilings. The top half of the smooth plaster had been painted a brilliant white above a dado rail; below the paint was a dusky orange. Rose put on her huge sunglasses as a statement: it was clearly not to her taste.

Pam pulled a piece of paper from her pocket. It was the remnants of an old envelope with shopping items scrawled on it in biro. 'How about we have a sort of lottery? I'll tear the paper into different sizes. Those of us with the three longest strips of paper get to go together in the triple room and the two shortest take the double.'

'Fine by me.' Jen watched Pam tear paper into five strips

then fold them and juggle them in her palm. She chose one. 'Here goes.'

'Fine by me too.' Della took a piece of paper. 'As long as no one snores like Sylvester does, I'll be happy whoever I go with.'

'I'll sleep with anyone.' Tess winked as she made her selection. Rose gave a light sound of disapproval and chose her piece of paper, leaving Pam unrolling the final one.

The five women scrutinised their separate scraps of paper and held them out with a flourish. Pam had the shortest one, then Rose.

'Right, that resolves it.' Tess grinned at Jen. 'You've got me and Della.'

Rose smiled at Pam. 'The two singletons are left with each other. We'll be fine, won't we, Pam?'

'*Mais oui.*' Pam doled out the swipe cards: three with number 216 and two with number 218: adjacent rooms. 'OK, let's unpack and meet when we've finished, shall we?'

'In the bar?' Tess suggested.

'I don't think there's a bar here...' Jen wondered if she'd made a bad choice.

Rose laughed. 'Paris is full of bars. We'll come to your room, Jen, and then we can decide from there.'

15

'Oh, this room is beautiful.' Jen clapped her hands.

'Gorgeous.' Tess plonked her suitcase on a single bed with a white duvet with pale orange circles. 'I'm in the shower.' She disappeared into an adjoining room marked *Douche* and yelled, 'Oh, this is lovely, girls. Really swanky.'

Jen and Della gazed around the room. The walls were white but three elongated orange tulips with delicate stems had been stencilled over each bed. The beds were singles, but perfectly spacious, with matching duvets reflecting the delicate orange of the tulips. On the far wall was a huge framed black and white picture of a woman in a wide-brimmed hat. Her eyes were in shadow and her mouth held a straw leading to a cocktail glass. The woman had the graceful neck of a swan and the picture stopped at her bare shoulders. Jen thought it looked chic.

Della moved to the window and stared down at the cobbled pavements of the precinct below, at the pedestrians interweaving and pausing to gaze into the shops. 'Paris,' she breathed.

Jen poked her head around the corner of the en-suite. Steam had already started to rise: Tess was in the chrome-framed walk-in shower. Her blurred shape could be seen behind the glass, her arms in the air, and she was singing a song that could have been Abba's 'Voulez Vous'. Jen looked around; the en-suite was enormous, plenty big enough for the three of them. There were two white basins, fluffy white towels on rails and two tall chrome-framed mirrors. The floor tiles were black squares and the walls were a mosaic of small black and white tiles. Della peered over her shoulder and gave a low whistle. 'I want this in my house.'

Jen grinned. 'What a lovely room,' she breathed. 'I think we're going to have a great time here.'

Inside room 218, Rose was less than impressed. 'Really?' Her face was disgruntled. 'The designer was clearly drunk… or mad.'

'It's not too bad.' Pam put her suitcase down. 'I think I quite like it.'

'Purple walls?' Rose's face held the expression of someone smelling something putrid, a rat that had been dead for days. 'It's grotesque.'

Pam shook her head. 'It has a modern feel to it. It's – fresh.'

'It's fresh out of Barbie's boudoir.' Rose shook her head. 'Really – is this the best décor we can have?'

Pam stared at the walls. They were, it had to be said, purple, or at least a deep shade of lavender. The curtains were the burnt orange and red of a stripy sunset. The furniture was white except for the headboards of each bed, which were gigantic black squares with integrated cabinets. The floor was tiled with cream-coloured flagstones. Rose tutted loudly. 'This will give me a headache.'

Pam gave her a good-natured smile. 'I could ring the desk and ask for another room?'

Rose sniffed. 'What if they are all this bad? I hope Jen's triple room is better.' She moved towards the en-suite. 'Let's see what's in here. Oh no.'

Pam followed her into the en-suite. It looked fine to Pam: the tiles were white, as was the little shower, which hid behind a frosted Perspex saloon door at the top of a step. The towels and toilet roll were bright pink against the white. Pam took in Rose's disappointed expression. 'Is it the colour?'

'It's poky.' Rose shook her head sadly. 'And it would be easy to slip down that step after a shower.' She moved over to the bed and sat down. 'I just wanted a bit of luxury while I was in Paris. And this is – well, this is just bog standard.'

Pam plonked herself down next to her and placed a gentle hand on her shoulder. 'Shall I pop into Jen's room and see if someone wants to swap with you?'

Rose didn't move; she was thinking. Suddenly, she turned her gaze on Pam, as if noticing her for the first time. 'No, no, it'll be fine.' She took a deep breath. 'I'm being a diva, aren't I? I'm glad it's just us two in here, Pam. I mean, I'm up for a party while we're in Paris, but, well, we'll be quieter than the group of three, won't we?' She sighed. 'And if I stop being such a prima donna, perhaps I'll get to enjoy the cheeriness of the room and the compact practicality of the en-suite?' She patted Pam's hand. 'No, I'll be fine. I'm sorry.'

'I'm happy to ask for a different room.' Pam sat upright. 'I know the English don't usually complain, but I don't mind requesting something else.'

Rose smiled, a weak curve of her lips. 'Pam, I've become a fussy old lady, on my own for too long. No, I need to learn to be adaptable, flexible, to accept what life throws at me and maybe this room is a challenge. I need to see the good in everything and not be so pessimistic. I'm determined to be a glass-half-full person.'

Pam grinned. 'Or even a glass-completely-full person.' She went to the window. 'There's a great view of the street below – all the cafés and the shops. It's not too noisy but it's central and buzzing and full of the essence of Paris.' She turned round, her hands on her hips, and chuckled. 'Rose, I think the universe is giving us experiences all the time and perhaps we grow and become better because of them, however really hard some of them have been. What do you say?'

'I think I agree with you, Pam.' Rose stood up and brushed a hand through her new smart hair. 'Now, let's freshen up and put our things away, then we can pop next door and have a look at Jen's room.' She pressed her lips together. 'This room is plenty good enough to sleep in. It will suit us just fine. Paris is out there, waiting for us to explore it, to capture each moment and savour it. And there will be a café out there or a bar with a few nice drinks with our names on them. What do you say?'

'I say bring it on.' Pam was grinning. 'Or as they say here, *allons-y*.'

* * *

It was almost half past seven. The decision about where to eat was easy: they'd find the Moroccan restaurant the taxi driver had recommended. It was two minutes from the Hotel Sirène and, as Tess had said, they could have a meal and then tumble back to their rooms and into bed for a good night's sleep; they'd be rested and fresh for sightseeing on Thursday.

The taxi driver had told them that the restaurant was called the El Madani and that Chafik made the best couscous in Paris and for a price that couldn't be beaten outside Rabat, his home town. Based on Faik's directions, the friends were confident that the restaurant was almost next door to the hotel. The problem had been about what to wear.

Rose and Pam had been ready first, Rose in a chic black dress and heels and a warm grey coat, Pam in jeans and a bright shirt. Della had found a gold top and black trousers and Jen had put on a pretty green dress with white polka dots. But Tess had changed three times. The jeans had been thrown aside for a dress when she'd seen what Jen was wearing, then she decided that jeans would be a good idea after she saw Pam's casual clothes. Finally, she settled for a shiny silver sleeveless top over black denims, but she couldn't make her mind up about accessories. Della was wearing a pretty diamanté clip. Rose had pearl earrings. Jen was wearing her chestnut hair up so Tess found huge golden hoops for her ears and put her hair up in a clip. She then complained that it made her look too old, her face was haggard – not that Jen didn't look fabulous with her hair up but Tess insisted that it wasn't a style for her, so she backcombed her blonde hair into a mane and stared into the mirror. 'What do you think, girls? Too Debbie Harry? Too punk rock?'

Finally, she had smoothed her hair into its usual sleek style, found the black jacket she'd worn in the taxi and they were ready to go. They took the lift downstairs, greeted Marion at the reception desk with a pleasant *'Bonne nuit,'* and followed the paved street away from the hotel. The skies were dark; street lamps created a honey haze around the bulbs. Shops and cafés were illuminated with glittering signs and various strains of music sounded as they passed.

It was still busy; although many of the shops were closed now, the air was buzzing with chatter and thrumming melodies from the cafés, which were filling with people wanting to eat, drink and socialise. Pam suddenly had a thought.

'*Bonne nuit* means goodnight. We should have said *bon soir* to Marion at the desk.'

'Does it matter?' Jen looked anxious.

'Perhaps she'll think we're staying out all night and lock the door.'

'It's a twenty-four hour reception – we'll be fine.' Rose's face was positive.

Della inhaled. 'Can I smell cooking? Definitely – spices, saffron, harissa, something is making my mouth water. Do you think we're close to the Moroccan restaurant?'

The women passed a café, a shop selling souvenirs and a small supermarket, which was still open. A man loitered outside, smoking a cigarette. Next door there was a boutique with several signs in the window announcing the word '*soldes*'. Jen wondered if the shop was closing down but Pam thought it meant that sales were taking place. Tess pressed her nose on the window. 'I might come shopping here tomorrow.'

Suddenly, Della called out, 'This is it, isn't it? El Madani?'

It was a building with a vast window and red fronting, with curved writing in gold across the window showing that it was a Moroccan restaurant. Pale yellow light glimmered from inside.

A voice behind Tess called, '*Madame?*' and someone tapped her on the shoulder. She turned to see a young man in his twenties staring at her. He had dark hair, a leather jacket and jeans. '*Madame?*' It was the young man outside the supermarket, the one they'd passed moments before. He had finished his cigarette and now he was following them.

Tess turned to her friends and pulled a face, mouthing, 'Help.'

Jen took her arm and tugged her away. 'Let's keep walking.'

Pam, Rose and Della caught up with them. Pam whispered, 'We should just go in to the restaurant. It's back there – we're going away from it.'

'He's following us,' Della hissed.

The five women increased their pace, linking arms. 'We must be conspicuous,' Jen suggested.

'*Madame?* English? Wait *un* moment.' The man was behind them, taking strides that brought him closer. Rose glanced over her shoulder. 'What do we do? Walk faster.'

'Perhaps he's a scammer?' Tess was alarmed.

Della's voice was low. 'Perhaps he has a knife?'

'*Madame*. English. *Attendez* – wait.'

Rose stopped where she was. 'This is silly – the restaurant is the other way. And there are people everywhere.' She whirled round, staring at the man who was walking towards them. 'What do you want?' Her tone was fierce.

Pam was at her side, using a more affable voice. '*Qu'est-ce que vous voulez, monsieur?*'

Tess stood her ground and then the five friends clung together. The young man had reached them. His eyes roamed from face to face. He looked at Tess, took in her blonde hair, scrutinised her ears and smiled. 'It is you – I think?'

Tess frowned. 'Pardon?'

The young man held out his hand. In his palm was Tess's gold earring. 'Your *boucle d'oreille*? I think you let it fall... in the street.'

'Oh, my earring, yes. Thank you so much.' Tess giggled, grabbing it from his hand.

'No problem, *madame*.' He met her gaze with serious eyes. *'Bonsoir.'*

'Thank you,' Tess breathed, but the young man was walking away. She turned to her friends. 'Thank goodness – I love these earrings.'

'I thought he was a scammer.' Jen gasped. 'Eddie warned me we'd meet them in Paris.' She smiled. The thought of Eddie, his caring nature, his concern for her safety, gave her a warm feeling. She wondered how he was getting on in Las Vegas, if he was missing her as much as he'd said in his texts.

Rose sighed. 'It was just a young man being kind.'

'I suppose we can't be too careful,' Della admitted. 'But you can be too suspicious of people. He was just a nice young man.'

Pam nodded. 'Well, I think it shows that most people in the world are basically good.' She shrugged, a grin on her face. 'Now, I don't know about you, but I think we should go back the way we came, find El Madani again and have some of the best couscous in Paris. What do you say?'

16

'Ladies, ladies, you are most welcome.'

Chafik was a tall, well-built man in his forties with a beaming grin that stretched between two rounded cheeks below twinkling brown eyes and heavy brows.

Rose gave him her most charming smile. 'The taxi driver recommended you.'

'Faik, yes – he is my cousin. Come in, please. I will find you a good table.'

'I hope they are all good,' Tess quipped and Chafik put his arm around her. 'Oh, yes, all good, but you will have the very best tonight.'

He led them to a large round table in the corner, its surface shining gold metal. There was an ornate lamp in the middle, the glass bulb a tessellation of small mirrors and tiny holes. The light twinkled gold and a jewel of colours. The five friends sat down on red velvet chairs and gazed around them. Two couples were eating and drinking at smaller tables on the other side of the restaurant. Rhythmic music came from loudspeakers, the beat of drums and the breathy, reedy sound of a flute. The curtains were rich gold, reflecting the soft light that gleamed from low-hanging lamps. There were paintings on the wall, one depicting an array of colourful pots, another showing a souk market in full swing underneath a sweeping archway, a third was a simple painting of a young woman in a headdress holding up a heavy bunch of grapes. Pam sighed. 'This place is lovely.'

Chafik was delighted. 'Can I bring you drinks?'

'Red wine!' Tess exclaimed.

Rose met the waiter's eyes. 'What do you recommend?'

He chuckled. 'You are in Paris, *madame*. I suggest the French reds. Perhaps a *Côtes du Rhône* or even a Loire red, if you are having tagine or couscous.'

Jen gazed at her friends. 'Shall we have both? There are five of us...'

'Why not?' Rose agreed, and Chafik was at her elbow with menus, suggesting the best choices and recommending starters, praising the *beghrir*, explaining how the pancakes were made, offering Pam roasted pepper hummus or feta and pine nuts, extolling the virtues of *zaalouk* to Della and giving her a detailed account of how to make the dip from aubergine, tomatoes, olive oil and garlic. Jen sat back in her seat, her eyes shining. 'This is wonderful. I am so glad we came here.'

The dishes arrived and the rapid chatter between the five women became quieter as they munched, pausing to comment on how delicious the food was, to share mouthfuls between them, sampling the other's choice. The bottles of wine were soon empty and Rose ordered a third.

Chafik hovered with the dessert menu. Tess wanted to try *basbousa*, an almond semolina cake with orange and cardamom syrup, and Rose asked for cheesecake. Jen decided coffee later might be nice. Her mind flickered to Eddie, to the evening he'd come round to her house for coffee and she'd wondered if he would stay the night. She thought about him in Las Vegas, at the roulette wheel, and she smiled.

'What's tickling you, Jen?' Pam asked.

'I was just thinking about Eddie...'

Della met her eyes. 'Are you missing him?'

'No, not really.' Jen was surprised at herself. 'I was just thinking how much nicer this is, the five of us here in Paris, and how much I'm going to enjoy it. I know Eddie was really looking forward to his trip but I don't think I'd get much out of Las Vegas.'

'I went to Florida once.' Tess paused as Chafik put a dish of golden semolina cake in front of her and she gazed at the lashings of syrup. 'Mmm, looks delicious. Where was I? – Florida. It was nice enough. Alan and I had a sort of second honeymoon.' She pulled a disgusted face. 'The less I say about that, the better.'

'Why?' Rose was interested. 'What happened in Florida?'

'Tess might not want to say.' Pam looked alarmed. 'Sometimes there are things in our past we'd rather forget about...'

'We might want to hear it, though.' Jen giggled. 'Go on, Tess – tell all.'

Tess breathed in deeply and reached for her glass of wine. 'It was years ago – thirty years, maybe a bit less. My youngest, Gemma, had just left home for a job in London and I was doing a bit of work with an estate agent, showing people around houses, selling properties – sometimes really big ones. I was quite good at it.' She paused to see four pairs of eyes staring at her. Pam's fork was poised in mid-air. Tess forced a grin. 'I got quite friendly with one of the bosses, a man called Jeff, and he used to invite me and Alan out with him and his wife, Christine. We became quite pally.'

Pam squeezed her eyes shut, as if she knew what was coming; Della leaned forwards. 'So, what did you do?'

'We all became best buddies, the four of us –Jeff and Chris didn't have children and my two had flown the nest. So we used to meet up a lot, go out for dinner or have boozy feasts round our homes; we went away for odd weekends together and, suddenly, things changed. Alan said we should see less of them – he wasn't so keen on Jeff and he thought Chris wasn't a good friend for me, she was too loud, and she drank too much.'

Jen sighed. 'So, did you do what he said – did you all stop being friends?'

'Yes, but all for the wrong reasons. Then I was out one day, showing a client a house in Exmouth, and I saw Alan drive past – it was his car – and I was sure Chris was in it. I challenged him about it that evening but he said it couldn't have been him, I'd made a mistake.'

'Was it a mistake?' Della's mouth was open.

'Well, two days later, Jeff told me in the office that he and Chris had split up. He knew she'd been seeing another man. I was sure I knew who it was. I went home and challenged Alan and he admitted it eventually. He'd been having an affair with Chris.'

Rose frowned. 'What did you do?'

'I threatened to leave him. I was going to find my own place. I told him to sell the house, we'd get a divorce. I was furious.'

The women were quiet. Tess's dessert was unfinished. Then Pam whispered, 'But you didn't go, Tess. You didn't leave Alan.'

She shook her head. 'He persuaded me not to, begged me. He said he'd made a huge mistake – he didn't love Chris, he loved me and it was because I'd been neglecting him and concentrating too much on my work. I wasn't sure, but he kept going on about how it would break the girls' hearts and how he'd change, he'd make it up to me and we should go on a second honeymoon, to get our mojo back. So we did –we went to Florida.' Tess shrugged. 'That was it.'

Pam's voice was still hushed. 'And are you glad you stayed together, Tess?'

Tess shook her head. 'I don't know – sometimes... I mean, I don't think Alan has played away since but...' She swallowed a mouthful of wine. Tears glistened in her eyes. Jen reached over and took her hand, squeezing it. Della sighed. Rose picked up her glass and gave a low laugh.

'I almost had an affair once.'

'Really?' Tess made an effort to smile. 'You cheated on your husband? On Bernard?'

'Almost.' Rose gave her most enigmatic Mona Lisa smile. 'I thought about it.'

Jen reached over and stole a teaspoonful of Tess's *basbousa*. 'Delicious, Tess. So – Rose – what happened?'

'It was like a scene in a romantic film... complete with background music.' Rose closed her eyes. 'We were living in Exeter. Bernard was at work. Paul was at secondary school and we'd let the spare room to a student at the university. Gerry, his name was – he studied history. He wasn't good-looking – a bit scruffy, skinny, glasses, but he had something, you know, about him. And I knew he liked me.'

'Why was it like a film?' Della stole a teaspoonful of Tess's *basbousa* and Tess launched an attack on the back of her hand with her fork, but Della was quicker and swallowed a morsel of cake and syrup in one cheeky mouthful.

'It was the afternoon and I'd been playing music in the lounge. Rachmaninov on the piano – a passionate piece – and Gerry came in. He'd been upstairs in his room, working. I knew he was there, watching me from the doorway, but I kept on playing. He walked up behind me, put his hands on my shoulders and I kept playing. He kissed the top of my head, my ear, my neck, but I kept moving my hands across the keys, feeling the passion that was drifting like a powerful force in my direction, waiting for what would happen next.'

'My days,' Della breathed.

'Then what?' Tess clearly wanted the juicy scenes.

'Then I stopped and turned around. Gerry clasped me in his arms, told me he had feelings for me. He kissed me on the mouth.'

'What happened next?' Tess didn't notice Rose steal the last of her dessert. 'What did you do? Fall on the floor, have passionate sex?'

'Bernard came home for his tea. The door went click and Gerry bolted to his room like a frightened rabbit. And that was it.'

'You weren't tempted after that?' Pam filled everyone's glass with wine.

'He was twenty-four – I must have been well into my thirties.' Rose laughed. 'He moved out soon after that.'

'How did you feel?' Della asked.

'I'm not sure.' Rose shook her head. 'I was brought up by strict parents – they filled me full of words like duty and honesty and responsibility. I rebelled a little as a teenager, but I think my final rebellion was to marry Bernard. After that, I sort of fell into a routine for years and didn't rebel again.'

'Until now,' Pam suggested.

Jen sat upright. 'My boss tried to have an affair with me. It was in 1974. Colin and I had been married for four years and I was desperate to have a baby. We'd just had a miscarriage at ten weeks. I suppose I was a bit vulnerable. I was a secretary. The man I worked for, Vic, was known for being a bit of a...'

'Ladies' man?' from Rose.

'Casanova?' from Della.

'Pig?' from Pam.

'Dick?' from Tess.

Jen giggled. 'All of those. He started with the compliments – you know, my darling Jenny, my love – then I was his dolly bird, his favourite girl.' Pam pulled a face, but Jen laughed. 'He'd make a fuss of me in front of the other girls, put his arm round me, and then he started to pat my bottom whenever he could.'

'You should have complained.' Rose was indignant.

'You should have kicked his butt.' Pam gritted her teeth.

Jen shook her head. 'He tried it on once too often, when I was on my own late one night. It was awful. He was stronger than me and he kept kissing me. His hands were all over me and I was so scared I couldn't scream. I managed to wriggle free and run away. He just stood there and laughed.' Tess shook her head. Jen's face was sad. 'I left after that – handed in my notice.'

'That's disgusting.' Pam's face was flushed with anger. 'Men like that should be punished. It's always the women that get the blame.'

Della made a fist. 'Men got away with too much in those days. It was always the women's fault. I mean, I never cheated on Sylvester, but once, when the boys were small and we were living in London, there was this milkman...'

'Milkman?' Rose hooted.

Tess grinned. 'Did he give you a free pint a day? A ride on his milk float?'

Della shook her head. 'He kept singing that Rolling Stones song at me, "Brown Sugar". He kept making comments about wanting to try it out with a Caribbean woman—'

'Revolting man,' Pam shouted.

'He thought it was fine for him to make suggestive comments to me, say the things he wanted to do to me when my husband was at work. Sylvester would have killed him if he'd known.'

'You didn't tell your husband?' Jen asked.

'No, I'd had enough. He thought he could say all sorts of things to me and I wouldn't retaliate. Then, one day he was telling me that he'd never seen a black woman's – you know what – I lost my temper and threatened to bash him with a rolling pin – and from then on, I got my milk from the Co-op.'

The women laughed, except for Pam, whose face was still furious. Rose poured the last of the wine into glasses and Jen waved Chafik over and asked for coffee. The friends were quiet for a moment, thinking. Then Tess asked, 'What about you, Pam? Have you ever had crazy affairs?'

Pam shook her head. 'No, that sort of thing doesn't really happen to me. I've had – you know – relationships and I've lived with people, but I always end up by myself.'

'Don't you mind?' Jen sat back in her seat as Chafik placed cups of coffee on the table.

'No, not really.' Pam ruffled her hair until it stood upright in peaks. 'It tends to be safer that way. I've travelled by myself a lot too. In my thirties and forties, I dabbled in photography for a while and I went all over Europe, to India, Borneo, all by myself. It wasn't a big deal.'

'I'd have been terrified, weren't you?' Jen admitted.

Pam grinned. 'Oh, yes, at first. But I lived in an ashram for a bit; I worked with kids in a school in Africa; I did a bit of charity work. So, I'm used to being by myself.'

'You're so independent – that's incredible.' Tess leaned back and stifled a yawn. 'Well, we've certainly got to know each other a bit better tonight.'

Rose winked. 'I'm sure there's a lot more where that came from. This holiday is going to be interesting.'

'It's been a lovely evening.' Jen smiled.

Della sipped her coffee. 'This is going to be such a great trip.' She felt someone touching her sleeve and looked up into Chafik's smiling face. He handed her the bill.

'You come back tomorrow, lovely ladies, and I make you a special Moroccan banquet?'

Rose took the bill from Della's fingers and eased herself upright. She delved into her handbag and found her credit card. 'It's been a lovely evening, *monsieur*. Thank you very much. And yes, we will certainly be back again before we leave. Are we ready, ladies?'

Tess stood up on shaky legs. She was feeling the effects of the wine. She put a hand to her ear and checked the gold hoop was still in its place. 'I'm ready for bed.' She grinned. 'And then, tomorrow, I'll be ready for breakfast and a spot of sightseeing.'

17

Rose sipped coffee from a small cup and gazed out of the window. Outside the hotel, even at eight o'clock, people were already on the move in the little cobbled shopping precinct, heads down accelerating, heads up sauntering or moving languidly, chatting into phones, all on their way to some destination Rose knew nothing about. She glanced at her three friends who were also on their phones: Pam was staring out of the window in a world of her own, but Jen was thumbing through her mail, Tess was busy messaging someone and Della was looking at the screen, sighing.

'Sylvester won't send me anything.' She smiled sadly. 'He has a mobile but he won't ever use it. He says the screen's too small for texting. I rang him this morning and told him that I was here safely, so that's the main thing. He said I should go off and enjoy myself and not to worry about calling him again. He said he'd be fine and to stop fussing over him. So that's what I'll do – he'll be out in the van selling snacks most of the time, I expect, and then he'll fall into bed at the end of the day.'

Tess continued to text, picking up a croissant with her free hand and nibbling the end. 'Alan says he's missing me and that Elvis is having a great time.'

Pam's face brightened at the mention of the little cocker spaniel. 'What exactly did Alan say, Tess?'

'He texted that Elvis is enjoying the golf club; he went for a long walk last night and he's going for another today. Alan says the weather is lovely back in Exmouth...'

'It's lovely here too.' Rose's voice was bright. She looked around the breakfast room, with its neat tables and white cloths, the high ceilings, the scent of roasting coffee beans hanging on the air. There was a single man in his forties at the adjacent table, concentrating on a newspaper, and a couple with a teenage daughter engrossed in conversation at another. Rose reached for her cup and drained the last dregs.

'Eddie's sent me a photo of his hotel in Las Vegas.' Jen giggled. 'It looks amazing. So plush.'

Rose wrinkled her nose and decided to say nothing. She was surprised how irritated she felt when she thought of Jen's fiancé. It was irrational of her, but she couldn't help thinking it was slightly unfair: Eddie was away on his stag do and he was still filling Jen's time with news about himself. 'I hope you'll send him a few photos of Paris. We're going to have a great time here.' As an afterthought, she added, 'I wouldn't like Las Vegas.'

'He's going to a casino tonight.' Jen was still smiling. 'He says if he wins, he'll buy me something nice.'

Tess put her phone away and reached for a second croissant. 'I hope it's not perfume – men have an odd idea of what we like.'

Jen beamed. 'I've got the Chanel on you gave me, Tess – it's wonderful.'

'We're going to a casino tomorrow, aren't we?' Rose held up her cup as a young woman in a black dress and starched apron filled it to the brim. 'Thank you, Claudette.'

'We're not going there to bet though.' Della shuddered. 'Those places are dens of iniquity.'

'It'll be fun.' Tess grinned. 'I might have a flutter.'

'Let's chat about today,' Rose suggested. 'We've got sightseeing to do. Are we all agreed we'll start at the Louvre?'

'It's on the spreadsheet.' Jen watched Claudette fill up her cup, moving skilfully to one side to do the same for Tess.

'What about old bookshops?' Pam leaned forwards, her face eager. 'It would be good to find something interesting, to browse a bit.'

'Won't the books all be in French?' Della glanced up at Claudette, who had filled her cup. 'Thank you – *merci*.'

The young waitress smiled. 'There are many old bookshops down by the Seine, not far from La Louvre. The *bouquinistes*. You will find many interesting things.' She picked up Jen's empty plate. 'And perhaps you will enjoy the street art at rue Dénoyez?'

'That sounds lovely.' Della nodded. 'Can you add that to the list, Jen?'

Pam picked at her croissant. 'I think I'll go for a run before breakfast tomorrow. It feels strange to do no exercise for a whole day. My body feels itchy under my skin.'

'You're missing little Elvis.' Rose squeezed Pam's arm. 'I'm not sure you slept well last night.'

'He usually sleeps on my bed. It was strange being without him.' Pam ruffled her hair.

Della giggled into her hand. 'I had a wonderful night's rest. I missed Sylvester but, oh, the peace and quiet was lovely.'

'I slept like a log.' Tess stretched her arms over her head. 'No Alan taking up three quarters of the bed.' She thought for a moment. 'I wonder if I ought to ask him if we should have twin beds. Mind you, there would be nobody to keep my feet warm at night...'

Jen sighed. 'I have all this to come, when I share my home with Eddie. Cold feet, snoring, taking up all the space.' She forced a grin. 'Maybe that's married life.'

'Yes, but don't forget the passion,' Tess reminded her, thinking immediately that she was not describing her own marriage.

'And the hugs – the love,' Della added, thinking of Sylvester.

Rose shook her head. 'You'll have company around the house, someone to share everything with.' She was determined to encourage Jen, to make up for her previous, probably misjudged, feelings of frustration towards Eddie. 'I'm sure you'll both be deliriously happy.' Rose noticed Jen shoot her an alarmed look and she wondered if she had overdone the optimism. She pushed back her seat. 'Shall we go, ladies? The Louvre awaits us.'

'Is it far? 'Della asked. 'I don't mind walking but my back aches if I overdo it.'

'We could get a taxi between five of us.' Tess looked hopeful.

'It's a couple of stops on the Metro.' Pam smiled, stretching in her seat. 'And the Metro is only a few minutes away. The hotel's ideally placed for sightseeing.'

'That's why I chose it.' Jen grinned, watching Claudette clear their table. 'That and the great reviews, and the fact that it's not too big, and the price, of course, and that it's close to amenities.'

'It's perfect,' Rose agreed. 'Right, shall we get going? You never know – if we're early, we might walk straight into the gallery.'

* * *

The queues were four people deep, stretching back from the glass pyramid entrance across the square. Pam shivered. 'We should have bought advance tickets online.'

'But look at this beautiful building.' Della's face shone as she gazed at the golden turrets of the Louvre, the rounded arches and ornate windows. 'I could gaze at this all day.'

'It's quite chilly though.' Jen pulled her coat around her, lifting the collar. 'When I get in, I'm heading straight for the *Mona Lisa*. I want to take a selfie with her to send to Eddie.'

Rose grunted. 'The queue isn't too bad. I think we'll be here for a good half an hour though. Then they'll want to check the bags before we go in.'

'They'll have fun checking mine.' Tess brandished her huge bag. 'It's full of all sorts – sweet wrappers, a toilet roll, receipts – I've even got cutlery, in case I need it. And there's enough medication to start my own pharmacy.'

Rose feigned a worried expression. 'Drugs and weapons? They won't let you in, Tess.'

For a few seconds, Tess looked genuinely concerned. Jen's face held traces of panic. Then Rose burst out laughing. 'Oh, come on. We're hardly gangster material, are we?'

'We're five dangerous English pensioners...' Pam giggled.

Della had tears in her eyes. 'Imagine the headlines. *"Granny Thrown out of French Museum for Attempted Vandalism with a Spoon."*'

Tess rummaged in her bag and brandished a dessert

spoon. 'Be careful what you say – I can do considerable damage with this.'

'You could probably devour an entire cheesecake,' Rose suggested.

Pam frowned. 'Who was it in a film that was going to cut someone's heart out with a spoon?'

'Alan Rickman in *Robin Hood*.' Jen jumped up and down with the memory. 'He was the Sheriff of Nottingham. I thought he was lovely.'

Suddenly the people in front of them shifted forward several paces. Tess nudged Della. 'Right, we're on the move. I reckon we'll be inside in less than ten minutes.'

It was forty-five minutes later when they paid the entrance fee and assembled in the entrance to have their bags checked. A sombre-faced man with thin hair shook his head as he handed Tess's bag back to her with no comment. She stifled an effervescent giggle and they were in, climbing the curved steps and gazing up at vast glass honeycomb ceilings up through the pyramid.

Della held her breath. She had never seen anything so beautiful. The room was full of blinding white light and the walls reflected a golden glow as she looked up to the majestic building outside. Jen clutched her handbag to her chest. The gallery was vast but swarming with so many visitors; she recalled Eddie's warning about pickpockets.

Pam brought the group together. 'We've probably done this all wrong.' Her friends glanced at her. 'We should have worked out in advance where we want to go in terms of exhibitions. I mean, this place is so huge we'll never get round it all today. So, what are the things we really want to see?'

'The *Mona Lisa*.' Jen had her answer ready.

'Van Gogh. I like him.' Tess was pleased with herself but Pam's expression was confused.

'Van Gogh's not here – his works are in the Musée d'Orsay.'

'Is that in Paris?' Tess pulled a face. 'Perhaps we should have gone there instead.'

'There's some interesting Egyptian stuff here, isn't there? Rameses the Third or someone?' Rose folded her arms.

'I'd like to see him,' Tess spluttered.

'And Botticelli?' Della suggested. 'Some sculptures too – Michelangelo? I read up about the *Dying Slave* on the Internet.'

'I don't mind.' Tess shrugged. 'It's all pictures to me.'

'Right, we need a plan.' Pam grinned. 'We'll do the Louvre in less than three hours then we'll get some street food for lunch. How's that?'

'Will that be long enough?' Rose wondered.

'Three hours will be loads. I'll be insane at the end of three hours.' Tess chuckled. 'I won't even remember what paintings I've seen.'

'*Mona Lisa*,' Jen insisted, pouting.

'OK.' Pam turned to lead the way. 'I have a list – Egyptian artefacts, Botticelli, Michelangelo, *The Gioconda*.'

'And *Mona Lisa*,' Jen insisted.

Pam rolled her eyes. '*The Gioconda* is *Mona Lisa*. Right – we'll do Mona first, then we'll go to the Apollo Gallery, then the Sully Wing and I desperately want to see Caravaggio's *Death of the Virgin*.'

Rose was staring at Pam. 'Do you know your way around here?'

Pam nodded. 'A little. I've been here a couple of times

before. I know that three hours is probably enough for one day in the Louvre for most people.'

Pam led them down a spiral staircase and onto an escalator, following a signpost to the Denon Wing. When they entered the huge gallery, Jen let out a little cry. 'My goodness – look at the crowds over there. What's happening?'

A dense group had thronged around a small painting and there was a great deal of pushing and shoving. Some people were calling out, shouting; others had fixed selfie sticks to their phones and were taking snaps. Rose said grimly, 'That's the *Mona Lisa*.'

'That little painting behind the crowds?' Jen's little voice sounded disappointed. 'But it's so small.' She stared at her mobile phone, clasped between delicate fingers.

'More to the point...' Della sighed '... However will you get your photo taken with all those people around? You're tiny. You'll never get to the front.'

Jen's shoulders sagged; her face was despondent. Inside her warm jacket, she looked shrunken. 'I'll just have to give up. Maybe I can take a photo with the Eiffel Tower. That's big.'

The friends were quiet for a moment. Then Tess's face brightened. 'I know. Come with me, Jen.'

She hooked an arm through Jen's and dragged her towards the crowd. Tess attempted to infiltrate the clump of huddled bodies, turning sideways and then wriggling hopefully, but she and Jen were still at the back of the crowd. Then she patted the shoulder of a burly man in a raincoat who was standing in front of her and grasped his arm, tugging the sleeve. He turned a savage face towards her. Jen frowned as Tess stood on tiptoes and whispered something into his ear. The man appeared baffled, so Tess said something else. The enormous man, his neck wide and his thick dark hair cropped close, nodded in understanding and turned his attention to Jen. '*Madame, vous permettez...*'

Jen was confused. She felt herself seized by the wrist and propelled to the front of the crowd. The man grunted something in a low voice to the bystanders, moving forward like a rampaging bull, tugging Jen with him. People on both sides scattered, moving back. Jen saw a woman in her fifties gaze at her with sad brown eyes. Someone else patted her gently and murmured something in a gloomy voice. Then Jen was at the front, standing in front of the small portrait of the *Mona Lisa*. The man had extracted her mobile phone from her fingers and was holding it up in front of him. '*Madame...*' he grunted, waving at her to move to the left. Jen complied, putting on her sweetest photo face. The brawny man took a few snaps, nodded at Jen and wrapped a tree-trunk arm around her, shepherding her back through the throng. Someone started to clap and suddenly Jen was surrounded by applause. She gazed up at the kindly man, muscular in his tight raincoat. 'Thank you, *monsieur – merci beaucoup*,' she breathed.

'*De rien, madame. Bonne chance à vous.*'

Jen was breathless, confused, as Tess whirled her away from the moving horde that had begun to lurch forwards again. They reached their friends and Rose laughed. 'Excellent move, Tess – you told them Jen was a bride-to-be and they let her go through. I heard them all clapping. Brilliant ploy.'

Tess gritted her teeth. 'Well, not exactly.'

'Whatever you did it worked like a dream.' Della was peering at Jen's smiling face in front of the *Mona Lisa* in the photo. 'He's taken some great pictures too.'

Tess shrugged nonchalantly, her face reflecting pure

mischief. Pam pressed her lips together. 'Go on, then, Tess – tell us. What did you say?'

'Well, let's just say it was lucky the big man understood some English.'

'What did you say to him, Tess?' Rose frowned.

'I said my sister was a sick old lady and she had three weeks to live and her last wish was to have her photo taken with the *Mona Lisa* before she passed away.' Tess winked. 'It worked though.'

'I suggest we make ourselves scarce, before they notice how much like a healthy blushing bride-to-be our Jen really is.' Pam led the way. 'Right. We've some galleries to visit. First we'll go to see the Egyptian stuff, then Botticelli, Michelangelo. Then we'll have a look at a few more rooms, end up with my Caravaggio and finally we'll have coffee somewhere, I think.'

Jen trooped after her, waving the phone, her face animated. 'We can do better than boring coffee. Tess has earned everyone a glass of something nice. On me, I think!'

18

The painting was mostly composed in dark reds and pale yellows; it depicted a life-sized gathering of men bending over a body lying on the bed. Above their heads, blood-red drapes hung down. Pale fingers folded over faces in mourning or were clasped tight in supplication. A woman at the front of the picture was seated in a chair, her body folded forwards in grief. The virgin, in red, lay stretched out on a board, a hand across her abdomen, her head lolling to one side, her face soft as if she'd found final peace. A pale light reflected on flesh: bare shoulders, bald pates, foreheads, naked feet, but the background was the dark burgundy of dimly lit shadows. The virgin herself, her eyes closed, seemed to be slumbering with a serenity that the living bodies in the painting somehow failed to notice. Pam's face was wet with tears. 'I love Caravaggio,' she breathed.

'It's so sad,' Tess whispered.

'When was it painted, Pam?' Rose asked.

'And what's her story, the virgin?' Jen stood on tiptoes. 'Who are all the people around her?'

'It's massive – the scale, I mean. The people are as big as we are.' Della's eyes shone. 'It must have been a work of devotion.'

Pam didn't realise tears were still trickling down her face. 'Caravaggio painted it in the early 1600s as a commission, I think, for a chapel. He used a prostitute as a model – maybe it was his mistress, I think I read that – and the Church found out and rejected his painting.'

Tess gasped. 'He was a character then, this Caravaggio?'

Pam nodded. 'He got into brawls with people – he killed a man during a sword fight after a game of tennis.'

'Too much testosterone.' Jen giggled.

Tess guffawed. 'Remind me to avoid sporty men.'

'Look at the dazzling light and creeping shadow.' Pam wiped her cheek with the back of her hand. 'Caravaggio was a Baroque master. He makes the virgin look so divine. That's Mary Magdalene at the front, weeping, and those are the apostles.'

'I can see why you love it so much.' Della took Pam's arm. 'It's beautiful and blessed, yet so sad too.'

Tess shuffled her feet. 'Well, I'm ready for lunch. My legs ache. I don't want to sound like a philistine, but I'm done with the Louvre. I'd give anything to sit down somewhere and have a cheese sandwich.'

'Shall we go outside and find somewhere nice?' Rose suggested. 'It might be really expensive in here.'

Pam took a breath. 'Right. We could find a street seller and have some falafel?'

'Not at all,' Jen protested. 'I'm buying a bottle of wine for us to share. I've had my photo taken with Mona this morning. I'll message Eddie later and show him what a great time we're having here. I'm in a fabulous mood.'

* * *

Della wasn't used to wine at lunchtime: even one glass of house white made her feel fuzzy around the edges, soft as sponge. She had eaten all of the croque-monsieur, a toasted sandwich, and was leaning with her head on her elbows, listening to Tess chat about how badly behaved she had been in school as a teenager and how she wished she'd paid attention in the French classes but Madame Pooley had taken an instant dislike to her. The others were laughing – Tess had called the teacher Mrs Chicken, a bad translation of her name from French, and that hadn't gone down well with Madame Pooley who, apparently, had a thin red neck that resembled wattles when she became angry and shouted.

Rose said her French had been quite good sixty years ago but it was very rusty now and she was too embarrassed to try it out on real French people, and Pam was telling them how she'd worked in West Africa and had spoken French all the time and it had made her hone her very average linguistic skills. Jen related how in her school they had a choice between languages and secretarial studies and she'd done a shorthand typing course, which had led her to find reasonable jobs, and then Pam said something about men and their secretaries, hierarchy and the patriarchy.

Della closed her eyes. She was thinking that while she was enjoying a relaxing lunch with her friends, poor Sylvester was shivering on the seafront with the hatch of his van open, serving coffee and sandwiches, ice cream and sweets. He'd be taking the brunt of the harsh sea winds. She wished he could retire – he was seventy-five – but she could hear his voice in her head saying what he always said when she brought the subject up. She imagined his brow creased, his hand over hers. 'And what damn fool thing will we live off, Della? Fresh air? You know my pension isn't enough.'

Della sighed. It didn't seem fair that he was working in the van, the sharp breeze from the sea biting the exposed flesh of his chest. He will insist on wearing his shirt buttons open at the front, she thought, and a smile crept across her face as she imagined him, his shirt undone, dancing with her in the kitchen, wiggling his hips.

But here she was in Paris, spending the money he'd so carefully saved, the funds he'd given to her without a second thought about himself or their tight budget. And now he was at home, selling coffee from disposable cups on Exmouth seafront, buffeted all day by the elements. It made her ache heart with worry: they weren't young any more. Della felt her age each morning when she woke, in the ache from her lower back and, at times, the twinge in her hips. She thought again of his wide smile, the crinkle around his eyes, his smooth head. She wished Sylvester were here with her to enjoy Paris. The *Dying Slave* in the Louvre would have made him chuckle – such a perfectly muscled Greek body and only a tiny willy. Della chortled to herself, imagining the two of them in the Louvre, whispering about the perfect lines of the alabaster statue and the one unmistakeable defect. Jen patted her hand. 'What's tickling you?'

'The Michelangelo statue – the one with the little willy. It made me think about Sylvester.'

Tess didn't miss a beat. 'Are you telling me your man isn't well endowed? Tough luck, Della.'

'Oh, no, quite the opposite,' Della blurted and felt her cheeks tingle. She put both hands to her face and giggled. 'I was just thinking about him, that's all – he'd find the statue so funny...'

Pam rested gentle fingers on her arm. 'You must miss him.'

'We've never been apart, not really.' Della was shocked to feel hard tears prickle her eyes. She waved a hand in front of her face, as if to make the silliness go away. 'I'll take him something really nice back – as a present.'

Rose gazed across the table at five empty plates and five empty glasses – every drop of wine had been drained. 'Time to go for a stroll down the Seine, I think, girls. Shall we stretch our legs and try to walk off the effects of lunch?'

Pam saw the stalls from the other side of the road: books and magazines, stretching out across a backdrop of trees in front of the river. She squealed with delight. 'Look at all these wonderful books. They say the Seine is the only river in the world that runs between two bookshelves.'

Jen couldn't really understand the excitement over a few old books with dusty covers, but she felt the tug of the river and wriggled behind a bookstall to lean over the wall. She gazed at the river, taking her phone out and holding it in front of her to frame a photo. The water was grey, corrugated iron with a mottled surface, and Jen brought the leaves of a budding tree into the frame. In the distance she could see the repeated curve of bridges. On the banks at the other side were tall buildings several storeys high, with windows repeated in an identical pattern. The sky was a rich blue; the blue of Eddie's eyes. She took several photos. Paris was beautiful. She'd send them to him later.

She returned to the bookstalls, where Pam was raving about a book she'd bought by Molière. Rose had found some sheet music by Fauré and Satie, which she'd bought, despite the high price. Della had bought a colourful poster of the Louvre and Tess was chatting to a bookseller, a man in his forties with a jaunty trilby hat, about French wine, quizzing him about which was the best value. The man waved his hands, smiling and joking. 'Champagne, always, *madame*. You do not understand – you are English – champagne is the nectar of love.'

Tess's eyes sparkled mischievously. 'Do you mean that it makes a woman drunk, so that she's putty in a man's hands?'

The salesman shook his head. 'Not at all. Just think. A beautiful woman is sitting across the table from a man. He pours the champagne, his hand on hers, and they drink, their eyes meet. The champagne is intoxicating – not because of the alcohol. Because of the lightness of the bubbles, the tickle of the taste, the delicate balance of romance and desire as their lips kiss the glasses and their eyes melt together like warm chocolate.'

Tess giggled. 'I must try some champagne, then, while I'm here, if it has that effect on a woman. Mind you...' She grabbed Jen's hand. 'You're the one intoxicated with romance. I'm just an old lady that nobody loves.'

'You are never too old to have a love affair in Paris, *madame*,' the man called across as Tess linked Jen's arm and they walked away.

She chuckled. 'Some French men are so full of shit.'

Pam linked her other arm and whispered in her ear. 'He's certainly used those lines before. He had it off pat – not a grammatical mistake in sight.'

'They are good salesmen,' Rose agreed. 'They are used to chatting up the punters.'

'Some champagne might be nice, though, while we're here,' Jen suggested.

Della shook her head. 'I bet it's not cheap.'

Tess spluttered with laughter. 'Then maybe we'll have to get someone else to pay for it.'

'You're incorrigible, Tess,' Rose said grimly.

'I'm happy for anyone to encourage me.' Tess winked.

They had arrived at a wide pavement where several men and women had set up canvasses on easels and were in various stages of painting the scenery. The artists seemed engrossed in their work and didn't mind at all when the five women stopped to peer over their shoulders. Most paintings were in watercolour or rich oils, although one older man in a blue tunic was sketching in charcoal. Rose was watching a young man with a straw hat and a small ponytail. He was engrossed in a type of impressionist painting of the river flowing under a bridge, concentrating all his efforts on creating white clouds with mauve bellies in a pale sky.

Pam began to chat to a striking woman, probably in her fifties, with short vibrant red hair, wearing a light grey sweatshirt and jeans. The woman seemed happy enough to talk while she worked, pointing at the evening depiction of the river that she was creating with splodges of red and yellow paint, the colour of jewels. The almost-completed sunset on the Seine was a cauldron of colour. Pam muttered something that was clearly a compliment and the woman delved in her pocket and brought out a business card. Pam beamed at her friends. 'Marie-Laure says she will sell me this painting for thirty-five euros. Isn't that wonderful? I'm going to meet her on Sunday afternoon at the hotel and she's going to wrap it up for me.'

Jen walked up to the painting. 'I might buy one too. They are really lovely.'

Pam nodded. 'She loves working in oils, doing sunsets

and sunrises, creating light and shadow and energetic colours. It's such a powerful representation of the river.'

A woman in a green dress, her hair in long russet curls, touched Jen's shoulder. She had deep-set blue eyes that glittered, a tanned face and a serious expression. 'English?' She patted Jen's arm, moving her away from her friends. 'You are English.'

Jen looked towards her friends for advice and then nodded at the woman. 'Yes, I am.'

'You give me five euros and I tell your future.'

'Tell her no,' Rose muttered quietly. 'Just walk over here, Jen.'

The woman's gaze held Jen's. It was difficult to look away. The woman repeated, 'I tell the future you need to know it. You are concerned about something. A decision.'

Jen gaped, fascinated. 'It can't hurt.' She plunged a hand into her purse and tugged out a ten euro note. It was in the russet-haired woman's fingers. 'Ten euros – I tell you and your friends what will happen to you all.'

'You should move away, Jen,' Rose suggested. The woman whirled round, her green dress swirling.

'You, *madame*.' She stared at Rose. 'You are on the brink of a big change. But you, *madame*.' She pointed at Jen. 'You cannot change anything in your life even if you wish it.'

'Rubbish,' Rose scoffed. 'That's completely the wrong way round.'

'You, *madame*, you...' She touched Della's wrist. 'You should be careful. You must hold onto what you have.'

Della's face was alarmed, but the copper-haired woman was staring at Tess, who was intrigued. 'You are the lucky one here. You will know the meaning of love.'

Tess sniggered. 'I don't think so... not with my Alan.'

'And you, *madame*.' The woman turned all her attention to Pam. 'You who have the secret – you need to let it go from you. It is time.'

'That's ridiculous,' Rose spluttered. The friends stared at each other. The woman in the green dress had walked away.

'She got us all wrong.' Tess's mouth was open. 'Jen's the one with the love – I'm the one who should probably hold onto what I have. Who's on the brink of change, then? Jen – perhaps the predictions are all about Jen? But what about the secret and letting it go?'

'What a waste of ten euros,' Rose muttered.

'It was all so vague,' Della admitted. 'It could all be any one of us.'

'She was just a con artist,' Rose spat.

'So, what's your secret, Pam?' Tess giggled but Pam had moved over to the painter with the red hair, Marie-Laure, who turned over her shoulder and shook her head, saying something in French. Pam murmured a reply.

'What did she say?' Jen asked.

Pam blinked, thoughtfully. 'The woman in the green dress is called Elodie. She comes here from time to time to ply her trade and she selects people she knows need to hear something important.' She took a breath. 'Marie-Laure says that Elodie's never wrong. She's made predictions before that have come true. Marie-Laure says we should pay attention to everything she has said.'

19

Della lay on the bed, her back aching, complaining that she had walked too far. She'd rest her feet and have a shower before she put on her glad rags, then she'd be fine. Tess was already in front of the mirror in her new lacy underwear, determined to be every bit the Parisienne, holding up two dresses, the little black one and the short silver-and-black one, to decide which to wear.

'The plain black one.' Della opened one eye to peer before closing them both and leaning back on the pillow. 'The silvery one will do for the casino tomorrow.'

'But it's a jazz club tonight,' Tess protested, holding up the shimmering dress. 'I might need a bit of glam.'

'You'll out-glam the stage acts in that.' Della grinned, her eyelids still closed. 'It's a beautiful dress. So is the fitted black one. You will look wonderful in either of them.'

'The plain black one it is, then. What are you wearing, Della?'

'A skirt, a blouse.' She sighed. 'I'm waiting for Jen to come out of the shower before I get dressed. I'm desperate for a shower. Mind you, I'd give everything for a long soak in a hot bath...'

* * *

Jen was covered in lather, her hair dripping around her head and neck. She allowed the water from the shower overhead to thunder on her scalp, beating out a dull rhythm. Her eyes were squeezed tightly closed against the water droplets but she was deep in thought. Elodie's words were scratching and scratching in her mind: *You cannot change anything in your life even if you wish it.* Of course, that was nonsense, as Rose had said – she could change things. She was going to marry Eddie – that would change everything. And she did wish it. It would change her life completely. She would not be alone. She would have a partner, a husband, someone to share her time with, day and night. The days would be gone where she'd have no one to talk to, no one to do things for. And Eddie was the perfect companion: he was smart, polite, charming, handsome, and considerate. What more did she want?

But still the water beat out a steady pulse in her brain. She loved Eddie. Not as she had loved Colin: she had been younger then. With Eddie, she hadn't yet developed the synchronisation, the habit, the loyalty and passion and day-to-day rhythm that came with living with a life partner, but he was someone she respected, admired and enjoyed spending time with. Eddie was pleasant. He seldom grumbled; yes, he had his opinions, but he was sensible, careful, wise. Of course she loved him. *You cannot change anything in your life even if you wish it.* Elodie's words were ridiculous – so wide of the mark. She was actively making changes: she was getting married, for goodness' sake.

She thought for a moment about marriage as the hard droplets of water pounded against her face. In sickness and in health, for richer or for poorer. Jen wondered about what was to come in the future. She had lost one husband – what if Eddie became ill? What if her own health failed? It would, of course, happen to them both one day, although she still felt young, in her early seventies, but time had its way of running out all of a sudden, as it had for poor Colin. Jen felt comforted that she would have Eddie to advise her and support her if there were problems ahead. That was what a partnership was all about. She'd have a fabulous hen party, a wonderful wedding and a happy life with Eddie. She was certain of it. It was what she wanted, more than anything.

The shower still thrummed, dripping heavy water on her head. She wasn't sure what it was about Elodie's words that disturbed her. She reached for the shampoo and lathered her hair again, massaging her scalp with strong fingers. She was in Paris. She was the centre of everything, the bride of the hen party, and she was with friends. They shared laughter, jokes, solidarity – they understood each other in a way that was special. And Jen was really enjoying herself. Tonight they were off to a jazz club; they'd reserved a table at Chez Maman, and they'd dress up to the nines, have supper and chatter together.

Jen rinsed her hair and reached for the conditioner. She'd have a fabulous time, forget about Elodie and her strange incantation. She turned around under the water, a little sprite in a waterfall, and laughed out loud. *'J'adore Paris.'* She'd choose a dazzling dress, jewellery, and go out on the town. But first she'd have time to send Eddie the photo of her smiling face as she posed alone in front of the *Mona Lisa*.

She was ready, in a fitted floral dress and a velvet wrap,

when Rose and Pam arrived. Pam was relaxed in a pale silky blouse and dark trousers, her ankles ending in pixie boots. Rose had put on a grey silk dress and long sparkling earrings. Tess was resplendent in her little black dress and a black fascinator hat with a mesh bow. Della was wearing a long black skirt and a soft cream top and had borrowed a black shawl from Tess. They gawped at each other, making appreciative noises, and checked handbags, keys and phones before Pam reminded them that Faik, the taxi driver, would probably already be waiting for them outside.

Chez Maman was a small building twinkling with glowing lights at the end of a long, winding alley. Inside, a man in a white shirt, black trousers and black dickey-bow tie nodded when Pam asked for *'table réservée au nom de Jen Hooper'* and led them to a square table close to the stage, already laid with cutlery, glasses and napkins, with five simple chairs backed in green material. It was dark inside, like a cavern, the walls made of dark wood with lanterns gleaming, pouring honey-soft lighting from all sides. They sat down stiffly and gazed around. The club was already busy, most tables occupied with people of all ages – couples, groups, all talking, eating and drinking. A huge neon sign above the bar flashed the name Chez Maman and waiters in black and white weaved expertly between the tables, trays balanced on their hands. Rose's eyes went straight to the stage. Three musicians were playing: a round cheeked man on a double bass, a portly man on a trumpet and a young woman on a huge grand piano. The music fizzed, a rampaging rhythm of energy and mischief, and Rose sighed and leaned back in her chair.

Tess was already examining the menu. 'It's all in French. You'll have to help me out, Pam. What's *Dos de Cabillaud*?

It's the cheapest thing on the menu and it's twenty-six euros.'

'It's cod loin, with broad beans and a salad, I think. This is jazz-club prices.'

Della made a shocked face. Jen put a little fist on the table. 'We can have what we like. Eddie is gambling away in Las Vegas now and we've saved lots on the wedding. Tonight's on me – so eat what you like, Tess.'

Pam shook her head and opened her mouth, about to argue, but Rose interrupted. 'As long as you let us push the boat out for you on the last night, Jen. We could come back here. The music is great.'

'It's lovely,' Della breathed, looking around at the stage area swathed in a canopy of little twinkling lights. 'Like a fairy grotto but with the coolest music.'

The trio had finished playing and applause rippled around the club. The portly man on the trumpet muttered his thanks and said something in French, laughing at his own humour before putting the trumpet back to his lips and blowing three full notes. The trio swung into action again, the music rampaging furiously.

Pam was gazing at the menu. 'There's nothing vegetarian – absolutely nothing.' Her brow was furrowed. 'Perhaps I can ask someone to make me a salad sandwich...'

'You could fill up on the wine?' Tess suggested.

'They must have chips?' Della wondered and Pam pulled a dissatisfied face.

'They have a starter I could order – Salade *tomate-mozzarella*– that's just cheese and tomatoes, a few olives – maybe they'll throw some bread in.'

'It sounds lovely.' Della smiled.

'I might try *filet de veau*?' Rose suggested. 'That's veal, isn't it? Might be nice.'

'They have *foie gras de canard*. That's delicious.' Jen gasped. 'I'm having that as a starter. It's heaven.'

Pam covered her eyes with long fingers. 'This is my worst nightmare.'

Della was concerned. 'What is it, Pam?'

Pam sighed. 'A vegetarian in Paris.' She rubbed tired eyes. 'Cruelty on the menu. You don't want me to tell you how they treat veal before they kill it? Or how they make the poor ducks' livers so fatty that...'

Tess looked horrified. 'I'm not eating that, then.'

'No, nor am I,' Della agreed.

Jen grinned. 'Well, I certainly am. I'm sorry about the cruelty and all that but it's already dead and on a plate, so I'm going to enjoy myself. It's my hen do.'

Rose gazed from Pam to Jen and took both their hands in hers. 'There's a bottle of Cabernet Sauvignon on the wine list, with our names on. Shall we order?' She nodded over to the waiter, who immediately turned in their direction. 'The music is excellent.'

Pam nodded. 'It's a lovely place.'

'Let's enjoy ourselves.' Jen turned to the waiter. *'Vin, monsieur, s'il vous plaît. Vin rouge.'*

Tess grinned up at him, her hand poised, her blonde hair swishing beneath the black fascinator. *'Deux, Monsieur.* We'll have *deux* bottles.'

The jazz trio finished playing and some background music came on. Rose recognised it as John Coltrane's 'A Love Supreme'. The food arrived: Pam enjoyed her starter, which the chef had made more substantial with some *pommes de terre sautées* and a salad, and Jen moaned, 'Mmm, delicious,' with every mouthful of her *foie gras*, despite Pam sighing and demonstrating her frustration by giving an irritated cough and pointedly refilling her own wine glass. Tess was in fine form, regaling everyone with the story of her own hen night, when she'd become so drunk she had danced on the table of a Greek restaurant, cavorting with one of the waiters and then having to fight him off before taking a taxi home. She laughed. 'It's about time I calmed down, I suppose. That was almost fifty years ago but I'd still be up for a bit of table dancing now.'

'Not with the waiters, I hope.' Della shuddered.

Tess grinned. A group of musicians had just moved to the stage: three men in smart black suits, one holding a double bass, another seating himself at the piano and the third making himself comfortable behind a drum kit. Tess indicated them with her head. 'They look like they might be up for a good energetic bop on the tables.'

The piano player ran his fingers up and down the keys with panache; the drummer brushed the snare softly and the bass began to thrum. A glamorous woman, tall and lean in a long silver dress, sashayed onto the stage. Her lips were scarlet and her black hair had been swept onto her head and pinned with a bright orange flower.

Pam gasped. 'She looks like Josephine Baker.'

'More Dinah Washington – with a dash of Nina Simone,' Rose whispered.

The singer put her lips close to the microphone and muttered something, her voice sultry and soft. Then she began to sing. Rose recognised the song at once. It was 'My Funny Valentine', in English; the singer's accented vowels resonating with emotion. Rose sighed, taking in the aching beauty of each note. Jen closed her eyes and remembered

Eddie's proposal on Valentine's evening, recalling the thrill of his words. She peeked at the ring twinkling on her finger, the row of three diamonds. It was too large – it moved around easily – but a wedding ring would hold it fast. Tess gazed at the musicians, the gentle sway of the pianist's head as he waved his fingers across the keys.

Della sighed, imagining dancing to the music with Sylvester, swaying in the kitchen. She wondered if she could find a CD by the singer to take home to him, so that she could share the sad sweetness of the song. Pam put her head in her hands, enjoying the moment, the rounded beauty of each note, the tenderness and the tragedy of a love song. She smiled to herself, thinking about the stupidity of love: it was merely a transient foolish thing based on weakness, emotion, or worse, unbridled lust. Love between people could only hurt. Now, in her early seventies, Pam didn't really believe in love, that it could last; she thought it was just human folly, a trap to make sure people procreated and life continued. The song ended with a flourish of instruments. Pam brought her hands together and clapped, sharing the applause with everyone in the room. Someone whistled, someone called out 'Bravo'.

The singer spoke in French, introducing the pianist as Bruno, the drummer as Sacha and the double bassist as Jean-Francois. Then she told the audience that she was Cassandra Hibou and that she would sing a song called 'J'ai deux amours'. The musicians began to play a soft introduction and Cassandra began to croon in her scratchy, smoky voice. Rose leaned over. 'She is really wonderful. What a find.'

Jen beamed and clapped her hands together softly. Tears shone in her eyes. Pam gazed at the singer, whose arms rose and fell as she sang. She was elegant, her long neck stretched towards the microphone, her body a slim sheath of silver. Rose watched the pianist carefully. His melody had enchanted her. Della was shifting in her seat, a soft sway, as if she were back home in Sylvester's arms. Tess pushed her chair back. 'I need the loo.'

Tess moved deftly between the tables towards the pink neon sign with the shape of a lollipop wearing a skirt: *Dames.* She felt confident wearing the snug black dress, her heels and the cheeky black fascinator. Five minutes later, she was examining her reflection in the mirror. Her blonde hair shone and her face was flushed, a pink tinge to it. She applied a little light dusting of powder, more lipstick and smiled at herself. She would do. She adjusted the fascinator and broadened her grin. She was enjoying Paris; she liked the feeling she had of being independent, of making her own decisions, of doing things she wanted away from Alan, away from his judgement and criticism. It occurred to her that she felt lighter, brighter, as if she was free of constraints, free from the likelihood that he would find something wrong with her appearance, her actions or something she'd said without thinking first.

She stood up straight, pulling the dress into shape around her figure, and winked at her reflection. '*La vie est belle,*' she told her cheerful face in the mirror. She knew exactly what the phrase meant at this moment – her life was full, for living. She swivelled on her heel and made her way back towards the buzzing sounds of the jazz club. She stood in the doorway for a moment, surveying the scene. Her four friends were at the table: Della swaying gently; Rose staring at the musicians; Jen's face a picture of soft emotion and Pam, thoughtful as ever. To her right, the lights of the bar area twinkled. Cassandra was on stage, singing a song in English. It was a mournful song, the lyrics 'But not for me' repeated with the poignant tones of someone who had loved, lost and would not love again. Tess sighed, and was about to return to her seat when she felt a hand on her arm. She turned and stared into the face of a broad shouldered man about her own age, tall, in a dark suit. His eyes glittered beneath thick brows as he considered her face and he spoke to her in a voice that rumbled like distant thunder.

Tess frowned. She had no idea who the man was or what he had just said to her. Her immediate thought had been that he was a doorman, a bouncer, judging by his hefty appearance and the impeccable suit. He spoke again. It was certainly not French; it had the guttural growl of an Eastern European language, perhaps Albanian or Serbian – she had no idea. Tess took in his serious expression, the dark hair greying over the temples, the sombre suit, the full lips and small perfect teeth, and she looked wildly about her for help. Her mind was racing. She was in trouble. This man was either a policeman – or a kidnapper.

20

Tess stared at the enormous man. His hand was still on her arm. He spoke again, the deep rumble of an unknown language from a far-off country. Her eyes were wide. She wondered whether she should make a run for it, rush back to the table to the safety of her friends. The man said something else, lifted the bushy brows and smiled. His eyes shone.

Tess gasped. 'I'm sorry – I've no idea what you have said to me.'

The man chuckled. 'English? Oh, I am so sorry.'

Tess frowned. The huge man had a heavy accent, as if his words were all stuck together with toffee, but she could understand him. 'English, yes.'

He shook his head and waved a hand. 'I saw your dress, your hair. I was sure you must be a Russian woman.'

Tess laughed a peal of relief. 'Russian? Oh, my goodness, no. I'm from England. I'm here with my four friends over there – we're on a hen party.'

The man smiled. Tess thought he looked kind now, not so threatening. He nodded. 'Hen party. That is the tradition of many women enjoying time together before a marriage. I am right, I think.'

'Yes.' Tess beamed, all enthusiasm. 'Your English is good. Are you Russian, then?'

'I am, although I live in Paris now. Once I lived in England, in London. I did a Masters at King's for one year, so I can speak English quite well.' His eyes met hers. 'You are not the hen of your party?'

Tess didn't understand what he meant at first, then she trilled a laugh. 'No, it's my friend, Jen, who's getting married. She's the small one in the flowery dress, over there. There are five of us.'

'Are you staying here in Paris for a long time?'

'Four more days.' Tess raised her voice to speak over the music as the man leaned his head towards her. 'Jazz club today, casino tomorrow. We're having great fun. We're staying at the Sirène hotel. It's lovely.'

The man nodded. 'If you are looking for a casino, I recommend La Rêve. It isn't too far from the Sirène, a short taxi ride, and it is a beautiful building in a wonderful location. The cocktails are very nice there too – they do a particularly good Moscow Mule. You should try it.'

'Thanks, that's really kind.' Tess held out her hand. 'I'm Tess Watkins, by the way. Pleased to meet you.'

The man gave a little bow then stood upright and took her hand. 'It is my pleasure to meet you, Tess. Vladimir Borovik-Romanov.'

Tess gave a little trill of delight. 'My goodness, that's a mouthful.'

'Vladimir.' He smiled at her again. 'Good to meet you, Tess.'

'Indeed. Nice to meet you too, Vladimir.' Tess flashed him

a smile and sauntered away, twisting between tables. She was looking forward to telling her friends all about the Russian spy she'd just met outside the ladies' toilets.

As she sat down, all eyes were on Cassandra, who was singing a powerful ballad called *Ma mélancolie*. Tess picked up her wine glass and decided to wait until after the applause to tell the others about her brief encounter. Cassandra was at the dramatic climax of her song, her arms in the air, the long dress scintillating, sending out diamond shards in the lights around her. The jazz club was silent apart from Cassandra's full hypnotic voice. Every table was occupied now, but all eyes were on the singer, entranced by her sultry song and the melodic accompaniment. Rose was transfixed, her gaze moving from Cassandra to watch the pianist's moving hands. Della and Jen were swaying with the slow rhythm. Tess looked for the man, Vladimir, across the room, but she couldn't see him.

She imagined he might be at one of the larger tables, surrounded by several other men. They would be business partners in equally sharp suits, watching the singer with appreciative eyes, glasses of expensive brandy clutched in enormous fists. But Vladimir wasn't with any of the groups of entranced people at the larger tables; Tess searched around the room for him through narrowed eyes. Perhaps he'd be in a shadowy corner with a Russian woman, blonde like Tess – his wife, perhaps, immaculately dressed and much younger, in her thirties or forties, with a serious stern face. He would be leaning back in his chair, his hand resting on hers on the table. But Tess could not see him. She wondered if he was having a clandestine liaison with a Frenchwoman. Tess's mind began to invent stories: the woman would be a stunning flame-haired high-class prostitute called Manon or

Babette, dressed from head to toe in Gucci or Oscar de la Renta – all paid for by Vladimir, of course. They would sip champagne before heading back to his penthouse suite, every room done out in glossy white with fluffy black carpets. Tess stared around the club again, but she could not see him.

Then she caught sight of a man at the bar speaking to a waiter: he had wide square shoulders, now in an overcoat. She thought it was him, Vladimir. She recognised the back of his head, sturdy and solid. Pam leaned over and whispered in her ear. 'What are you looking for, Tess?' Cassandra had finished singing; Tess brought her hands together in applause and waited for the cheering to subside. She grinned at Pam. 'I met someone just before…'

Pam shook her head; she couldn't hear Tess's words over the applause. Cassandra was speaking through the microphone, her voice low and conspiratorial, saying, 'Thank you,' several times in French, English and German to her audience. Then there was a waiter at Jen's elbow, carrying a tray, two bottles and five fluted glasses. Jen looked alarmed as the man began to place the glasses on the table. 'What's this? We didn't order…'

The waiter tried his best English. 'It is for the hens. Monsieur Borovik-Romanov ask me to bring best champagne, two bottles, for you as a gift, with his compliments. He says enjoy your evening here and congratulations to the bride.'

Jen looked puzzled. 'What gentleman?'

Tess spluttered, pleased with herself, and put on her most innocent expression. 'Oh, that will be the Russian spy I met outside the toilets a few minutes ago. Vlad the Impaler. He obviously understood the bit I told him about the hen party and wanted to buy us champagne as a token of his appreciation...'

'What have you done, Tess?' Rose's expression was shocked. 'How have you got us all this?'

The waiter was pouring the champagne into glasses, the creamy bubbles fizzing to the surface. 'Monsieur Borovik-Romanov is a frequent customer here. The champagne is a gift from him.'

Tess sat upright and offered a serious face to the waiter. *'Merci, monsieur.* Tell Vladimir we are all very grateful for his kindness.'

'Vladimir?' Della grabbed Tess's hand. 'Tell us all about it – have you been up to mischief, Tess?'

'I'll tell you everything.' Tess giggled. 'But first, let's drink the champagne.' She raised her glass. 'To Jen and to the best hen party ever.'

'To Jen – and the hens...' they chorused, lifting their glasses and giggling like the rising pop of the bubbles. The first mouthful exploded on their tongues, chilled, with the tang of lemon and the sweetness of honey at the same time.

An hour later, the five friends were in a taxi being driven back to the Hotel Sirène. They had all drunk far too much and were chattering, their voices loud and exuberant.

'I love champagne,' Della hooted. 'I just love the way it makes you feel – so warm and happy and like there's not a care in the world.'

'There isn't a care in the world,' Tess agreed. 'I'm having such a wonderful time.'

Rose leaned forward. 'Did I ever tell you about the time I drank champagne in Berlin?' Her four friends leaned forward too. 'Bernard and I went there years ago on a city break. We wanted to see some cabaret and went to a club. It was wonderful – a real dive, underground, all dark inside with a real feeling of being clandestine, illegal, as if we were doing something we shouldn't. And there was a band playing, five men – piano, accordion, drums, double bass, and the singer – oh, the singer had a voice like an opera star, a tenor. Such a huge voice, even though he was only a little man, about five feet three.'

'When was this?' Tess asked.

'I'd have been about forty-five. Paul was a student, away in Loughborough. It was just me and Bernard, we had five days in Berlin, so it would be –what? Thirty years ago. Well, this cabaret band – I remember they were called Das Unheil. Such a strange name, I thought, but their songs were really – you know – a bit near the knuckle and very well performed. Heartbreakingly beautiful melodies. I loved them – I clapped and cheered and I think the singer noticed and took a bit of a shine to me. He kept nodding in my direction and grinning as I applauded. Well, Bernard and I used to bicker a lot – that was normal for us – and, that night, he became very cross with me. He said I was "behaving like a floozy" and he insisted we leave before the band had finished. Well, of course, I said no. I could be quite stubborn at times. I told him I wasn't going anywhere until the band had finished their set and he got up from his seat and said that he was going back to the hotel and he left. I was so shocked he'd just leave me like that.'

Della's brow wrinkled with concern. 'He shouldn't have done that. In a city you didn't know, so far from home...'

'The hotel was quite a way away. I knew it was called the Hotel Königshof but I had no idea where it was or how to get back. I didn't know if Bernard had walked back – it was a long way, a mile, maybe two. So, I just sat where I was and watched the cabaret band for an hour. Then, at the end of their set, the singer came over to me – he walked straight over to my table and started saying something in German. Well, I didn't understand him, and I told him so, but he spoke excellent English. His name was Maximilian and he was really nice. It turned out that he was around the same age as me and single. We chatted about music – about his background, his training, the cities and venues he'd played across Europe and how he'd actually been an opera singer in his twenties. I was fascinated. He bought champagne and we talked and talked and drank and talked...'

'And then you snogged each other's faces off?' Tess butted in, her expression hopeful.

'Not at all. Max was a gentleman – he was lovely. And really interesting – much more so than Bernard. And so polite and respectful. We chatted about music into the early hours... then he called a cab to take me back to the hotel.' Rose's eyes misted over.

'You're such a dark horse, Rose,' Jen murmured.

Pam made a soft sound. 'Often platonic relationships are so fulfilling.' She thought for a moment. 'I went travelling with a man called Todd when I was twenty-three. He was lovely – so easy to be around, such a sense of humour. He was generous to a fault but a really free spirit. We went to Australia, worked out there for a while picking fruit, vegetables, grapes – we shared the same tent, even the same bed sometimes...'

'And you never shagged him?' Tess's eyes were wide. 'Really?'

'Not every relationship is about sex, Tess,' Rose chided.

Della was puzzled. 'But if you're close to each other

emotionally, and he's so nice, and he's a man and you're a woman...'

'Perhaps Pam wasn't attracted to him.' Jen chewed her lip. 'Perhaps he was ugly.'

'Butt *uuuugly*,' Tess spluttered and began to roar with laughter.

'We were best friends.' Pam sighed. 'He'd loved someone once, someone who'd broken his heart. He didn't want any sort of emotional relationship. I understood that. We got on well. And it was just the right time in our lives for a strong friendship to be what we both needed.'

Tess was confused. 'But there must have been some nights, you know... when you were in need of a hug or maybe you were talking and felt close and you thought about it... the need for intimacy, love, that special way of sharing?' Tess grinned. 'I know I would.'

'Not for me and Todd. We were the closest of friends though.' Pam shrugged and her brow creased with a sad thought. 'He died years ago, in the 1980s. I went to visit him in hospital just before... It was horrible. He didn't look anything like the old Todd – I hardly recognised him. It was tragic.'

For a while, it was silent inside the taxi, the five women lost in their own thoughts. Faik murmured from the cab in the front. 'Hotel Sirène here now, ladies. I bring you back safely.'

'Thank you, Faik.' Rose searched in her handbag for the fare. 'And please tell your cousin I'll be in touch to book a table at his wonderful restaurant. Probably for Saturday evening.'

Faik accepted the twenty euro note she waved at him. 'That is good. He will be very happy to see you.'

'We'll call you tomorrow, Faik,' Jen muttered as she held the taxi door open for Della. 'We're going to a casino.'

'We're off to Casino La Rêve,' Tess added.

'Really?' Pam linked her arm through Tess's. 'Where's that?'

'Not far. And highly recommended, apparently.' Tess grinned as they sauntered into the hotel reception. 'It serves great cocktails.'

Della hooked her arm through Tess's other elbow and the three women strolled towards the lift together. Tess wasn't sure if they were holding her upright or if she was helping them to walk in a straight line. Her mind was on other things. She was thinking of a huge Russian man in a dark suit who had bought them champagne and had been so courteous.

21

Pam's feet pounded out a rhythm on the pavement as she pattered past a man emptying bins into the cavernous rear of a dust lorry. He grunted *'Bonjour'* as she sped on for another half mile, then she paused at the kerbside, waited for her moment and jogged across the road. She was at the bottom of the cobbled precinct that led to the Hotel Sirène on the corner; she'd be back in ten minutes. The run had cleared her head, the air rushing against her face, and her body felt better for the exercise. Her shoes drummed on the ground and the beat made words echo into Pam's head. She pushed them away but, with each slap of her shoe, a syllable reverberated in her brain. Elodie's words: *You who have the secret.* Pam ran faster, increasing the rhythm, hoping the effort would dull the repeated words, now an incantation inside her head. *You need to let it go from you. It is time.* She could see Elodie's serious face, the glittering intensity of her blue eyes. *Let it go.*

Pam sprinted past the last few shops and cafés, pausing outside the hotel to bend forward, stretch out her legs and breathe deeply. *Let it go from you.* She recalled the fortune teller in the green dress, the gentle hand on her arm and how her words had hit Pam like spraying shrapnel, each sound awakening something inside her she wanted to keep hidden. *You who have the secret.* Pam knew exactly what she was talking about. She knew it was something she'd held fast for years, as an injured person clutched a wound to stop further bleeding, to force the pain to stay inside, to prevent it feeling any worse. *Let it go from you.* But she couldn't. It still hurt: the images still haunted her at night sometimes, when she closed her eyes to sleep, and she would put out a hand and find Elvis's soft fur, his warm tongue licking her hand, and she'd feel better. Pam stood up, breathless, and ran a hand through her hair so that it stuck up from her head. She shook her anxiety away, walked into the hotel and flashed a smile towards the receptionist. *'Bonjour, Marion.'*

The receptionist wore a black jacket and crisp white blouse. She glanced up from her paperwork. *'Bonjour, madame. J'espère que vous avez bien dormi. Le petit déjeuner est servi dans la salle à manger.'*

Pam nodded and caught her breath. Yes, breakfast was what she needed. The scent of fresh coffee filled the air, drifting from the dining room. She decided she'd have a quick shower. It was just eight o'clock. She strolled over to the lift, selected the second floor and leaned back against the metal walls, closing her eyes.

By half past eight, the five friends were seated at a table while Claudette, neat in her starched apron and black dress, filled coffee cups. Jen was staring at her phone. 'Eddie says he hasn't won anything yet. But he says the casinos are very bright and busy places – he's having a great time. But he misses me, of course.'

'Did he send a photo of the casino?' Della asked. 'I've only ever seen one in films.'

Jen shook her head. 'Just one of him and Harry outside the Golden Nugget yesterday afternoon.' She showed Della the screen and rolled her eyes, imagining the snug, safe feeling of being next to Eddie in his car, his hand on her knee. 'They are both looking very smart, aren't they? And he's missing me so much.'

'Oh, he looks like his father, the young man!' Della exclaimed. 'Both my boys look exactly like Sylvester. I swear there is none of me in them. Except Linval has my trusting nature – he was always in trouble for being gullible. He makes the wrong decisions all the time – he married this woman, Sariah, and she was very controlling. She left him, took their two children with her. Poor Linval only sees them alternate weekends.'

'That must be hard for him,' Pam sympathised. 'And for you, Della.'

'That's Harry, Eddie's son.' Jen aimed the screen towards Tess, who was lathering jam on her croissant.

'Handsome, both of them.' Tess filled her mouth and rolled her eyes. 'There's nothing like fresh croissants and coffee first thing in the morning. And French ones taste so much better than back home.'

'It's because we're in Paris,' Della agreed. 'That reminds me – I must send Linval a card. Aston too. And one for Sylvester and for Jan and Ian, our neighbours.'

'I need to send some too,' Pam murmured. 'I might send one home to Elvis – just for fun.'

'I expect Eddie and his son have spent a mint in the casinos,' Rose chided. 'Those places swallow money like a drainage system.'

'We'd better not get carried away tonight, then.' Tess chortled.

'We agreed – just one small bet for the fun of it – we'll be there mostly to take in the atmosphere,' Pam reminded them.

Tess almost choked on her croissant. 'And the cocktails. Moscow Mules all round – they come recommended.'

'By Vlad the Impaler,' the four friends chorused, rolling their eyes. Tess had mentioned her Russian encounter twice already before breakfast.

Della glanced at her phone sadly. 'Of course, I have heard nothing from Sylvester. That man drives me crazy sometimes with his hatred of technology. He won't use his phone. He says he can't see the screen well enough. I promised not to bother him while I'm here but I sent him a photo this morning, the one of us all outside the Louvre. I couldn't help it, in case he'll just give it a glance. It'd make him chuckle. It's a shame he can't just reply with a kiss.'

'I had a text from Alan this morning.' Tess reached for more butter. 'He's been playing golf...'

Pam sat up. 'How's my boy? How's Elvis?' The thought of her little spaniel reminded her with a sharp pang just how much she was missing him.

'Elvis is fine.' Tess chuckled. 'Apparently he loves the golf course. Alan says he can't keep him away. He's been walking there every day with – I can't remember the woman's name – Clara, Celia? Cliff's wife, the one Alan says is dull, poor thing – I expect she's glad of a bit of company. Alan and Cliff must be playing golf non-stop. He's clearly enjoying his freedom.' Tess thrust out her chin. 'And so am I.'

'Cliff's wife must be a bloody saint,' Rose grumbled.

Jen stared at her phone, sighing. 'I wonder how much Eddie has spent in the casinos. You'd think he would have won something. He promised me a present.' She sat up, smoothing her hair. 'I can't imagine what's so good about a casino. It's just gambling.'

'The atmosphere – and the lights and cocktails. I bet it's so exciting,' Tess breathed.

'Not to mention all the glamorous croupiers looking like Bond girls.' Rose frowned. 'I can imagine Eddie and his son are like moths to a flame, placing their bets right, left and centre.'

Jen frowned. 'Well, we'll see what casinos are like for ourselves later. And they have male croupiers, don't they? I'm so glad we're going to a casino. I'm not letting him come back with all the stories, telling me all about it and I have to listen with no idea what he means. No, I want to be able to say, "When the girls and I went to a casino in Paris..." and show him we had a better time than he did.'

'We'll have lots of fun playing roulette.' Rose covered her smile, secretly impressed by Jen's determination.

'And drinking Moscow Mules,' Tess added, crumbs around her mouth.

'Right.' Pam finished her coffee. 'Time to go. What's on the agenda first thing this morning?'

'Sightseeing. Lunch. Then the graveyard.' Della pushed her chair back eagerly, her face excited.

Della's mouth was open as she gazed up at the Arc de Triomphe. Her eardrums vibrated with the rattle of the circulating traffic, but her eyes were full of the huge monument. To Della it epitomised Paris even more than the Eiffel Tower. It was a majestic square block, immovable, with a straight top like a table framed by blue sky. Its size, its alabaster whiteness and its deep ornate carvings took her breath away. In her head, she practised what she would say to Sylvester: 'It's not at all like the pictures. There is a kind of reverence about it, strength – it is a symbol of victory. It's truly stunning.'

Della could imagine Sylvester chortling, tears in his eyes, saying, 'Damn fool building has been there a long time, Della. And it'll be there long after we're gone. But it doesn't breathe, it can't talk. You and me and life are what matters.' And he'd hug her and they'd laugh together. But she wished that he could see it now, that he had shared this trip with her. Della missed him. She wondered if they could come back together, maybe in the autumn, and she could show him around.

Pam was chattering about history again. 'Napoleon the First ordered it to be built at the beginning of the 1800s to celebrate his armies' victory. But it is nice to see it at night-time. The flame on the Tomb of the Unknown Soldier is lit every evening.'

Jen sighed. 'Look at all the cars zooming past, just like it's an ordinary day, just sweeping through the arch on their way to work and here's us, tourists, amazed by it. To Parisian commuters, it's just ordinary.'

'The pyramids are like that.' Pam was thoughtful. 'Outside Cairo, you pass through the middle of a residential area and suddenly, wow – there are the pyramids. Incredible, exquisite, all that history and they are just across the road from a block of flats where people look out of the windows every day and see the Sphynx as their normal view.'

Tess was suddenly interested. 'Did you go there with your friend, Todd?'

Pam shook her head. 'I went with a woman called Shelly in 1990. Todd had died by then, years before.'

Rose held up her mobile phone. 'Come on, girls. Let's take some snaps. "The hens do the Arc de Triomphe". Let's make sure we have some good pictures.'

There was a great deal of shuffling, swapping of phones and selfies. The Arc was behind them, solid on its giant pillars as if holding up the azure sky. Rose breathed out. 'What a perfect spring day. What's next on our list?'

Jen jerked up her chin, excited. 'Let's go and see the love locks on the bridge. I want to put one there for Eddie and me.'

Tess's face lit up. 'Does it bring you love forever?'

'It's a symbol of a strong relationship. Some people even throw the keys into the river now.'

'I'd love to see that,' Della breathed.

Jen sighed. 'A million locks, inscribed with lovers' names and messages, miles of them permanently stuck to a bridge, to remain there to eternity.'

'It sounds romantic,' Tess enthused.

'It sounds barmy.' Rose folded her arms.

'Sadly, I'm not sure we can see it any more.' Pam shook her head. 'A few years ago they closed the bridge. Sections of fencing collapsed under the weight of the locks. I think they had some of the railings removed. I think it's illegal to put locks on the bridge now.'

Jen pouted. 'What shall we do, then?'

'We could go for morning coffee and a cake?' Tess suggested.

'What about going a bit closer to the Eiffel Tower and taking some photos?' Rose suggested. 'We could see the sights, find a bistro, have a light lunch and then this afternoon we'll do the Montparnasse cemetery and if we get time we could go up the tower.'

'Sounds like a good idea,' Della agreed.

Fifteen minutes later, the five women stood beneath the straddling metal legs of the Eiffel Tower, disagreeing. Tourists were brushing past them, thronging in huge groups. The friends couldn't decide on a plan of action.

'I'm in Paris. I want to go up the tower,' Jen insisted.

'I'm not sure how I'd be with the height,' Tess muttered.

'Look at the queues, though,' Rose whispered. 'It's probably a rip-off.'

'But we'll regret it if we come to Paris and don't see the view from up there,' Jen grumbled.

'You can see views from the Montparnasse tower,' Pam suggested. 'It's not as expensive and the queues will be much shorter.'

Jen stamped her foot. 'We can walk to the second floor and it's only a few euros from there. I can pay for everybody.'

'Heights, though.' Tess pulled a face.

'I don't really mind, as long as we do something,' Rose grumbled. 'The queues aren't getting any shorter and it's draughty standing here.'

'I'd like to see Paris from the top of the tower.' Della's eyes shone.

'I just want to sit down and have a rest,' Tess grumbled. 'And a pastry.'

'It's expensive around here,' Rose warned. 'All the cafés will be full and I bet the food is just tourist-style rubbish.'

Pam was immediately enthusiastic. 'Rue Cler is just a few minutes away. They have street vendors and pastries there. Divine things to eat for the refined Paris palette, Rose.'

'Let's go there, then,' Tess agreed. 'The tower is just like the one in Blackpool. It's a carbon copy and not really interesting.'

'I'd like to see from the top, though.' Della sighed.

Jen stared up at the huge iron construction. 'Come on, Della – you and I can go up there together.'

'Should we split up? Really?' Pam looked concerned.

Rose nodded enthusiastically. 'It might be a good idea. We could meet back here at two o'clock – that gives us almost three hours – and we'll all be happy and ready for the cemetery.' She pulled a grim face.

Pam took a few seconds to understand Rose's comment. 'Oh, at Montparnasse, you mean?' She sighed. 'Well, I've been up the Eiffel Tower before so I'll go with Tess to Rue Cler and maybe afterwards we could go to the Hotel des Invalides...'

'Are you calling me an invalid?' Tess shrieked, laughing.

'It's lovely there. We could see Napoleon's tomb.' Pam pointed into the distance. 'Over there is La Trocadero. It's beautiful. Fountains and lawns, ice cream. It might be nice to relax in the sun if you like, Tess.'

'OK, it's a deal.' Tess swung her handbag. 'Right – Pam and I are going for the cake and ice cream option. Della and Jen are going to gaze from the top of the tower and look at the tiny ant people below, if they can survive the queues and – what about you, Rose?'

Rose rubbed her hands together. A breeze had started to shift between the metal network of the tower and the air seemed suddenly chilly. She smiled. 'I think I'll take off by myself for a bit, have a mooch around. Two o'clock, did you say, Pam? Right. I'll see you all back here, then.'

She turned on her heel and wandered off, an elegant lady in a smart coat carrying a Burberry-style handbag. Della linked her arm through Jen's. 'You ready, Jen? Shall we aim for the giddy heights?'

Tess tucked a hand through Pam's arm. 'And we'll take the gourmet option. Pastries it is, then. See you later. Have fun, hens.'

22

'Right.' Rose turned and stared back at the Eiffel Tower. It stood tall, a giant beacon, and she smiled to herself. 'I won't get lost because I know where I have to head back to, by two o'clock. I can hardly miss it.' She swivelled around and began to march away. She had no idea where she was going but it felt good to be by herself – somehow she felt empowered. Here she was, an older lady in the city of love all alone, and yet strangely she did not feel lonely. She had been so desolate and solitary in her house in Exmouth. Yet here in Paris, Rose saw couples of all ages from all over the world, holding hands, embracing, chattering together, their faces animated, but she didn't feel excluded.

Paris was all-encompassing: it was for everyone and she was part of its energy, its joy, its life. She considered what she might do in her free time. She could buy herself lunch, sitting outside a little bistro in the sunlight at a bright blue table with a parasol, choosing something nice for herself – oysters, perhaps, with wine. She decided that she would stop if she saw a place that she liked the look of, a simple street-side café with a friendly, beckoning waiter to show her to a single table. But for now she was going to stroll through Paris at her ease and pretend she'd lived there all her life.

In her imagination, she was a Parisienne widow, a singer, a classical concert pianist whose husband had been a composer. He had died two years ago – he might have been called Bernardo – but the woman she was now was another Rose. She was independent, sophisticated, a woman of means, a woman of taste. She was *chic*. She imagined living in a spacious flat in one of the nearby *arrondissements*. Her home would be tastefully decorated, with antique furniture, velvet hangings and a painting she had mischievously stolen from a famous artist as a young girl – a head and shoulders portrait of herself, her hair long and dark over cream skin, a look in her eye that challenged, that declared her *insouciance* to the world. Rose was enjoying inventing the new person she could be in Paris.

In her reverie, Rose was admired by men – so many men. One was a rich widower, a millionaire who sent her bouquets of lilies every day. He would be called Michel or Maurice – a musician, of course, probably the conductor of a great orchestra. Then there would be Gaston, a celebrated composer of popular melodies and a successful opera who had loved her since they were young. She had spurned him but he was still on fire with passion for her. He had written the opera especially for her, *La Seule*: the woman alone. It had been a huge success. People cried at the end when the beautiful heroine chose music over love and turned her devastated Romeo away. Rose increased her pace, turning into a small back street that wound behind the main path. She would have another admirer, a film star in his fifties. Robert –

no – Raoul – a successful actor who had been married several times to famous models but who held a strong passion for Rose, ever thwarted by her aloofness, her need to be separate and in charge of her own destiny.

Rose imagined her life as an opera being performed for the public. There would be a grand piano in the centre of the stage, pure white, the footlights and spotlights dazzling the audience with the sheer purity of her music. And she would be illuminated, seated at the piano in a dress so light and diaphanous it would look like mist. Her hair would be spangled with diamonds, her skin translucent. Rose smiled. She felt warm in Paris, safe, as if its anonymity, its huge buildings, its busy people were a protective shield that kept her secure.

She turned another corner and stopped. Opposite, there was a small church constructed of red brick, with an arched wooden door. Rose could see two stained-glass windows, mostly red but with blue and yellow panels. She narrowed her eyes to examine the pattern; there were figures in pale yellow, supplicants on their knees praying and the blue glass was shaped as Mary, the Virgin, holding out her hand. Rose glanced at the little watch on her wrist. It wasn't twelve yet. She liked the look of the little building: although she had no real religious belief herself to tempt her inside, the church seemed inviting, perhaps because it was a little secluded and intriguing. Her fingers felt the brass door handle and she pushed. The door opened easily, with the soft creak of an ancient voice whispering.

Inside, dust twirled in front of her eyes as she stared into the soft gloom. The smell of musty wood and decay filled her nostrils and found its way to the back of her throat. The silence hit her; the tangible lack of any sound surrounded her and made her feel separate, an intruder. She blinked into the dim light, a soft haze of colour from the stained-glass windows, a deep red glow that made her vision blur. Two rows of pews flanked either side of the aisle. To the right were huge copper organ pipes. Rose walked forward, towards the altar and tall gold cross. A sense of reverence pressed down on her shoulders, keeping her silent, making her conscious of the softness of her footfall, of each dull echo. There was someone in the middle of one of the pews, a man in a dark coat, his head down. Rose imagined him in silent supplication. She arrived at the altar, moved towards the crucifix and stared up at the figure of Jesus hanging down from the cross.

The wax figure had melancholy blue eyes, the lids low as if he was blessing those who looked up at him. The scarlet drops of blood on his brow contrasted sharply with his deathly pale skin. His hair was long and brown, matching a neat beard, and his robe shone white. Rose sighed, thinking that Jesus would probably not have looked at all like the alabaster statue. She asked herself how she felt about it and the answer came instantly. It was a shame love and devotion had to mean so much suffering. Rose wondered if Jesus had felt lonely in his last hours, carrying the weight of mortal sin on his shoulders, the burden of the cross.

For a moment she was filled with sadness, as if melancholy was the first, most primitive emotion, the most natural feeling of human existence, to grieve, to feel loss. There was a kindness in Jesus' face, a sense of purity and Rose thought that he must have been compassionate; the best of people, and the society of his time had treated his kindness with suspicion and aggression. Rose wondered if things were better nowadays; she doubted it. She shook her head. She had no idea what she felt. She'd hardly thought about religion since school, certainly since her wedding to Bernard, which, although it had been traditional in style, in a church, the service led by the local vicar, had been more about the guests and the dress and the music than a pact with God.

The thought of church music made her turn her head and she saw the steps that led to the organ in the corner. She moved quietly, her feet shuffling on the stairs. She pushed the small door and it opened. Rose caught her breath. The pipe organ was small but it was a beautiful construction of wood and shining metal. Rose allowed her fingers to touch the keys, to run over the stops. She positioned herself on the seat with its heavy cushion, made herself comfortable, pressing her feet on the pedalboard. She knew how to operate a church organ – Bernard had played in churches regularly and she had often filled in for him. Her fingers trembled as they hovered over the keyboards, couplers, expression pedals. She put her hand down to feel for the 'on' switch, pressed it, took a deep breath and pulled the stops. She heard the whistle of the bellows and began to play.

It was 'Jesu, Joy of Man's Desiring' by Bach. The music grew, swelled and filled the church, resonating against the walls and rising as insistent as an offering. Rose's fingers found the right keys – she knew the music well; she'd played it so often with the notation that her fingers naturally touched the right notes. She had first played it as a ten year old, her back straight in a blue checked dress, her hair pulled back from her brow with a white silk ribbon. Her teacher had been Claude Fisher, the local church organist, and he had always been a stickler for accuracy, pace, the power of emotion created by playing a piece louder or softer. Rose played easily, her fingers fluid, sweeping over the notes, a smile on her face. This, to her, was how she could interpret any religious faith, in the vibration of the music around her. It was celestial.

Her fingers pressed the final deep chord and held it down. Then she removed her hands; the music softened, faded and then there was silence. Rose was conscious of the sudden claustrophobia; she was alone, seated at the organ in silence. She flexed her fingers and thought for a moment. There had been a song her mother had sung to her as a child, years ago, a silly song from her mother's own youth. Rose frowned. How did it go? She touched a middle C. Then it came back to her: 'Oh Tough, Mighty Tough of the West'. It was a cowboy ditty.

With confident hands, she waved her fingers across the keys, belting out the daft song, a smile on her face. It was for her mother, for the years gone by that would never come again, for nostalgia and naïve times when she'd gone to the shop on the corner and bought four chewy sweets from old Jeanette Neville for a farthing; for the times when she'd sat on her dad's knee at six years old and painted lipstick circles on his bald head while he snoozed on a Sunday morning while her mother, pregnant with baby John, had made Sunday dinner. Rose even remembered their Bakelite radio – it was called a wireless then – rattling all morning, playing family favourites. They were good times, and the simple tune swept them back, chord after chord, note after note, replicating the emotion exactly as if it were yesterday.

She finished the song and the thought of her mother kept her fingers moving. Her fingers played two jangling chords. Then she was banging out the Abba song: 'Does Your Mother Know'. The lively tune was easy enough to interpret on the organ, her left hand accompanying the melody with improvised chords. Rose realised that the song was forty years old now. She had been thirty-five when it had come out. She had been teaching music from home every day, with a reputation for captivating the interest of the youngsters who sat at her piano. She'd interested them by showing that all music, pop and classical, jazz and show time, could be enchanting when played with belief, with an understanding of its power to entertain and to communicate a feeling. She finished the Abba song with a flourish and sat back in her cushioned seat, her face filled with a smile.

The sound of soft clapping made her turn, her heart leaping in shock. A young man stood behind her, fresh faced, probably in his late twenties or early thirties. He had neat dark hair, soft hazel eyes below arched brows. He was wearing a navy-blue overcoat, a carefully tied cream scarf at his throat. Rose remembered the figure who had been praying in the pews, the man in the shadows bending forward, his shoulders hunched as she'd passed him. He was smiling now, his face animated, a little breathless.

'*C'était merveilleux, madame.*'

Rose saw him beaming at her and she understood the compliment. She was not sure how to reply – her schoolgirl French was rusty now. She stammered, '*Je ne parle français. Je suis anglais – anglaise.*'

The young man greeted her anxious words with an even broader smile. 'English?' He burst out laughing. 'Well, that's just insane. I mean, I was just saying a little prayer – not that I pray much, but there you are – and then, lo and behold, you came along and the organ started up and the music filled the whole church.'

Rose stared at him. He had a northern English accent and the most open, friendly face. He held out a hand and clasped hers, his palm warm. 'I'm Darren Chadwick. From Salford, in

Manchester. I can't believe you came in here and played the organ, just like that. And today of all days. It was wonderful. Simply wonderful. A miracle even. I can't believe it. I mean, it was spot on and, as Abba might say – well, "thank you for the music".'

23

Rose wasn't sure why this young man, with his infectiously warm personality and easy smile, had insisted on taking her to lunch at a little bistro round the corner that he claimed he went to 'all the time' and promised that 'they make the best Brie en croute' she'd ever taste. As she sipped a glass of Sauvignon Blanc and talked about her hen-trip holiday, she was surprised that a young man of his age wanted to spend time with a woman forty years his senior. Most of the people she knew were older women – she was baffled that this young man wasn't sitting with a group of trendy youngsters in their thirties, discussing politics and the last series of *Game of Thrones*. But he was leaning forward across the table, holding a glass of wine and chattering animatedly, his hazel eyes shining.

'And I loved that piece you were playing at the beginning, the one that goes up and up and then down again. I've heard that before. The classical one. It was wonderful.'

'Johann Sebastian Bach. "Jesu, Joy of Man's Desiring".'

'Yeh, that's the one. It was such an uplifting tune. Mind

you, Rose – you don't mind if I call you Rose, do you?' She shook her head and he sipped more wine. 'Mind you, Rose, I was proper uplifted when you started banging out the Abba tune. I couldn't believe it. I'd just been trying to pray – I don't pray very often, mind – and I'd just said, "Right, please, God, show me the way I can make my music better" – honest to God, I did – and straight off, the organ music filled the church. It was surreal.'

'Are you a musician, Darren?' Rose asked.

'Daz – call me Daz, Rose. Everyone calls me Daz – except for my mother, who calls me Darren, even when I'm in her good books, which isn't often nowadays, especially since I left home. And my brother Jason – he calls me Dazzer, but that's a bit too familiar, isn't it?'

Rose smiled at him. 'The Brie is lovely – you were right. So – are you a musician, Daz?'

He nodded, his mouth full of food. He chewed for a while, waving a fork to indicate that he'd speak when his mouth was empty again. 'I'm a singer – in a club. Monty's. It's not far from here. That's why I live locally. I do four nights a week. I do ballads mostly, a few country and westerns, some-times stuff from the musicals.' His eyes twinkled. 'But I'd love to do Abba.'

Rose leaned forwards. 'It must be such a wonderful life, being a young Englishman in Paris, singing in a nightclub.'

'Oh, it is, it is.' Daz drank more wine. 'I've been here in Paris for six years now. It wasn't easy at first – I had to build up a reputation, get a good name for myself here. I'd done the Salford clubs for years, all over the north west. Two of us came over, my mate and me – we were a duo, proper popular with the crowds, we were. We rented our little flat, not too far from here. It's a right dive, our place, a poky attic with three rooms and a kitchenette, but we can afford to pay the rent every month and Monty's is a good place to be a regular – she pays well, Monty, and the crowds are always very appreciative. I get good tips too, mostly at the weekends.'

'It must be nice to be on stage with someone else. Performing by yourself would be so much more stressful.'

'It is, Rose. You're so right. But I am on my own now.' Daz pushed his plate away. 'That's why I went to the church. I'd been feeling right low. My mate, Simon, left a fortnight ago. He wanted to travel, to perform somewhere else. He said he was bored and he had this offer in Amsterdam. I would've gone with him but he said it was just for one person and we'd reached the end of the road, and that was it. He was gone.'

'Oh, dear.' Rose looked sad. 'That must've hit you hard after all this time.'

'It did, Rose – I was proper upset. I mean, I can perform by myself, but we were popular as a duo, you know, and I always felt it was Si who pulled in the crowds, not me. He had a great stage presence, you know, always laughing and joking with the audience. To tell the truth, I'd begun to worry I wasn't going to be able to do it by myself. I've done my best these last couple of weeks and Monty's been very sweet to me, but somehow it just hasn't felt right.'

'Is that why you went to the church?'

'Oh, it is, Rose. I felt proper lost, as if I doubted myself and I thought I'd ask Jesus – I always believed in someone being out there for me. I get the religious bit from my gran – she was always at the church. Even scrubbed the church steps, did the church flowers and that. Anyway, I just woke up today and I said to myself, "You know what, Daz – you should get out there and go and pray." And I did. And then, just as I said the words, I heard your music.' Daz chuckled. 'You're my guardian angel, Rose.'

'I'd hardly describe myself as a guardian.' Rose thought for a moment. 'Or an angel.'

Daz pushed away his plate, leaving half of his food untouched. 'Are you on your own, Rose? Back in England?'

'I'm a widow, yes. My husband passed away two years ago. My son, Paul, has a family – he's usually busy but we catch up on the phone, mostly on Sundays.'

Daz's brow wrinkled. 'Aren't you lonely?'

'I was.' Rose took a breath. 'Very lonely. Do you know, Daz, I'd let things slide I'd become sorry for myself, boring, dowdy.'

'No way.' Daz gaped. 'When I first saw you after you'd played the organ, Rose, I thought, she's a proper classy Frenchwoman, her – I was a bit scared to talk to you. I thought, I bet she's in the Paris Philharmonic Orchestra or something.'

Rose chuckled. 'I wish.' She thought for a moment. 'No, I am here in Paris with my four friends, having a wonderful time sightseeing and...' She took a breath. 'I'm glad you came to talk to me, that you took the chance to tell me you were feeling a bit low. Do you know, Daz – life is for living. I know it's an old cliché but it's easy to forget that there is beauty in each moment and we should try not to let the world get us down when really there's so much fun to be had.'

'That's proper philosophical, that is – we've been given this one life and the best we can do is live it properly.' Daz grinned. 'And you've cheered me up no end. I'm right glad we met too, Rose. You know, I'm going to go down to Monty's tonight and do the performance of my life. You've set me on the path to – to bouncing right back.'

'I'm glad I have,' Rose said. 'Now, shall I pay for our lunch?'

'Not at all – this is on me.' Daz reached into his jeans pocket for his wallet and brought it out with his phone. 'It's the least I can do. How long are you in Paris for?'

'Just until Monday, sadly.'

'Let me have your mobile number.' Daz patted her hand. 'I can send you photos of me on stage tonight. I'm going to do a song for you. Do you like Avril Lavigne's "Girlfriend"? No, I know – Cyndi Lauper – "Girls Just Wanna Have Fun". I'll do that one especially for you, shall I? I'll announce it over the mic – "This is for my new friend, Rose, sent today by the angels." Oh, no, I'd better not say that – it sounds like someone died.'

Rose smiled. She had found a piece of paper in her handbag and was scribbling her phone number down. 'If you can send me a film on your phone of you singing, Daz, I'd be so pleased. I'm off to a casino tonight with the girls but it would be lovely to see a video of you on the stage.' She handed him the paper. 'And thank you so much for lunch. It has been a real treat. And it's been such fun meeting you.'

'No, no.' Daz stood up, came round the table to Rose and immediately hugged her. 'The pleasure has been all mine, meeting a proper musician, a proper muse – that's what you are, Rose. Thank you for the music earlier on in the church and for inspiring me.' He waved his phone. 'And for letting me stay in touch.'

He hugged her again. He smelled of something fresh and tangy, like newly picked apples. Rose smiled at him and gazed beyond to the clock on the wall. It was ten minutes to two.

* * *

Tess stretched her legs out on a bench in the gardens of La Trocadero. A fountain shot frills of water towards the sky behind her. She was staring up at the Eiffel Tower, dipping her tongue into the soft ice cream in the cone. She sighed. 'Rue Cler and the pastries were lovely. But we should have gone up the Eiffel Tower. I wish we'd gone to the top with Jen and Della.'

Pam frowned. She'd hardly touched her cone. 'I thought you didn't like heights. You said you'd hate it.'

'I can be really silly sometimes about things like that.' Tess shook her head sadly. 'I don't let myself do things and then I realise I want to. You know, I get invited out and I want to go but I say, "No, thank you," or, "I'd love to but I'm busy." It's crazy, because I'm not busy at all. A woman I know from the post office asked me to go with her and some friends to yoga, just a weekly class, and I said, "No, I don't think so – yoga's not for me." Then when I went home, I wished I'd said yes. I'd have loved the company, a chance to get out.' She gave a hollow laugh. 'It's a miracle I ever went to aqua aerobics and met you all. I nearly didn't go.'

'Yoga is so good for the body, Tess.' Pam licked her cone tentatively. It made her tongue cold. 'Why did you think about not going to aqua aerobics?'

'Alan said I'd look silly in a swimsuit at my age.' Tess had almost finished the cone. 'That's why I didn't want to go up the tower with Jen and Della.'

'Because of the swimsuit?'

'No, because of Alan. His voice gets in my head some-times and makes me think, oh, I won't do that, I won't enjoy it. Or I think, I'd better not do that, I'll just look silly. You know, it's as if I sort of don't deserve anything nice for myself. I don't have a right to have fun.'

Pam breathed out, a huff of annoyance. 'That's not fair. I mean, you are such a happy person, Tess. You have such a gift for fun – you are the life and soul of everything we do here in Paris.'

'I wish I thought so.' Tess licked her fingers. 'I try so hard. I mean, I do enjoy myself, I want to have a good time and yet sometimes, in the middle of the laughter and the fun, I sort of stop and remind myself that I probably look like a fool and I wonder if Alan's right, if I am a bit silly and I open my mouth too much and I should just be quiet and say nothing.' She laughed. 'And then a few minutes later, off I go again, having too much to say and laughing too loudly.'

Pam folded her arms. 'Alan's affected your confidence.' She thought for a moment. 'Really, Tess – you should just carry on being who you are. You're lovely – a joy to be with.'

Tess's eyes were shining, filled with globes of tears. 'Thanks, Pam.'

Pam squeezed her hand. 'And next time there's anything happening, like a trip up the Eiffel Tower, you're definitely going to the top. Because you're worth it.' She sighed. 'I'd never have thought, knowing you, that you were having problems with self-esteem. You are so outgoing and effervescent. I admire you for it, Tess. Everyone does.'

'Do you think so?'

Pam nodded. 'You are definitely the social animal of the group. We all follow your lead.'

Tess wiped her eyes. 'I always think you are the confident one. I wish I were more like you, Pam – calm, self-assured. You are so strong, so certain.'

'I am, when I put my mind to something.' Pam gave a short laugh. 'It's got me into trouble a few times.'

'Go on – give me an example.' Tess chuckled, linking her arm through Pam's.

'Well, in 1983, I was arrested for shouting my mouth off.'

'No!' Tess's eyes were wide. 'You are my idol now! Tell me everything.'

Pam smiled, remembering. 'I was at the women's peace camp at Greenham Common in 1982 or 83. We made a fourteen mile long human chain from Greenham to Aldermaston, protesting about nuclear weapons. I wanted to be noticed. I had on a rainbow CND T-shirt, bright blonde hair, short and spiky. I had it cut short when I was twenty-two –I never grew it long again. Well, it was bitterly cold, December, I think, and all the other women were in warm coats and scarves and gloves. The woman next to me told me to wear a hat, to cover up my hair and stop drawing attention to myself, but I was determined to stand up for what I believed. So I shouted in this policeman's face... and I was arrested.'

'What did you shout?' Tess's eyes were huge.

Pam giggled. 'I shouted, "So I'm a Common woman. What are you going to do about it, Officer Dibble?" It was a bit unwise...'

'Then you were arrested? Did they lock you up?'

'Two officers manhandled me into a van, took me down the station. They kept me overnight. I was back on the fence the next day with a caution.'

Tess looked impressed. 'What a rebel.'

Pam sighed. 'Common sense was never my forte. I mean, I've got better as I've become older, I've learned to be sensible and take less risks... but I've got myself in some daft situations in my time, in some nasty scrapes.'

Tess leaned her head against Pam's shoulder. 'Tell me more.'

Pam thought for a moment, her brow creased, then she spotted two figures walking towards them, waving happily. She waved back. 'Another time, maybe, Tess – here are Jen and Della. Now, where's Rose?'

24

Della couldn't stop talking about the view from the top of the tower. 'Oh, my, it was so incredible. It made the waiting worth every second. The man behind us said the queues weren't too bad for a Friday – he was from Sweden. It was his fifth time up the tower. He was such a nice man. And then at the top floor, you could see the whole of Paris stretched out in the sunshine like a flat map – the greys of buildings and the green parks and the gardens, the Tuileries, like a big leafy plant. Oh, I felt quite dizzy. It was so amazing.'

Tess bit her lip. 'I wish I'd come up with you.'

'I wish you'd come, Tess,' Jen breathed. 'Della and I were saying, it would have been lovely to see your reaction – you'd have been so full of excitement.'

Pam winked at Tess. Jen frowned. 'Where's Rose? It's quarter past two.'

People were walking around them, some at a fast pace, intent on a destination. Others stood still, pointing phones and cameras. A striking young woman in a long colourful coat was twirling around, her hair a sweeping trail of light behind her, while a young man in jeans took photographs. A crowd of people were watching them, several paces back. The friends were surrounded by the bustle of pushing throngs and darting individuals, all in a hurry. 'We can't move from here.' Pam sighed. 'This is where we said we'd all meet.'

'I'm starving,' Della grumbled.

Tess reached into her bag. 'I knew you would be – I bought you each a pastry from the Rue Cler. It'll do for lunch – we can eat later, before the casino.'

Jen took her small package warily. 'Oh, so much cream – and look at all this jam.'

'And almonds – they're heavenly,' Tess explained.

'I'll never fit in my wedding dress if I eat all of this...' Jen shrugged. 'But who cares? I'm in Paris.' She took a large bite.

Della had cream on her nose. 'The pastry is so flaky. Thanks, Tess – you made the right choice.'

'There were shops full of so many cakes – colourful macaroons, brioches, fruit tarts – it was incredible.'

'What was incredible? What have I missed?' It was Rose, her face shining. She had arrived just behind them, clutching her handbag. Her cheeks were pink; she had clearly been walking fast.

'Pastries, Rose.' Tess thrust out a wrapper. 'Have one – I saved it for you.'

'Thanks, but I couldn't.' Rose smiled mischievously. 'Not after eating the best Brie en croute in Paris and a lovely glass of Sauvignon.'

'You're late and you've had lunch.' Jen put on a face of mock disapproval. 'What have you been up to?'

Rose closed her eyes. 'I had the most wonderful adventure – and I met a lovely young man.'

'A young man?' Della repeated, her eyes wide with disbelief.

'His name is Daz and he's from Salford in Manchester. He's thirty-two and he bought me lunch.'

'Rose, you're such a cougar!' Tess pretended to be shocked. 'We can't leave you alone for five minutes.'

Pam put her arm around Rose. 'You can tell us all about it on the way to Montparnasse. There's a Metro station just round the corner. It'll take us about half an hour. Shall we go?'

'I want to hear all about this young man, all the details – where you met him, what he's like and how you came to have lunch.' Tess grinned. 'I should have skipped the pastries and gone with you, Rose.'

* * *

Despite the milky haze of the sunshine, a chilling wind blew around the north wing of the cemetery. Stone statues surrounded them: sad faced angels, a grey woman in a robe, weeping, ornate crosses, quartz gravestones, tombs hewn from sparkling granite. The friends had been wandering around Cimetière du Montparnasse for over three hours. It was ten to six. Pam was staring at the phone held out in front of her, researching on the Internet. 'They should be around here somewhere...'

Tess shuddered. 'Who are we looking for?'

'Jean-Paul Sartre and Simone de Beauvoir.' Pam looked around at the tombs and statues. 'They should be here.'

'They'll wait where they are until you find them,' Rose said grimly.

'It's very calm here.' Della breathed in slowly. 'A really peaceful place.'

Tess wrinkled her nose. 'I'm looking forward to the casino, so we can spend a bit of time with the living.'

Jen shook her head. 'Serge Gainsbourg's tomb was so beautiful. All those wonderful flowers people had left. And that young man, sitting on the grass, crying.'

'I thought it was Serge himself at first,' Rose muttered. 'I nearly had a heart attack.'

'It's good you can research things while you're here, Pam.' Della pulled her jacket tightly around her against a gust of wind. 'Or we'd never have known the background of the sculpture by that Romanian man, Brancusi. It was such a sad story, poor Tania from Russia killing herself for love.'

'You didn't spot the security cameras around there?' Rose met Della's gaze. 'Poor Tania could have done with people paying more attention to her when she was alive. Perhaps she wouldn't have topped herself for love.'

'It was good to see Beckett and Ionesco.' Pam waved her phone. 'Ah, here they are – Jean-Paul and Simone. My literary idols.' She bent down to take a photograph. Her five friends copied, their bodies huddled together in an attempt to discern what fascinated Pam so much.

'Can't we see Jim Morrison?' Tess grumbled.

'He's in the other cemetery with Oscar Wilde and Edith Piaf,' Jen replied.

'We should have gone there, then.' Tess suddenly stiffened. 'What's that noise? Someone blowing a whistle?'

'Perhaps it's the police?' Rose suggested. 'Chasing a criminal? Oh, look – Simone lived longer than Jean-Paul. That just shows women have more resilience.'

'I love the angels in here – all sorts of sculptures. Some

look so pure and others look menacing.' Della looked around her. 'I thought I heard a whistle too.'

'Maybe it's someone walking a dog, calling it back – you know, like they do with sheepdogs.' Jen looked up at the sky, blank parchment, a few tattered clouds, and shivered.

Rose sniffed. Her nose was pink in the cold wind. 'My favourite grave was the Charles Pigeon family tomb. I liked the sculpture of the woman lying down asleep and the man sitting up holding a pencil and a notebook, both people covered up in bed. It was as if they'd died but he was getting up again. I wonder what the story was behind that.' She paused for a moment. 'Do you think there are ghosts here?'

Jen's face was pale. 'I wouldn't like to be here late at night...'

'What time is it?' Tess asked, pulling out her phone. 'Five past six. Shouldn't we be thinking about going back and getting ready to go out?'

Pam looked up sharply. 'Five past six? This place closes at six.' She leapt up. 'That will be why we heard the whistles – they were blowing whistles to tell the public the place was closing.'

'Oh, no.' Jen's hands went to her face. 'We'll be locked in.'

Della looked around. 'We could scale the walls maybe – give each other a bunk-up?'

'No one could bunk me up there.' Tess was horrified.

Pam had broken into a sprint and was heading towards the north gate. Rose stared at her friends. 'What's she up to?'

'We'd better follow her.' Della shrugged.

Jen was troubled. 'I'm freezing now. I'm not staying here all night. Come on, girls – Pam will find a way out for us.'

When they reached Pam she was speaking to a small man in a dark jacket. His face was creased with exasperation and he was jangling a set of keys. Pam was waving her hand apologetically and speaking in French. The man shook his head in disbelief as he noticed the four friends approaching. His tone was annoyed, blowing air through closed lips, but he opened the huge gate and ushered the women outside, muttering to himself. Pam puffed out a sigh of relief. 'I reached him just in time. Thank goodness for that. Right – I'm not sure we have time for the tower now. Shall we get back to the hotel?'

Tess nodded. 'Can we get a taxi? I'm desperate for a shower.'

'What I'd give for a nice hot bath.' Della groaned.

Jen grinned. 'We can get some food – just a bite – and then we'll hit the casino.'

It had been Jen's idea to go out and buy something to eat in her room, and the five hens gathered together to share supper – charcuterie, cheese, bread, fruit and a salad in a bag. She and Della had popped out to the supermarket in the street and brought back groceries and two bottles of wine. Tess said a light meal before the casino would make them lean and hungry and ready to gamble, and Rose suggested that they should eat at El Madani tomorrow night as a treat after the Friday night frugality. She picked up her phone and made a reservation with Chafik, who promised them a wonderful banquet at the best table in the restaurant. Pam was sitting on the floor, her back resting against Della's bed, her feet bare, chewing bread and reading a book. Jen had already showered and was wrapped in a kimono. Tess was painting her toenails red, a piece of cheese sticking out of her mouth. Della stood in front of the wardrobe mirror, repeatedly asking it if the long dress in silky red material was too showy for the casino.

'Wear the dress, Della,' Tess grunted without looking. 'You always look a million dollars, even in the tattiest jeans.'

'I don't know about this dress though – the neckline is so low.' Della frowned. 'I don't want to be mutton dressed as lamb.'

'Lamb is overrated.' Tess giggled, helping herself to wine.

'We should be getting ready, Rose,' Pam murmured. Rose had been quiet – she'd hardly touched the food. She stared at the screen of her phone.

'I'm not coming with you.'

Jen was puzzled. 'To the casino? Why not?'

'I'm going to Monty's.'

'Who's Monty?' Tess asked, interested.

'It's the club where the young man I met, Daz, sings. I'd like to go there tonight, to see him perform. To give him a bit of encouragement.'

'But what about the casino?' Della was disappointed.

'I'm sorry.' Rose breathed deeply and took some money from her purse. 'I've been thinking about that. Della – here. Take this – it's fifty euros. Place a bet or two for me.'

'What if she wins?' Jen asked.

'We'll split it,' Rose replied, and offered them an apologetic smile. 'I really want to go to the club.'

Pam sat upright. 'You shouldn't go there by yourself.'

'I'll get a taxi. It's twenty minutes' ride. Then at the end of the evening, I'll get a taxi back.'

'I'll come with you, Rose.'

'I don't want to spoil your evening though, Pam.'

Pam turned to Jen, then Tess and Della. 'What do you

think? I don't mind. Rose shouldn't go by herself. I'll be as happy at a nightclub as I will at a casino.'

Jen nodded. 'It makes sense, I suppose. The three of us will be fine.'

Tess brightened. 'Maybe if the club is nice we can all go there on Sunday evening – for Jen's big hen do. I mean, the casino is just for the experience really – it's not like we'll be seasoned gamblers after just one visit.'

'So, we can go and check Monty's out, Pam.' Rose's eyes sparkled. 'I'm looking forward to hearing Daz sing.'

'We'll miss you both.' Della sighed. 'But I know how important music is to you, Rose.'

Jen agreed. 'It won't be the same without you, but Della and Tess and I will have a fab time. But I do understand how much you want to hear the music. I hope it's a lovely club.'

Rose waved her phone. 'Let's keep in touch – like the youngsters do. We'll send photos and texts to each other of what we see and what we do, shall we? That way it will be like we'll all be together.'

'Perfect,' Tess agreed. 'And we'll make it interesting too – a sort of competition? Let's see who has the best time. After-wards, we'll rate our evening out of ten.'

Rose nodded, imagining what Monty's might be like. There would be soft lighting, tasteful décor, sophisticated guests with expensive clothing, smart singers crooning smooth music. She was already sure the club was going to be at least five points better than the casino.

25

As they stood on the steps outside the casino, the three friends linked arms. Tess couldn't stop smiling; the sparkling lights were gaudy but behind them lay the glitz and glamour of the roulette wheel and cocktails. Jen shivered with apprehension as a gust of wind blew her hair. Della stared up at the sign, *La Rêve*, emblazoned in a gold arch, simple black lettering above a half-moon stained-glass window depicting a woman in a frilly dress, dancing wildly. She glanced over her shoulder as Faik's taxi pulled away and, behind her, the Eiffel Tower stood out against a velvet horizon like an illuminated needle, little yellow stitches of buildings tacked below. Della had to catch her breath. She had been up to the very top of the tower today and now, swathed in a red dress and sequin encrusted black shawl, she was stepping inside a huge casino, being greeted by two identical burly men in impeccable black suits with starched white shirts, neat dickey bows and fastidiously cut hair.

Jen was determined to enjoy herself. She was desperate to appear confident in her surroundings, wearing a knee length, off-the-shoulder dress in vibrant green. Eddie had texted her before she'd left, full of his sightseeing in Las Vegas, and now he was filling her thoughts – she was missing him. She imagined he was already in the casino with his son playing blackjack, although she had no idea what blackjack was. He would be there on holiday, not in Las Vegas and, of course, in her imagination, he hadn't met Jen, not yet – he was still a lonely widower, but an extremely rich one, of course. Eddie would be wearing a black tuxedo, his craggy handsome face frowning as he was immersed in the game, then, as she appeared in a distant corner, Jen would catch his eye and he'd look up from his cards – Jen wasn't sure if there were cards in a blackjack game, but in her reverie, Eddie was definitely hunched over cards – and he would gasp and stare. He wouldn't be able to pull his gaze from her and Harry would be impatient, waiting. 'What's the matter, Dad? Concentrate on your game.' But Eddie wouldn't be able to concentrate, not ever again. He'd have lost his heart in an instant to a woman in an emerald dress.

The friends were inside the casino, walking up thick carpeted steps. Banks of slot machines whirred on either side of them, flashing shuddering lights and spitting cash. Tess strode forwards. Wearing a short silver and black sparkling dress and dangling diamanté earrings, her hair shining and smooth after half an hour with the hairdryer, she imagined she was a Russian woman, Svetlana, twenty-seven years old and single. Now out to conquer Paris as a socialite, she was already the toast of Moscow where her moody rich mother lived alone, except for her Pekinese pup. She tried to imagine she was calm, in control, in her comfort zone inside the casino, Paris being her second home – she had a luxury suite in the Rive Gauche – but, as she looked around the noise and the vast expanse of space filled with shifting people, all focused on gambling, dazzled her and she was suddenly out of her depth.

She stood with her friends at the edge of a long room filled with tables, a plush red and gold carpet covering the floor. There were chandeliers hanging from gilded ceilings, closed-circuit televisions blinking from all walls. This was the main gambling room, the table game pit spread in the centre, but there were small walkways leading away, more opportunities to tempt the customer to find new exciting ways to spend money. The décor was ostentatious. A flashing gold sign, comprised of little white bulbs, proclaimed that they were inside Casino La Rêve. Gaudy neon strips flashed candy colours, pinks and oranges and blues, and the punters strolled by. Tess stared at glamorous couples talking excitedly, several groups of men with frowns on their faces, already working out strategies, where to place the next bet.

Tess gazed towards an adjacent room. Gaudy flashing machines side by side like garish sentries caught her eye. The ceiling seemed to move, a neon blue and yellow projection of an underwater scene with flickering fish and shifting sea life. Two sturdy silver pillars, swathed in carvings of climbing leaves and twirling vines, linked the floor and the ceiling. Tess glimpsed a higher level, an ornate white staircase leading to a balcony where even more gaming was taking place. She breathed out slowly. 'I think I need a drink.'

* * *

Rose and Pam leaned against the bar in Monty's. The club wasn't bright or glitzy, as she'd thought it might be. It was very dark, like being underground in a long rabbit warren;

the walls were clad in ebony the tables and carved chairs were heavy oak and the bar was a tessellation of dusky blocks of mahogany. Soft lights gleamed from the ceiling, pale yellow bulbs hanging inside opaque globes. Behind them, there was a stage area in shadow, an unlit glitter ball overhead and a white grand piano with a microphone to one side. Music came from speakers and Rose recognised the pop tune – 'The Power of Love' by Frankie Goes to Hollywood. Pam was talking to a barman, while buying two white wine spritzers.

The people around them varied from casually dressed people like themselves – both Pam and Rose had decided to wear jeans, a light top and a jacket – to some of the most devastatingly glamorous women Rose had ever seen. Her eyes were drawn to one woman in particular at the bar next to Pam, who spoke loudly to her friends in French and then to someone else, a tall lean man, in heavily accented English. Rose thought she was probably South American, by the lilt of her accent. She was at least six feet tall. Her raven hair cascaded down her back and her face was stunning, with carmine lips and thick false eyelashes. Her black strappy dress was cut low, almost to the navel, and so figure-hugging it seemed to be part of her own skin. Rose wondered with a smile how the woman kept her bosoms in place yet, at the same time, she was thrilled by the idea of wearing such a daring dress herself. In her twenties, she could have carried it off, although Bernard would have certainly been unimpressed and called her a floozy.

Rose tugged herself away from her thoughts as Pam passed her a spritzer and pulled at her sleeve. 'There's a little table over there, to one side of the stage. Come on, Rose – let's sit down.'

They squeezed between tables to a space in a dim corner of the room, past the edge of the stage, towards simple chairs with curved backs. They made themselves comfortable just as the taped music faded and a flurry of little white lights, soft as snowfall, spattered across the stage. Dramatic music began to boom from the speaker overhead and then a circular spotlight snapped onto the curtain at the back. A voice from offstage announced the artist who had just walked into the lights as Filmah something – Rose couldn't hear the surname.

Filmah was a strikingly attired woman in a long figure-hugging black and grey lace dress and black gloves that extended all the way up her arms. She wore a cream and black hat that was enormous – much wider than her shoulders – and the bow on it must have been at least four feet long, finished off with a plume of pink feathers so high that Rose wondered how she could move without the hat falling off. But Filmah was poised and assured, glamorous in the style of a Second World War film star, with pencilled brows and crimson bow lips.

Suddenly she began to sing. Rose recognised the song immediately as the 1930s song 'Falling in Love Again'. Filmah sang it in a husky voice, all cigarette smoke and sulky tones, waving her gloved fingers to accentuate the drama in the lyrics. Rose watched, rapt, as the singer hung onto the last notes and raised tormented brows. The audience clapped, a trickle of applause, and Filmah pouted and muttered something that was clearly rude in French. Pam laughed. Then Filmah began a second song in German, the same moody drawl and studied insouciance on her face. Rose glanced at Pam, who seemed to be enjoying the song, and scanned the club to see if she could see Daz. There were several young men at the bar, in the corner, wearing jeans and white vests, chatting happily and ignoring the singer, who was now knitting her brow and singing the final strains of the song as if she were suffering the agonies of lost love. Rose clapped warmly. 'She sounds just like Marlene Dietrich.'

Pam grinned and raised her glass. 'Of course she does. It is Marlene Dietrich.'

Rose shook her head. 'No – Marlene has been dead for—'

Pam spluttered a laugh. 'I know. The singer's called Filmah Boots. But it's a Marlene song and Filmah's doing lip-sync.'

'Lips sink?' Rose shook her head.

Pam laughed and carried on applauding as Filmah frowned, swore in French and marched off stage, the hat perfectly secure despite the speed of her stride. 'She's miming, Rose.'

'Miming? Really? Why?' Rose frowned. She couldn't see the point in that. She was meant to be watching someone perform. It couldn't be right. Miming wasn't singing – miming was cheating, wasn't it?

* * *

Jen, Della and Tess stood in the gaming room, sipping chilled white wine. Tess pulled a face. 'You should have asked for a dry martini, shaken not stirred.'

'I only knew the words *vin blanc*,' Jen stammered. 'Otherwise I'd have asked for the cocktails – Moscow Mules.'

Della giggled. 'You should have said it all in English – "Give me a dirty martini, bartender, and make it fast."' She laughed again, a wide smile. 'I've always wanted to say that.'

'If we win on roulette, I'll buy us some Moscow Mules.'

Jen's brow furrowed. 'I've no idea how you bet, though. What do we do?'

'We buy some chips and go over to the roulette wheel,' Tess said. 'I saw it on a James Bond film. You get the chips and put them on a number, red or black, and then the croupier spins the wheel and – unless you're really lucky – you lose it all. That's it.'

'I have Rose's fifty euros.' Della shivered. 'I'm too scared to spend it.'

'I have fifty euros too.' Jen's face was determined. 'Will you go first, Della? If we just buy some chips and then have a few goes – maybe we can win something. That would make Eddie jealous.'

Tess shook her head. 'How much has he won in Las Vegas?'

'Nothing yet.' Jen frowned. 'I texted him earlier. He says he's playing poker tonight. And craps.'

'It's all crap if you ask me.' Tess looked around her. 'If he's been in Las Vegas for several days and won nothing yet, he must have lost a small fortune.'

'Harry won a little at baccarat last night.' Jen forced a smile, imagining her fiancé in a dinner jacket, a handsome man of leisure, his son an identical copy but younger, gazing over his father's shoulder. 'And Eddie says he's feeling lucky tonight. He's going to play roulette too.' She sniffed. 'So, I'm going to play roulette. It would be just great if I won something, wouldn't it? To show him I can play on the wheel in a casino too.'

Della looked concerned. 'There are what – thirty-seven numbers? That gives you the chance of a thirty-seven to one win. So, if you played the wheel thirty-seven times, you might win once. That's not great odds, is it?'

'How do you know all that?' Tess was impressed. 'Della, you must be a mathematical genius.'

'I have to be. Sylvester likes a little flutter on the football every now and then. He's such a huge West Ham fan. I have to keep an eye on him. I mean, he's very sensible. But everyone knows betting can run away with you. You think, just one more bet – it's a dead cert this game – I'm bound to win.' She waved her hands emphatically. 'So, I have a rule. I say to him, "Sylvester, you can bet so much – say, five pounds – but when it's gone, the betting stops right there and that's that."' She put her hands on her hips. For a moment, she was waggling her finger, telling Sylvester to put his wallet away.

Jen's forehead was creased with anxiety. 'So, we'll bet fifty euros each, then? How many chips is that?'

'I suppose it depends what the chip you buy is worth.' Della spread her fingers. 'If you buy five euro chips then you get ten. If you could buy one euro chips then you'd get fifty.'

Jen grasped Della's wrist excitedly. 'So, you and I can both play together? We'll get the five euro chips and, with my fifty euros and Rose's fifty euros, that's twenty goes. We're bound to win.'

Della shook her head. 'Not with a thirty-seven to one chance of success.'

'That's where the excitement comes in, I guess,' Jen breathed. 'I'm not feeling excited yet, though. Quite honestly, I'm terrified.'

Tess pulled a face. 'I'm not convinced about all this betting. I think we'll just pour a hundred euros down the drain. That's an evening meal for us all – or a day out in Paris shopping.'

'Come on.' Jen tugged at Tess's hand eagerly, trying to appear confident. 'We are three intrepid women in Paris,

gambling in a casino. Let's hit the big time, shall we, girls?'
She grasped Della's wrist tightly. Tiny inside the emerald
dress, she didn't look the confident Paris gambler.

They walked over to the desk where money was
exchanged for chips. Jen hesitated.

'I don't know what to say... how to buy some chips.' Jen's
eyes were wide. 'I can't speak French. Pam's not here – Rose
has got a bit of French. I don't know what to say...'

'Just ask the man for chips.' Tess whispered. '*Les chips*?
Perhaps you say... *pommes de terre*? *Frites*? I don't know...'

Jen was shaking. 'It's too scary. What if I lose all my
euros?' She grabbed Tess's hand. 'I want to do it but – I'm so
nervous. This gambling business is terrifying. The tension is
too much... I can't do it. Will you go first, Della?'

Tess propelled Della forward towards a young man in a
suit. Della reached into her purse and took out Rose's fifty
euro note, holding it out. 'Can I play roulette? *Chips, s'il vous
plaît, monsieur*. Fifty euro chips... please?'

The man at the desk took it without looking at her and
handed her a single chip. The three friends walked away,
frowning.

By the time they had reached the wheel, Jen's confidence
had completely drained away. Della's hand was shaking,
holding the chip. They huddled together in silence, flanked
by a throng of men and women leaning forward, cheering
and waving arms or fists, while the wheel whirred and the
ball spluttered to a halt. A man with a clipped beard and a
paunch, playing with chips of five euros, had lost three bets
consecutively and slunk away, dejected. A woman, possibly in
her sixties, her hair piled high on her head and a diamond
necklace with a huge blue stone nestling in her cleavage, won

on her second bet. Jen was breathing rapidly. 'Shall we have a go, Della? Shall we try a bet?'

The wheel whirred before Della could answer. She seemed mesmerised. A young man in an open-necked shirt and an effusive manner placed his chips on number four, watched the wheel whir and won. He said something in Italian to his girlfriend, a slim woman with short blonde hair. Tess glanced at her friend nervously. 'Go on, Della.'

She stared at the chip. Fifty euros was about forty pounds – maybe forty-three. Some days, Sylvester didn't bring much more than that home after a quiet session in the van. But the wheel was whizzing round again and, as it slowed, the ball rattled, teasingly twirling and finally coming to a standstill on the number four. The young Italian man whooped and cheered. *'Ho vinto – di nuovo.'* His blonde partner threw herself at him, kissing him enthusiastically. 'You won again.'

Della wondered whether, if the young man's luck was good, then hers might be too. Besides, someone had to get the ball rolling, literally. Jen's face was pale with fear. Della knew she'd have to bet first, then perhaps Jen would feel braver. She stared again at the single chip and imagined losing all Rose's money in one moment of play. Her hand trembled. In her nervousness, she hadn't been thinking straight: she'd made a mistake.

Jen stared at her friend. 'Go on – just do it.'

Tess frowned. 'Where are the rest of the chips, Della? What's happened? Have you been scammed?'

Della's heart was thumping against her ribs. The chip in her hand was damp with her perspiration. 'I think I've done something really stupid,' she gasped. 'I think I've just bought a single fifty euro chip...'

26

Rose was really enjoying the live acts at Monty's. So far, the performers had all been extremely glamorous women. Rose wondered if Daz would come on stage at the end, as the grand finale act. She imagined him singing 'New York, New York' and other songs made famous by Frank Sinatra, dressed in a smart suit, or maybe wearing a leather jacket and skin-tight jeans, like James Dean. She glanced at Pam, who was swaying steadily to the ballad that the blonde singer was crooning, and she looked entranced, a smile on her face.

Rose sipped the last of her second spritzer. She'd loved the last singer, a woman popular with the audience, called Elton Joan, who wore oversized glasses and a glittery jacket. Her lipstick was black, shaping her lips in a sullen snarl, and her red hair stuck up around her face like a wild flaming fan. She'd really played the piano well and she'd sung all the songs herself too, her strong voice bellowing out 'Rocket Man' and 'Crocodile Rock'. Rose had watched her feet in tall platform boots pressing the piano pedals and wished she, Rose, could be in the singer's place, sitting at the stool of the beautiful white baby grand and tinkling on the keys. She doubted that she'd wear what Elton Joan was wearing although, in fairness, Joan didn't seem to care about wearing age-appropriate clothes, despite being not too far from Rose's own age. The singer had so much make-up on that, from where she was sitting, Rose could see the cracks in the porcelain foundation on her face beneath the spangled glasses and, she was sure, the flame-red hair wasn't natural.

But now there was an extremely buxom singer in a yellow fringed dress, an oversized cowboy hat and high leather boots. She had blonde curls beyond her shoulders, the thickest, healthiest hair Rose had ever seen. She was pretty, although her eyes and lips had been enlarged so much with make-up that she resembled a Barbie doll. Her name was Wheezy Anna and she was very fond of country songs. Rose had watched her lips carefully all the way through 'Jolene' and 'Nine to Five'; now she was singing 'I Will Always Love You' and Rose realised that Pam had been right – she was definitely miming or lip-syncing, as Pam called it.

But Rose had to admit, Wheezy Anna was very convincing and she had the emotion off to a tee, including the wobbling lower lip and the large, quivering Adam's apple. Rose thought that perhaps the enlarged Adam's apple spoiled her good looks a bit but then, as Rose knew only too well and Bernard had reminded her quite often, she had knobbly knees and skinny chicken thighs herself, so she couldn't really criticise anyone else. And Rose didn't intend to be critical – she was enjoying the music and the spectacle immensely.

Wheezy Anna finished her final song to a trickle of disinterested clapping. Many of the audience were chattering and not paying attention. Then a woman walked onto the stage in a black strappy dress cut low to the navel; her hair was a cascade of black curls. It was the stunning woman Rose had noticed at the bar. She greeted the audience in French, Spanish, German and English and the applause resounded. She introduced herself as *'votre amie, Montserrat Tabueña'*. As she spoke, moving easily from one language to the other, Rose realised that she was Monty, the owner of the club. She was muttering something about a friend of hers called Ashley, a popular singer who had recently left the club for pastures new.

Rose thought this might be a good opportunity to go to the bar and buy two more white wine spritzers. She put her hand on Pam's arm and gestured that she was about to refill their glasses and then she slid back her chair and began the difficult journey between closely grouped tables and throngs of people buying drinks. Behind her, another act had started on stage. Rose glanced over her shoulder to see a slim woman in a long leopard-skin dress and a mane of pale pink hair. She was singing a song Rose had never heard before but the lyrics, 'shut up and drive', drifted across to her ears. Rose grinned at the barman, repeating the words she'd heard Pam use earlier. *'Deux spritzers de vin blanc, s'il vous plaît.'*

She carried the drinks carefully back to the little table, avoiding a tall woman in a bra top and leather trousers, who almost elbowed one of the glasses from her hand. Rose felt the need to mutter, *'Pardonnez-moi, madame,'* under her breath. She finally reached her seat and wriggled in comfortably, staring up at the performer. The leopard-clad singer was in the centre of the stage, energetically shaking her pert backside and waving her arms. Pam leaned over and took the drink, grinning. 'Thanks, Rose. This one's good. She's called Greta...'

Rose didn't hear the rest of Pam's words. The song had finished, the woman was curtseying theatrically and blowing kisses to a lacklustre applause. Someone from the back made a loud owl noise. The singer, Greta, turned an angry face to the crowd and said something in French and her quip was greeted with a smattering of laughter. Greta appeared not to care. She ran fingers through her pink-white mane and introduced her next song. *'Voici une chanson pour mon amie qui est venue à mon secours aujourd'hui. Elle s'appelle Rose.'*

Rose was taking a mouthful of white wine spritzer. She sat up straight in her seat. She'd just heard her name, Rose. Pam had, too – she seemed to have understood all the words in French. Pam turned to her and blinked, her face surprised. The singer Greta continued. *'La chanson s'appelle* "Girls Just Wanna Have Fun".'

Rose clutched her glass, her mouth open. That was the song Daz had promised her. She stared up at Greta. Beneath the strawberry hair, the pouting prawn-pink lips and the huge eyelashes, she recognised the soft hazel eyes, the gentle infectious smile. A lively musical intro boomed through the speakers and Greta cavorted and danced before belting out the lyrics in lip-sync and shaking a leopard-clad bottom as she strutted across the stage, but Rose could only stare. She leaned over to Pam, tapped her arm and in a squeaky voice, she muttered, 'Pam... that's Daz...'

Pam nodded. 'I thought it might be – as soon as she came on stage and introduced herself as Greta Manchester.'

The music rolled along with such energy and Daz – Greta Manchester – was so full of enthusiasm and panache, pouting and cavorting, that Rose wanted to leap up and dance. The song was for her and she was desperate to jump up, climb on the chair and bop along. Instead, Rose wiggled in her seat, tapping her feet and, finally, she bounced up and down on her bottom, clapping her hands. Daz finished the song with flair, blowing kisses to the audience, and Rose and Pam applauded and cheered.

Flamboyantly, Daz called, *'Pour mon amie, Rose,'* and Rose clapped until her hands hurt.

Someone shouted something loud and raucous from the back of the club and Pam frowned, turning to Rose. 'That's not nice.'

'What?' Rose felt suddenly defensive. 'What did they say?'

Pam shrugged. 'Apparently, Greta used to be part of a duo and the other singer left. When she dedicated the song to you, someone called out, "Why doesn't your friend Rose come on stage and help you now? She'd be an improvement."' Pam folded her arms indignantly.

Rose gazed up at Daz. She could see that he was flustered for a second, then he flashed a professional smile and began to introduce the next song. Rose felt her heart thud in her chest. Injustice, unfairness, always made her blood boil. She had to do it: she had no choice now. She pulled herself onto shaky legs and turned to the audience. 'I am Rose. *Je suis Rose.* I am here. Hey – give me a hand up, will you, Daz?'

Greta leaned forward. 'Rose?'

'Come on – pull me up on the stage with you – I need a hand.'

Greta gave a whisper from the corner of her mouth. 'What are you up to?'

Rose found herself standing next to Greta on the stage without a clue about what she would do next. She could sing, a bit – she'd been cast as Yum-Yum in *The Mikado* at school. She'd been a promising fifteen year old musician, usually self-conscious and awkward, but on stage in costume and make-up, she had felt a sudden irrational confidence., Suddenly, she had become a completely different version of herself, a tantalising Yum-Yum playing opposite a handsome sixteen year old boy called Gerald in the role of Nanki-Poo. Since then, she'd sung in a few choirs, but never solo on stage and certainly never with a performer like Greta Manchester. She gazed towards the piano. 'Daz, can you sing – I mean, sing live?'

'Yes, but—'

'If I play the Abba song I did in the church – can you give it a go?' Rose was aware of the audience. They had been clapping and cheering when she first dragged herself onto the stage but now there was silence. Stunned faces stared, surrounding her on three sides. Someone at the back wolf-whistled. Rose caught Pam's eye and her thumbs-up good luck sign.

Daz nodded. 'Go for it, Rose,' and he turned towards the audience, Greta Manchester in all her sensual and mischievous glory, full of bravado. *'Mesdames et messieurs – voici mon amie, Rose – et une chanson de Abba...'*

Rose seated herself at the white piano, her fingers trembling. She breathed in, determined to calm her thudding heartbeat. She'd played the song earlier – 'Does Your Mother Know' – so they'd rehearsed it, in a manner of speaking. She stretched her fingers, took a breath and began the opening chords, banging her hands on the keys for all she was worth. Then suddenly, Greta Manchester was off across the stage, all arms and legs and stiletto heels, shaking narrow hips and throwing back the strawberry-pink mane of hair before launching in with the first cheeky, tantalising lines of the song. It was working. The audience joined in with the chorus, and Greta and Rose were a team, listening to each other, feeding from each other's energy. They were on fire. Pam raised her phone, clicked a photograph and pressed *send* to Jen.

Rose began to enjoy herself, nodding her head up and down as she played, gazing towards the audience and grinning widely, just as the keyboard player in Abba – Björn or Benny, she wasn't sure which – used to do. She leaned towards the microphone and tried the backing vocals, making her voice high, like a little girl's voice, to create a comedy effect. The audience roared at her exaggerated attempt to be Agnetha or Anni-Frid, and gave her a resounding cheer.

Something clicked in Rose's brain – a primeval need to perform, to be seen centre-stage, to be flamboyant, to strut her stuff and to be adored. It was suddenly the most natural thing in the world to be at the piano, singing Abba melodies in an energetic voice and belting out a rhythm on the keys. Daz noticed. He – or rather, Greta – turned and waved encouragingly at Rose, setting off another round of yelling and clapping from the audience.

As the song ended, Rose couldn't stop her fingers moving to begin the opening notes of another Abba favourite. She hadn't played 'Mamma Mia' on the piano since a lesson she'd given to nine year old Jamie Riley five years ago, but the notes were falling from her fingers as if she'd just practised it. Greta didn't miss a beat. The song was clearly a familiar one and the moves came naturally. Greta sauntered towards the audience, leaning forward in the leopard-skin dress, and launched into the first line, striking a pose very reminiscent of the two front women in the Swedish group. The audience went wild, cheering and hooting.

Rose played for all she was worth. Her face ached from

grinning and her throat felt strained from the singing, but she couldn't escape the thrill of excitement, the tingle just beneath her skin, the heaving nervous energy in her lungs. They ended the song, Rose trilling on the final chords and joining in the chorus, Greta waving long limbs and pursing pouting lips towards a screaming audience, rapturous with appreciation. Greta curtseyed, then held out a hand for Rose, who came over and took a tentative bow. Wolf whistles screeched from the back of the club. Someone shouted, '*Vive la Rose!*' and then Greta was easing her down, as she slid from the edge of the stage towards a pink-cheeked Pam, breathless with excitement and appreciation, who helped her down and handed her the white wine spritzer.

'Just magnificent,' Pam gasped, hugging Rose. 'A star is born.'

Rose beamed. 'Greta was something quite special, wasn't she?'

'I don't mean Greta Manchester.' Pam chimed her glass against Rose's in a gesture of celebration. 'I mean you.'

27

Della clutched her chip, the single chip worth fifty euros, and wondered what to do. The well-groomed croupier had just called for people to place their bets. The young Italian man who had won twice in succession had positioned his chips on number four. Tess pressed her hand on Della's shoulder for encouragement, but there was nothing she could do to help. On the other side, Jen grabbed her arm. Della's breath shuddered in her chest. 'I'm not sure – should I just place the bet on any number and see what happens?'

Tess whispered, 'You said it was one chance in thirty-seven. We'll lose it all.'

Jen's tiny voice came from behind her. 'Can you go back to the desk and ask them to swap it for several smaller chips?'

Tess shook her head. 'Perhaps they'll understand if we explain we made a mistake.'

'I don't know how to say that.' Della's voice was a whisper.

The croupier's face was serious and his voice was clear, professional. *'Faites vos jeux, mesdames et messieurs.'*

Della squeezed the chip hard in her hand, unsure what to

do. The moment was filled with awkwardness, embarrass-ment, the feeling that she had strayed too far somewhere and had lost her bearings.

Tess muttered, 'What shall we do, Della, Jen?'

A deep voice drifted towards them from behind Tess's shoulder. 'Please allow me to help.'

Della and Jen turned to see a tall, broad chested man smiling at Tess. He had taken her hand and lifted it towards his mouth in a gesture of greeting. Tess was staring at him. 'Vlad – Vladimir.'

He gave a small bow. He was impeccable in a grey suit, his eyes sparkling below thick brows. 'You and your friends are placing a bet? I think perhaps you cannot decide on the number to choose.'

Tess nodded. 'Yes – we bought a fifty euro chip...'

Vladimir chuckled. 'I am impressed by your panache. Fifty euros will bring a good return. If you will permit me...' He turned to Della and leaned forwards to whisper in her ear. She nodded, relief spreading over her face. Vladimir spoke to the croupier at the wheel. '*Numéro dix-huit pour madame.* Number eighteen.'

The croupier nodded as Della placed her chip down. The young Italian man smirked with confidence as the wheel began to spin fast. His girlfriend with short blonde hair rested her chin on his shoulder, her arm around his chest. The woman with the blue pendant in her cleavage had placed several chips on number twelve. Several other people had made bets. A man with an Australian accent was talking about the reliability of the Fibonacci sequence of betting and how his bet couldn't fail with number twenty-two. His companion laughed and told him to order the champagne in advance. Jen put her fingers to her throat and felt her heart beat faster there. Della made her hands into fists and put them in front of her mouth. Tess couldn't help reaching for the thick material of Vladimir's sleeve and clutching it. The wheel whirred; the ball rattled across the numbers so fast it was a blur.

The croupier ended the betting with a steady voice. *'Rien ne va plus.'* Then the wheel began to slow down, the fast thrumming of the ball becoming a tantalising rattle. The pace decreased rapidly until the metal ball was rolling in the centre, each number of the wheel clearly visible. The throng leaned forward and Della felt herself squeezed between the Australian and a large man whose aftershave smelled of disinfectant. She held her breath and felt dizzy. Jen couldn't see anything except broad backs in suits and the wide shoulders of a woman in a fur wrap, her hair piled high. Jen sneezed as the dusty scent of the fur irritated her nose. Tess gripped Vladimir's cuff.

He turned to her and winked. 'It is exciting, playing roulette. But not so if you lose.' She grinned up at him, her breathing shallow.

The ball was almost at a standstill. The numbers rolled past: number twenty, fourteen, thirty-one, nine. The ball lurched from the centre, almost pausing at number twenty-two. The Australian gave a guffaw, a winning yell. Then the ball slid forwards, finding its home. It came to rest on number eighteen. Della closed her eyes, feeling her legs become weak beneath her. Jen heard the crowd breathe out, a sigh of disappointment, a grunt of disbelief, but she couldn't see what was happening. With a determined thrust of an elbow, she shoved the fur-clad woman to one side and peeked through the gap between Della and the Australian. She could see the roulette wheel. The metal ball was nestling neatly in the groove of number eighteen. Della passed a hand across her warm brow and murmured, 'Thirty-seven to one? That means we've won…'

'One thousand, seven hundred and fifty euros, plus the fifty you bet with, based on the odds that are paid out, – so that's eighteen hundred euros.' Vladimir seemed very calm. 'A good evening's betting on one chip, I would say.'

Della faltered, almost slipping to one side. The Australian man put a hand on her waist to steady her, almost knocking Jen over. 'You OK, love?'

Della nodded. 'I need some air, please.'

Jen was at the front now, slipping her arm through Della's. She gazed at her friend and then back at the roulette wheel. 'We won. Oh, my goodness, Della – you won.'

Vladimir steered Tess, Della and Jen away from the wheel. 'Please allow me to accompany you to the bar.'

'Cocktails – how brilliant,' Tess enthused, but Vladimir put his hand on her shoulder.

'I think I should buy us all some champagne to celebrate.'

Tess looked up into his blue eyes. 'Vladimir – these are my friends, Jen and Della.'

Vladimir offered his little courteous bow. 'My pleasure.'

Jen was staring at him. 'Back there – you chose the number. How did you pick it?'

Della's face was pure disbelief. 'You whispered to me – put it all on number eighteen. It is a lucky number.' She gasped. 'How did you know that it would win?'

Vladimir shrugged. 'I did not know.' He smiled at Tess. 'But I am a lucky man, where money is concerned. In love, I have no luck, but in investments, it always seems to work for me. Besides…' he gave a soft chuckle '… I have played at that wheel before and I understand it well. I have – shall we say – a strategy.'

They reached the bar by way of a wide staircase and Vladimir led them to a table with plush red seats beneath a glittering chandelier. He stopped to talk to a waiter, speaking to the smartly dressed young man quietly.

Della breathed out. 'What just happened back there? I can't believe it.'

'Vladimir happened.' Tess was smiling.

Jen clapped her hands. 'We won. It was insane. Our first try at the roulette wheel and we won. Just wait until I tell Eddie. He'll be so impressed.'

Vladimir joined them, sitting next to Tess. He nodded politely towards Della. 'I have arranged for the money you won to be brought to you as cash. Meanwhile, we can have something to drink, to celebrate your success.'

'You're very good at all this, aren't you?' Della asked.

'The casino manager is a client of mine. He will put your money in an envelope and—'

'No, I mean – you know how to behave in a casino. You're very sure of yourself.' Della was impressed

'I suppose I am.' Vladimir leaned back in his seat. A young woman arrived, wearing a black dress and carrying a tray with champagne and four glasses. Vladimir smiled at her. *'Merci, Mireille.'* He watched her pour the sparkling wine into the glasses. 'I am an accountant. I have an accountancy business – my son runs it mostly now – and many of my clients in Paris know me well. And let me say, I am quite good with money matters, with numbers. I have been lucky in my life.' He raised a glass. *'Santé.* To you, Tess, and to your friends.' He lifted the glass in Jen's direction. 'And to your forthcoming marriage, *madame. Na Zdorovie. Cheers.'*

Tess sat back in her seat and smiled. The champagne bubbles dissolved on her tongue, sending little bursts of sharpness to tickle her nose. She took a breath. 'Thank you, Vladimir. Thank you for coming to help us at the roulette table. We were like three fishes on a hook, twisting and gaping with no idea where to wriggle.'

Vladimir chuckled. 'I am glad to be of service, Tess.'

Jen took out her phone. 'I'm going to text Eddie now – I'm going to tell him we won, first try.' She thumbed carefully and sent the text. A message had arrived from Pam; Jen decided she'd look at it later. She held out her phone and took a selfie, a photo of the group at the table with the champagne, and sent it to Pam.

Jen put her phone away and sat up straight. 'Oh, I've just remembered – I've brought fifty euros too. Should we go back to the table and try our luck again?'

Vladimir shook his head. 'I think we have already used up our lucky chip. I'm not sure the manager will be too pleased with us if we win two times with two chips.'

'You've bought us champagne again, Vladimir.' Della frowned, thinking. 'We should be buying you champagne. You have been so kind, helping us.'

'It is you who have been kind, spending your time with me.' Vladimir loosened his tie. 'Show me another man here who is sitting with three wonderful women, drinking good champagne. Tonight, I feel like a king.'

'So, Vladimir.' Tess clutched her glass and sat forward in her seat. 'How long have you lived in Paris? What part of Russia did you say you were from? Moscow? Tell me all about yourself.'

Vladimir shifted in his seat until he was facing Tess. 'Well, my dear, I came to Paris over thirty years ago with the dream of making my life here. I was married then, and my son, Vassilly, was ten years old...'

Della caught Jen's eye and winked. Jen nodded. 'Shall we pop to the ladies' room, Della? I think we can have a little stroll around too, maybe stretch our legs a little.'

As Jen and Della sauntered away, arm in arm, Tess and Vladimir were leaning close, their heads together, chattering. Neither noticed the others had gone.

* * *

In Monty's club, it was almost one o'clock. The bar was closed and the punters were leaving. Monty was standing in the doorway, relaxed in the low-cut dress, speaking loudly in several languages, hugging clients and waving as they left. At the table in the corner by the stage, Rose and Pam were sitting with Daz, now scrubbed and relaxed in a white T-shirt and faded jeans. He swigged from a bottle of sparkling water.

'So, my friend, Simon, left for Amsterdam. We were really popular here – we were a duo act, Greta Manchester and Ashley De La Zouch. We were top of the bill and Si was proper funny. He did all the jokes with the punters so, when he left, I suppose they thought I was a bit of a disappointment by myself.'

'You were brilliant,' Pam told him.

'I thought you were very good.' Rose patted his hand encouragingly. 'The miming was wonderful, but you have a really strong singing voice.'

'Thanks, Rose. Well, I had to carry on working, didn't I?' Daz scratched his head. 'But I was right worried – I thought it was all going downhill for me. Monty's been very good, keeping me on here, but the punters loved us as a duo and some of them were right unhappy with me just doing my stuff by myself. I thought, Well, Daz, you could end up being out on your ear. If they don't like me, I can't work, can I? Then what?'

Pam grinned. 'Then Rose turned up.'

Daz threw his hands in the air. 'I know. Out of the blue. My guardian angel.' He took her hand in his, holding it affectionately. 'I'll never forget what you did for me tonight, Rose. It was right funny, though, how you just scrambled onto the stage and sat at the piano, just natural like you'd done it all your life, and started playing Abba.'

'But you responded so well, Daz.' Pam met his eyes. 'You were so quick to pick it up.'

Daz guffawed. 'I'm a proper pro, me, Pam. But honestly – when Rose started to sing the backing vocal bit, you know – I was gobsmacked.' He burst out laughing. 'I thought it was Agnetha up there with me on the stage. I was flabbergasted.'

'You looked in control. It was really impressive.' Pam looked at Rose. 'And you were a superstar.'

Rose put a hand to her head. 'I'm not sure what came over me. I just felt so – you know – annoyed, listening to the crowd shouting at you, Daz, and I thought, Right, I'm going to help him out. And I did.' Rose sighed loudly. 'And do you know what? I haven't enjoyed myself so much in ages.'

Pam took out her phone. A message had come in from Jen. She decided to look at it later. Daz gazed over his shoulder. The club was almost empty. Monty was at the door, saying goodbye to a large balding man in pale clothes and round spectacles. The man waved over at Daz. *'Au revoir, mon ami. A demain.'*

Daz looked up and lifted a hand. *'A bientôt, Maurice.'*

Rose glanced at the portly gentlemen. 'Who's Maurice?'

Daz picked up his jacket, tattered faded denim. 'He's one of the performers – he was on earlier. Elton Joan. Lovely fella – he has a heart of gold, Maurice.'

'Maurice was Elton Joan?' Rose shook her head. A thought had just come to her. 'Daz – all the singers in the show tonight – were they all men?'

Daz laughed. 'You're kidding me, Rose. Have you never been to a drag club before?'

'No, never.' Rose pulled a surprised face.

Pam lifted her phone and pushed it into her handbag. 'We should be getting back to the hotel.'

Daz clambered to his feet. 'I'll come with you to the street, make sure you get a taxi. Then I've to come back and have a chat with Monty. She's asked me to stay behind for a few drinks.' He gave Rose a hopeful look. 'I can ring you though, can I? It's been such fun working with you.'

Rose nodded. She felt suddenly very tired. Her legs ached – she was exhausted. The excitement of the performance had wearied her. She offered Daz a smile. 'Yes, please do ring me. Oh, Daz, it's been such fun.' Daz hugged her, lifting her from her feet, and Rose breathed out, drained of energy. As he put her gently down, she wondered if she'd ever be the same person again.

28

No one noticed as Claudette poured black coffee into cups and placed a tower of warm croissants in the centre of the table. Everyone was talking at the same time and no one was listening.

'I sent Eddie a text last night that we'd won almost two thousand euros. He told me he'd made in excess of a hundred dollars yesterday so I trump him.' Jen was elated.

'You should have seen her.' Pam waved her hands. 'On the piano, playing Abba's songs – and singing too. She was incredible.'

'Vladimir is seventy-three. He is divorced, three times. His first wife was called Galina. She was Vassilly's mother. Then he married a woman called Tamara who was an architect. She went back to Russia and he married a Parisian woman called Mathilde who turned out to be very money-grabbing...' Tess noticed the croissants and picked one up.

Rose reached for the coffee cup. 'I mean, they mime to all the songs but you'd never believe it wasn't live. It's called lip-sync. And I've never seen such glamorous women. I know it's all wigs and frocks but it was astonishing how lovely they all are. And Daz actually sang live – he has a really good voice.'

'Eddie didn't seem pleased that we went to the casino...'

'Sylvester will be surprised we won all that money – I can't wait to tell him when we're back. I have it in an envelope in my bag – Vladimir counted it out to make sure it was all there. What do you want to do with it, Rose?'

'... of course, Eddie is gambling again today. I don't know why he isn't bored with it. The casino is great but once was enough for me, just for the experience, to say we...'

'I haven't even been for a run this morning. Rose and I got in so late. We slept like logs after all those white wine spritzers – I'm sure we had four...'

'I wish Alan had his beautiful manners. Vladimir is an absolute gentleman. I don't think I've ever met someone who is so refined, so cultured and so knowledgeable about...'

'I'd love to buy the white piano and take it home with me to practise on. It sounded so good, the tone was so...'

'If we're shopping today, I'd like to buy Sylvester a Paris sweatshirt...'

They stopped, all at once, and Jen burst out laughing. 'What are we all like?' She grinned at the faces around her, all so happy, so full of their holiday mischief, and she remembered a photograph she had discovered on her phone earlier that morning. 'Do you know, Pam, I saw the photo you sent of Rose on stage last night. It was incredible.'

Pam nodded. 'And the selfie you sent – the photo of the three of you and the glasses of champagne. Wow.'

'I wish we could have gone to both. The casino and the club.' Della sighed. 'What a good time we're having here – aren't we?'

'I love Paris,' Rose said.

Tess agreed. 'I know. I don't want to go home.'

'Right.' Jen lifted her coffee cup. 'Today is all about shopping.'

'And being five again instead of a three and a two,' Della suggested.

'I've booked a Moroccan feast tonight,' Rose reminded everyone. 'With Chafik. Best table in the restaurant.'

Pam wagged a finger as Tess reached for a second croissant. 'Maybe we should skip lunch or just have a smoothie somewhere – so we'll be really hungry.'

Jen put her elbows on the table and rested her chin on her hands. 'Tomorrow is the last full day.' She sounded disappointed. 'We need to plan it out properly.'

'Tomorrow night is Jen's big hen party,' Tess reminded them.

Rose was thoughtful. 'We should all talk about what we want to do... plan where we're going... We could do that over lunch, even if we're just having a smoothie?'

'What about last night's competition?' Tess waved her arms in excitement, lifted by the sudden memory. 'We were going to decide which place won – the casino or the nightclub.'

'Ten out of ten for the casino.' Jen giggled.

'At least ten – maybe even ten and a half.' Tess nodded and Della agreed.

Pam raised her voice. 'You should have seen our Rose, though. I say ten out of ten for Monty's.'

'We're all winners,' Rose offered, making the peace. 'A great night was had by all.' She put a fist firmly on the table. 'Talking of winners, Della, I want to divide up the winnings from the casino. Now, here's what I thought. We have eighteen hundred euros. Now, my arithmetic isn't good, but I thought if we divide it by six, we get three hundred euros each towards our shopping trip, and I'll put some of mine to a good charity. That's fair. What do you think?'

'The charity idea's great,' Pam said.

Jen was confused. 'Why are you dividing it six ways? There are five of us.'

'Della gets double.' Rose smiled. 'She put the bet on. I mean – I'm happy to give her all of it if you like.'

Della put her hands up. 'No, I want to share – we should all be equal.'

'You should have double,' Jen insisted. 'You put the bet on. It was terrifying. I couldn't have done it.'

'I agree.' Tess's voice was loud with excitement. 'Della gets double.'

'Three hundred euros is far too much to go shopping with...' Pam sighed. 'I'm going to put half into a charity...'

Tess had a sudden thought. 'You should buy Elvis something really nice.'

'We can all treat ourselves.' Jen patted Rose's hand. 'Thank you, Rose.'

'No, thank Della,' Rose asserted. 'We'll enjoy ourselves in the shops now, thanks to her.'

'Pardon, please?' Claudette was holding up the coffee jug. 'More coffee for anyone?' She looked steadily from face to face. 'Also I have to tell you that Madame Tess Watkins...'

Tess sat upright and grinned. 'That's me – Tess Watkins.'

'You must please go to Reception as soon as you can. There is a message for you.'

Tess frowned. 'I don't understand.'

'What kind of message?' Della asked.

'We'll all go to Reception together, shall we?' Jen suggested.

'Now.' Tess was standing, suddenly alarmed. 'Oh, my goodness – you don't think something's happened to Alan?'

Pam was on her feet. 'Or Elvis? We should go straight away.'

The five friends trooped to Reception, where Marion was talking on the phone, impeccably dressed in a black suit and red blouse. She held up a finger to indicate that she'd be finished in a moment and continued to converse on the phone. She put the receiver down with a smile. 'Good morning.'

'You have a message for me?' Tess asked. Her mind was racing. Marion might have just been on the phone talking to the French police. Something awful might have happened in Exmouth and the English police had contacted the French ones to find Tess. She wondered how she'd feel if Marion told her that her husband had been in an accident. Tess was confused – she didn't know. She'd be devastated, of course – but another presiding worry was that she'd have to go home early, cut her holiday short. Immediately, she felt guilty – and worried about Alan at the same time.

Marion frowned. 'A message?'

Tess put on her most hopeful face. 'For Tess Watkins? Claudette mentioned at breakfast.' She felt her four friends move closer to her, a gesture of physical solidarity. Della put a hand on her shoulder.

Marion's face suddenly changed from serious to pleased. 'Ah, yes – one moment – I have it here, for you.' She turned round to bend down and when she stood again, she was carrying a huge bouquet of red roses. She handed them to Tess. 'This came for you.'

Tess held the bouquet away from her body. 'It's not my birthday.' She frowned. 'Alan doesn't send me flowers.' She laughed, a bubbling sound of surprise. 'Perhaps he's missing me.'

Jen's eyes twinkled. 'Red roses? There must be a dozen of them. I bet they're not from Alan.'

'There must be a card with it, some sort of message.' Della put out a finger to touch one of the roses. Its petal was soft as a baby's skin.

Tess found a small envelope, a card inside, and read aloud. '"For my friend, Tess, thanking you for the pleasure of your company last night. I would be delighted if you would have dinner with me at the Colombe Blanche this evening. I have taken the liberty of reserving a table for eight o'clock. Yours..."'

'Vladimir,' Jen and Della chorused together, clapping their hands.

'I can't go.' Tess shook her head. Marion was watching her.

The receptionist took a breath. 'Most people in Paris would die to have dinner at the Colombe Blanche. It is very exclusive – very hard to get a table there. I myself have never been...'

'I'll have to say no.' Tess looked at her friends. 'We're having a night out together at the Moroccan restaurant, at El Madani.'

'Does Vladimir know you're married?' Jen asked.

Pam shrugged. 'Do you want to go? It's an experience, Tess.'

'We can all go out together tomorrow night,' Rose suggested.

Jen agreed. 'Tomorrow's our big hen night out. I don't

mind if you have dinner with Vladimir tonight. In fact, I think you should. But would Alan be offended?'

'Don't tell him,' Della blurted and the friends stared at her, surprised.

'You'd never cheat on Sylvester,' Jen whispered.

'I know. But Tess isn't cheating. She's having dinner with a man who likes her – they get on well.' Della frowned. 'And what an experience – dinner at one of the best restaurants in Paris. He's just a friend – a nice man who likes your company, Tess. I mean – we're only here for two more days. Why not go?' Della's eyes flashed. 'And you don't need to tell Alan.'

'That's true,' Rose agreed. 'To hell with Alan.'

'I'm not sure...' Tess hugged the roses. 'It's all of you I'm thinking of. We should all be together, having fun at El Madani, joking with Chafik. I mean, dinner with Vladimir would be lovely but—'

'Then go,' Pam insisted.

Jen folded her arms. 'I tell you what – we'll get you dressed up and send you off in a taxi, then we'll go to El Madani, have a lovely evening and meet you back in our room to hear all about it.'

'It's an experience, Tess.' Pam put an arm round her friend.' You have to go.'

'Are you sure?' Tess was quiet for a moment, thinking, and then a loud grunt of disapproval came from the other side of the reception desk.

Marion leaned over towards the friends, wagging a finger, a stern expression on her face. 'If I had been invited to *la* Colombe Blanche for dinner by a man who sent me those roses, I would put on my best dress and go, and I wouldn't care about my husband at all.'

Tess grinned. 'That's made up my mind. I'm having

dinner with Vladimir tonight at the Colombe Blanche. You're all so sweet. Thanks, girls.' She laughed out loud as she found herself hugged in a five-way embrace and squealed with joy. 'Don't squash my flowers...'

29

'I can't buy this – it's almost three hundred euros. That's all my winnings.'

Jen winked at Tess. 'If it's from your winnings, think of it as a free dress.'

The women stared at Tess in the frock, gazing at herself in the long mirror: a black and gold cocktail dress that came to just above her knees. The chic middle-aged assistant in the black suit hovered, watching them carefully. They were the only customers in the little shop just off the main street, its orange sign proclaiming its name, Le Tilt. Della put out her fingers and touched the material.

'You look gorgeous, Tess.'

'Is it too tight? Is the neckline too low?'

Rose grunted. 'I've seen lower.' Her mind slipped back to Monty at the club, with the figure-hugging dress, the neckline plunging to her navel.

'Is my bum too big in this dress?' Tess wailed.

'No, it's not – you look perfect.' Pam shook her head. She'd never paid anything like three hundred euros for a dress – the two frocks she owned rarely came out of her wardrobe. But she loved the way Tess's face flushed with excitement, how the dress fitted her so well and gave her an air of sophistication.

Tess's knees were shaking. She loved the dress – she'd known, the minute she set eyes on it, that it was just what she wanted to wear at the Colombe Blanche. And, now she had tried it on and was staring at herself in the mirror, she wanted to buy it. But Alan would say it was a waste of money, it was too expensive. Alan would say that three hundred euros would buy him a decent golf iron. Alan would say that she was overdressed.

Tess sighed. 'Do I look like mutton dressed as lamb?'

'Lamb is overrated.' Rose, Della, Pam and Jen chorused and fell about laughing.

'You look lovely, Tess,' Della purred.

'Vlad will be knocked out.' Jen nodded.

'You'll be the belle of the Colombe Blanche,' Pam agreed.

Rose folded her arms. 'Just buy the bloody dress, Tess.'

An hour later, the five friends were sitting in a sushi bar. Tess had the dress and shoes in stylish carrier bags. Della had bought several items for Sylvester, including the Paris sweat-shirt. Pam had bought Elvis a dog bowl with his name on and etched pictures of the Eiffel Tower in black, and several old books from the Marché Vernaison. They had spent most of the time marvelling at the three hundred stalls, Jen looking at all the second-hand jewellery. She had bought a little glass representation of an old French car for Eddie. It had cost her a lot of money but Eddie was worth it. The salesman, his cigarette in his mouth, had assured her that it was a perfect glass carving of a 1959 Renault Caravelle Cabriolet. She thought Eddie would love it. Jen imagined him in her house, their house, unwrapping the soft tissue, smiling at her and pressing his lips against hers, then handing her a present he'd brought back from Las Vegas, an expensive necklace, perhaps. It would be wonderful to see him again. And he'd be so delighted to see her, kissing her neck as he wrapped the diamonds around her throat, murmuring her name in a voice thick with desire.

Tess found a black beret for Alan and said it might look good on him while he was on the golf course. She leapt at a set of wooden Russian dolls, buying them despite Pam telling her they weren't good value at fifteen euros. Rose had bought several CDs, excited by finding a copy of Fauré's 'Requiem' and Rameau's 'Hippolyte et Aricie'. Pam was delighted to find a copy of Abba's Greatest Hits and, despite Rose's protestations of, 'I thought you didn't like Abba,' she bought it to remind her of the wonderful evening at Monty's.

They sat in the small sushi bar feeling exhausted, nibbling at a selection of rolls. Della and Jen were skilful with chopsticks. Tess's California roll fell from the slack pincers onto the tiled floor. Pam used her fingers to lift and nibble her avocado sushi, with an expertise that showed she'd done it many times before. Tess and Rose thought it better to copy Pam and eat their sushi as finger food, although the wasabi made tears appear in Rose's eyes. She picked up her mobile phone from the table and smiled. 'I have a message about tomorrow night from Daz.'

Pam leaned forwards. 'What does he say?'

'Good news.' Rose dabbed at her mouth. The wasabi made her lips tingle. 'We have a table reserved right next to the stage. Monty is delighted we're having a hen party there. Daz says she'll take good care of us. Daz says Sunday nights are always a riot at Monty's.'

'I'm so looking forward to it.' Della stared at her phone. 'Still nothing back from Sylvester. That is so typical of him. I have to do everything at home that involves a computer. I wish that man would learn to use technology.'

'You must miss him.' Jen patted her hand.

Della sighed. 'Of course I do. I wish he could share all this with me. But I'm determined we'll come again, just the two of us in Paris – maybe in the autumn.' She offered her friends a grin. 'And I'm so glad to be here with you all.'

Pam nodded. 'To think I nearly didn't come. I'm so glad I did.' She caught Tess's eye. 'Elvis is still fine with Alan?'

'Oh, yes.' Tess spluttered a giggle. 'I think Alan's enjoying my absence, golf every day without being nagged, and Elvis is a favourite with everyone at the golf course.'

Pam's face clouded. 'Is the woman still walking him every day? Is he having lots of fresh air? He's not getting wet in the rain?'

'He's fine, Pam.' Tess pushed the last of her sushi away. She seemed to have lost her appetite for the food. 'Alan just said everyone loves Elvis there and everyone makes a fuss of him. I bet he's having a whale of a time.' She paused for a moment, thinking. 'I hope it will all be all right tonight at the restaurant with Vladimir. I mean, I hope I don't do anything stupid, or make a fool of myself.'

'Relax, Tess – you'll enjoy it.' Della reached over and patted her hand.

'You're going there for all five of us.' Jen gave her an encouraging smile. 'We'll all be desperate to hear about it.'

Rose agreed. 'Vladimir must be a really nice man to treat you to dinner at such an expensive place.'

Pam frowned. 'I hope his intentions are honourable.'

'What do you mean?' Tess's face was anxious.

'I'm being silly – ignore me.' Pam ran a hand through her pixie cut. 'You're in a restaurant, a public place. You'll be fine. Only...' She stared into the corner, thinking, then her eyes moved back to Tess's face. 'It might not be a good idea to go back to his home afterwards.'

'For coffee...' Jen giggled, remembering Eddie. Her mind slipped from the night he proposed to her to thoughts of their honeymoon in Lyme Regis. It was only a week away. The thought came to her with several emotions – excitement, nervousness and a feeling in the pit of her stomach that she couldn't identify. 'That is, unless you want to, Tess...'

'Tess is married, Jen.' Rose was unimpressed.

'She's in Paris having fun.' Della met Tess's anxious gaze and winked. 'Don't worry, Tess. Have your meal with Vladimir and then take a taxi back to the hotel. You'll be fine. He's just a lovely man who is friendly and generous and likes you.'

Tess was alarmed. 'But what if he wants to go somewhere afterwards – a casino, a club?'

'Play it by ear,' Jen suggested.

'Keep in touch with us by phone,' Rose advised.

'Or don't go anywhere with him – just eat the pudding, drink the wine and come back to the hotel,' Pam warned.

Della laughed, a gurgling of bubbles. 'You've been alive for seven decades, Tess. You are a big girl now. Do what you want. Go and enjoy yourself. I'm sure you'll be fine.'

Pam took out her purse to pay the bill. 'What shall we do now?'

Jen produced her spreadsheet from her handbag with an exaggerated flourish, pretending to consult the list carefully. 'Boat trip down the Seine. Everyone agreed?'

'Agreed,' Rose replied. 'The river, the views, the fresh air –
how lovely. That'll give us an appetite for dinner.'

Tess shivered, her body already prickling with nerves.
'I've no appetite at all for dinner. I don't even know why I'm
going tonight. I'll be terrified.'

* * *

Pam had suggested a hop-on-hop-off river cruise but Jen had
spotted a huge boat with a glass top and sides and everyone
agreed that it looked like the best way to see Paris from the
Seine. The sky was pale blue, crammed with faded clouds,
and there was a light breeze, so Rose suggested the friends
find a seat downstairs near the window so that they all had a
good view of the cityscape. The boat was packed with
tourists, so Jen and Della found themselves sitting together,
Jen's face pressed against a window while a noisy family filled
the spaces beside them. Pam, Rose and Tess sat behind,
gazing into the tin-grey water.

Tess closed her eyes, feeling the lilt of the river beneath
them, and the sway of the boat seemed to remind her that
she should try to be calm, slow down the heart-pounding
panic in her chest and enjoy the holiday. Today was Saturday
and that meant they would be flying home in two days. She'd
see Alan and then normality would return: Alan would be
away at golf all day, there would be endless evenings staring
at the television screen, Tess making his meals, bringing him
a cup of tea while he watched the sports channels. She
breathed in deeply. Paris felt different. She felt different. In
Paris, Tess was an individual, a person in her own right. She
was Tess, not the diminishing half of Alan-and-Tess. She
frowned and wondered where her marriage had gone wrong,

how she and Alan had become so lazy, how they now required so little affection from each other, drifting from one day to another with no purpose, no conversation, no real love.

Their girls, Lisa and Gemma, had families of their own. Gemma and her husband, Andrew, were well off, their three children in private education, all in their teens. Lisa was by herself now, independent: 'between partners' was her phrase. Her son, Richie, was twenty-one, living in Edinburgh and working with wildlife conservation. Tess saw more of Lisa than she did Gemma – they had more in common. Tess wished she could talk to Lisa now; tell her about the hens' trip to Paris. Lisa would be so impressed.

Tess imagined telling her daughter about Vladimir. In her imagination, she saw them drinking coffee in Exeter, Tess chattering about her gold and black dress, about dining in the Colombe Blanche. She imagined Lisa, her short glossy red hair, her slender fingers with the bitten nails, a habit she'd had since she was a child, wide-eyed and impressed as Tess described the sumptuous food, the champagne, the delightful company. In her mind, Tess was telling Lisa how Vladimir offered to take Tess back to Hotel Sirène in his Bentley – Tess had no idea why Vladimir would drive a Bentley – and how he'd take a detour, driving up to a hill on the outskirts of the city, and they'd sit, looking down at Paris, at the Eiffel Tower with its shining beam, the dark city lit by the shimmering lights, and he'd put an arm around her and she'd sigh. The feeling would come over her that she was safe, cared for and important. Tess wondered how she'd feel if Vladimir tried to kiss her. She suddenly felt cold, opened her eyes and stared through the glass window. The boat had drifted beneath a bridge and they were lost for a few seconds in a confusion of glistening water and shifting shadows.

Rose had been leaning out of the window, taking photos on her phone. She wanted to see all of Paris. She wanted to see all the sights, to keep them and remember everything when she was back in Exmouth. She wanted to be able to keep Paris close to her. She thought with a smile that if Paris were a photograph; she would carry it next to her heart. Paris was a strange city, filled with so many unknown people and places, but Paris also belonged just to her. She felt at home in Paris – it was a bizarre thought to have, but Rose felt that this was the most natural air she had ever breathed. She took more photos: a curved bridge with stone-carved gargoyles twisted through the arch; a tall statue of a golden creature, its wings spread; a domed building with a tiny tricolour flag at the top, furled in the breeze. Rose sighed. This was her Paris – she was a part of its fabric and now she was being carried on its waters, borne from one historical site to another. Rose felt the history, the traditions of bygone ages, the pride, the culture, seep into her bones.

Pam was lost in thought. She could see artists painting the Seine from the top of a bridge and she remembered Marie-Laure, the woman whose painting she had promised to buy. Tomorrow she would meet the artist and take the painting as promised. Pam knew exactly where she'd put it in her home – over the fireplace, where it could be enjoyed from the sofa where Pam and Elvis snuggled after dinner. Pam smiled at the thought of seeing Elvis again, and her mind drifted back to Marie-Laure on the bridge, the solid block detail of her oil painting, the smudges of dappled colour of the sunset. Pam recalled the fortune teller in the green dress, Elodie, the intense glittering eyes, and her hushed words. *You who have the secret. You need to let it go from you. It is time.* Pam squeezed her eyes to block out the uncomfortable memories that flooded back.

'Look.' Della squealed with delight. 'The Eiffel Tower. The Place du Trocadéro. We've been there. But look how beautiful it is from here.'

'Let me take your picture, Della – with Paris in the background. Pass me your phone.' Jen took the mobile and pointed it at Della, framed her smiling face, and then took several more. The five friends huddled together, with Tess, Rose and Pam in the seat behind, wriggling close and grinning their widest smiles, while Jen stretched out her arm and narrowed her eyes to check all five of them were included in the snap. The others took out their cameras in turn and photos were taken. Della sat comfortably back in her seat, gazing at one of her photos: five happy women with their arms round each other and she, Della, in the middle with the Eiffel Tower sticking out like an antenna from the top of her hair. She giggled softly. 'Sylvester will love that one.'

30

'Ladies, my ladies, come and sit over here, please. I bring you wine – the best wine from France tonight, from the south-west region. You will taste the sunshine in each glass. Please sit here, most comfortable seats, and I will bring you the menu. But tonight I have made a tagine especially, if you like it, with couscous and dates and apricots, pomegranate and cinnamon and lamb. And for you, *madame*...' Chafik turned to Pam '... I make with artichokes, preserved lemon, my special spices, garlic, mushrooms, green vegetables.'

Pam sat down, smiled up at Chafik, her hair still damp from the shower. 'That sounds lovely, Chafik.'

'I'd like that too – rather than the lamb,' Della agreed.

Chafik's face was round with happiness, his smile broad. 'But first the wine: a delicious full-bodied red, no? I bring you a bottle of vin de Pays de la Haute Vallée de l'Aude.'

Rose nodded. 'Yes, please – one bottle to begin with, for us all.' She turned to her friends. 'Just listen to me ordering wine like an expert. A few weeks ago I hardly drank at all.'

'We've corrupted you, Rose.' Jen giggled.

Rose shook her head sadly. 'I'm not sure how I will cope back in Exmouth. Drinking wine is for Paris, with friends, not alone in my little house with a meal for one. Perhaps I can change? I hope I shall be able to cook couscous and have wine with it just for myself instead of skipping meals or having cheese on toast. What's that old saying? "Today Lucullus dines with Lucullus." I hope I can do that when I'm back home.'

'What does that mean – the Lucullus thing?' Jen asked.

Pam's face shone. 'That we should enjoy our food just as much if we dine alone as if we were with others. It's a motto of mine, too – I don't want to eat cereal out of a box or just grab a sandwich because I am single. It's important to take care of ourselves and treat ourselves well.'

Jen shook her head. 'I think that's one of the reasons I want to marry Eddie. It's nice to have someone to cook for, to share things with.'

'You don't have to marry someone to share with them.' Rose frowned.

'I enjoy cooking and sharing food with Sylvester,' Della agreed. 'But sharing fun is far more important. We share things all the time.' She beamed at Rose. 'And now it's nice to share this lovely meal with all of you. Poor Sylvester won't be dining well with Sylvester tonight, I bet. He'll be eating a casserole from the freezer or...' she glanced at Pam '... cereal out of the box.'

Chafik was pouring wine into glasses. Della sipped hers. 'You're right, Chafik – I can taste sunshine.' She giggled.

Rose was thoughtful. 'Things are changing. I mean – this break to Paris with you all has made me – I don't know – stop and re-evaluate things.'

'In what way?' Della asked.

'At home, I was just wasting away.' Rose shook her head sadly. 'I don't want to sound morbid, but it was as if I was just waiting for death. Bernard had gone – the rhythm of my life as I knew it had gone – and I was just treading water. I needed to move forward but I couldn't see it.'

Jen shuddered. 'That's what the fortune teller said – Elodie said that – she said you were on the brink of a big change.'

'I don't believe in fortune tellers – but maybe I am changing.' Rose sipped her wine. 'Maybe things are changing and I'm ready to go with the flow.'

'But if Elodie was right about you – what about me?' Jen raised anxious brows. 'She told me I couldn't change anything even if I wanted to. But I'm just about to get married – I'm about to change my life completely.'

'Perhaps she meant you are happy now and your life with Eddie will be just as happy?' Della soothed. 'Perhaps she meant you are not going to change the positive attitude to life you have.'

'Perhaps I won't be happy with Eddie, though.' Jen was alarmed.

Rose shrugged. 'I wouldn't set too much stock by what a fortune teller says.'

Della wasn't sure. 'She told me to hold onto what I have. All I have is Sylvester and my boys in London. I'll hold onto them with every fibre of my being.'

'But they'd never leave you.' Jen reached for her wine. 'She's got me thinking. What if she's right – I was lonely before and, if I marry Eddie, I'll still be lonely?'

'If?' Della's eyebrows shot up. 'The wedding's in a week's time.'

Rose waved Chafik over, ready to order more wine. He

placed small trays of olives, dates and walnuts on the table. She helped herself to a green olive. 'I wouldn't even think about the fortune teller again.'

Jen turned to Pam. 'You've been quiet – what do you think, Pam?'

Pam gave a brief grin. 'I don't know – I'd forgotten all about the fortune teller.'

Della's eyes were wide. 'She said something very strange to you, Pam – she said it was time to let go of a secret.'

Pam sighed. 'Oh, well – I suppose we all have secrets.' She laughed, too loudly. 'I wonder which one of mine she was referring to – I have so many.'

Della was watching her carefully. Jen reached for an olive and sighed. 'Well, I'm worried about it, about what she said to me. And what did she say about Tess?'

'I can't remember.' Pam shrugged.

'She said she'd know the meaning of love.' Della's eyes were wide.

'Well, that's rubbish.' Rose guffawed. 'She's married to Alan and he seems a strange sort of man – nice to her one minute and offhand the next, more interested in his golf. Della's the one who knows what true love is – you and Sylvester are still loved up after all these years.'

'I'm very lucky. And Pam...' Della said generously. 'She and Elvis are soul mates.'

'What about me?' Jen made a little fist, her eyes misting. 'I ought to be the one who knows what love is. I'm about to get married. But I'm a bit worried... Eddie...'

'What about Eddie?' Rose asked.

'He texted me earlier – he was a bit off with me. He said we'd all been foolish going to the casino and winning on the roulette – that it wasn't the place for a group of older women.

He said it was unwise to be drinking champagne with strangers. He wrote this long message about women of my age and decorum.' She breathed out. 'He sounded grumpy. I expect it's the distance between us. He's probably missing me.'

'I'm sure it's just the normal problem with text messages,' Pam suggested. 'You can never pick up what people really mean – their tone – in texts.'

Rose muttered under her breath, 'Eddie's an idiot.'

Jen put small hands to her mouth. 'It was like he was really unhappy with me – I've never seen that side of him before.'

Della sighed. 'Love can be complicated.'

'It certainly can,' Jen agreed. 'We've never had a lover's tiff before.' She thought for a moment. 'We haven't really been together long enough.'

Rose looked up at Chafik, poised with his notepad, about to take their order. 'I think we'll have more wine, please, Chafik – we need some sunshine in a glass. And I'll have the couscous and the tagine with lemony artichokes.' She gazed at her friends. 'This is going to be such a feast. I wonder how Tess is managing with her haute cuisine.'

Jen grinned mischievously. 'I wonder how Tess is managing with Vladimir...'

* * *

Tess was staring at the menu. Vladimir was staring at Tess. He breathed out deeply. 'You are a vision, my dear. The dress suits you well. It brings me happiness that you bought it especially for our dinner.'

Tess grinned. 'I didn't have a thing to wear.' She waved

towards the menu. 'And I'm not sure I'll be able to have anything to eat. I don't understand this menu at all – neither the French nor the English version.'

'Allow me to explain.' Vladimir reached over to pat her hand. 'This is a seasonal tasting menu. There are five courses made by five different top chefs. They are small courses – tasters, if you like – but a feast for the eyes and the palette. The wine that accompanies each course is chosen specially to complement it.'

Tess clapped her hands. 'It sounds lovely –do you know, I'm really hungry now. I've hardly eaten all day.' She was thoughtful for a while. Sitting opposite Vladimir, she felt relaxed in this beautiful restaurant where everything was modern and clean and white – the walls, the tablecloths and chairs. Huge black and chrome Anglepoise lamps hung overhead, projecting a soft yellow beam onto the tables below. The bar at the far end was finished completely in chrome, with black seats and a grey brick wall behind. Everything oozed modern efficiency and style.

Vladimir was handsome in a dark grey suit and a red tie, which he had loosened as he sat back in his seat. Tess was no longer anxious – she felt warm with anticipation. 'So, what are we going to eat, Vladimir?'

He smiled at her. 'Our first course is a sort of mousse of vegetables. Then we will sample the artichoke and caviar. The third taster is ricotta and salsify with asparagus and lavender foam. Then we have the chicken, endive and garlic course and finally the rhubarb and sorrel cream.' He watched her face carefully, seeming to enjoy the fact that her eyes had widened. 'All with excellent wine.'

'It sounds lovely, Vladimir.' She leaned forward. 'Do you come here all the time?'

'Often.' He noticed the waiter at his elbow, a slim young man in a white shirt, and nodded. 'Thank you, Michel.' Vladimir turned his attention back to Tess. 'But dining alone is no fun.'

'Why do you dine alone?' Tess blinked in astonishment. 'There must be lots of glamorous young women who would be delighted to be your dinner date.'

'Ah.' Vladimir sipped his wine. 'I am a cautious man. Yes, I am sure many women would like to have dinner here. But they would not like my company so much as they would like to be dining in this restaurant.'

'I don't understand.'

He sighed. 'It is better to dine alone than with a companion who cares only that you will pay the bill.' He met Tess's eyes. 'That is why I am here with you tonight, Tess. You are a special sort of woman, the sort a man does not meet often in his lifetime.'

'In what way?' Tess felt her skin tingle; she was flattered.

'You have such a personality – like bubbles in a champagne glass. The first time I saw you, when I spoke to you in the jazz club and thought you were a Russian woman, I felt I knew you. And I was right. You have the face of an angel, yes, but when you smile, it is like the world bursts with happiness.'

Tess made a face of mock-horror. 'Are you sure it's me you're talking about?'

He chuckled. 'And so modest. The sort of women I meet in Paris, they worry that they must have a perfect appearance and they always ask what things cost to buy. You are different – you are joyous, natural. You are funny and you make me feel happy to be alive.'

Tess stared into his eyes, her face suddenly sad. 'I'm a married woman, Vladimir.'

'I thought so.' He lifted up her hand for a moment, gazing at the ring on her wedding finger, and he was quiet, then he spoke, his voice a rumble. 'Does he make you happy, your husband?'

'No, not really.' Tess scanned her heart for feelings of unfairness, disloyalty or unkindness towards Alan. She found none – instead, she found the need to be honest with Vladimir, to make sure she didn't mislead him. 'We've been together for a long time, Alan and I – we have children, grandchildren. Our life is a bit of a habit. We're sort of stuck in an old marriage.'

Vladimir sighed. 'How can he not appreciate such a woman? Tess, you are a woman of beauty – you make a man happy with your laughter and your sense of being alive.'

Tess giggled without meaning to. 'I can't imagine Alan thinking such a thing. He can't wait to be away from me – he plays golf all day, every day.'

'Was it Mark Twain or someone else who said that golf is a good walk spoiled?'

'Golf is a good walk for dogs,' Tess retorted, thinking of Elvis.

'I like that better.' Vladimir chuckled, sipped his wine. 'Does your Alan know you are having dinner with me tonight?'

'No – I didn't tell him.' Tess took a mouthful of wine. It was incredibly delicious. 'He wouldn't care anyway.' Tess met his eyes, her own flashing with defiance. 'We're friends, Vladimir, you and I. We like each other. Soon I have to go back home. We're having fun in Paris. Let's just enjoy ourselves. No one will get hurt.'

Vladimir reached out a huge hand and covered hers. 'I hope we can be friends, Tess. I enjoy being with you immensely. You make a tired old man feel full of life, full of joy and optimism. Thank you for dining with me tonight.'

Tess grinned and turned her attention to the dish that the waiter had set in front of her. 'Oh, just look at this,' she gasped. There was a whirl of creamy froth nestling in the centre of a pure white bowl, the mousse decorated with leaves of green watercress and a smear of orange sauce, small peas and tiny jewels of purple flowers. She gazed at Vladimir, her eyes twinkling. 'Do I have to eat this or can I just take it home and frame it?'

Vladimir chortled as the waiter poured wine. He lifted his glass. 'Na Zdorovie. Bon appétit, my dear Tess. To you, to a good life and to our friendship.'

Tess chinked her glass against his. 'To friendship, Vladimir.'

31

Pam slept fitfully, her dreams filled with confusion. In her nightmare, she was separated from Elvis and she couldn't find him. Then, with a jolt of panic, she knew where he was. He was in a whirlpool, under water, drowning, and she waded in and tried to find him but she was being tugged down into the depths. Beneath the surface of the water, she could see Elvis's head; his ears were spread wide, and as he turned his eyes stared at her, cold as glazed marbles. She was sure he was dead. She reached for him, her arms stretched out, screaming his name, and woke with a start. It was six thirty. Rose was sleeping, making happy snuffling noises. The four friends had eaten and drunk wine until almost midnight, talking about life and love and their hopes for the future and how much they all adored Paris. It had been a wonderful evening but, as she often did, Pam felt a little like the odd one out. She shared none of their experiences: a marriage, children, having to share decisions and compromise on a day-to-day basis. She was too independent, too set in her ways, too aloof now. Pam slid out of bed and reached for her jogging pants, a T-shirt and her running shoes. She'd begun to feel sad, a bit sorry for herself, but she knew she'd feel better after some exercise.

* * *

Jen opened her eyes and reached for her phone, blinking in the gloomy half-light that streamed through the curtains. Someone in the room was snoring softly. Jen stared at the screen of her mobile. There was a text from Eddie. She read it quickly. He was apologising to her for being overprotective; he'd felt anxious about her being at risk in the casino but he had good news from Las Vegas. He had won some money on the roulette – over three hundred dollars – and he and Harry had quit while they were ahead. Eddie was going to buy Jen a present today with some of his winnings. He would see her in a few days' time. He was looking forward to their wedding.

Jen sighed. She wasn't sure what was wrong, but she felt unsettled about something. Eddie was kind, he was cheerful; he was caring, protective of her, concerned. Then she realised what the worry was, the uncomfortable thought scratching in the back of her mind. His message had been polite and sympathetic, but there was no real emotion in what he said to her in the text. He didn't say that he missed her terribly, that he loved her madly, that he was looking forward to taking her in his arms.

Jen wondered if it was because Eddie was an older man – that was the reason he lacked passion. Perhaps, as Pam had implied, the emotion of his words was lost in the process of texting. Of course he loved her – they were about to be married. Jen opened her eyes wide, suddenly startled – she wasn't sure she could ever remember Eddie telling her that he loved her. She told herself that this panic was pre-wedding nerves. She was in Paris, missing Eddie. It would all be fine again when she was back home in Exmouth. Besides, she had a wedding to look forward to. She sat up straight in the bed.

Della was breathing deeply, her hair visible from beneath the duvet cover. Jen gazed across at Tess's bed. It was empty. It hadn't been slept in. Jen picked up her phone to check the time – it was quarter to seven. Jen wondered what to do. She would wake Della, then go to see Rose and Pam. Tess had stayed out all night; the thought worried her that something might have happened to her. Jen slithered out of bed and rushed over to Della, gently shaking her by the shoulder. 'Della – Della. Tess isn't here. She hasn't come back.'

* * *

Rose held her coffee cup out. 'Yes, please, Claudette. I can't eat a thing this morning, but I will have black coffee, and lots of it.'

Della pushed her cup towards the waitress. 'Me too. Thank you.'

'I'm still full after last night's meal.' Jen sat back in her seat. 'Where's Pam? She can't still be out jogging?'

'She is. It's half past eight. I texted her and I've messaged Tess twice. There's no reply from either of them.'

'I'm worried about Tess.' Della pushed away her plate, the croissant unfinished. 'It's strange she hasn't sent a message to any of us.'

'What did we have planned for today?' Rose asked. 'And what do we do if Tess isn't back soon?'

Della was thoughtful. 'Reception might be able to help

us to trace Vladimir. Tess and he went to the Colombe Blanche last night – we can check what time they left the restaurant.'

'I expect she went back to his place.' Rose gave an expansive shrug, a gesture that meant more than she was saying. Della and Jen raised their brows so Rose decided to elaborate. 'For goodness' sake. She'll have gone to his penthouse suite, drank too many cocktails and then he'll have seduced her or she'll have seduced him. After all, Alan isn't interested in her – who can blame poor Tess for finding a bit of affection?'

'Really? Do you think she'd do that?' Della's face was frozen in disbelief.

'Tess? You know what a character she is.' Rose chuckled. 'They are probably at it like rabbits in the four-poster bed at this very moment.'

'Rose!' Della exclaimed, clamping a hand over her mouth to stifle a snigger.

'But what if they didn't go to his home?' Jen's hands flew to her mouth. 'What if he's kidnapped her? What if she's in his basement, all tied up? What if she's a hostage or, worse – he might have murdered her.' She met her friends' eyes. 'You hear of things like this – innocent women on holiday being lured and trapped and held for ransom. I mean – he's a powerful man. Maybe he has got minders, big men in suits and glasses with Kalashnikovs. Maybe he's taken a special liking for Tess. Maybe she's his sex slave...'

'Who's a sex slave?' They turned to see a blonde woman standing in the doorway, smiling, overdressed in a gold and black cocktail dress.

'Tess – thank goodness,' Jen breathed.

'Move over – I need food.' Tess sat down. 'This cordon

bleu stuff in posh restaurants is lovely but I'm ready for breakfast. And coffee.'

'Tell us everything.' Della giggled. 'Where have you been?'

'Or shouldn't we ask?' Rose grunted.

'You've been to his penthouse apartment, haven't you, Tess?' Jen was all eyes.

Della watched Tess ripping up a croissant and reaching for the butter. 'Well, you have an appetite on you, Tess Watkins. What have you been up to, all night, with Vladimir?'

Tess paused for effect. 'I spent the night on his boat, on the Seine. And Vladimir is a gentleman.' Her three friends leaned forward. Tess's face shone. 'We talked all night – well, until I fell asleep and he covered me with a blanket. He's such a nice man. We chatted about ourselves, our lives, our dreams. He's so interesting – fascinating. He sails, paints, writes – he is so talented. And such good company.'

'He didn't try anything on with you?' Jen looked disappointed.

Tess laughed. 'He kissed me – on the cheek – twice, when he dropped me off this morning outside the hotel.' She stuffed croissant in her mouth. 'He's a lovely man.'

'Well, I'm glad to hear that.' Rose folded her arms. 'Thank goodness you're safe, Tess. Now we need to find Pam.'

'I passed her in Reception – she'll be down to join us soon.' Tess was still chewing. 'She's having a shower after her run.'

'That's good news,' Rose said. 'So – we have a light Sunday schedule today before the hen party tonight.'

'What's on the list to do this morning?' Della asked.

'Well, I've had an idea,' Tess spluttered between mouthfuls. 'A change of plan. I've organised something that I want to do and I've got an appointment for ten o'clock. She can do one of us or all of us together, if you're keen. I just thought it would be something great, to remember the special hen-party occasion, a sort of souvenir of Paris.'

'What do you mean, she'll do all of us?' Della was suspicious.

'What have you organised, Tess?' Rose asked.

'Oh, I got Vlad to organise it – he rang someone he knows of and I'm booked in – we all are – for ten o' clock.'

Della raised an eyebrow. 'What are we booked in for? A massage? A facial?'

Tess grinned, and stretched out a hand for a third crois-sant. 'No, nothing half so relaxing and boring. He said he wanted to buy me something – just a little gift to remember Paris. So then it came to me – something for us all to share.' She giggled. 'It's all booked – Vladimir will pick up the bill. We're all going to have a tattoo.'

* * *

'So, Vladimir said to me, "What can I get for you?"' Tess had put on a ridiculously deep voice and an accent that was closer to Merthyr Tydfil than Moscow. '"I want to get you a souvenir to remember your time here, my dear—" Ouch! That hurt.'

Inès chuckled and waved the instrument of torture. 'It should not hurt you too much, *madame*. It is on a part of you with most fat.'

Tess giggled, her bottom in the air as she lay on the treat-ment table and winked at her friends. She assumed Inès, the young tattoo artist, must be right about the pain and which parts hurt the most: she had tattoos all over her body, across her brow, down her neck, on the visible parts of her chest and her arms. They were mostly beautiful flowers in all colours, embellished with twisting leaves and delicate butterflies. Inès must be a good tattooist, Tess thought, as she had had so much practice. With her colourful body and her amber dreadlocks piled on top of her head, she was spectacular. The inside of the parlour was equally impressive, the white brick walls plastered with posters of men and women, their bodies pierced and tattooed with snakes and maps, names and faces. There was a man with the face of a baby across his entire back and a woman who had Napoleon's face and shoulders across her belly, complete with tricorn hat and the phrase, '*L'état, c'est moi.*'

'Ow – this hurts,' Tess repeated, still laughing. 'Who's next?'

Inès sighed. 'It won't take long, *madame*. I just write "Paris" in calligraphy style and a small heart, yes? You don't want the Tour Eiffel as well?'

'No – this is enough pain for today.' She caught Jen's eye. 'Alan will never see it on my bum anyway, so he won't have any reason to grumble. But I bet it's going to hurt to sit down.'

'I give you follow-up pack with cream – all will be well,' Inès muttered, her tattoo machine whirring.

'What does it feel like, Tess?' Jen whispered.

'Bee stings on sunburn – cat scratches on top of old scratches. It's not too bad.' She winced. 'Ow! That hurt!'

'I almost finish,' Inès muttered again.

Pam lifted her sleeve to show her upper arm. On her shoulder, there was a red heart containing the word 'Elvis' in black. 'I had this done three years ago.'

'So – are you going to join me for a special Paris souvenir today?' Tess asked.

'I don't see why not.' Pam grinned. 'I've always wanted a second tattoo.'

'I'm up for it,' Rose said and her friends gaped at her with admiration. 'On my forearm.'

'I'll have one on my ankle,' Pam decided.

'Oh, all right – so will I.' Della folded her arms.

Four sets of eyes were staring at Jen. Tess muttered, 'It's your hen party, Jen. You need a tattoo to remember it for ever.'

Inès turned her gaze on Jen. 'So, all five of you for the word *Paris* and a little heart, yes?'

Jen was anxious. 'Eddie won't like it. He'll disapprove, I know he will.'

Tess sniggered. 'Then he's no fun.'

Jen offered her most optimistic look. 'Then again, he might find it really sexy. Maybe on our wedding night, when I take off the dress...' She imagined Eddie's lips on the tattoo, kissing her shoulder, murmuring sounds of appreciation. Perhaps he'd undress in their honeymoon suite in Lyme Regis, and reveal a new tattoo across his chest, the words Las Vegas, or even Jen's name in a heart.

Rose barked a laugh. 'Bernard would have called me a floozy. He was a lovely man, but I listened to him too much when he was alive – I'm not listening to him now.'

Jen was thoughtful for a moment. 'Oh, to hell with it – you're right. It's my hen party. I'll have a memento of Paris – the tattoo's only a small one. Across my shoulder, on my upper arm, where it won't show much.'

Inès looked at them, her eyes shining. 'I think you are very wonderful to have this tattooing. In my shop I don't get any old ladies at all.'

Tess pulled a face at her friends and giggled. She

squirmed on the treatment table with happiness – her tattoo was done. 'Thank you, Vladimir,' she cooed. 'I won't ever forget this trip to Paris.'

'Vladimir has nice friends, I think,' Inès observed.

'How do you know Vladimir?' Tess asked, suddenly interested.

'I don't – I know his son, Vassilly. He comes here many times – he has many many tattoos, on every part of his body. He is addicted to them.' Inès flourished her tattoo machine. 'Well – you are finished, *madame*.' Her eyes moved to Rose. 'So – who is next?'

32

It was past one o'clock as the five friends sat in Jen's room, eating take-away sandwiches and massaging cream into their tattoos. Rose brandished her arm. 'It's lovely, so simple – just the word "Paris" and a little heart. It's really cute. I don't know why I never had a tattoo before. It didn't hurt a bit.'

Jen was rubbing cream into her shoulder. 'Well, mine was agony, like being stung by a bee over and over, but then I've always been a wuss.'

'I'm so glad we had them done,' Pam agreed.

Tess giggled. 'We're a sisterhood of Paris hens now.'

Rose sighed. 'I can't believe we're going back home tomorrow.'

'Nor can I.' Jen was pensive for a moment.

'What are we doing this afternoon?' Della asked. 'My schedule says "free time". Does that mean we can just chill out here? I could do with a rest, although I have to say, my backache is so much better since I've been in Paris.'

Pam sat upright. 'I have to meet Marie-Laure at half past one –do you remember the painter on the bridge? I'm buying her oil painting of the Seine and she's bringing it to Reception. I thought I'd take her for a coffee to say thank you.'

Jen consulted the spreadsheet. 'I left this afternoon free so that we could get some rest before the big hen night. We haven't arranged this evening properly, have we?'

'It's all sorted. We can eat at the club.' Rose's eyes widened in anticipation. 'We're booked in for seven o'clock; Monty has reserved us a table for five, next to the stage. Daz says it's going to be great fun. In fact – ' she looked a little sheepish ' – I'm going over there now. I said I'd give Daz a hand with his – you know – preparations for the evening. He's going to show me his playlist.'

'Ah.' Tess took a breath. 'I promised I'd meet Vladimir at half past two for afternoon tea. You don't mind, do you, Jen? It said "free time" on the spreadsheet...'

'It's not a problem at all.' Jen grinned and squeezed Della's hand. 'I've booked a facial for three o'clock in a hotel down the road. They have beauticians that work on Sundays. I'll call them and see if they can fit you in too and we can go together, Della.'

'That would be wonderful.' Della grinned.

'So we'll all meet back here at – say – five thirty and get ready, shall we?' Pam suggested.

'Can you four meet me in Monty's?' Rose scratched her head. 'Daz and I might be busy – I'll take a change of clothes with me. Is that all right?'

'It's all perfect.' Jen's smile broadened. 'It's my very own hen night and I'm looking forward to it. I never had one the first time round, with Colin. I was just a youngster then and – well – I never even thought about it. Do you know...?' She stretched out her hands and took Della's and Tess's; the five women in turn grasped each other's fingers and clasped them tight, sitting in a circle. 'This has been the most wonderful trip I've ever had. I couldn't have had a nicer time and shared it with four nicer people.'

'This is going to be a hen party to beat all other hen parties,' said Rose. The hens clasped hands, then leaned forward and hugged each other, their eyes shining.

* * *

Pam had paid Marie-Laure the thirty-five euros for the painting and stowed it behind the reception desk with Marion and invited the painter for a coffee. She and Marie-Laure were sitting in a café across the road from the hotel, drinking grand café crème. Marie-Laure was explaining that she painted for seven days a week, especially in spring and summer.

'In winter, I paint from home.' She ran a hand through her short red hair. 'So, for the tourists, I paint Paris, the Seine, the tower, to make enough money to live. For myself, I paint things inside my head – impressionist stuff.'

'Sounds lovely,' Pam murmured. 'What sort of impressionist things do you like to paint?'

'My favourite is one of the rain on the window panes. I paint it in grey and silver, little droplets of oil. I have another of blue flowers in a field – it is based on a photo I took on holiday many years ago in Picardie with my daughter.'

'Does your daughter live with you?'

Marie-Laure laughed. 'Oh, no – she is thirty-seven years old. She has children of her own. I am almost sixty. But I brought her up by myself from when she was ten years old.'

'That can't have been easy.'

'No.' Marie-Laure shook her head. 'It was very difficult. But it was better that way, alone. Sophie's father was a pig.'

Pam laughed. 'Was he untidy?'

'No, he was the opposite. Very tidy. He would shout at me if the house wasn't perfect.' Marie-Laure waved her hands. 'But that's not why he was a pig. He would yell bad things at me– insult me. Then, when he was angry, he would threaten me, throw things about the house.'

'That's awful,' Pam breathed.

'Oh, it's not the worst thing.' Marie-Laure blew air between her lips, a sound of disgust. 'One day, he was angry about something I did wrong – he pulled my hair and Sophie came between us to defend me and he pushed her out of the way, to the ground, very hard. She broke her wrist.'

Pam's face was drained of colour. 'That is terrible.'

'I left him. I could not live with someone who had put my child in danger. That was it, finished. I came to Paris with my daughter and we made our own way. I painted by day and I cleaned houses at night to keep us both fed and with shelter. I never took money from Phillippe – I never wanted to speak to him again. He came to find me one time, said he was sorry, that he would change, and I told him to stay away or I would go to the police. I moved to another flat. I did not see him again and he didn't try to find us ever.'

'That must have been hard for you and Sophie.'

Marie-Laure lifted her coffee cup. 'It would have been harder to stay. Since then, I have been a single woman, a mother to Sophie, an artist. I have been happy that way.'

Pam nodded. 'I know what you mean. There's just me and Elvis at home – Elvis is my spaniel.'

'It is much better that way, if you ask me.' Marie-Laure pressed her lips together. 'I was unlucky – I met the sort of man who was just too dangerous to be close to. There are not many of them out there, but when you find yourself with one, it is very bad.'

'I can understand that,' Pam said.

'You have had the same experience?'

Pam shook her head. 'No – yes, no – well, not the same exactly.'

Marie-Laure's eyebrows shot up towards her bright hair. 'Why? What happened? Did you know someone who was aggressive?'

Pam looked away into the distance and pressed her lips together. She could feel tears pricking at her eyes. It was an image she had pushed away and blanked out for years but there it was, back in front of her, the struggle, the feelings of helplessness, of anger, of terror. She wondered how she could avoid the subject – her mind raced for something to say, but nothing came to her. Marie-Laure put a hand over hers. 'Something happened to you?'

'I've never told anyone about it.' Pam could feel her throat constricting. It was hard to swallow, difficult to speak. She shook her head but the images were still vivid in her imagination; she was powerless, too afraid to scream, too terrified to fight back.

Marie-Laure moved her head close to Pam. 'Then tell me, here in Paris – tell a complete stranger you will never see again. Sometimes it is better to share a secret with someone. Then maybe the pain of it will go away.'

Pam blinked and a single tear rolled down her cheek. Her lips quivered. 'I never told my mother. I never told my friends. It was awful – awful.' She placed her palms over her eyes and wiped away tears; Marie-Laure was staring at her. Pam took a deep breath. 'I was twenty-two, working in a hotel at the seaside as a chambermaid, a cleaner. It was a summer job. At that time, I wanted to earn enough money to go travelling through the winter, to visit India and Australia. So I was doing a lot of shifts. Well, there was a man who worked in the kitchen, a commis chef, called Des. He was about thirty. He took a shine to me. He was always – you know – seeking me out at break times, making a joke with me. And, of course, I wasn't interested in him – but I used to joke back, just to be friendly.' Pam breathed deeply. Her fingers were shaking.

Marie-Laure put a hand on the top of Pam's and met her eyes with a steady gaze. 'Go on, Pam.'

'Well, it developed into a sort of game with him – he'd call me his girl, his dolly bird, and bring me little things, cakes, biscuits, and he'd make personal comments – my hair was nice, my skirt was a pretty colour – and then he started saying other things – about my body, about how he was aroused, touching my arm, asking me to kiss him, that sort of thing. I ignored him altogether. I just steered clear of him. That worked for three days. Then he...'

Pam caught her breath, swallowing the words that might come next, squeezing her eyes tightly to shut out the memory. 'It was early morning, a Tuesday. I was in one of the bedrooms, changing the sheets. I heard a noise behind me and I turned round. It was Des. He came into the room and closed the door...'

Pam closed her eyes. She could say no more. The images were like a film strip, each frame still vivid, one moment after the other. Marie-Laure squeezed her hand and spoke softly. 'Did Des rape you?'

Pam nodded. A tear trickled down her cheek. Marie-Laure frowned. 'You should have told the police – you should have had him locked up.'

'I couldn't. It was what he said to me afterwards. About how it had been my fault – I had led him on; I had flirted with him; my skirt had been too short – that sort of thing.'

'That is horrible.'

'It was over fifty years ago.' Pam shook her head. 'No one would have listened to me.'

Marie-Laure placed Pam's coffee cup in her shaking hands, guiding it towards her lips. Pam sipped gratefully and sighed. 'I've never told anyone, not ever. It has affected me all my life... stayed with me...'

Marie-Laure leaned forward. 'You have told someone now. It is over. You can forget this man. You are a strong woman, Pam. We are both strong women.' She gave a short laugh. 'We have been hurt and we have worked through it.'

Pam nodded. 'I hope you're right, Marie-Laure.'

'I am.' Marie-Laure reached in her handbag, finding a pen. 'You can speak more of this to me if you want to. I'll give you my phone number. You can call me from England.' She scribbled a number on a cardboard beer mat. 'We are both survivors. But it is good to have a friend to talk to about these things.' She pushed the coaster in Pam's direction.

Pam took it in both hands. 'Thank you, Marie-Laure. Thank you for listening, for telling me about Phillippe. You're right. The past is gone – maybe now I can leave it behind me and move on.'

'I agree,' Marie-Laure said. 'Let us have another café crème and talk about good times. I want to hear all about your little dog, Elvis. And I will tell you about Manon, my ginger and white cat, and how she loves to leave paw prints all over my impressionist paintings.'

* * *

It was three o'clock. Tess and Vladimir were sitting across from each other at a table in La Mouche, a quaint tea shop in the basement of an art gallery, sharing a pot of Darjeeling tea and cream cakes. Tess was chattering about how she'd love to come to Paris again one day, the many things she'd like to do next time. Vladimir's eyes were fixed on her face, watching her every expression, smiling at the way the corners of her mouth moved when she spoke, when she laughed. He nodded, amused, and said, 'One day I will show you Montmartre, Vallée Village, Le Bon Marché, Rive Gauche, Palais de Tokyo. There are so many places I want to take you to see.' His eyes gleamed. 'Would you like that, Tess?'

Her face shone. 'I think I'd like that very much indeed...'

Monty's club was empty, the bar in shadow. Two figures huddled on the stage, a single light overhead. Rose had installed herself at the white piano, moving her fingers gently across the keys, working out the chords to Abba's 'Take a Chance on Me'. Daz stood next to her, smart in a T-shirt and faded jeans, singing the lyrics, frowning and moving his head up and down to keep a rhythm. As she played the final notes, he put a hand on her shoulder. 'I think we've got that one, Rose. It's right racy now. What about trying "Fernando" next?'

Rose looked over her shoulder. 'We could have a go at "The Winner Takes It All" and "SOS" too. Have you got some moves worked out?'

Daz grinned, his eyes twinkling. 'Oh, yes, Rose – I've got all the moves. You must let me show you the ones I've worked out to "Dancing Queen". Proper lively they are – I might finish with that one. What do you think?'

Rose grinned, playing the opening chords of 'SOS' with renewed energy. 'It's sounding good. Come on, then – strut your stuff. I think it's going to be a really special night, Daz.'

* * *

Della and Jen took the lift to Le Zip, the beauty parlour at the top of a four storey boutique-style neighbouring hotel, Paris Lune. On the top floor, there was a neon sign in tangerine and yellow. They were greeted at Reception by a therapist, a tall woman, possibly in her thirties, with a white uniform, her dark hair in a tight chignon, the pearliest teeth the friends had ever seen. The therapist beamed. 'Madame Hooper? Madame Donavan? I am Françoise. Follow me, if you please.'

Jen and Della exchanged glances and followed the woman who was sashaying ahead of them, her long legs ending in high heels, to a treatment room where two beds were covered in fluffy white towels, the room lined with shelves, bottles and ointments, to be welcomed by another therapist with shining teeth, dark hair, flawless skin and a crisp white uniform. Françoise gave them her friendliest grin. 'Welcome, *mesdames*. This is Chantelle. I hope you will enjoy here the best beauty treatment of your lives. When you leave in one and a half hours, your faces will be twenty years younger.'

33

Jen and Della lay on their backs on the treatment tables. Their hair had been tied back with Velcro-fastening white headbands and their faces were covered in lime-green sludge. Soothing cotton wool pads had been placed over their eyes. Gentle music, the chatter of dolphins echoing from beneath the deep seas, flowed through speakers, and the friends both breathed out simultaneously.

Jen spoke, trying not to damage the mask that was tightening her skin. 'I'll be a married woman soon, Della.'

Della muttered through the corner of her mouth, her lips restricted by the shrinking mask. 'I hope you'll be very happy, Jen.' She thought for a moment. 'Marriage is certainly a wonderful thing. I wouldn't be without Sylvester.'

'I thought the same about Colin – he was a lovely person.' Jen sighed. 'Eddie's a lovely person too.'

'I've known Sylvester for fifty years now and I can honestly say married life has been pure bliss. I mean, we had ups and downs – the boys were boys, you know – money was hard to find sometimes, but through it all we had each other.'

'Eddie and I won't have any troubles like that. His son lives a long way away, in Chester. I don't have children. Eddie will rent out his house. We'll do fine together – we'll be better off, Eddie says. It will be good.'

Della thought for a moment. 'What does marriage mean to you, then, Jen?'

'Company.' Jen considered Eddie, his fine manners, his good looks. 'Being with someone you can be proud of – someone who is presentable and refined and pleasant.'

Della giggled. 'That's not my Sylvester. He has bendy toes and hairy nostrils. I don't think he's the most presentable of men.' She smiled at the thought of him. 'You should see him sometimes at night, when he's sleeping, one eye half open, his glasses still on, snoring, wearing his vest, his little pigeon chest all hairy.'

Jen tried not to wrinkle her nose beneath the mask. 'You make it sound awful.'

'Not at all,' Della protested. 'He's so cute. I love it.'

Jen pressed her lips together. 'So, Della – what does marriage mean to you?'

'Love.' Della didn't need to think about it. 'Sylvester's my soul mate, my best friend, the love of my life. Without him, I'd be less of a complete person. If he died, I couldn't ever find another Sylvester – and I'd never settle for anyone else, for anyone less. He is all man and he makes me feel appreciated, like a real woman, a beautiful woman. My Sylvester is passionate, he's hot, he's a handful and we bounce off each other like electricity. He's just funny, warm, loveable and he lets me know I am the one for him. He tells me he loves me twenty times a day – he *shows* me in so many ways.' Della giggled. 'I miss being with him. I can't wait to see his sweet little face tomorrow.'

Jen was glad her eyes were closed and her face was pulled tight under the thick green gunk. At least she looked composed. But inside, her thoughts were racing. Della's words were about love and about how right she and Sylvester were for each other, but nothing she had said applied to Eddie. Jen didn't miss him, not that much. He didn't make her feel like a real woman; he didn't bounce off her like electricity and he didn't tell her he loved her twenty times a day. Jen couldn't recall him saying it once. Her heart thudded harder. She had never told him she loved him either.

So, what was their relationship about? Passion? Love? Company? Or was it the sterile, polite exchange between two older people who thought they had no other choices and were prepared to settle for something that was, in reality, not ever going to be good enough?

Della's breathing became regular and deep: she was asleep. But Jen couldn't relax. Her mind was slithering down a helter-skelter and she was terrified. She was getting married in less than a week and, right now, she wasn't sure if she wanted to marry Eddie at all.

* * *

They were ready. Four women, dressed to the nines for Jen's wild hen party and, outside, next to Monty's lurid pink and gold neon sign, they were taking photos of each other, singly, in groups, posing for all they were worth. Tess had on her expensive gold and black cocktail dress and was wearing a 1920s-style feather headdress, a white feather boa and black velvet gloves. Pam was in a short red skirt and a glittering black vest, her blonde hair spiked, red earrings dangling, shivering with cold but laughing.

Della had opted for a black velvet mini dress and a little coquettish hat with a veil on an Alice band. But Jen had fully entered into the hen party spirit. She was dressed as a schoolgirl, her chestnut hair in bunches, a skewed tie against a white blouse, a short grey pleated skirt, stockings and suspenders. She had drawn freckles on her nose. Round her neck, she had an L-plate on a long string and she had written a huge question mark after the red L in black marker pen. They were laughing, giggling like youngsters, their arms around each other.

Pam chuckled. 'We should have all done the schoolgirl thing.'

Jen was triumphant. 'Eddie will disapprove when he sees these pictures,' she brayed. 'I don't care.'

'Sylvester will frame them on the mantelpiece,' Della spluttered.

'We look fabulous, darlings,' Tess chuckled.

'Let's go in and find Rose.'

They were greeted at the door by a very tall willowy woman in a full length lace dress the same coffee tone as her flesh, with a plunge neckline and a low back. Her hair was a mass of black curls spilling over her shoulders. She held out spiky-nailed fingers spattered with diamond rings and greeted the friends in a voice that was smoky, whisky-soaked. 'Welcome. I am Montserrat Tabueña. It's a pleasure to have you here at Monty's. I hope you will have a wonderful night.'

'Oh, we will – thank you,' Jen enthused.

Monty guided them to their table, where Rose was already seated, wearing the clothes she'd had on at breakfast – jeans, a blouse and a light grey jacket. A young waiter with slicked-back hair brought a tray of cocktails to the table, pale sparkling drinks in flute glasses. 'Sgroppinos, compliments of Monty.'

Tess sat up and held a glass to her lips, swigging a mouthful. 'Mmmm. What's in them, *monsieur*?'

The waiter gave a small bow. 'Lemon sorbet, vodka, champagne.'

Tess clapped her hands. 'Perfect. I must introduce Vladimir to these.'

Rose and Pam exchanged glances and raised their eyebrows meaningfully. Jen took a sip and squealed with delight. 'Delicious.'

'You didn't get changed, Rose – you're still in jeans.' Della took a tentative taste of her Sgroppino. 'Mmmm.'

Rose shrugged. 'I have something to wear with me – I've been helping Daz get ready. I'll go off and change in a minute.'

Pam gulped a mouthful of her cocktail. 'This is so nice. I could drink these all night.'

Another waiter, his hair in a neat ponytail, arrived with a tray containing five plates of steaming rice. He placed the food on the table.

'What's this?' Pam asked. 'We didn't order food yet.'

'Compliments of Greta Manchester,' the waiter muttered. 'It is wild mushroom risotto with truffles.'

'Daz told me he'd organised this.' Rose chortled. 'We can't drink on an empty stomach.'

At that moment, a woman in red leather strutted onto the stage. A voice through the speakers introduced her as Queen Caliente. She had long dark hair to her knees and the angriest face, arched eyebrows and a red mouth that turned down in a snarl. She was a rock chick, carrying a long microphone on a stand, launching raucously into 'Bad Reputation' by Joan Jett. Jen gaped at Queen Caliente, her mouth open and her fork poised in mid-air. Della flashed a wide grin. 'She's really good.'

Queen Caliente sang several more songs, concluding her act with Suzi Quatro's 'Devil Gate Drive'. Pam finished her risotto just as the ponytailed waiter came to collect the dishes. Then the waiter with slicked-back hair brought a tray of Sgroppinos. 'Compliments of the house, *mesdames*.'

Jen was shocked. 'Has Monty paid for these as well?'

The waiter shook his head. 'No, *madame*, the acts back-stage knew you were coming and that it was a special night for a special friend of Greta so they buy you these more cocktails.'

Tess reached for her glass. 'Tell them thank you from us all.'

'What a great evening.' Rose clapped her hands. 'I'll go and get changed after this next act, shall I?'

A woman was already prancing on stage, announced over the speakers as Miss Peaches Beaverhausen. Peaches was dressed in a school gymslip, shirt and tie, ripped fishnet stockings and her blonde hair stood out in bendy plaits, ending with oversized red ribbons. Her mouth was a cupid's bow and her eyes were wide and innocent. Peaches noticed Jen immediately and greeted her with a wave. *'Ma jumelle,'* she cooed.

'She's saying you're like her twin,' Pam translated and Jen waved at the performer enthusiastically. Peaches was already pouting and lip-syncing away to Britney Spears' 'Oops!... I Did It Again', waving her bottom at the audience, showing lacy knickers.

By the time Peaches had finished 'I'm a Slave 4 U', the five women were standing up, clapping their hands. When she launched into 'Toxic', Jen clambered on her seat and began waving her arms. She was quickly joined by Pam, Della and Tess, standing on their chairs and dancing on the spot. Rose, seeing an opportunity, sneaked off backstage. Peaches finished her song to loud applause and began to say something in French. Pam nudged Jen gently and then Peaches walked to the end of the stage and held out a hand. Jen was puzzled.

'She's asking you to join her on stage,' Pam whispered.

Jen clambered up beside Peaches and stood shyly in her school uniform while the audience cheered. Peaches took her hand as the intro to '... Baby One More Time' sifted through the speakers. Up close to Peaches, Jen could see that the singer was a little too old to be a schoolgirl – she was probably in her thirties – but she was extremely glamorous and very enthusiastic about performing the song, wiggling her bottom in time to the music. Jen copied her every move, turning round to shake her hips almost as Peaches was doing. After two Sgroppinos, Jen was losing any feelings of awkwardness; as the audience yelled and clapped, she followed Peaches across the stage, twirling and strutting and pouting. The audience responded with increased cheers and applause. Peaches threw her arms around Jen and said in her best English, 'This lady steal my show,' before planting a huge lipstick kiss on her cheek. Jen curtseyed several times, grinning to hear the rapturous appreciation as Pam and Della reached out to help her down to her seat.

Pam went to the bar to order another round of cocktails, including one for the absent Rose. Tess had threatened to drink it if Rose wasn't back in time. Meanwhile Ida Heaux, a blonde country and western singer in a short, fringed dress and an oversized rhinestone cowboy hat, lip-synced to 'Stand

By Your Man'. When Pam returned, Ida was just finishing her final song, 'Coal Miner's Daughter', snarling at the hecklers at the back who were catcalling and laughing. Someone had thrown a pair of lacy knickers at Ida and she was holding them up by the elastic and yelling something rude in French. She curtseyed, waved a finger in a gesture of disapproval, and strode off.

Then Monty was on stage, exuberant in the skin-tight dress and huge eyelashes, speaking in French, Spanish and German. Applause and cheering greeted her. She waved her arms towards the hens' table and spoke directly to Jen. 'My friend is getting married in six days' time. It is my honour to have her party here.' She threw out a long arm. 'And here to entertain us all, from England, is the gorgeous Greta Manchester.'

Greta sauntered on stage in animal print hot pants and a halter neck top, long pink hair flying behind her like liquid candyfloss. She blew a kiss to Jen and began to lip-sync to 'Can't Get You Out of My Head' by Kylie Minogue. Jen climbed up on the chair next to Pam, Della and Tess and they began to bop, Tess with two cocktails in her hand. 'Rose is missing this,' she shouted.

Pam was bobbing up and down, her face relaxed and happy. 'It makes me smile how the French audience don't understand the pun in Greta Manchester's name but they all love her anyway.' She wiggled her hips, copying Greta's movements. 'Daz told us that Greta had made a name for herself in the UK long before she came here and she wasn't going to change it.'

'She's very good,' Della shouted over the applause as Greta launched into 'Murder on the Dance Floor', making a cheeky face at the front row.

Jen squealed with delight. 'This has to be the best place in Paris to party. I'm having so much fun.'

The hens shook their shoulders and wiggled throughout the song, waving their arms and clapping their hands hard, reaching for their cocktails and taking a sip to cool down. Then Greta purred into the microphone, saying something in French, translating for Jen. 'We have a one-time special guest for tonight. This is the only place you can see her in the whole of France, my partner in crime, the devastatingly beautiful and the best pianist in Paris – Rose-On-Wye.'

Rose was on stage. Except that it wasn't Rose. The friends blinked in amazement. Marie Antoinette, in a tall, white powdered wig that resembled a giant Mr Whippy ice cream, stood in a long blue silk dress, tight across the bodice, with a low neck, a sweeping skirt, puffed sleeves with white lace at the edges. She wore tight white gloves that came past her elbows. She gave an elaborate curtsey, waved an elegant hand towards the audience as if she were the Queen, and took her position at the piano. Greta strutted downstage as Rose played the opening bars of 'Mamma Mia'. The crowd whooped in delight and applauded enthusiastically. The hens exchanged glances, squealed with delight and began to dance on their chairs, bopping for all they were worth.

Rose beamed at the audience as 'Mamma Mia' became 'Gimme! Gimme! Gimme! (A Man After Midnight)' followed by 'Thank You for the Music'. And, as a grand finale, 'Dancing Queen'. She nodded her head in time to Greta's swaying hips and she winked in Jen's direction, blowing a kiss. Pam yelled, 'She's been practising this all afternoon.'

'She's glorious,' yelled Della.

'The girl's definitely got talent.' Tess twirled where she stood, a cocktail in each hand, almost toppling over.

Jen raised both arms, singing along to the words, her head thrown back, her freckle-painted face smiling as if she'd never stop. She was having the time of her life. 'I'm getting married in six days,' she whooped, waving her cocktail glass and wiggling her bottom. 'And I'm having so much fun in Paris. Thank you for the music, Rose. Thank you to my friends for being here with me. This is the best, best, best hen party ever.'

34

It was raining heavily the next morning as Jen, Tess and Della huddled in the covered entrance to the Hotel Sirène waiting for Faik's taxi to arrive, their suitcases by their ankles. It was almost ten o'clock; they'd arranged to be picked up at ten, leaving them plenty of time at the airport. After breakfast, the friends had gone upstairs to their rooms to finish packing, heavy hearted, and bleary eyed.

Tess was sulky. 'I wish we had another week here.'

'It's been lovely,' Della agreed. 'It's done us all the world of good. Have you noticed how happy Pam seems this morning? She was out jogging before breakfast in all this rain, and she was the life and soul at breakfast. I've never seen her so chirpy.'

'Which is more than can be said for me,' Jen grumbled. She had drunk several cocktails last night and she assumed that was why she felt as if she were carrying a breeze block on her head. She sighed. 'We've had such a good time.'

'Where are Pam and Rose? They are a bit late.' Jen sighed.

'The weather is horrible.' Tess wrinkled her nose. 'We

were so lucky that it's been warm and dry this past week – this rain would have made sightseeing so difficult.'

Della gazed down at her suitcase. 'I'm sure I'm taking much more back than I came with.'

Tess shrieked with laughter. 'I've got my new dress...'

'And my bag's full of presents – T-shirts, Eddie's glass carving of the classic car...'

'Pam's got a painting to take back too, all wrapped up in her case. She seems to have made a friend of Marie-Laure – they've exchanged numbers.' Tess giggled. 'And she's bought Elvis a doggie bowl with the Eiffel Tower on it...'

'This rain's getting heavier. I hope Rose and Pam come soon.' Della stared into the distance. 'Is that Faik's taxi slowing down?'

'No, it's not Faik.' Tess gasped as a black Bentley drew up outside the hotel. She recognised the smoky windows and the man in the overcoat behind the wheel. 'It's Vladimir.'

Jen and Della watched as she rushed towards the driver's side as the window slid down. In one movement, Tess had pushed her head through the window and kissed Vladimir on the cheek. They were talking. Jen and Della could hear Tess's pealing laughter and Vladimir's low rumble. Jen winked at Della. 'She seems much taken with him.'

Della shook her head. 'She told me they're just friends.'

'I wouldn't be too sure.' Jen made a face and cocked her head towards the Bentley where Tess was kissing Vladimir again.

Then the car eased away slowly and, when Tess reached her friends, her hair was dripping and there were tears in her eyes. She gave a brave giggle. 'That was Vladimir.'

Jen nodded. 'You seem very close, you and him, Tess.'

'He's really nice – I'll miss him.' Tess sniffed.

Della touched her on the shoulder. 'Are you OK?'

'I think so.' Tess wiped her face with the back of her hand. 'It's silly – I haven't known him for long but we get on so well.' She forced a smile. 'But I'm going back to Alan, back to watching golf on the television and waiting for him to come back late from the golf club.' She shook her head. 'Silly, isn't it?'

'It was good timing that Vladimir turned up, just as you were leaving,' Jen observed.

'He asked if he could text me, keep in touch.' Tess swallowed. 'He offered us all a lift to the airport. I said no – Faik has been so good to us. Then Vladimir said he's very fond of me... That's what started me off, made me a bit weepy.'

Jen put an arm round Tess. 'I'm sure it will all be fine when you get back to Exmouth.'

Tess sighed. 'I'm not sure I'll ever be all right.' She brightened, deliberately forcing a giddy laugh. 'But we've had such a good time here, haven't we?' Tess rubbed her bottom. 'I still can't sit down after that tattoo. I'll be in agony on the plane...'

The rain was spattering against the canopy of the hotel entrance, making thudding sounds above their heads. Puddles formed in the road, passing cars swishing heavily through deep water and sending splashes into the gutter. Pam and Rose arrived, hauling their luggage.

'Sorry we're late,' Pam breathed. 'It's only just after ten.'

A taxi careered round the corner and stopped with a squelch at the kerb. Faik appeared from the driver's seat, wearing a heavy sheepskin jacket. '*Mesdames* – I am here.' He opened the boot and took Jen's luggage, then Tess's bag, stacking them in the boot. Della offered him her holdall and Pam tugged her suitcase towards the boot. Faik stacked the bags carefully and reached for Rose's suitcase. Rose held onto the handle firmly. 'No,' she said.

Faik blinked. 'I take suitcase, *madame*.'

'I'm not coming.'

The four friends turned to Rose. Jen's brow wrinkled. 'Rose?'

'I'm staying here.'

'What do you mean, you're staying here?' Tess was anxious. 'You can't – we have a flight booked...'

'I'm not going back to England yet.' Rose reached into her pocket and thrust a set of door keys into Tess's hand. 'Will you check my house is all right, please, Tess? Just until I'm back?'

Tess took a breath. 'What are you going to do, Rose? How can you stay here in Paris?'

'I've spoken to Daz. I'm staying at his flat for a while.'

Della frowned. 'I don't understand.'

Rose smiled, her face illuminated. 'Daz asked me to stay on here and I said yes. Monty so enjoyed our performance last night that she's offered us more work together, as a duet. I'm doing a week or two in the club as Rose-On-Wye with Greta Manchester, playing Abba songs live. We went down a storm.' Her eyes shone with happiness. 'I'd be mad to turn it down. Daz has a spare room in his little flat, where his friend Simon used to stay before he went to Amsterdam. So – he'll be my flatmate and I'll be away for as long as I want.' She squeezed Tess's hand containing the key. 'Just check everything is OK in the house from time to time, would you?'

'Of course.' Tess was baffled. They had been five and now they were four.

Jen's brow furrowed. 'Will you be all right here though, Rose? Don't you think it's a bit risky?'

'You have to take risks sometimes.' Pam folded her arms.

Rose put out a hand. 'You're right, Pam. And I need to stay here. When I was on stage last night, I felt that I'd come back to life. I was performing, playing the piano, and it was as if there was a point in me being on this earth. I felt happy, really happy.' Rose turned to Jen. 'Thank you so much, Jen, for the hen week. Thank you so much for everything. I've had the time of my life – it's been the best ever. It's been life changing for me, it truly has. I know what I want to do now.' Rose threw her arms around Jen and hugged her tight.

Jen winced – the flesh around the tattoo on her shoulder was still tender. She cuddled Rose, kissing her cheek. 'If you're sure...'

'I've never been surer about anything.'

Pam put her arms around Rose. 'I'm so pleased for you.'

Rose gazed at her friends. 'Daz is so thrilled I'm staying. He has big ideas for our show. But the thing is – I want to do this. I've got a purpose now and – and it makes me happier than I've ever been – ever.'

Della hugged Rose. 'That's all that matters.'

Tess threw her arms wide. The five hens enfolded each other in a tight embrace. When they pulled apart, there were tears and shining eyes.

'Take care, Rose,' Tess called as she wriggled into the taxi, followed by Della, Pam and Jen.

'We love you,' Jen yelled as the door slammed.

Rose shouted, 'Good luck with the wedding. Good luck with Eddie.'

The taxi pulled away, smoke chugging from the exhaust pipe, and Rose waved an arm. Her face was wet from the streaming rain and her hair stuck to her head, soaked, but she was smiling. Daz would be here at any moment in a

borrowed car to pick her up. They'd have lunch later at the
little bistro that served the best Brie en croute she'd ever
tasted and then, afterwards, they'd go to Monty's to rehearse
the new act. Rose looked up at the skies, metal grey and
heavy with rainclouds, and laughed out loud. She was in
Paris, she was alive and she was having fun.

* * *

Somehow, by some miracle, they had managed to be allo-
cated seats next to one another on the flight home. Pam was
seated by the aisle, her head on Della's shoulder, asleep.
Della was smiling: Pam was clearly having no trouble
sleeping at the moment. She had snuggled down in her seat,
resting against her friend, breathing lightly, her eyes closed.
Della knew how edgy Pam had been about leaving Elvis
behind and now, Della supposed, because she was on her
way home to her beloved spaniel, Pam was relaxed again. But
there was no doubt the trip to Paris had been beneficial
for her.

Della could trace the change to yesterday afternoon, the
moment where Pam returned to the hotel from her coffee
with Marie-Laure and brought the painting of the Seine up to
her room, a smile on her face. It was as if she'd shrugged off a
burden – she was lighter in some way, more comfortable with
life. Della thought she understood how Pam felt. Leaving
Elvis was a little like leaving Sylvester. Della's smile broadened. Husbands and dogs, both were a bit dependent, both
full of love, bounding up with affection, loyal. Once you
found a good one, you couldn't live without him. And Della
would be seeing her Sylvester soon, holding him in her arms,
planting a kiss on those pursed lips and listening to him

cackle with delight. Della closed her eyes, leaning her head against Pam's, and felt the lift of the aeroplane taking her home.

* * *

'I told Vladimir he could text me. Do you think I did the right thing, Jen?'

Jen gazed through the window at the clouds, skeins of drifting cotton in an azure sky. She sighed. Pam and Della were asleep in the seats behind them. Jen pressed her lips together. 'I'm not sure, Tess. What will Alan say?'

Tess was sandwiched in the middle seat between Jen, at the window, and a grey-blonde-haired woman who was possibly in her fifties who was reading a romance novel. Tess glanced at the woman, to check if she was listening to their conversation. She was a pleasant looking woman with a friendly face, a yellow jacket and faded jeans. The book she was reading was about a Cornish love affair. There were fat red hearts all over the turquoise cover, swirling calligraphy surrounding the figures of a man and woman holding hands in silhouette. Tess turned back to Jen.

'The thing is, I've decided not to tell Alan. I mean, if he knew I'd met a friend in Paris and we're texting, he wouldn't be interested. Unless the friend played golf.'

'Are you being honest with Alan?'

Tess frowned. 'How do you mean?'

Jen gave Tess her full attention. 'Are you being honest with yourself about Vladimir, Tess?'

Tess sighed. 'In what way?'

'I'm not sure if it's just a friendship with you and Vladimir. You talk about him non-stop.' Tess gasped and Jen pressed her arm gently. 'Of course, I don't mind. It's lovely, to hear you telling us all about him and it's lovely that you get on so well. But I think you might be deceiving yourself a bit. I think you like him more than you're saying.'

'Do you think so?' She was conscious that the woman with the long grey hair had not turned a page of her novel in a while. Tess met Jen's eyes. 'I think you're right, Jen. I might have feelings for him. And I know he has feelings for me. He said so.'

'And so, what about Alan?'

'He's my husband. I have to make the best of it when I get back.' Tess closed her eyes, remembering her date with Vladimir, how they'd talked on his boat until three in the morning, how she'd fallen asleep, her head on his knee, as he stroked her hair. She recalled the gravelly emotion in his voice as he'd told her he'd never met a woman he had been drawn to so instantly, that he had cared for so deeply and so quickly. 'Alan is my husband, but I don't love him, Jen. I haven't loved him for a while. I think I'm falling in love with Vladimir.'

'Can't you try to love Alan again? What about a weekend away? What about spending quality time together, a romantic dinner, like you had in Paris with Vladimir?'

Tess sighed. 'You're right. I should try to make it work with Alan.'

The woman next to Tess hadn't shifted position; she was still reading the same page. Tess took a deep breath. 'But Alan isn't interested in me, Jen. He isn't interested in going out unless it is a night at the golf club. He neglects me. Vladimir is affectionate, warm; he listens to me, he pays attention to me, and he cares about what I think. Alan just shuts me out.'

Jen shrugged. 'Alan's your husband. You should try your best to win him round.'

'It's not a competition. If it is, we both lost some time ago.' Tess raised her voice. 'Alan never listens to me. He never pays me compliments or tells me I'm interesting. Everything is on his terms – he does what he likes without considering me. He's always been like that, ever since we married, making all the decisions, doing whatever he wanted, putting himself first. He'll never change. He's that sort of person – selfish, I suppose. A wife is just a status symbol, someone to sort out things around the house while he swans off doing his own thing. I'm just someone nice to come home to – a bit of company in front of the television at night. Someone to keep the house tidy and the bed warm.' Tess was almost shouting. 'And in that department, Alan's not really interested any more. He has no passion, no warmth. He never tells me he loves me – Vladimir said those words to me on his boat: that he cares for me deeply, that I was precious. Jen, Vladimir's company is worth so much more than a night in front of the telly watching the golf with a hot cocoa.'

The woman next to Tess closed her romance book with a dull thud. Her voice was a warm Cornish burr. She put her hand on Tess's arm. 'Well, I'd go off with that Vladimir if I was you, my lovely – your Alan don't deserve a look-in. He's just a selfish bastard, if you ask me.'

Tess met the woman's eyes, the intense blue of Cornish oceans, and sighed. 'I think you're probably right. I need to give it some serious thought, don't I? But thank you.'

Jen grinned and stared out at wispy cloud trails. Tess was a lively character. Jen loved her for her warmth, her impetuosity, her kindness and loyalty, her good nature. Tess didn't deserve someone as cold as Alan. Jen recalled him in the

Olive Grove, smiling, winking at her, oleaginous. It was clear he was not really interested in Tess and she would probably be happier with Vladimir. After all, the broad shouldered, impeccably dressed Russian was drawn to Tess, magnetised by her energy, her sense of fun. Jen had seen how they talked together, their heads close; how they made each other laugh; how they craved each moment of the other's company, relished it as if it was a precious gift. Jen thought about Vladimir in Paris and Tess in Exmouth; how they might text each other frequently; how their friendship might blossom into something that would last and how Tess's marriage to Alan might wilt and fade. After all, Vladimir had declared his love after just a few days and Alan didn't care – to him, Tess was just a habit.

Jen shivered. It was as if someone had thrown icy water straight in her face. She stared out of the window; below the plane, she gazed at the green and grey coastline of England, fields and houses carved in the landscape like little scars. She would be home soon, and in five days' time she would be marrying Eddie. It was all organised: the ceremony, the reception, the dress. She had wanted the security, the presence of another person in her life. And what had Tess said about Alan? That he was the one *'making all the decisions, doing whatever he wanted'*. That was exactly how Eddie seemed to be.

And then Tess's words were loud, screaming in her ears. *'He never tells me he loves me – Vladimir said those words to me on his boat: that he cared for me deeply, that I was precious. Jen, Vladimir's company is worth so much more than a night in front of the telly watching the golf with a hot cocoa.'* Jen caught her breath. Tess had described her life with Alan, but it was exactly true for her own relationship with Eddie. They'd be sitting in her living room in front of the screen, silent, Jen and her new husband, two separate people in one house. Jen's skin was covered in goose pimples. It was clear as the blinding sun shining through the drifting clouds outside the window. Eddie was not right for her: he was not what she needed. She was making a huge mistake.

35

The taxi ride from the airport didn't take too long. Jen asked for Della to be dropped off first – she was wriggling in her seat, impatient to see Sylvester and to tell him all about Paris. She had texted him that she was on her way but, as usual, he was technologically too inept and too myopic to reply. Della waved her phone. 'I told him we'd be back at half past five. I expect he's waiting for me to come home and cook dinner for him. I hope so. I told him to leave the snack van early and make sure he is home on time.'

'Are we back at half five?' Tess gasped. 'Oh, goodness – it's just after five now. I texted Alan that I'd see him at half seven. For some reason, I was sure we'd be back at half seven.'

'You've probably got into the swing of the continental clock.' Pam grinned. 'Seventeen thirty is half five, not half seven.'

'I doubt it will be a problem.' Tess shrugged. 'He'll be out playing golf.'

Jen was quiet, deep in thought, staring out of the window as the taxi swerved into familiar Exmouth streets. Pam narrowed her eyes. 'Jen? Are you all right? You were somewhere else then...'

'Oh – I'm fine – thanks, Pam.' Jen's eyes moved back to the window, to the houses gliding past. She was thinking about Eddie, who was due to return tomorrow, Tuesday. Then there would be four days until their wedding, at three thirty on Saturday. Their wedding day was hanging over her like a threat.

Della hugged her. 'Are you thinking about the wedding, Jen?'

Tess chuckled. 'Or daydreaming of Paris? I wonder how Rose is getting on. I bet she's in the dressing room right now with Daz, putting on that huge wig and powdering her nose.'

Pam nodded. 'I'd like to go back to Paris and take Elvis.'

'I'd love to go back and take Sylvester,' Della agreed.

Tess breathed out deeply. 'I'd love to go back.'

The taxi slowed down outside Della's house. The taxi driver helped Della with her luggage and she hugged her friends, mumbling thanks and promises to text and ring. Then the taxi chugged away, leaving her at the kerbside, rooting in her handbag for her door keys.

She stepped inside the house and closed the front door behind her. The smell hit her straight away. It was overcooked meat, bacon fried to such an extent that the stench hung heavily on the air. Della left her luggage where it was, just inside the door, and tightened her grip on her handbag. Something didn't feel right. 'Sylvester?' she called.

She blundered into the kitchen and stopped still. The litter was everywhere – plastic take-out cartons, half-eaten food, discarded empty paper bags. She rushed over to the cooker. A large frying pan was full of grease, burned oil, bits of bacon, crisped yellow smudges of overcooked egg. She turned towards the sink. Unwashed plates were piled up, thick with slimy smears of food. There were empty coffee cups, several beer cans. Della felt her heart thud. It was all wrong. She had made Sylvester all of his meals, put them lovingly in cartons in the fridge, and labelled them carefully. But the kitchen was a mess – Sylvester would never leave it so untidy. He knew it was her domain – he respected how she kept the kitchen spotless and in order.

'Sylvester? Are you here?' She charged into the living room. There were socks on the floor, curled, worn, now discarded and a thick coat she didn't recognise, an anorak with a huge furry hood. 'Sylvester?' She heard her voice rise and waver. Her heart thumped.

Della charged upstairs, into their room. The bed was smooth; the duvet in place, but there was no evidence of Sylvester – no coffee cup, no slippers, no clothes. She frowned.

A scratching sound came from the spare bedroom, not the box room she used as an office, the second bedroom next to hers. Della caught her breath. She wondered if there was someone in there – a burglar. She looked around her for something to arm herself with and found a vase on the landing, full of dried flowers. She threw the flowers on the floor and clutched the vase in her fist. If there was a robber in there, she would smash him in the face with it. Her heart pumped and made the blood in her ears sing. Della moved softly towards the bedroom door and flung it open, lifting the vase high, and stared at the man lying on the bed, playing a game on his mobile phone. It was Linval. Della stood still, staring at her eldest son.

'What are you doing here?'

'Mommy, I wasn't expecting you to be back yet...'

'I can see that by all that mess in my kitchen. Linval, what's going on? Where's your father?'

Linval stood up, a small, slender man in his late forties, wearing a black sweatshirt and jeans. His hair had started to recede at the temples. He grinned at his mother, Sylvester's easy, confident smile. He came over and hugged her. 'Good to see you, Mommy.'

Della pulled away from him and gave him the look she'd always given him, from the time he was a three year old child at her knee and he'd told her a lie. Her eyes grew large, a round, hard stare.

'What's going on, Linval? Where's your daddy?'

'He made me promise not to tell you...' Linval took a step back. 'I don't want you taking on now. Everything's all right.'

Della's hands were on her hips. 'What's happened?'

'Daddy's fine, it's just a little thing.'

Della glared. 'Linval?'

Linval shuffled his feet. 'How to tell you, Mommy? I rang him on the landline from Stepney to check he was all right and he had this kind of bad cough and, I mean, it was really bad, hacking, you know. I hardly knew it was him, he was wheezing so bad, and then I rang the next morning from work and he sounded terrible, so I came straight down here. He was in bed. He had chest pains and a fever. He couldn't breathe so I called a doctor and...'

'Linval.'

'I've got the car outside, Momma. I'll take you to the hospital in Exeter. I took some days off work so that I could check on him every day and stay here. I've been here since Friday. He's in Bluebell ward...'

Della's eyes pricked with sharp tears. 'Linval – be straight with me – is he all right...?'

Linval rushed to her and wrapped his arms around her. 'He's all right now. Come on, we'll go and see him. I'll drive you there.' He manoeuvred his mother gently towards the door. 'My car's outside –it's the black Focus across the road. Come on, Mommy – we'll go and visit him now.'

When they arrived, Sylvester was sitting up in bed, propped up by thick pillows. His pyjamas were open at the neck, showing his vest beneath. He was wearing his glasses and Della thought he looked small and shrunken in the hospital bed, which had been cranked to full height. She scanned the walls for information about his condition, his treatment, but found nothing except his name, Sylvester Donavan. She rushed over to him, throwing her arms around his neck. 'Sylvester. You, here? What happened?'

Sylvester gave a light laugh, but his face was strained and weak. 'You've come home to me, my angel.' He chuckled. 'I'm not dead yet.'

Della turned a grateful gaze on her son. 'Thank goodness you came down, Linval. Who knows what might have happened? You should have phoned me straight away,' She met her husband's eyes, her own large brown ones misty and soft with emotion. 'How are you feeling, my love? I shouldn't have left you.'

Sylvester coughed, a tight wheeze in his chest. There was a film of sweat on his forehead and across his lip. He laughed again, but it came out as a creak. 'Damn fool pneumonia.' He frowned. 'The doctor says I have to stay here for a while. But it's not too bad. I'll get better in a few weeks.'

Della's eyes were wild with worry. 'Pneumonia? Out in the cold, no proper coat, no scarf, in that awful snack van on the cold beach, the wind blowing right at you...'

Sylvester squeezed her hand. 'The nurse is a nice

woman. She's skinny but tough as hell. She makes me do these foolish lung exercises. You should see it, Della – I have to take long slow deep breaths while she counts at me and then she gets me blowing through a straw into a glass of water. Crazy thing...' He began to cough, covering his mouth with a fist and hacking into his hand.

She reached for a glass of water and held it out, rubbing Sylvester's back with her free palm. 'I'm here now, my love. I'm home. Oh, Sylvester – what would I have done if you...? I should have been here for you.'

'I told Linval not to say a damn fool thing.' He took the glass and drank slowly, thankful eyes on his wife. 'I didn't want your holiday spoiled, you fussing, coming back home just for me...' His words were lost in a paroxysm of choking.

'Of course I'd have come back.' Della turned to Linval. 'What kind of woman am I, swanning off to Paris, having fun and enjoying myself and leaving your father all by himself like this?'

Linval sat on a chair, crossing his legs easily. 'It's all fine now. You're back home and Daddy's going to get well.'

Della sighed. 'I wish you'd told me.'

'No, Della – I wanted you to enjoy your hen party and not fret and worry yourself.' Sylvester swallowed a gulp of water and clasped her hand. 'Linval has been a good boy – he's looked out for me. My lovely Della is come home now. I'll be out of here soon, I promise. Then we can get back to normal, have some fun again.'

'Things will change, Sylvester. That job on the seafront can go, for starters.' Della wrapped him in her arms. 'I won't leave you again, my love. I'm going to get you well. When you're ready, we'll take you home, get you strong. You're all that matters. Then everything will be all right again, you wait and see.'

Sylvester gazed up at Della, his eyes shining through the glasses. 'And how was Paris, my angel? Did you miss me?'

Della sighed. 'Let's get you well first, my love. Then, maybe we can talk about Paris. Maybe we can go together – we can have a holiday, a sort of convalescence, and I'll take you up to the top of the Eiffel Tower. Oh, it's lovely up there, Sylvester. You feel on top of the world up there.'

Sylvester pulled his wife onto the bed, using all the strength he could muster, so that he could wrap both arms around her and hold her as tightly as his weakened state would allow. He coughed, and grinned, spluttering, 'I'm on top of the world, Linval. I have my lovely wife back with me here. And that's all that matters to me now.'

Pam and Tess gave Jen a hug and pushed the taxi door open. Jen was in the taxi by herself now. It felt too big without the laughter and support of her friends. She was alone. She'd be home in five minutes. Then she'd have some thinking to do. She had some decisions to make.

As the taxi pulled away, Tess and Pam tugged their cases towards Tess's door, waving and smiling. Pam turned to Tess. 'I'll just get Elvis and say thanks to Alan and then walk home, Tess. It'll only take me ten minutes.'

Tess's phone buzzed and she took it from her pocket and checked the message. 'It's Vladimir,' she breathed. 'Asking if I'm home and if everything is all right.' She raised her eyebrows. 'Alan's car is over there, so I'm guessing he's in and Elvis is probably tired out after a long walk. But you could stay for a cup of tea – stay for dinner if you like?' Tess looked hopeful. 'Stay for ever?'

'Thanks, Tess, but I won't have a cup of tea. To tell the truth, I'm looking forward to seeing Elvis, to getting him home and having some quality time with him.' She grinned. 'I want to put the painting up, the one I bought from Marie-Laure. We can meet tomorrow for a coffee though, if you like? Or after aqua aerobics on Wednesday.'

Pam gave Tess her best smile. She knew why her friend was keen for her to stay on and not to rush home. The expression in Tess's eyes told the story – she was worried about seeing Alan, about having to close the door on the outside world and resume the life she'd had before Paris. Clearly, the Tess that had returned to Exmouth was not the Tess that left five days ago. Pam winked and offered a brave face. 'Come on, Tess – let's go in and face the music, shall we?'

Music was, in fact, coming from the kitchen, a bass speaker booming. As they stood in the hallway, Tess recognised the voice of Percy Sledge crooning 'When a Man Loves a Woman'. It was her CD – she'd bought it thirty years ago and she loved the old soul classics on it: Marvin Gaye, Al Green, Ben E. King, and The Temptations. She wondered why Alan was playing it – he was never much of a music fan. She blinked, imagining him in the kitchen in an apron and not much else, cooking her supper. She wondered if he was playing the soul music to get her in the mood for love – perhaps he'd missed her. Tess was baffled. She made a face at Pam, showing her surprise that Alan had any romance in him whatsoever, and led the way into the kitchen.

Tess stopped, shocked, in the doorway and Pam caught her breath. Elvis was in the kitchen, on his lead, the leash tied to the table leg. He'd been lying down, his face on his paws, despondent, but when he saw Pam, he leapt up, tugging so hard the table inched forward.

Pam gasped. 'Elvis?' She rushed to her little spaniel, jerking the lead from the table leg with shaking fingers and hugging her dog, who was licking her face with so much gratitude, Pam almost fell backwards. She stared at Tess. 'I don't understand. Why is Elvis tied up? Where is Alan?'

Tess stood tall, her face grim. She was still wearing her jacket, her phone clutched in her hand. An instinct, a feeling deeply rooted in her knowledge of her husband, led her to the hallway and she walked up the stairs softly. On the landing, there was an overpowering smell of too much perfume. Tess knew the scent instantly – it was Chanel. She stopped outside her bedroom. She could hear them in there, on the bed, an unpleasant grunting, a giddy giggle. She pushed the door open with one smooth movement, so hard that it banged against the wardrobe. The smell of Chanel filled her nostrils.

Alan and the woman stopped in an instant, frozen, their arms still around each other, turning to stare at her with their mouths open. They were naked and Tess's vision was filled with bare flesh: Alan's pale shoulders, the sweep of his blotchy back, the woman's loose breasts, the folds of her belly. Then Tess caught the expression in their eyes: the woman was surprised, her eyes wide with shock, and Alan's face was horrified.

'Tess – Tess, you're early – you said half past seven...' He wriggled across the bed from the woman, pushing her roughly away. 'It's a mistake – Celia was just helping me walk the dog up at the golf course – then she got cold... It's not what it looks like.'

Tess couldn't keep her lips together. She spluttered a giggle and, before she could stop herself, she'd raised her phone and clicked a photograph. She turned on her heel and marched down the stairs, away from Alan calling her name, away from the overwhelming stench of Chanel.

She called towards the kitchen, 'Pam – bring Elvis – we're leaving.' Tess strode out through the front door, the cool breeze buffeting her face. She had her jacket on, she was tugging her case behind her and the keys to Rose's house were in her handbag. She laughed out loud, breathing fresh air. Alan could go to hell.

36

Jen had slept very badly. She woke after a few hours' sleep at two o' clock in the morning and couldn't calm her racing thoughts. Eddie would be back later this afternoon, and she'd have to decide. She dozed fitfully, drifted off to sleep and opened her eyes to see a floating white spectre in the corner of the room. Her heart lurched and she flicked on the light to stare at her ivory wedding dress hanging from the wardrobe door. She breathed out, went downstairs for a glass of water, drank it in thirsty gulps and crawled back to bed, flicking off the light.

Her thoughts whirled. She didn't love Eddie. She had loved the idea of sharing her life with someone, the idea of company, a partner, a man to call a husband. But she'd been wrong. Yesterday, she'd suggested to Tess that she try again with Alan. Jen felt guilty. She shouldn't have given such poor advice. She'd been holding onto the wrong idea, to the idea that a bad husband was better than none at all. She should have told Tess to leave Alan, to ring Vladimir and tell him how she felt, to chase her dreams and not stick with something that was outdated, broken and not fixable. Jen would ring Tess later and apologise, then tell her to follow her heart. She understood how important that was she needed to follow her own heart.

Then the pendulum of her emotions swung back. Jen felt embarrassed – she had deceived Eddie by promising to marry him, by offering him a chance of happiness before she snatched it away again. She had led him to believe that they were compatible, they were happy enough, that they'd have a future together. She had deceived herself. All the arrangements for the wedding had been made: there were so many people to tell that the wedding was off– her sister, Anna, and her husband, Pete, Eddie's son and his wife… Jen wondered if it wasn't easier to go through with the charade and put up with Eddie rather than face the humiliation of telling people that she'd changed her mind.

And how was she going to tell Eddie? He'd be here later, in the evening. He was staying for supper. His text said he had so much to tell her about Las Vegas. He and Harry really enjoyed themselves. Eddie hadn't mentioned Paris or asked her if she'd had a good time.

Jen rolled over, pulled the duvet tightly around her body and squeezed her eyes shut. She had to tell him. She had to explain that she'd been to Paris and changed her mind; that she'd thought she loved him, that she wanted to marry him, but she'd made a mistake. And it would be a big mistake to marry someone she didn't love, someone who was just there to prop up her old age and to bump around her house so that the silence wasn't so excruciatingly lonely.

Jen wondered what she would do if she didn't have Eddie. She'd be alone. Rose had been alone. Rose had been dowdy and depressed but she'd seized her opportunity and found work in Paris. She had a life now, she had options. Della had Sylvester – she was one of the lucky ones, still in love, still cherished. Tess had Alan. Jen couldn't think about that – about how awful it must be to live with someone who stifled someone else's happiness, whose selfishness suffocated someone's life to the point that they felt empty. Jen knew then that she couldn't marry Eddie now. She couldn't turn into Tess, into the way Tess was before she went to Paris, the Tess who was a poor second best to her husband's all-consuming hobby.

Jen wondered if she should get a dog, a little spaniel like Elvis, who would keep her company. Pam clearly adored Elvis and the pair of them had a symbiosis that many married couples would be fortunate to emulate. But Jen wasn't Pam. She wasn't as strong and independent and self-sufficient as Pam clearly was.

She sat up in bed with a shiver. She remembered a clear-eyed woman in a green dress, her russet curls twirling as she spoke. *'You cannot change anything in your life even if you wish it.'* Jen listened as Elodie's words whispered in her ear one more time, and she understood. If she married Eddie, she'd still be the same Jen. She'd still be widowed, unsatisfied, separate and alone. She needed to make changes to her life, certainly, but the changes could not include being married to Eddie. That was what Elodie had meant – any change had to come from within herself: an off-the-peg quick-fire solution would still leave her lonely and vulnerable. She had to tell Eddie later today. She had to call the wedding off. Jen closed her eyes and sighed deeply. Ten minutes later, she was asleep.

* * *

She spent the day hovering near the phone, wondering whether to call the Olive Grove and cancel the reception, or to phone the register office and explain that she was no longer in need of a ceremony. She decided to wait until she'd told Eddie, to do everything in the right order. She folded the wedding dress; put it in its box. She would return it to the shop in Plymouth tomorrow and hope they'd give her a full refund. Jen drank coffee, six cups in succession through the day, as she watched the hands flick slowly across the clock. A text message came in from Eddie at three o'clock that he was running late but that he'd be with her by seven in time for supper. There were no endearments, no anticipation or thanks for the meal she'd cook; just a simple laconic state-ment of time and place. Jen decided she wouldn't cook a meal for him; he wouldn't stay long enough to share food. That was what couples did: they shared a meal, and talked across the table. She'd just tell him the wedding was off when he came in and ask him to leave. It didn't seem appropriate to serve up a last supper and simper over the casserole dish before she told him to be on his way for ever.

By seven o'clock, Jen was showered and dressed. She had turned up the central heating to stop herself shivering, feeling a mixture of awkwardness, guilt and sheer fear. Then, on a whim, she changed her clothes from the flowery dress to a pair of skinny jeans and a skimpy vest with thin straps. When she checked herself in the mirror, her Paris tattoo, the calligraphy and small heart, was clearly visible at the top of her arm. Jen sighed. Eddie would be sure to notice it; it had to be done.

A sudden rattle sounded at the door, the dull echo of approaching thunder that made Jen's heart knock. She heard his key in the lock, and then he was in the doorway, Eddie, handsome in his overcoat, a serious look on his face.

'Hello, Jen,' he murmured. 'I'm sorry I'm late.'

'Come in, Eddie, please.' Jen was astonished how formal she sounded. They stood in the living room and stared at each other like strangers. Jen sighed. 'Shall I take your coat?'

Eddie shrugged off the overcoat and puffed out air. 'It's hot in here, Jenny. Central heating's a bit of a luxury for this time of year.' He noticed the strappy vest. 'You could always put a jumper on.'

Jen nodded. She wasn't sure what to say.

Eddie paused, gazing around the room. 'It's good to see you, my dear. You look well.' He hugged her briefly. 'What's for supper? I'm famished. It was a long drive back from London.'

'I haven't made anything.'

Eddie raised his brows, surprised. 'Never mind, Jen. We could eat out. I could ring the Olive Grove and book a table. We could have a bite to eat and then I could tell you all about Las Vegas and you could tell me—'

'Eddie…'

He was staring at her. Then he was staring at her arm. 'I do hope that thing washes off, Jen.'

She held out her arm. 'It's permanent, Eddie. We all had them done in Paris.'

His look was sheer disapproval. 'I knew you'd behave like teenagers once you were there. Never mind. I dare say you can cover it up with some foundation stuff or something when we're out. Do you want to get changed and then we can go? There's a lot to discuss about the wedding on Saturday, about the photographs and—'

'I don't want to get changed – or cover it up.' Jen was

aware of the sulky tone in her voice. She did sound like a teenager. But then Eddie was behaving like an admonishing father. Jen took a breath. 'Eddie – I have something to say.'

An empty silence followed. He was staring at her, frowning. Jen wondered if he knew already. At first, she wasn't sure how to say it and then the words came out. 'I don't want to get married.'

He rubbed his chin. 'Wedding nerves, my dear?'

'No, it's not that, Eddie.'

Eddie forced a grin, opening his arms to hug her. 'What's the matter, Jen? I'm sure we can sort it all out.'

She stood back from him and blurted quickly, 'I don't want to marry you. Not now. Not at all.'

'I don't understand.'

Jen sighed. She wondered why he didn't rush over, put his arms round her and try to change her mind. The thought sifted through her head that, if he kissed her hard and told her he couldn't live without her, she'd give him a second chance. But he faced her, his frown deepening.

'I don't want to get married, Eddie.'

His frown became a deeper crease. 'I'm not sure I want to just shack up, Jen...'

'I don't want to be with you, Eddie.'

'But the wedding's all booked, paid for.'

She shook her head. 'I'll pay you back – half—'

'But I'd have to tell everyone that the wedding's off.'

Jen wiped a tear from her face, one solitary streak of water sliding down towards her mouth. 'I'm sorry.'

'Are you sure this is what you want, Jen? For us to call it a day?'

'I'm sure.'

She saw him turn, hesitate, turn back. She thought he

was about to plead with her to change her mind, to hold her in his arms and tell her how deep his feelings ran. He coughed. 'All right. I'd like the ring back, if I may. It was Pat's, my wife's...'

'Of course.' The diamond ring slipped easily from her finger and she dropped it into his palm.

He gave a low grunt. 'Can I ask – what changed your mind? Was it those women – the hen-party crowd in Paris?'

'No – it was me.'

'Well, I have to say, it's not what I expected...' He frowned. 'I thought you and I could have...' Eddie turned away. Jen wondered if he was upset. She hoped he wouldn't cry.

Jen put out a hand and touched his sleeve. 'Eddie, it's my fault. I shouldn't have said yes when you asked me to marry you. I should have given myself more time to think about it. Perhaps we can be friends. Perhaps if...'

Eddie faced her again, his eyes sad, and he sighed. 'No, I think you're probably right. I'm sorry, Jen, that it didn't work out. We could have been all right together.'

Jen chewed her lip. 'I know, Eddie. But all right isn't good enough for me – or you. It just wouldn't have been enough for either of us, would it?'

He shook his head sadly and reached for his coat. He pulled it on, buttoned it up, placed his key on the coffee table, turned and left her without another word. The door closed crisply and Jen breathed out slowly. She had done it. She was single again.

* * *

It was Friday evening. Della was sitting on the hospital bed, feeding Sylvester grapes. He was opening his mouth like a little thrush while she dropped them in, one by one, and he chuckled, the cackle developing into a rasping cough. Della rubbed his back in the green Paris sweatshirt and hugged him. The hospital staff were pleased with his progress. The doctor had suggested that he stay on Bluebell ward for a few more days and they'd review his condition, but he was definitely improving. Della was showing him her photos of Paris on her phone, and Sylvester was squinting through his glasses, pointing and snickering mischievously. Della snuggled closer to him and pointed at another picture. 'There – look, that's me outside a bar called Monty's. You and I will definitely go there to see the acts. As soon as you're well, we'll book a week in Paris. I can't wait to show you the delights of Miss Peaches Beaverhausen, Ida Heaux and Greta Manchester.'

Sylvester squinted at the screen, stifling a cough. 'They all look like lovely ladies to me. But who's this one with the big hair? I think you'll have to keep me away from that one, Della. She looks very naughty.'

Della brandished the photo. 'Oh, that's one of the naughtiest of all of them. That is the talented pianist, Rose-on-Wye.' She held his hand in hers, tightly. Elodie's words drifted into her mind. *'You must hold onto what you have.'* The fortune teller had been right, Della thought. And she would hold on, for all she was worth, with both hands.

* * *

Pam was sprawled in front of the blazing fire with Elvis on her lap. Over the fireplace was a vibrant oil painting of the Seine, the sunset a cauldron of colour. Pam fondled the little dog's velvet ears and he looked at her with round, trusting eyes. She lifted a glass of wine to her lips and sipped it slowly. Life was good. Then she remembered something. Her handbag was on the floor by her feet and she delved into the bottom and pulled something out. It was a cardboard beer mat, with something scribbled on it. Pam read Marie-Laure's name and her mobile number and she smiled. It was time to give her a call.

* * *

Tess was in Rose's house. She'd found an Abba album, an old-fashioned long player still on the turntable, and she was playing it loud, listening to the words of 'Take a Chance on Me', singing along and wiggling her bottom, which had now healed nicely from the tattooing. She'd been at Rose's for four days. Alan had texted her eight times and, foolishly, she had told him where she was staying. He'd been round twice: once to tell her that she was mistaken about what she'd seen in the bedroom – it was merely Alan keeping Celia warm after she'd developed hypothermia on the golf course walking Elvis – and another time to explain that Cliff's wife, Celia, was a dull woman of low morals who had seduced him against his will and he couldn't help it. On both occasions, Tess had shut the door in his face.

Tess had packed her case, choosing casual clothes and something special to wear in the evening. She and Vladimir were going sightseeing, shopping, to the opera and he was taking her to a restaurant where she'd be able to see the whole panorama of London from a great height. She had booked her ticket to Paddington. She'd go up on the overnight train and Vladimir would meet her at the station in the morning. They were going to stay in a hotel for four days, together. After that, Tess thought – who knows? But she imagined Elodie had been right – in fact she was sure of it. Tess said Elodie's words out loud and smiled. 'You are the lucky one here. You will know the meaning of love.'

Jen had the heating on full and was in her pyjamas, drinking hot chocolate. It was almost eight o'clock; she'd been sitting at the laptop for an hour, the takeaway pizza box on the table. She was looking for something that would fit the bill, something that would excite her and take her somewhere she'd never been before. She clicked the mouse and a bright array of pictures came up: an ocean liner, a picture of ice-blue fjords, an expanse of water, mountain peaks piercing turquoise skies. She read the offer: *Singles Cruise to Norway – Sail through deep fjords that slice through snow-capped mountain ranges in breathtakingly beautiful scenery. Experience Norwegian serenity in a trip of a lifetime specially designed for adventurous singles over fifty who want to make new friends.*

Jen clicked on the picture and nodded, smiling. The dates she wanted were available, starting from June the first. The price was reasonable and the itinerary of activities and visits made her pulse quicken. She would be on board the *Freyr* in two months. She was going to enjoy a three week cruise, and then she would have as many more of them as she could afford. It was time to travel, to see the world, to take control of her life.

Rose and Daz were in the glitzy dressing room with the huge

mirror that covered one wall, in costume, breathing deeply, five minutes before they were due to go on stage. Monty was out front, introducing them in four languages, her white dress with gold brocade slashed to the navel. Greta Manchester was in a pink wig and a silky leopard-print jumpsuit with a plunging neckline. Rose wore a long yellow dress with satin sleeves, a huge blue wig piled on top of her head in indigo pleats and a beauty spot painted above crimson lips. She winked at Greta. 'So – we start with "Money, Money, Money", right?'

Greta winked back. 'Right. And we finish with "Dancing Queen"? Ready to go, partner?'

Rose reached out and they clasped hands. 'I'm ready, Greta. Ready for anything.'

'Right, Rose – let's go out there and give our all again. Let's rock and roll,' Greta breathed, her hands shaking as they always did with pre-performance nerves.

'Rock and roll?' Rose winked mischievously. 'We don't rock and roll, Greta, we *sash-ay*. You and I are the best act in Paris. We are pure unadulterated divas, darling.'

Greta winked. 'Oh, we're the new name on everyone's lips. Tonight we'll take Paris by storm.'

'Not only tonight.' Rose turned, her face determined, her hands on her hips. 'This show is on every night, Greta. Each moment we are out there, giving it 100 per cent, that's what life is about. My eyes are wide open and I love what I'm seeing. This is my time now and I'm not looking back. I'm here living the dream, and this is just where I intend to stay.'

ACKNOWLEDGMENTS

Thanks to my agent, Kiran Kataria, for her support, kindness, wisdom and integrity.

Thanks to Sarah Ritherdon, Nia Beynon and all at Boldwood Books for their warmth, professionalism and inspirational approach, and to those wonderful people who have worked hard editing, designing and putting this book together.

Thanks to the many talented and lovely people who continue to support me on this journey, especially Erika Denham-Linney, Rich Linney, Shaz Godfrey, Frank Deveux, Ian Wellens, Susie Honnor, Bim Bollard, Dianne Hopkins, Kathy North, Julie Mullen, Martin Seager, Rach Cornish, Rog and Jan Gardiner, Bill Parry, Jan Mullen, Ken and Trish Rutherford, Kay Graymore, Ruchi Singh, Slawska G Skarso, Sarah Eddy, Sarah and Jim Forbes, Beau CC, Zach Jackson, Katie Holmes, Jennifer Lane, Stephanie Evans, Peter Blaker and Jonno Watts. Special thanks to Ivor Abiks at Deep Studios and to Planet Rock for the music.

A special mention for the talented Solitary Writers, the

Dorset Chapter of the RNA and my wonderful neighbours whose humour and warmth are always deeply appreciated.

Thanks to my family: Irene and Tosh, always in my heart; to my best brother, Tony Leigh; to Kim Leigh, Angela and Norman Hill, Maddie Hoffman, Ellen Simpson, with my love.

Best love always to my beloved Liam and Caitlan and to Big G, who is the source of it all.

Thanks to everybody who has taken the time to read something I've written and smiled.

MORE FROM JUDY LEIGH

We hope you enjoyed reading *Five French Hens*. If you did, please leave a review.

If you'd like to gift a copy, this book is also available as a ebook, digital audio download and audiobook CD.

Sign up to Judy Leigh's mailing list for news, competitions and updates on future books:

http://bit.ly/JudyLeighNewsletter

ABOUT THE AUTHOR

Judy Leigh is the bestselling author of *A Grand Old Time* and *The Age of Misadventure* and the doyenne of the 'it's never too late' genre of women's fiction. She has lived all over the UK from Liverpool to Cornwall, but currently resides in Somerset.

Visit Judy's website: https://judyleigh.com

Follow Judy on social media:

> facebook.com/judyleighuk
> twitter.com/judyleighwriter
> instagram.com/judyrleigh
> bookbub.com/authors/judy-leigh

ABOUT BOLDWOOD BOOKS

Boldwood Books is a fiction publishing company seeking out the best stories from around the world.

Find out more at www.boldwoodbooks.com

Sign up to the Book and Tonic newsletter for news, offers and competitions from Boldwood Books!

http://www.bit.ly/bookandtonic

We'd love to hear from you, follow us on social media:

facebook.com/BookandTonic

twitter.com/BoldwoodBooks

instagram.com/BookandTonic